What the critics wrote about *A God in Ruins*

'Triumphant . . . Atkinson gives Teddy's wartime experiences the full treatment in a series of thrilling set pieces. Even more impressive, though, is her ability to invest the more everyday events with a similar grandeur . . . almost as innovative as Atkinson's technique in *Life After Life* – possibly more authentic as an expression of how it feels to be alive . . . extraordinarily affecting'
James Walton, *Daily Telegraph*

'A novel that cares deeply about its characters and about the purpose of fiction in making sense of our collective past . . . Atkinson's finest work, and confirmation that her genre-defying writing continues to surprise and dazzle'
Stephanie Merritt, *Observer*

'Her command of structure is extraordinary . . . She writes with terrific compassion for her characters . . . also shows off a brilliantly brittle sense of humour that on several occasions made me laugh out loud . . . *A God in Ruins* stands as an equally magnificent achievement'
Matt Cain, *Independent on Sunday*

'Particularly lovely and melancholy . . . one of those writers that really can make you weep on one page and laugh on the next'
Gillian Flynn

'Horribly funny . . . every page has some vividly original phrase . . . But the tour de force is her treatment of Teddy's experience as a bomber pilot, recreated as memorably as the Blitz scenes in *Life After Life* . . . a really affecting memorial to the huge numbers of bomber crew who died'
Evening Standard

'Better than most fiction you'll read this year . . . I can't think of any writer to match her ability to grasp a period in the past. No, not even you, Booker-winning Hilary Mantel'
The Times

'An amazing accomplishment, a breath-taking literary sleight of hand but, unlike chilly experimental novels, this one is brim-full of heart-breaking emotion and with characters that mean the world. This is an unmissable book'
Sunday Express

'Hugely impressive and immensely moving . . . Atkinson's descriptions of the life of a pilot in Bomber Command are harrowing, edge-of-the-seat stuff. Yet there is plenty of the sharply observed humour that makes Atkinson's work a treat . . . The twist, when it comes, is well earned and revelatory'
Erica Wagner, *New Statesman*

'Atkinson's novel does indeed deserve to be taken seriously because it interrogates – as the best war novels do – what happens when the fighting stops'
Times Literary Supplement

'A sprawling, unapologetically ambitious saga that tells the story of post-war Britain through the microcosm of a single family, and you remember what a big, old-school novel can do . . . especially impressive'
New York Times Book Review

Also by Kate Atkinson

A God in Ruins

Kate Atkinson

BLACK SWAN

TRANSWORLD PUBLISHERS
61–63 Uxbridge Road, London W5 5SA
www.transworldbooks.co.uk

Transworld is part of the Penguin Random House group of companies
whose addresses can be found at global.penguinrandomhouse.com

Penguin
Random House
UK

First published in Great Britain in 2015 by Doubleday
an imprint of Transworld Publishers
Black Swan edition published 2016

A CIP catalogue record for this book
is available from the British Library.

ISBN
9780552776646 (B format)
9781784161156 (A format)

Typeset in 10¾/14pt Giovanni Book by Falcon Oast Graphic Art Ltd.
Printed and bound by Clays Ltd, St Ives plc

Penguin Random House is committed to a sustainable
future for our business, our readers and our planet. This book is made
from Forest Stewardship Council® certified paper.

MIX
Paper from
responsible sources
FSC® C018179

7 9 10 8 6

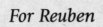

For Reuben

A man is a god in ruins. When men are innocent, life shall be longer, and shall pass into the immortal, as gently as we awake from dreams.

Ralph Waldo Emerson, *Nature*

The purpose of Art is to *convey* the truth of a thing, not to *be* the truth itself.

Sylvie Beresford Todd

On one occasion [St George] came to a city named Salem, near which lived a dragon who had to be fed daily with one of the citizens, drawn by lot.

The day St George came there, the lot had fallen upon the king's daughter, Cleolinda. St George resolved that she should not die, and so he went out and attacked the dragon, who lived in a swamp close by, and killed him.

When he was faced by a difficulty or danger, however great it appeared – even in the shape of a dragon – he did not avoid it or fear it, but went at it with all the power he could put into himself and his horse. Although inadequately armed for such an encounter, having merely a spear, he charged in, did his best, and finally succeeded in overcoming a difficulty which nobody had dared to tackle.

This is exactly the way in which a Scout should face a difficulty or danger, no matter how great or terrifying it may appear to him or how ill-equipped he may be for the struggle.

Robert Baden-Powell, *Scouting for Boys*

30 March 1944

The Last Flight

Naseby

He walked as far as the hedge that signalled the end of the airfield.

The beating of the bounds. The men referred to it as his 'daily constitutional' and fretted when he didn't take it. They were superstitious. Everyone was superstitious.

Beyond the hedge there were bare fields, ploughed over last autumn. He didn't expect to see the alchemy of spring, to see the dull brown earth change to bright green and then pale gold. A man could count his life in harvests reaped. He had seen enough.

They were surrounded by flat farmland. The farmhouse itself stood square and immoveable over to the left. At night a red light shone from its roof to stop them crashing into it. If they flew over it when they were coming in to land they knew they had overshot and were in trouble.

From here he could see the farmer's daughter in the yard, feeding the geese. Wasn't there a nursery rhyme in

11

there somewhere? No, he was thinking of the farmer's wife, wasn't he? – cutting off tails with a carving knife. A horrid image. Poor mice, he had thought when he was a boy. Still thought the same now that he was a man. Nursery rhymes were brutal affairs.

He had never met the farmer's daughter nor did he know her name, but he was disproportionately fond of her. She always waved them off. Sometimes she was joined by her father, once or twice by her mother, but the girl's presence in the farmyard was a constant for every raid.

She caught sight of him now and waved. Rather than return the wave, he saluted her. He imagined she would like that. Of course, from this distance he was just a uniform. She had no idea who he was. Teddy was just one of the many.

He whistled for the dog.

1925

Alouette

'See!' he said. 'There – a lark. A skylark.' He glanced up at her and saw that she was looking in the wrong place. 'No, over there,' he said, pointing. She was completely hopeless.

'Oh,' she said at last. 'There, I *see* it! How queer – what's it doing?'

'Hovering, and then it'll go up again probably.' The skylark soared on its transcendental thread of song. The quivering flight of the bird and the beauty of its music triggered an unexpectedly deep emotion in him. 'Can you hear it?'

His aunt cupped a hand to an ear in a theatrical way. She was as out of place as a peacock, wearing an odd hat, red like a pillar-box and stuck with two large pheasant tail-feathers that bobbed around with the slightest movement of her head. He wouldn't be surprised if someone took a shot at her. *If only*, he thought. Teddy was allowed

– allowed himself – barbaric thoughts as long as they remained unvoiced. ('Good manners,' his mother counselled, were 'the armour that one must don anew every morning.')

'Hear what?' his aunt said eventually.

'The *song*,' he said, mustering patience. 'The skylark's song. It's stopped now,' he added as she continued to make a show of listening.

'It might begin again.'

'No, it won't. It can't, it's gone. Flown away.' He flapped his arms to demonstrate. Despite the feathers in her hat, she clearly knew nothing about birds. Or any animals, for that matter. She didn't even possess a cat. She was indifferent to Trixie, their lurcher, currently nosing her way enthusiastically through the dried-up ditch at the side of the road. Trixie was his most stalwart companion and had been by his side since she was a puppy, when she had been so small that she could squeeze through the front door of his sisters' dolls' house.

Was he supposed to be educating his aunt, he wondered? Was that why they were here? 'The lark's known for its song,' he said instructively. 'It's beautiful.' It was impossible to instruct on the subject of beauty, of course. It simply *was*. You were either moved by it or you weren't. His sisters, Pamela and Ursula, were. His elder brother, Maurice, wasn't. His brother Jimmy was too young for beauty, his father possibly too old. His father, Hugh, had a gramophone recording of 'The Lark Ascending' which they sometimes listened to on wet Sunday afternoons. It was lovely but not as lovely as the lark itself. 'The purpose of Art,' his mother, Sylvie, said – instructed even – 'is to *convey* the truth of a thing, not to *be* the truth itself.' Her own father, Teddy's grandfather, had been a famous artist, dead long ago, a relationship that gave his mother authority on the subject of art. And beauty too, Teddy supposed. All these things – Art, Truth, Beauty – had capital letters when his mother spoke about them.

'When the skylark flies high,' he continued rather hopelessly to Izzie, 'it means it's fine weather.'

'Well, one doesn't need a bird to tell one if it's good weather or not, one simply looks about,' Izzie said. 'And this afternoon is glorious. I adore the sun,' she added, closing her eyes and raising her painted face to the skies.

Who didn't, Teddy thought? Not his grandmother perhaps, who led a gloomy drawing-room life in Hampstead, with heavy cotton nets drawn to prevent the light entering the house. Or perhaps to stop the dark escaping.

'The Knights' Code', which he had learned by heart from *Scouting for Boys*, a book he frequently turned to in times of uncertainty, even now in his self-exile from the movement, demanded that 'Chivalry requireth that youth should be trained to perform the most laborious and humble offices with cheerfulness and grace.' He supposed entertaining Izzie was one of those occasions. It was certainly laborious.

He shaded his eyes against the sun and scanned the skies for the skylark. It failed to make a reappearance and he had to make do with the aerial manoeuvres of the swallows. He thought of Icarus and wondered what he would have looked like from the ground. Quite big, he supposed. But Icarus was a myth, wasn't he? Teddy was going to boarding school after the summer holidays and he really must start getting his facts in order. 'You will need to be a stoic, old chap,' his father advised. 'It will be a trial, that's the point of it really, I suppose. Best to keep your head below the parapet,' he added. 'Neither sink nor float, just sort of paddle about in the middle.'

'All the men in the family' went to the school, his Hampstead grandmother said (his only grandmother, Sylvie's mother having died long ago), as if it were a law, written down in ancient times. Teddy supposed his own son would have to go there too, although this boy existed in a future that Teddy couldn't even begin to imagine. He didn't need to, of course, for in that future he had no sons, only a daughter, Viola, something which would be a sadness for him although he never spoke of it, certainly not to Viola, who would have been volubly affronted.

Teddy was taken aback when Izzie unexpectedly started to sing and – more startling – do a little dance. *'Alouette, gentille alouette.'* He knew no French to speak of yet and thought she was singing not *'gentille'* but 'jaunty', a word he rather liked. 'Do you know that song?' she asked him.

'No.'

'It's from the war. The French soldiers sang it.' The fleeting shadow of something – sorrow, perhaps – passed across her features, but then just as suddenly she said gleefully, 'The lyrics are *quite* horrible. All about plucking the poor lark. Its eyes and feathers and legs and so on.'

In that inconceivable yet inevitable war still to come – Teddy's war – *Alouette* was the name of 425 Squadron, the French Canadians. In the February of '44, not long before his last flight, Teddy made an emergency landing at their base at Tholthorpe, two engines on fire, shot up as they crossed the Channel. The Quebecers gave his crew brandy, rough stuff that they were nonetheless grateful for. Their squadron badges showed a lark above the motto *Je te plumerai* and he had thought about this day with Izzie. It was a memory that seemed to belong to someone else.

Izzie did a pirouette. 'What larks!' she said, laughing. Was this, he wondered, what his father meant when he said Izzie was 'ludicrously unstable'?

'Pardon me?'

'What larks,' Izzie repeated. '*Great Expectations*. Haven't you read it?' For a surprising moment she sounded like his mother. 'But, of course, I was making a joke. Because there isn't one any longer. The lark, I mean. Flown orf. Gorn,' she said in a silly cockney accent. 'I've eaten lark,' she added in an offhand way. 'In Italy. They're considered a delicacy over there. There's not much eating on a lark, of course. No more than a mouthful really.'

Teddy shuddered. The idea of the sublime little bird being plucked from the sky, of its exquisite song being interrupted in full flight, was horrible to him. Many, many years later, in the early Seventies, Viola discovered Emily Dickinson on an American Studies course that was part of her degree. In her scrawly, untamed hand she copied down the first verse of a poem she thought her father would like (too lazy to transcribe the whole of the short poem). 'Split the Lark – and you'll find the Music, Bulb after Bulb, in Silver rolled.' He was surprised she had thought of him. She rarely did. He supposed literature was one of the few things they held in common even though they rarely, if ever, discussed it. He considered sending her something in return – a poem, even a few choice lines – as a means of communicating with her. 'Hail to thee, blithe spirit! Bird thou never wert' or 'Hark, how the cheerful birds do chaunt their lays, and carol of love's praise' or 'Ethereal Minstrel! Pilgrim of the sky! Dost thou despise the earth where cares abound?' (Was there a poet who *hadn't* written about skylarks?) He supposed his daughter would think he was patronizing her in some way. She had an aversion to learning any-thing from him, possibly from anyone, and so in the end he simply wrote back, 'Thank you, very thoughtful of you.'

Before he could stop himself – the armour of good manners falling away – he said, 'It's *disgusting* to eat a lark, Aunt Izzie.'

'Why is it disgusting? You eat chicken and so on, don't you? What's the difference, after all?' Izzie had driven an ambulance in the Great War. Dead poultry could do little to ruffle her emotions.

A world of difference, Teddy thought, although he couldn't help but wonder what a lark would taste like. Thankfully, he was distracted from this thought by Trixie barking extravagantly at something. He bent down to investigate. 'Oh, look, a slow worm,' he said appreciatively to himself, the lark temporarily forgotten. He picked it up gently in both hands and displayed it to Izzie.

'A snake?' she said, grimacing, snakes apparently having no charms for her.

'No, a slow worm,' Teddy said. 'Not a snake. Not a worm either. It's a lizard actually.' Its bronze-gold-lustred scales gleamed in the sun. This was beauty too. Was there anything in nature that wasn't? Even a slug demanded a certain salutation, although not from his mother.

'What a funny little boy you are,' Izzie said.

Teddy didn't consider himself to be a 'little' boy. He supposed his aunt – his father's youngest sister – knew less about children than she did about animals. He had no idea why she had kidnapped him. It was a Saturday, after lunch, and he had been mooching around in the garden, making paper planes with Jimmy, when Izzie had swooped on him and cajoled him into going for a walk with her in 'the countryside', by which she seemed to mean the lane that ran from Fox Corner to the railway station, hardly nature wild in rock and river. 'A little adventure. And a chat. Wouldn't that be fun?' Now he found himself hostage to her whims as she wandered along, asking him strange questions – 'Have you ever eaten a worm? Do you play at cowboys and Indians? What do you want to be when you grow up?' (No. Yes. A train driver.)

Carefully, he placed the slow worm back in the grass and to make up for her failure with the skylark he offered Izzie the bluebells. 'We have to cross the field to get to the wood,' he said, looking doubtfully at her shoes. They appeared to be made of alligator skin and were dyed a rather lurid green that no self-respecting alligator would have admitted to. They were brand new and clearly not meant for tramping across fields. It was late afternoon and the dairy herd, whose field it was, was mercifully absent. The cows, huge baggy things with soft inquisitive eyes, would not have known what to make of Izzie.

She ripped a sleeve climbing over the stile and then managed to plunge one of her alligator-clad feet into a cow pat that would have been quite obvious to anyone else. She redeemed herself a little in Teddy's eyes by being admirably and carelessly cheerful about both mishaps. ('I expect,' his mother said later, 'that she will simply throw the offending articles away.')

She was, however, disappointingly unimpressed by the bluebells. At Fox Corner the annual exhibition was greeted with the same reverence that others accorded the Great Masters. Visitors were trooped proudly out to the wood to admire the seemingly endless blur of blue. 'Wordsworth had his daffodils,' Sylvie said, 'we have our bluebells.' They weren't *their* bluebells, not at all, but his mother's character was inclined to ownership.

Walking back along the lane Teddy felt a sudden unexpected tremor in his breast, a kind of exaltation of the heart. The memory of the lark's song and the sharp green smell of the great bouquet of bluebells that he had picked for his mother combined to make a pure moment of intoxication, a euphoria that seemed to indicate that all the mysteries were about to be revealed. ('There's a world of light,' his sister Ursula said. 'But we can't see it for the darkness.' 'Our little Manichean,' Hugh said fondly.)

The school was not, of course, unknown to him. Teddy's brother Maurice was up at Oxford now, but when he had been at the school Teddy had often accompanied his mother ('my little chaperone') to prize-givings and Founder's Days and occasionally something called

'Visitation' when one day each term parents were allowed – although not particularly encouraged – to visit their children. 'More like a penal system than a school,' his mother scoffed. Sylvie was not as enthusiastic about the benefits of education as one might have expected her to be.

Considering his allegiance to his old school, his father showed a marked reluctance for any kind of 'visitation' to his old haunts. Hugh's absences were explained variously by being tied up with affairs at the bank, important meetings, fretful shareholders. 'And so on, and so on,' Sylvie muttered. 'Going back is usually more painful than going forward,' she added as the chapel organ whined its way into the introduction to 'Dear Lord and Father of Mankind'.

This was two years ago, the prize-giving for Maurice's final term. Maurice had been deputy head boy, the 'deputy' in his title making him choleric. 'Second in command,' he had fumed when he had been appointed at the beginning of his final year. 'I see myself as a commander, not a deputy.' Maurice believed himself to be made of the stuff of heroes, a man who should lead other men into battle, although he would literally sit out the next war, behind an important desk in Whitehall where the dead were simply inconvenient tables of figures to him. No one in the school chapel on that hot July day in 1923 would have believed that another war could follow so swiftly on the heels of the last. The gilding was still fresh on the names of old boys ('the Honoured Dead') displayed on oak plaques around the chapel. 'Much good may "honour" do them when they're dead,'

Sylvie whispered crossly in Teddy's ear. The Great War had made Sylvie into a pacifist, albeit a rather belligerent one.

The school chapel had been stifling, drowsiness settling on the pews like a film of dust as the headmaster's voice droned on and on. The sun filtering through the stained-glass windows was transformed into lozenges of jewel-like colours, an artifice that was no substitute for the real thing outside. And now this would soon be Teddy's appointed lot too. A dull prospect of endurance.

When it came to it, school life was not so bad as he had feared. He had friends and was athletic, which always led to a degree of popularity. And he was a kind boy who gave bullies no quarter and that made him popular too, but nonetheless by the time he left and went up to Oxford he had concluded that the school was a brutal and uncivilized place and he would not keep up the callous tradition with his own sons. He expected many – cheerful, loyal and strong – and received instead the distillation (or perhaps reduction) of hope that was Viola.

'Tell me more about yourself,' Izzie said, wrenching a stalk of cow parsley from the hedgerow and spoiling the moment.

'What about myself?' he puzzled, the euphoria gone, the mysteries once more veiled from view. Later, in school, he would learn Brooke's poem 'The Voice' – 'The spell was broken, the key denied me' a fitting description of this moment, but by then – these sensations being ephemeral by their nature – he would have forgotten it.

'Anything,' Izzie said.

'Well, I'm eleven years old.'

'I know *that*, silly.' (Somehow he doubted that she did.)

'What makes you *you*? What do you like doing? Who are your friends? Do you have a thingamajig, you know –' she said, struggling for alien vocabulary, 'David and Goliath – a slingshot thingy?'

'A catapult?'

'Yes! For going around hitting people and killing things and so on.'

'Killing things? No! I would never do that. (His brother Maurice, yes.) I don't even know where it is. I used to use it to get conkers down from the tree.'

She looked disappointed by his pacifism but was not to be diverted from the catechism. 'What about scrapes? You must get into those, all boys do, don't they? Scrapes and japes.'

'Scrapes?' He remembered with a certain horror the incident with the green paint.

'Are you a Boy Scout?' she said, standing to mock attention and giving a smart salute. 'I *bet* you're a Scout. Dyb, dyb, dob and all that.'

'Used to be,' he muttered. 'Used to be a Cub.' It was not a topic he wished to explore with her but it was actually impossible for him to lie, as if a spell had been put on him at birth. Both his sisters – and even Nancy – could lie beautifully if necessary, and Maurice and truth (or Truth) were poorly acquainted, but Teddy was deplorably honest.

'Did you get kicked out of the Scouts?' Izzie asked eagerly. 'Cashiered? Was there some terrible scandal?'

'Of course not.'

'Do tell. What happened?'

The Kinship of the Kibbo Kift happened, Teddy thought.

He would probably have to spend hours explaining to Izzie if he so much as mentioned the words.

'Kibbo Kift?' she said. 'It sounds like the name of a clown.'

'How about sweets? Are you very fond of them, for example, and if so, what kind?' A little notebook appeared, alarming Teddy. 'Oh, don't mind this,' she said. 'Everyone takes notes these days. So . . . sweets?'

'Sweets?'

'Sweets,' she affirmed and then sighed and said, 'You know, dear Teddy, it's just that I don't *know* any little boys, apart from you. I have often wondered what goes into the making of a boy, apart from the usual slugs and snails and puppy dogs' tails, of course. And a boy,' she continued, 'is a man in the making. The boy in the man, the man in the boy, and so on.' This last said rather absently while considering the cow parsley. 'I wonder if you will be like your father when you grow up, for example?'

'I hope so.'

'Oh, you mustn't settle for ordinariness, I'm sure *I* never shall. You must grow up to be quite piratical!' She started to shred the cow parsley to pieces. 'Men say that women are mysterious creatures, but I think that's a ruse to deflect us from seeing their *absolute incomprehensibility*.' These last two words said rather loudly and very irritably as if she had a particular person in mind. ('She always has some man or other on the go,' he had heard his mother say.) 'And what about little girls?' Izzie said.

'What about them?' he puzzled.

'Well, do you have a "special friend" – you know, a girl

you particularly like?' She made a silly, smirking face which he supposed was her attempt (a very poor one) at miming romance or some such other nonsense.

He blushed.

'A little bird tells me,' she continued relentlessly, 'that you have a bit of a pash on one of the next-door girls.'

What little bird, he wondered? Nancy and her clutch of sisters – Winnie, Gertie, Millie and Bea – lived next to Fox Corner in a house called Jackdaws. A great many of these birds roosted in the woods and showed a preference for the Shawcross lawn, on to which Mrs Shawcross tossed cold toast every morning.

Teddy would *not* give Izzie Nancy, not under any circumstances, not under torture – which this was. He would not say her name to have it sullied on Izzie's lips and be made fun of. Nancy was his *friend*, his boon companion, not the stupid soppy sweetheart that Izzie was implying. Of course he would marry Nancy one day and he would love her, yes, but it would be the pure chivalrous love of a knight. Not that he really understood any other kind. He had seen the bull with the cows and Maurice said that was what people did too, including their mother and father, he sniggered. Teddy was pretty sure he was lying. Hugh and Sylvie were far too dignified for such acrobatics.

'Oh, my, are you blushing?' Izzie crowed. 'I do believe I've ferreted out your secret!'

'Pear drops,' Teddy said in an effort to put an end to this inquisition.

'What about them?' Izzie said. (She was easily distracted.) The ruined cow parsley was tossed on to the ground. She cared nothing for nature. In her heedlessness she would have trampled through the meadow, kicked over lapwings' nests, terrorized the field mice. She belonged in the city, in a world of machines.

'They're my favourite sweets,' he said.

Turning a corner they came across the dairy herd, nudging and bumping their way along the lane as they returned from milking. It must be late, Teddy thought. He hoped he hadn't missed tea.

'Oh, bluebells, how lovely,' his mother said when they walked through the front door. She was dressed in evening clothes and looked rather lovely herself. At the school he was about to start his mother had many admirers, according to Maurice. Teddy felt rather proud of his mother's status as a beauty. 'What on earth have you been doing all this time?' Sylvie asked. A question aimed at Teddy but intended for Izzie.

Sylvie in furs, contemplating her reflection in the bedroom mirror. Holding up the collar of a short evening cape to frame her face. A critical examination. The mirror was once her friend, but now she felt that it regarded her with indifference.

She put a hand up to her hair, her 'crowning glory', a nest of combs and pins. Old-fashioned hair now, the mark of a matron being left behind by the times. Should she have it cut? Hugh would be bereft. She had a sudden memory – a portrait in charcoal, sketched by her father not long before he died. *Sylvie Posing as an Angel*, he called it. She was sixteen years old, demure in a long white dress

– a nightdress actually, rather flimsy – and was half turned away from her father in order to show off her lovely waterfall of hair. 'Look mournful,' her father instructed. 'Think of the Fall of Man.' Sylvie, the whole of a lovely unknown life before her, found it hard to care very much for the subject but nonetheless pouted prettily and gazed absently at the far wall of her father's enormous studio.

It had been an awkward pose to hold and she remembered how her ribs had ached, suffering for her father's art. The great Llewellyn Beresford, portraitist to the rich and famous, a man who left nothing but debts upon his death. Sylvie still felt the loss, not of her father but of the life he had built on what had unfortunately turned out to be baseless fabric.

'As you sow,' her mother wailed quietly, 'so shall you reap. Yet it is *he* who has sown and *we* who have reaped nothing.'

A humiliating bankruptcy auction had followed his death and Sylvie's mother had insisted that they attend, as if she needed to witness every item they had lost pass in front of their eyes. They sat anonymously (one hoped) in the back row and watched their worldly goods being paraded for all to see. Somewhere towards the end of this mortification the sketch of Sylvie came up for sale. 'Lot 182. Charcoal portrait of the artist's daughter' was announced, Sylvie's angelic nature now lost apparently. Her father should have given her a halo and wings and then his purpose would have been clear. As it was she merely looked like a sullen, pretty girl in a nightdress.

A fat man with a rather seedy air had raised his cigar at each round of bidding and Sylvie was finally sold to him for three pounds, ten shillings and sixpence. 'Cheap,' her mother muttered. Cheaper now probably, Sylvie thought. Her father's paintings had gone quite out of fashion after the war. Where was it now, she wondered? She would like it back. The thought made her cross, a frown in the mirror. When the auction had finally limped to an end ('One job lot comprising a pair of brass fire-dogs, a silver chafing dish, tarnished, a large copper jug') they had bustled out of the room with the rest of the crowd and had chanced to overhear the sleazy man saying loudly to his companion, 'I'll enjoy myself looking at that ripe young peach.' Sylvie's mother shrieked – discreetly, she was not one to make a fuss – and pulled her innocent angel out of earshot.

Tainted, everything tainted, Sylvie thought. From the very beginning, from the Fall. She rearranged the collar of the cape. It was far too hot for it but she believed that she looked her best in furs. The cape was Arctic fox, which made her rather sad as Sylvie was fond of the foxes that visited their garden – she had named the house for them. How many foxes would it take to make a cape, she wondered? Not as many as for a coat, at least. She had a mink hanging in her wardrobe, a tenth-anniversary present from Hugh. She must send it to the furriers, it needed to be remodelled into something more modern. 'As do I,' she said to the mirror.

Izzie had a new cocoon-shaped coat. Sable. How had Izzie come by her furs when she had no money? 'A gift,' she said. From a man, of course, and no man gave you a fur coat without expecting to receive something in return. Except for one's husband, of course, who expected nothing beyond modest gratitude.

Sylvie could have swooned from the amount of perfume that she was wearing, spilt by a jittery hand, although she was not usually given to nerves. She was going up to London for the evening. It would be hot and stuffy on the train, even worse in town, she would have to sacrifice her fur. As the foxes had been sacrificed for her. There was a joke – of sorts – lodged in there somewhere, the kind that Teddy might make, not Sylvie. Sylvie had no sense of humour. It was a blight on her character.

Her eye was caught unwillingly by the photograph on her dressing-table, a studio portrait taken after the birth of Jimmy. Sylvie was seated. The new baby in his christening gown – a vast affair, worn by every Todd – seemed to overflow from her arms while the rest of her brood were arranged artfully around her in a semblance of adoration. Sylvie ran a finger over the silver frame, intending fondness but finding dust. She must have a word with Bridget. The girl had grown sluttish. ('All servants turn on their masters eventually,' her mother-in-law had advised when Sylvie was first married to Hugh.)

A commotion downstairs could only indicate the return of Izzie. Reluctantly, Sylvie removed her fur and put on her light evening duster for which only hard-working silkworms had been sacrificed. She placed her hat on her head. Her unfashionable hair didn't suit the neat skull caps and berets of the day and she was still wearing a *chapeau*. She accidentally jabbed herself with her long silver hat pin. (Could you kill someone with a hat pin? Or merely injure them?) She muttered an imprecation to the gods that caused the scrubbed innocent faces of her children to look reproachfully at her from the photograph. As well they might, she thought. She would soon be forty years old and the prospect had made her dissatisfied with herself. (*'More* dissatisfied,' Hugh offered.) She could feel impatience at her back and recklessness before her.

She gave herself one last appraisal. Good enough, she supposed, which was not necessarily a judgement that she liked to settle for. It was two years since she had seen him. Would he still think her a beauty? That was what he had called her. Was there a woman on earth who could resist being called a beauty? But Sylvie had resisted and had remained chaste. 'I am a married woman,' she had repeated primly. 'Then you shouldn't be indulging in this game, my dear,' he said. 'The consequences might be awful for you – for us.' He laughed at this idea as if it were appealing. It was true, she had led him on and then found there was nowhere to go.

He had gone abroad, to the colonies, doing important work for the Empire, but now he was back and Sylvie's life was running through her hands like water and she no longer felt inclined to be prim.

She was greeted by an enormous bunch of bluebells. 'Oh, bluebells, how lovely,' she said to Teddy. Her boy. She had two others but sometimes they hardly seemed to count. Her daughters weren't necessarily objects of affection, more like problems to be solved. Only one child held her heart in his rather grubby fist. 'Do wash before tea, dear,' she said to Teddy. 'What on earth have you been doing all this time?'

'Getting to know each other,' Izzie said. 'Such a darling boy. I say, aren't you looking glamorous, Sylvie. And I could smell you from a hundred yards away. Quite the *femme séduisante*. Do you have plans? Do tell.'

Sylvie glared at her but was diverted from a response when she saw the mucky green alligators on the Voysey hall runner. '*Out*,' she said, shooing Izzie towards the front door, and again, '*Out*.'

'Damned spot,' Hugh murmured, wandering into the hall from the growlery as Izzie flounced down the path. He turned to Sylvie and said, 'You look lovely, darling.'

They listened to the engine of Izzie's Sunbeam kicking into life and the unnerving sound of her accelerating away. She drove in the manner of Toad, much tooting and little braking. 'She'll kill someone sooner or later,' Hugh, a stately driver, said. 'And I thought she was penniless. What did she do to get the wherewithal for another car?'

'Nothing decent, of that you can be sure,' Sylvie said.

Teddy was free at last of Izzie's awful ramblings, but still had to suffer the usual interrogation from his mother before she was satisfied that one of her children hadn't been corrupted in some way by contact with Izzie. 'She's never without motive,' she said darkly. He was eventually freed to search out his tea, a somewhat put-up affair of sardines on toast as it was Mrs Glover's evening off.

'She's eaten a lark,' Teddy said to his sisters over the tea table. 'In Italy. Not that it makes a difference *where*.'

'"A skylark wounded in the wing,"' Ursula said, and when Teddy looked at her blankly she said, 'Blake. "A skylark wounded in the wing, a cherubim does cease to sing."'

'Let's hope that something eats *her* one day,' the more down-to-earth Pamela added cheerfully.

Pamela was going to Leeds University to study science. She was looking forward to the 'bracing north', the 'real' people. 'Aren't we real enough?' Teddy grumbled to Ursula, who laughed and said, 'What is real?' which seemed a silly question to Teddy who had no occasion to question the phenomenal world. Real was what you could see and taste and touch. 'You're missing at least two senses there,' Ursula pointed out. Real was the wood and the bluebells, the owl and the fox, a Hornby train trundling around his bedroom floor, the smell of a cake baking in the oven. The skylark ascending on his thread of song.

The evening's account for Fox Corner: after Hugh had driven Sylvie to the station he retired to his growlery again with a small glass of whisky and the stub of a half-smoked cigar. He was a man of moderate habits, more by instinct than conscious choice. It was unusual for Sylvie to go up to town. 'The theatre and supper with friends,' she said. 'I shall stay over.' She had a restless spirit, an unfortunate thing in a wife, but he must trust her in everything or the whole edifice of marriage would fall and crumble.

Pamela was in the morning room, her nose in a chemistry textbook. She had failed her Girton entrance exam and didn't really want to venture into the 'bracing north', but 'needs must' as Sylvie was wont – irritatingly – to say. Pamela had (quietly) hoped for glittering prizes and a brilliant career and now feared that she would not be the bold woman she had hoped to be.

Ursula, sprawled on the carpet at Pamela's feet, was

conjugating irregular Latin verbs. 'Oh, joy,' she said to Pamela. 'Life can surely only improve from here,' and Pamela laughed and said, 'Don't be so sure.'

Jimmy was sitting at the kitchen table in his pyjamas, enjoying his milk and biscuits before bedtime. Mrs Glover, their cook, was a woman who would brook no myth or fable and so, in the absence of her oversight, Bridget was taking the opportunity to entertain Jimmy with a garbled yet still remarkably bloodcurdling tale about 'the Pooka' while she scrubbed the pots. Mrs Glover herself was at home, dozing lightly, her feet propped up on the fender, a small glass of stout to hand.

Izzie, meanwhile, was on the open road, singing *'Alouette'* to herself. The tune was now lodged firmly in her brain. *Je te plumerai*, she bellowed unmusically, *je te plumerai*. I will pluck you. The war had been a dreadful thing, she wished she hadn't reminded herself of it. She had been a FANY. A rather silly acronym, in Izzie's opinion. First Aid Nursing Yeomanry. She had gone out to drive ambulances, although she had never even driven a car, but in the end she was doing all kinds of horrible things. She remembered cleaning out the ambulances at the end of the day, blood and fluids and waste. Remembered, too, the mutilations, the charred skeletons, the ruined villages, limbs poking through mud and earth. Buckets of filthy swabs and pus-soaked bandages and the terrible oozing wounds of the poor boys. No wonder people wanted to forget all about it. Have a bit of fun, for heaven's sake. She was awarded a Croix de Guerre. Never told anyone at home about it. Put it away in a drawer when she came home. It meant nothing when you thought about what those poor boys had gone through.

She had been engaged twice during the war, both men dying within days of proposing to her and long before Izzie herself had got round to writing a letter home with her happy news. She had been with one of them, the second one, when he died. By chance she had found him in a field hospital that her ambulance was delivering the wounded to. She hadn't recognized him at first, he had been so mangled by artillery fire. The matron, short of nurses and orderlies, encouraged her to stay with him. 'There, there,' Izzie soothed, keeping watch at his deathbed by the oily yellow light of a Tilley lamp. He called out for his mother at the end, they all did. Izzie couldn't imagine calling for Adelaide on her deathbed.

She smoothed her fiancé's sheets, kissed his hand as there was not much face left to kiss and let an orderly know that he was dead. No euphemisms here. Then she returned to her ambulance and went foraging for more casualties.

She ducked out when a third, a rather shy boy, a captain called Tristan, offered to tie a piece of string around her finger. ('Sorry, it's all I've got. There'll be a gorgeous diamond for you when this is all over. No? Are you sure? You'd be doing a chap an awfully big favour.') She had bad luck and would spare him it, Izzie thought – uncharacteristically selfless – which was ridiculous of her given that all those lovely subalterns were pretty much doomed with or without her assistance.

Izzie never saw Tristan again after her refusal and presumed him dead (she presumed them all dead), but a

year after the war ended she was riffling through the
society pages when she came across a photo of him
emerging from St Mary Undercroft. He was a member of
parliament now and, it turned out, filthy rich with family
money. He was beaming at the ridiculously young bride
on his arm, a bride who was wearing on her finger, if one
looked with a magnifying glass, a diamond that did
indeed look gorgeous. Izzie had saved him, she supposed,
but, sadly, she had not saved herself. She was twenty-four
years old when the Great War ended and realized that
she'd used up all her chances.

The first of her fiancés had been called Richard. She
had known very little about him beyond that. Rode with
the Beaufort Hunt, she seemed to recall. She had said 'yes'
to him on a whim, but she had been madly in love with
the second of her betrotheds, the one whose death she
had been a witness to in the field hospital. She had cared
for him and, even better, he had cared for her. They had
spent their brief moments together imagining a charming
future – boating, riding, dancing. Food, laughter, sunshine. Champagne to toast their good fortune. No mud,
no endless awful slaughter. He was called Augustus.
Gussie, his friends called him. A few years later she discovered that fiction could be both a means of resurrection
and of preservation. 'When all else has gone, art remains,'
she said to Sylvie during the next war. '*The Adventures of
Augustus* is art?' Sylvie said, raising an elitist eyebrow.
No capital letter for Augustus. Izzie's definition of
art was broader than Sylvie's definition, of course. 'Art
is anything created by one person and enjoyed by
another.'

'Even Augustus?' Sylvie said and laughed.

'Even Augustus,' Izzie said.

Those poor dead boys in the Great War were not so very much older than Teddy. There had been a moment with her nephew today when she had been almost overcome by the tenderness of her feelings for him. If only she could protect him from harm, from the pain that the world would (inevitably) bring him. Of course, she had a child of her own, born when she was sixteen and hastily adopted, an excision so clean and so swift that she never thought about the boy. It was perhaps just as well, then, that at the moment when she felt moved to reach out to stroke Teddy's hair he had suddenly bobbed down and said, 'Oh, look, a slow worm,' and Izzie was left touching empty air. 'What a funny little boy you are,' she said and for a moment saw the shattered face of Gussie as he lay dying on his camp bed. And then the faces of all of those poor dead boys, rank upon rank, stretching away further and further into the distance. The dead.

She accelerated away from this memory as fast as she could, swerving just in time to miss a cyclist, sending him wobbling into the verge from where he yelled insults at the retreating back bumper of the heedless Sunbeam. *Arduis invictus*, that had been the FANY's motto. Unconquered in hardship. Terrifically boring. Izzie had had quite enough of hardship, thank you.

The car flew along the roads. The germ of Augustus in Izzie's mind already sprouted.

Maurice, absent from this roll-call, was currently trussing

himself up in white tie and tails in preparation for a Bullingdon Club dinner in Oxford. Before the evening was out, the restaurant, as Bullingdon Club tradition demanded, would be wrecked. Inside this starched carapace it would have surprised people to know there was a soft writhing creature full of doubt and hurt. Maurice was determined that this creature would never see the light of day and that in the not-too-distant future he would become fused with the carapace itself, a snail who could never escape his shell.

An 'assignation'. The very word sounded sinful. He had booked two rooms in the Savoy. They had met there before he had gone away, but innocently (relatively) in public spaces.

'Adjoining rooms,' he said. The hotel staff would know the purpose of the word 'adjoining', surely? How shaming. Sylvie's heart was thundering in her chest as she took a cab from the station to the hotel. She was a woman about to fall.

The Temptation of Hugh.

'The sun whose rays are all ablaze with ever-living glory.' Hugh was singing to himself in the garden. He had emerged from the growlery to take a little after-dinner (if you could call it dinner) stroll. From the other side of the holly hedge that divided Fox Corner from Jackdaws he heard an answering lilt. 'Observe his flame, that placid dame, the moon's Celestial Highness.' Which seemed to be how he had found himself in the Shawcrosses' conservatory with his arms around Roberta Shawcross, having slipped through the gap in the hedge that the children had created through years of use. (Both he and Mrs Shawcross had recently taken part in a local amateur production of *The Mikado*. They had surprised both themselves and each other with the vigour of their unlikely performances as Ko-Ko and Katisha.)

Sun and moon, Hugh thought, the masculine and feminine elements. What would he have thought if he had known that one day these would be the names of his great-grandchildren? 'Mrs Shawcross,' he had said when he reached the other side of the hedge, rather scratched by the holly. The children who used this short cut were considerably smaller than he was, he realized.

'Oh, please, it's Roberta, Hugh.' How unnervingly intimate his name sounded on her lips. Moist, cushiony lips, accustomed to giving praise and encouragement to all and sundry.

She was warm to the touch. And without corsetry. She dressed in a rather bohemian fashion, but then she was a vegetarian and a pacifist, and, of course, there was the whole issue of the suffrage. The woman was a terrific idealist. You couldn't help but admire her. (Up to a point, anyway.) She had beliefs and passions outside of herself. Sylvie's passions were storms that raged within.

He tightened his hold on Mrs Shawcross slightly and felt her respond in kind.

'Oh dear,' she said.

'I know . . .' Hugh said.

The thing about Mrs Shawcross – Roberta – was that she *understood* about the war. It wasn't that he wanted to talk about it – God, no – but it was comforting to be in the company of someone who *knew*. A little, anyway. Major Shawcross had had some problems when he came back from the front and his wife had been very sympathetic. One had seen some awful things, none of them fit topics of conversation at home, and, of course, Sylvie had no intention of discussing the war. It had been a rip in the fabric of their lives and she had sewn it up neatly.

'Oh, that's a very good way of putting it, Hugh,' Mrs Shawcross – Roberta – said. 'But, you know, unless you can do very good invisible stitching there'll always be a scar, won't there?'

He regretted introducing the needlework metaphors. The overheated conservatory was full of scented geraniums, a rather oppressive smell in Hugh's opinion. Mrs Shawcross held the palm of her hand against his cheek, gently, as if he was breakable. He moved his lips nearer to hers. Here's a how-de-do, he thought. He was in uncharted territory.

'It's just that Neville,' she began shyly. (Who was Neville, Hugh wondered?) 'Neville can't . . . any more. Since the war, you know?'

'Major Shawcross?'

'Yes, Neville. And one doesn't want to be . . .' She was blushing.

'Oh, I see,' Hugh said. The geraniums were beginning to make him feel slightly sick. He needed some fresh air. He began to feel panicked. He took his marriage vows seriously, unlike some men he knew. He believed in the compromise of marriage, he acknowledged its circumscription. And Mrs Shawcross – Roberta – lived next door, for heaven's sake. They had ten children between them

– hardly a foundation for adulterous passion. No, he must extricate himself from this situation, he thought, his lips moving ever nearer.

'Oh, lord!' she exclaimed, taking a sudden step back from him. 'Is that the time?'

He looked around for a clock and couldn't see one.

'It's Kibbo Kift night,' she said.

'Kibbo Kift?' Hugh repeated, confused.

'Yes, I must go, the children will be waiting.'

'Yes, of course,' he said. 'The children.' He began to make his retreat. 'Well, if ever you need to talk, you know where I am. Just next door,' he added, rather pointlessly.

'Yes, of course.'

He escaped, taking the circuitous route of path and door rather than the vicious gap in the hedge.

It would have been wrong, he thought, retiring to the chaste safety of the growlery, but nonetheless he couldn't help but preen a little. He began to whistle 'Three Little Maids From School'. He felt rather jaunty.

And what of Teddy?

Teddy was standing in a circle in a nearby field, kindly provided by Lady Daunt at the Hall. The members of the circle, mainly children, were moving clockwise, performing a peculiar caper based on Mrs Shawcross's fancy of what a Saxon dance might have seemed like. ('Did Saxons dance?' Pamela asked. 'You never think of them dancing.') They held wooden staffs – branches they had foraged from the wood – and every so often stopped and thumped the ground with these sticks. Teddy was dressed in the 'uniform' – a jerkin, shorts and hood – so that he looked like a cross between an elf and one of Robin Hood's (not very) Merry Men. The hood was a misshapen thing because he had been forced to sew it himself. Handicrafts were one of the things Kibbo Kift was keen on. Mrs Shawcross, Nancy's mother, was forever getting them to embroider badges and armbands and banners. It was humiliating. 'Sailors sew,' Pamela said, in an effort to encourage him. 'And fishermen knit,' Ursula added. 'Thanks,' he said grimly.

Mrs Shawcross was in the middle of the circle, leading her little dancers. ('Now hop on your left foot and give a little bow to the person on your right.') It had been Mrs Shawcross's idea for him to join Kibbo Kift. At the very moment when he had started looking forward to graduating from Cubs to Scouts proper, she had seduced him away with the lure of Nancy. ('Boys and girls together?' a suspicious Sylvie said.)

Mrs Shawcross was a great enthusiast for the Kinship. Kibbo Kift, Mrs Shawcross explained, was an egalitarian, pacifist alternative to the militaristic Scouts from which its leader had broken away. ('Renegades?' Sylvie said.) Emmeline Pethick-Lawrence, one of Mrs Shawcross's heroines, was a member. Mrs Shawcross had been a suffragette. ('Very brave,' Major Shawcross said fondly.) One still learned woodcraft, Mrs Shawcross explained, went camping and hiking and so on, but it was underpinned by an emphasis on 'the spiritual regeneration of England's youth'. This appealed to Sylvie, if not to Teddy. Although she was generally hostile to any idea that had Mrs Shawcross as its origin, Sylvie nonetheless decided it would be 'a good thing' for Teddy. 'Anything that doesn't encourage war,' she said. Teddy hardly thought that the Scouts encouraged war but his protests were in vain.

It was not just the sewing Mrs Shawcross had failed to mention, there was also the dancing, the folk singing, the prancing around in the woods and the endless talking. They were in clans and tribes and lodges, for there were a good deal of (supposed) Red Indian customs mixed up with the (supposed) Saxon ritual, making an unlikely hotchpotch. 'Perhaps Mrs Shawcross has found one of the lost tribes of Israel,' Pamela laughed.

They all chose Indian names for themselves. Teddy was Little Fox ('Naturally,' Ursula said). Nancy was Little Wolf ('Honiahaka' in Cheyenne, Mrs Shawcross said. She had a book she referred to). Mrs Shawcross herself was Great White Eagle ('Oh, for heaven's sake,' Sylvie said, 'talk about hubris').

There were some good things – being with Nancy, for one. And they learned archery with real bows and arrows, not things that they had to make themselves from branches or such like. Teddy liked archery, which he thought might come in useful one day – if he became an outlaw, for example. Would he have the heart to shoot a deer? Rabbits, badgers, foxes, even squirrels occupied a tender place in that heart. He supposed if it were a matter of survival, if starvation were the only option. He would draw the line somewhere though. Dogs, larks.

'It all sounds rather pagan,' Hugh said doubtfully to Mrs Shawcross. ('Roberta, please.') This was in an earlier conversation, before their 'incident' in the conservatory, before he had thought of her as a woman.

'Well, "utopian" might be a better description,' she said.

'Ah, Utopia,' Hugh said wearily. 'What an unhelpful idea that is.'

'Isn't it Wilde,' Mrs Shawcross said, 'who writes that "progress is the realization of Utopias"?'

'I would hardly look to *that* man for my moral creed,' Hugh said, rather disappointed in Mrs Shawcross – a deterrent he would remind himself of later when his thoughts returned to the scent of geraniums and the lack of corsetry.

Teddy's idea of Utopia would not have included the Kibbo Kift. What would it have included? A dog, certainly. Preferably more than one. Nancy and his sisters would be there – his mother too, he supposed – and they would all live in a lovely house set in the green countryside of the Home Counties and eat cake every day. His real life, in fact.

In turn, the Kibbo Kift produced their own breakaway movement, the less eccentric Woodcraft Folk, by which time Teddy had managed to weasel his way out of the lot of them. At school he joined the OTC and enjoyed the concerted lack of pacifism. He was a boy, after all. He would have been surprised to know that in his sixties, when his grandchildren came to live with him in York, he would spend several months trailing backwards and forwards to a chilly church hall so that Bertie and Sunny could attend a weekly meeting of the Woodcraft Folk group that they were members of. Teddy thought that continuity would probably be a good thing for them, seeing as Viola, their mother, seemed to have provided so little. He gazed at his grandchildren's innocent faces while they intoned the hopeful words of the 'creed' at the beginning of the meeting – 'We shall go singing to the fashioning of a new world.'

He even went on a camping trip with them and was complimented on his 'woodcraft skills' by the group leader, who, despite being large, young and black, reminded him a little of Mrs Shawcross. 'Learned in the Scouts,' he said, even all those years later unwilling to admit that he had taken anything from the Kibbo Kift.

Sylvie paid the cab driver and the hotel doorman opened the door of the cab and murmured, 'Madam.' She hesitated on the pavement. Another doorman was already holding open the door of the hotel. 'Madam.' Again.

She moved closer, inch by slow inch, edging her way towards adultery. 'Madam?' the doorman said again, still holding the door, perplexed by this slow progress.

The hotel beckoned. She could see the lush tones of the foyer, the promise of luxury. Imagined champagne sparkling in engraved Bohemian glass, foie gras, pheasant. The dimmed lighting in the room, the bed with its starched hotel sheets. Her cheeks flamed. He would be waiting inside, just beyond the door. Perhaps he had glimpsed her, was already rising to his feet to greet her. She hesitated again, balancing what she was about to be given against what she was about to give away. Or – perhaps a worse outcome – everything would simply remain the same. And then she thought of her children, thought of Teddy, her best boy. Would she risk her life as his mother? For an adventure? A cold thrill of horror quenched the flames of sin. For sin it was, she thought, make no mistake. You did not need a God (Sylvie was an unconfessed atheist) to believe in sin.

She composed herself (difficult) and said to the doorman, rather haughtily, 'Oh, I'm so sorry. I've just remembered another appointment elsewhere.'

She fled, walking quickly, head held high, a purposeful woman with a decent, civilized destination beckoning her – a charitable committee, even a political meeting, anything but a rendezvous with a lover.

A concert! The lighted entrance of Wigmore Hall appeared ahead of her – a warm beacon, a safe harbour. The music struck up almost at once, one of Mozart's Haydn Quartets, *The Hunt*. Appropriate, she thought. She had been the hind, he had been the hunter. But now the hind had bounded free. Not quite bounded, perhaps, as she was in a rather poor seat at the back of the hall, squashed between a somewhat shabby young man and an elderly lady. But then one always paid a price for freedom, didn't one?

She had been a frequent attender of concerts with her father and knew the Haydn Quartets well, but still felt too flummoxed by her narrow escape to hear the Mozart. Sylvie was a pianist herself but she avoided attending recitals these days, they reminded her too painfully of a life that might have been. She had been told by her teacher when she was young that she could go on to 'play at concert level' if she took her studies seriously, but then of course the bankruptcy, the great fall from grace, had occurred and the Bechstein had been hauled unceremoniously away and sold to a private buyer. The first thing she had done on moving into Fox Corner was to acquire a Bösendorfer, her wedding present from Hugh. A great solace for marriage.

The *Dissonant* came after the interval. As the almost inaudible opening bars struck up she found herself weeping soundlessly. The elderly lady passed her a handkerchief (clean and pressed, thank goodness) to staunch her tears. Sylvie mouthed a thank-you to her. This mute exchange lifted her spirits a little. At the end of the concert the woman insisted that she keep the handkerchief. The shabby young man offered to escort her to a cab. How kind strangers were, she thought. She politely declined her would-be escort, a refusal she later regretted because in her disturbed state she took a wrong turn on Wigmore Street and then another and found herself in a far from salubrious area, armed with only a hat pin with which to defend herself.

She had once been at home in London, yet now it was a foreign city to her. A dirty, lurid nightmare of a place and yet she had willingly descended into this circle of hell. She must have been mad. All she wanted to do was to get home, yet here she was wandering the streets like a mad woman. When she eventually found her way back to a gleamingly busy Oxford Street she cried out in relief. A cab ride later and she was sitting demurely on a bench on the station platform as if she were returning from a day of shopping and lunch with friends.

'Goodness,' Hugh said. 'I thought you must be a burglar. You said you were staying up in town.'

'Oh, it was all deathly tedious,' Sylvie said. 'I decided I

would rather come straight back. Mr Wilson, the station-master, gave me a lift in his pony and trap.'

Hugh regarded his wife's high complexion, the slightly wild look in her eye of an overused racehorse. Mrs Shawcross, in contrast, was less of a thoroughbred and more of a good-natured Dobbin. Which, in Hugh's opinion, could be preferable sometimes. He kissed Sylvie lightly on the cheek and said, 'I'm sorry that your plans for the evening didn't work out, but it's very nice to have you home.'

Sitting in front of her mirror, unpinning her mound of hair, a fresh despair fell on Sylvie. She had been a coward and now she was chained to this life for ever. Hugh came up behind her and rested his hands on her shoulders. 'Beautiful,' he murmured, running his hands through her hair. She had to suppress the desire to flinch away from him. 'Bed?' he said, looking hopeful.

'Bed,' she agreed brightly.

But it wasn't just the bird, was it, Teddy thought as he lay in bed waiting for sleep to find him, the nightly oblivion kept at bay by meandering thought. It wasn't just the one lark that had been silenced by Izzie. (*A mouthful.*) It was the generations of birds that would have come after it and now would never be born. All those beautiful songs that would never be sung. Later in his life he learned the word 'exponential', and later still the word 'fractal', but for now it was a flock that grew larger and larger as it disappeared into a future that would never be.

Ursula, looking in on him on her way to bed, found

him awake and reading *Scouting for Boys*. 'Can't sleep?' she said with the offhand sympathy of a fellow insomniac. Teddy's feelings for his sister were almost as straightforward and uncomplicated as those he had for Trixie, who was lying at the foot of the bed, whining softly in her sleep. 'Rabbits, I suppose,' Ursula said.

Ursula sighed. She was fifteen and prone to pessimism. Although their mother would have vigorously denied it, this was her character too. His sister perched on his bed and read out loud, 'Be always ready with your armour on, except when you are taking your rest at night.' (Perhaps this was his mother's 'armour of good manners', Teddy thought.) 'A metaphor, I expect,' Ursula said. 'Knights can hardly have been expected to clank around all day long in a suit of armour. I'm always reminded of the Tin Man from *The Wizard of Oz* when I think of knights.' It was a book they were all fond of but Teddy wished that she hadn't put that image in his mind, the *Idylls of the King* and *Morte d'Arthur* dissolving into thin air in an instant.

An owl hooted, a loud, almost aggressive sound. 'On the roof, by the sound of it,' Teddy said. They listened together for a while.

'Well, night-night,' Ursula said eventually. She kissed him on the forehead.

'Night-night,' he said, stowing *Scouting for Boys* beneath his pillow. Despite the owl, which continued to hoot its unholy lullaby, he fell almost immediately into the deep and innocent sleep of the hopeful.

The Adventures of Augustus

~ *The Awful Consequences* ~

IT BEGAN innocently enough, in Augustus's opinion anyway. "It always begins innocently," Mr Swift sighed, although he doubted that Augustus's definition of innocence was the same as that of other people.

"But it wasn't my *fault*!" Augustus protested furiously.

"That will be written on your headstone, dear," Mrs Swift said, looking up from the sock she was darning. One of Augustus's, needless to say. ("What does he *do* to them?" she frequently puzzled.)

"And anyway, how could I have known what would happen?" Augustus said.

"There is no action that doesn't bring with it a consequence," Augustus's father said. "Only the short sighted don't consider the consequences." Mr Swift was a barrister and in court he spent his day prosecuting the guilty, relishing the to-and-fro of the courtroom battle. Some of this necessarily spilled over into his home life, which his son thought put his father at an unfair advantage.

"Innocent until proven guilty," Augustus muttered.

"You were caught red-handed," Mr Swift said mildly. "Isn't that proof of your guilt?"

"I wasn't *red*-handed," Augustus said indignantly.

"And, anyway, it was *green* paint. M'lud," he added solemnly.

"Oh, please," Mrs Swift murmured. "You're giving me a headache."

"How can I be givin' you a headache?" he asked, hurt by this further accusation. "To *give* you a headache I'd have to *have* a headache in the first place. You can't give something you don't have. And I don't have a headache. Ergo," he said grandly, pulling the word from some distant corner of learning, "I cannot have given it to you." Mrs Swift's headache was not improved by this barrage of reason. She flapped her hand at her son as if trying to get rid of a particularly annoying fly and returned to her darning. "Sometimes," she murmured, "I wonder what I did to offend the gods."

Augustus, on the other hand, felt rather pleased with himself. He was putting up a spirited defence. He was an innocent man in the dock, fighting for his rights. His sister, Phyllis, a "bluestocking", according to their mother, was always soapboxing about "the rights of the common man". And here I am, Augustus thought, they don't come more common than me. "I have rights, you know," he said stoutly. "I have been sorely used," he added grandly. He had heard his brother Lionel ("a prig", according to Phyllis) say this over some stupid pash he had on a girl.

"Oh, for heaven's sake," his father said. "You're not Edmond Dantès."

"Who?"

"You never seem to *think*," his father said. "Anyone

with an ounce of sense could have seen what would happen."

"What I was *thinkin'* was that I just wanted to see what was on the other side," Augustus said.

"Ah, how many times has that sentence been uttered as a prelude to disaster, I wonder?" Mr Swift said to no one in particular.

"And what was on the other side?" Mrs Swift asked, unable to stifle her curiosity.

"Well," Augustus said, moving a pear drop from one cheek to the other to give himself time to consider.

"Was it, by any chance, Mrs Brewster's wig?" Mr Swift asked in his courtroom voice, the one that implied it already knew the answer.

"How was I s'posed to know she wore a *wig*? It could have been any ol' wig! Just a wig lyin' around. And how was I to know that Mrs Brewster was bald? *You* wear a wig and you're not bald."

"In court. I wear a wig in court," an exasperated Mr Swift said.

"I don't suppose you have any idea *where* the dog took the wig?" Mrs Swift asked her son.

Jock, yapping with excitement and a little tainted with the aforesaid green paint, chose that moment to enter the room and Mrs Swift—

'Oh ye gods,' Teddy groaned, dropping the book to the floor.

Izzie had stolen his life. How could she? (The paint incident really hadn't been his fault.) She had taken his life and twisted it and turned him into a quite different boy, a stupid boy, having stupid adventures. With a stupid, stupid, stupid dog – a Westie, with a sketchy face and black bead eyes. The book had pictures, cartoony things that made everything so much worse. Augustus himself was a scuffed, badly behaved schoolboy, his cap glued permanently to the back of his head and a cowlick of hair in his eyes and a catapult hanging out of his pocket. The book had green card covers and gold lettering and on the front it said *The Adventures of Augustus* by Delphie Fox, which, apparently, was Izzie's 'pen-name'. Inside it was inscribed 'To my nephew, Teddy. My own darling Augustus.' What rot.

More than anything it was the Westie that had upset him. It wasn't just the wrong dog but it reminded him of his awful loss, of Trixie, who had died just before Christmas. It had never struck Teddy that she would die before him so he had suffered as much from disbelief as grief. When he came home from his first term at boarding school he found her gone, buried alongside Bosun beneath the apple trees.

'We tried to keep her going until you got here, old chap,' Hugh said, 'but she just couldn't hang on.'

Teddy thought he would never get over this bereavement, and perhaps he never did, but a few weeks after the publication of *The Adventures of Augustus* Izzie turned up with another gift, a tiny Westie puppy with the name 'Jock' engraved on his expensive collar. Teddy tried very hard not to like him as it would be not only a betrayal of his love for Trixie but a sign of his acceptance of the whole horrible fictionalization of his life. It was an impossible task, of course, and the little dog had soon burrowed its way deep into the caverns of his heart.

Augustus, however, would plague him one way or another for the rest of his life.

Ursula came into the room and picked the book up off the floor and started to read out loud, ' " 'Isn't that Augustus?' Miss Slee whispered in Mr Swift's ear. Quite a loud whisper, the kind that makes people in surrounding seats turn and look at you with interest." '

What *had* gone into the making of Teddy? Not slugs and snails, it was true, but generation upon generation of Beresfords and Todds, all coming to one singular point in a cold bed in the chill of an autumn night when his father had caught hold of the golden rope of his mother's hair and hadn't let go until he had hauled them both to the far shore (they had many euphemisms for the act). As they lay amongst the shipwreck of the marital bed they each felt slightly befuddled by the unexpected ardour of the other. Hugh cleared his throat and murmured, 'A voyage into the deep, eh?' Sylvie said nothing as she felt the seafaring metaphor had been stretched far enough.

But the grain had entered the shell (Sylvie's own metaphoric stance) and the pearl that would be Edward Beresford Todd began to grow until he was revealed into the sunshine that came before the Great War and lay happily for hours on end in his pram with nothing but a silver hare dangling from the pram hood for company.

His mother was a great lioness padding softly through the house, protecting them all. His father was more of an enigma, disappearing every day to another world ('The

Bank') and then without warning to another even greater and more faraway world ('The War'). His sisters loved him and swung him and tossed him and covered him in kisses. His brother, already away at school, already trained in the necessary stoicism, sneered at him when he came home in the holidays. His mother held her cheek against his and whispered, 'Out of all of them, you are my favourite,' and he knew it was true and felt bad for the others. (It was a relief, Sylvie thought, finally to know what love was.)

They were all happy, this much at least he was sure of. Later on he realized it was never as simple as that. Happiness, like life itself, was as fragile as a bird's heartbeat, as fleeting as the bluebells in the wood, but while it lasted, Fox Corner was an Arcadian dream.

1980

The Children of Adam

'Mummy, I'm hungry.'

Viola was too busy surveying the sea to acknowledge this statement. It was the frazzled end of a boiling-hot afternoon. 'Day at the beach!' Dominic had announced enthusiastically that morning. Too enthusiastically, as if going to the seaside had the potential to transform their lives in some transcendental way. Hardly a day passed without him having one great idea or another, most of which seemed to involve drudgery on Viola's part. ('I swear Dominic thinks of six impossible things before breakfast!' Dorothy laughed admiringly, as if that were a good thing.) The world, in Viola's opinion, would be better off without so many ideas. She was twenty-eight but already jaded. Twenty-eight seemed a particularly unsatisfactory age. She was no longer young and yet no one ever seemed to take her seriously as an adult. People still told her what to do all the time, it was infuriating.

Her only power seemed to be over her own children and even that was limited by endless negotiation.

They had borrowed the van from Dorothy for the five-mile journey and it broke down (no surprise) a mile from the beach.

A passing motorist, an elderly, rather frail-looking man in an old Morris Minor estate, had stopped and done something simple beneath the hood and – hey-presto – the van was fixed. Their rescuer was a local farmer, one of their neighbours, and both he and the Morris Minor were more robust than they appeared. Only the children recognized him but they gave no sign, already stunned by the heat and the general despair they were feeling at breaking down in Dorothy's van for the third time that month.

'You still need to take it to a garage,' the farmer told them. 'What I did was just temporary.'

Ever-helpful, Dominic offered his guru wisdom. 'Man, *everything*'s temporary.'

Unmoveable mountains and the wheeling stars in the heavens, not to mention the face of God, passed through the farmer's mind, but he was not inclined to disputation. He was bemused by them – the raggle-taggle infants (a touch of the Victorian poor) sitting morosely on the verge with their mother, herself a dishevelled young Madonna wearing an outfit that seemed to have come out of a dressing-up box.

Viola's faux-gypsy attire – peasant-style headscarf, DM boots, long velvet skirt, embroidered Indian jacket sewn with little mirrors – had all been put on hastily without a thought to the fact that they were going to a beach and that it was already hot and was only going to get hotter. It had taken so much effort to assemble everything necessary for this hegira – food, drink, towels, swimming costumes, more food, more towels, a change of clothes, buckets, spades, more food, more clothes, fishing nets, a small ball, more drink, a big ball, sun-tan cream, hats, wet flannels wrung out and put in a plastic bag, a blanket to sit on – that she had simply dragged on the first clothes that she could find.

'Nice day,' the old man said, tipping his tweed cap to Viola.

'Is it?' she said.

The mechanically inept head of the family meanwhile was playing the Holy Fool, or just the fool perhaps, prancing around in the road like a jester. He was wearing a tie-dyed T-shirt and jeans covered in patches, even where they didn't need patching, something that Viola resented as she was the one who had done the patching. Stylistically, the whole family was hopelessly out of date, even the farmer could sense that. He had seen the face of the revolting future – the local town's youth parading in the precinct, ripped and pierced and held together with safety pins, and the juvenile hedonists who had followed in their footsteps, dressed as pirates and outlaws and Civil War Royalists. When the farmer was their age he had dressed like his father and had never thought twice about it.

'We were children of the Sixties,' Viola liked to say in later years, as if that in itself made her interesting. 'Flower children!' Although when the Sixties were already over Viola was still wrapped neatly in her grey Quaker school uniform and the only flowers in her hair were from the occasional childish daisy chain, the flowers plucked from the edge of the school's lacrosse field.

She lit a thin roll-up and gloomily contemplated the bad karma that seemed to be her lot. She drew heavily on the cigarette and then, in a touching display of maternal responsibility, lifted her chin so that the smoke blew over her children's heads. When she got pregnant the first time, with Sunny, Viola had had no idea what it would involve further down the line. She wasn't sure she'd ever seen a baby, let alone held one, and imagined it would be like getting a cat, or, at worst, a puppy. (Turned out it was nothing like either.) Inertia was her only excuse really when a year later she found herself pregnant again, this time with Bertie.

'Our saviour!' Dominic beamed when the engine had coughed back into life. He dropped to his knees in front of the farmer, his hands in prayer position above his head, and touched his forehead to the tarmac. Viola wondered if he'd dropped acid – it wasn't always easy to tell as his existence seemed to be one endless trip, either going up or coming down.

It was only when this phase of her life was over that Viola realized that he was a manic depressive. The term 'bi-polar' came a little too late for Dominic. He was dead by then. 'Walking in front of a train can do that to you,' Viola said flippantly to her women's soul drumming group in Leeds, where she studied for a part-time MA in women's studies on the topic of 'post counter-culture feminism'. ('Eh?' Teddy said.) The north in the Eighties was a hotbed of revolt.

'Grinning nitwit,' the farmer said to his wife when he

got home. 'Posh, as well. You would think the rich would know better.'

'They don't,' the farmer's wife said sagely.

'I felt like bringing the lot of them back here and giving them a plate of ham and eggs and a hot bath.'

'They'll have been from the commune,' his wife said. 'Poor kiddies.' The 'kiddies' had appeared at the farmhouse door a few weeks ago and at first the farmer's wife thought they were gypsies sent to beg and was going to shoo them away, but then she'd recognized them as the children who lived on the neighbouring farm. She'd invited them in and given them milk and cake and let them feed the geese and visit the Red Devons' milking parlour.

'I heard they take drugs and dance naked in the moonlight,' the farmer said. (True, although it wasn't as interesting as it sounded.)

The farmer had failed to spot Bertie before he drove away. She was still sitting on the verge, waving politely at the retreating rear end of the Morris Minor.

Bertie wished he had taken her home with him. She had spied through the farmer's five-barred gates and admired his neat fields – the burnished cows and the fluffy white sheep that looked as if they had just been washed. She had seen the farmer in his battered trilby on his red storybook tractor trundling up and down those same neat fields.

She and Sunny had once wandered, unsupervised, into the farmyard and the farmer's wife had given them cake and milk and called them 'poor mites'. She had taken them to see the big red cows being milked (a wonder!) and then they had drunk the milk while it was still warm, standing right there in the dairy, and then the farmer's wife had let them feed the big white geese that cackled and honked with excitement so that Bertie and Sunny had broken into hysterical giggles as the geese milled around them. It had been wonderful until the moment Viola, like a dark cloud, appeared to take them home and started hyperventilating at the sight of the geese. She hated geese, for some mysterious reason.

Bertie had managed to rescue a feather and had brought it home with her as a talisman. This visit had the quality of a fairy tale for her and she very much wished that she could find her way back to the magic farmhouse. Or be taken there in an old Morris Minor.

'*Really* hungry, Mummy.'

'You're always hungry,' Viola said brightly, trying to show by example that it was not always necessary to whine. 'Try saying, "Mum! I'm hungry, is there anything to eat, *please*?" What would Mr Manners think?'

Mr Manners, whoever he was, dogged Sunny's life, especially when it came to food.

Everything Sunny said came out as a complaint, Viola thought, his name an ironic soubriquet if ever there was. She was continually trying to get him to take a more cheerful tone. 'Put a sparkle on it!' she would say, making jazz hands and an exaggerated happy face. When she was at school, at the Mount in York, they had a drama teacher who used to do this. The girls thought it was a ridiculous idea, but now Viola could see the value of sounding chirpy even when you didn't feel like it. You were more likely to get what you wanted, for one thing. And for another, your mother wouldn't want to strangle you every five minutes. Not that she followed her own advice. It was a long time since Viola had put a sparkle on anything. If ever.

'I'm *hungry*,' Sunny said more vehemently. He had a way of baring his teeth when he was angry that was horrible. He was a biter, too, when he really got going. Viola still shrank in horror from the memory of the visit they had made to her father last year, trekking north for Sunny's birthday. No Dominic, of course, he didn't do stuff like family. '*Family*?' her father puzzled. 'He doesn't do "stuff" like family? But he *has* a family. You. His children. Not to mention his own family.' Dominic was 'estranged' from his parents, something Teddy had a lot of trouble with.

'No, I mean traditional stuff,' Viola said. (Yes, 'stuff' is a very overused word in Viola's vocabulary.) If he hadn't been the father of her children, Viola might have admired Dominic for the way he was so easily able to absolve himself of all obligation simply by asserting his right to self-fulfilment.

Sunny had already been working himself up to a tantrum by the time he was helped by his grandfather to blow out the candles on his cake. Viola had made the cake that morning in her father's kitchen and then pricked out 'Happy Birthday, Sunny' in Smarties on the top of it, but with so little skill that her father thought it was Bertie who had done the decoration.

'When are we going to have the cake?' Sunny whined.

He had had to suffer (they had all had to suffer) his way through a stodgy wholemeal macaroni cheese that Viola had made, which was not birthday fare as far as Sunny was concerned. And besides, it was supposed to be *his* cake.

'Mr Manners wouldn't like to hear that tone,' Viola said.

Who was this Mr Manners, Teddy wondered? He seemed to have usurped parental authority.

Viola cut the cake and placed a slice in front of Sunny, who then, for no reason that Viola could discern, shot forward like a viper and bit her forearm. Without thinking, she slapped his face. The shock catapulted him into silence, a second stretched to infinity, as the room held its breath, waiting for the apoplectic shrieking to begin. As it duly did.

'Well, he *hurt* me,' Viola said defensively when she saw the look on her father's face.

'He's *five* years old, for God's sake, Viola.'

'He has to learn to control himself.'

'So do you,' her father said, picking up Bertie as if she might be in need of protection from further maternal violence.

'Well, what did you expect?' Viola said sharply to Sunny, masking the shame and remorse she felt at her own deplorable behaviour. The shrieking had turned now into howling, fat tears of anguish and distress smearing Sunny's already chocolate-caked face. She tried to pick him up, but as soon as she put her arms around him and lifted him his body spasmed into a rigid board that made him impossible to hold on to. When she put him back on the ground he started to kick her.

'You cannot go around kicking and biting people and not expect consequences,' Viola said, as prim as an old-fashioned nanny, betraying no sign of the messy stew of emotions that occupied her insides. She could feel a demon writhing inside her. The demon often spoke through the pruny lips of Prim Nanny. Mr Manners took a timid back seat to Prim Nanny.

'Yes, I can!' Sunny roared.

'No, you can't,' Prim Nanny said calmly, 'because a big policeman will come to the house and take you away to prison and lock you up for years and years.'

'Viola!' her father said. 'For God's sake, get a grip. He's a little boy.' He held out a hand to Sunny and said, 'Come on, let's go and find you a sweetie.'

He was always the voice of reason, wasn't he? Or The Voice of Reason in Viola's mind, awarding her father the capital letters of the Old Testament. Always nagging at her back. She wilfully failed to recognize it as the apprehensive murmur of her own conscience.

Viola, left alone at the table, now burst into tears. Why did everything always end up like this? And why was it always *her* fault? No one ever cared about how *she* felt, did they? No one made *her* a birthday cake, for example. Not any more anyway. Her father used to, but she hadn't welcomed his handmade offerings and had lusted after the kind of birthday cakes you saw in the windows of Terry's or Bettys, cake shops that faced off against each other on two sides of St Helen's Square, like a warring couple.

For her fiftieth birthday Viola ordered her own cake from Bettys, Terry's having long since left the battlefield.

'*Happy Fiftieth Birthday, Viola*' traced delicately in lilac on white, because despite heavy hints Bertie had failed to understand how significant reaching a half-century was. Viola had outlived her mother by more than three years, which was not a competition that she had particularly wanted to win. By then her mother had receded into an ephemeral past from which she couldn't be recovered. The more Viola forgot her mother, the more she missed her.

She told no one about the fiftieth birthday cake and ate it all herself. It lasted for weeks although it was very stale towards the end. Poor Viola!

She picked all the orange Smarties off Sunny's cake. They had been made in a factory – all of them, not just the orange ones – on the other side of town. Viola had been on a school tour of Rowntree's factory and seen the colours being tumbled together in what looked like cement mixers made of shining copper. At the end of the visit they were all given a free box of chocolates. Viola's were never eaten because when she came home she threw them at her father. She couldn't remember why now. Because he wasn't her mother probably.

She took the dirty cake plates through to the kitchen and put them in the sink. Through the window she could see Sunny and Bertie in the garden with their grandfather, who was showing them the daffodils. ('Millions of them!' Sunny said excitedly when he came running in.) Viola gazed at her children, kneeling amongst the flowers, their faces shining with reflected gold. They were laughing and chatting to her father. The sight made her feel incredibly sad. She felt as if she had been on the outside of happiness her whole life.

'Hungry!' Sunny bellowed at her. Viola, whose eyes remained on the sea, as intent as a lighthouse keeper looking for a wreck, reached behind into her rucksack and fumbled blindly around in its depths before producing the paper bag that contained the sandwiches left over from earlier – uncompromising things made of dense home-made rye sourdough with a filling of Tartex and limp cucumber. Sunny raged at the reappearance of this unattractive feast. 'I don't want that!' he shouted, throwing the sandwich back at her. His aim was terrible and the sandwich was snatched up and devoured by a pleasantly surprised Labrador that happened to be passing by.

'I'm *sorry?*' Viola said, in that tone of voice which indicated that she was very far from sorry.

'I want something *nice,*' Sunny said. 'You never give us anything *nice.*'

'I want never gets,' Viola said. (Not true of the Labrador, Sunny thought.) Prim Nanny had come with them to the beach apparently. She offered the sandwich to Bertie, who was digging a series of holes. Bertie said, 'Thank you, Mummy,' because she enjoyed the way her compliance made her mother pleasant to her. 'You're welcome,' Viola said. Sunny growled at this blatant pantomime of manners, performed, he knew, just to make him feel bad. It was like when they played Happy Families (too young for the irony of it) and if you didn't say 'please' and 'thank you' *every single time* you lost Master Mouse or Mrs Robin, even though you had simply *forgotten*. 'I hate you,' he muttered to Viola. Why was she *never* nice to him? 'Nice' was Sunny's ideal. One day his utopian vocabulary would be wider but for now he would settle for nice. 'I hate you,' he said again, more to himself than his mother.

'La-la-la,' Viola said. 'I'm afraid I can't hear you.'

He took a deep breath and shouted as loud as he could, 'I hate you!' People turned to look.

'I think there's some people out to sea who didn't hear you,' Viola said in that pretending-to-be-unruffled way she had that made Sunny want to destroy her. The cold weapon of sarcasm was an evil trick perpetrated by his mother against which he had no defence. A tempest brewed in his squally heart. He might explode. That would serve his mother right.

Just give in to her, Sunny, Bertie thought. You never win. Ever. She carried on digging serenely, one hand manoeuvring her short-handled little spade, the other holding the sandwich, which she had no intention of eating. After she'd dug placidly for a while she shifted her bottom along and started another hole as if she had a plan in mind, although the plan didn't go beyond digging as many holes as possible before the day was done.

Bertie had been christened 'Moon' – not christened, 'named', in a 'naming ceremony', a ritual devised by Dorothy and held at night in the woods behind the house with the whole commune present. Viola handed her new-born peacefully sleeping baby to Dorothy, who raised her up to the moon as if Bertie was an offering, and for one surprising moment Viola had wondered if her daughter was going to be sacrificed. Bertie held 'the privilege' of being the first baby born in the commune, Dorothy said. 'We give you the future,' she said, addressing the moon, who remained non-committal about the gift. It began to rain and Bertie woke up and started to cry.

'Now we must feast!' Dorothy declared as they headed indoors. Not on the baby, but on its placenta, fried by Jeanette with onions and parsley. Viola declined her portion – it seemed like cannibalism, not to mention utterly disgusting.

And, yes, Sun and Moon, those really were their names.

Luckily, Bertie had been given her grandmother's name as well. 'Moon Roberta?' Teddy said, trying to keep his voice expressionless on the telephone when informed of this. 'That's unusual.'

'Well, you don't want to be called the same thing as everyone else, do you?' Viola said. 'There are enough Sophies and Sarahs in the world. You want something that makes you stand out as different.' Teddy tended to believe the opposite, but kept his counsel. It didn't last long. Sun soon became Sunny and Bertie avoided being Moony by refusing to answer to any lunar version of her name until most people forgot it was on her birth certificate, her birth registered very reluctantly by Dominic who thought it was demanded by a 'totalitarian bureaucracy', which was the same reason he and Viola weren't married.

The only person whom Bertie permitted to remember her parents' lunacy was her grandfather, who sometimes called her Bertie Moon, which Bertie found oddly comforting.

She finished another hole, if a hole can ever be said to be finished, and dropped the sandwich in it.

Viola gave Sunny the rucksack and said, 'There's a satsuma in there. Somewhere.' Her son snarled at the idea of a satsuma.

'Oh, stop bellyaching, will you?' Viola murmured, too intent on the sea to be properly irritated with him.

('Why *did* you have children?' Bertie asked, later in their lives. 'Was it just the biological imperative to breed?'

'That's why everyone has children,' Viola said. 'They just dress it up as something more sentimental.')

Viola wished she had binoculars. The sun glinting off the water made it hard to make out anything clearly. There were a lot of people in the sea and from this distance they all looked pretty much indistinguishable, just shapes bobbing around in the blue like lazy seals. She had terrible short sight but was too vain to wear her spectacles.

Sunny retreated temporarily from the battle and returned to collecting pebbles. He loved pebbles. Rocks, stones, gravel, but sea-smoothed pebbles were best. He couldn't believe what a rich source this beach was. He probably wouldn't even be able to collect all of them.

'Where's Daddy?' Bertie asked, looking up suddenly from her digging.

'Swimming.'

'Where?'

'In the sea, of course.'

Near to where she was sitting Viola noticed a driftwood stick, bone-white and brittle, poking up like a skeletal fingerpost from the sand. She took it and idly started to sketch symbols in the dry sand – pentagrams and horned moons and the maligned swastika. She had recently taken up the study of magic. Or 'Magick'.

'What do you mean – like sawing a woman in half?' a bewildered Teddy asked.

'Ritual Magick. There's a "k" on the end. Witchcraft, the occult, paganism. The Tarot. It's not *tricks*, it's deep earth stuff.'

'Spells?'

'Sometimes.' Said with a modest shrug.

She had read the Tarot last night with Jeanette. The Sun, the Moon, the Fool, one after the other – her family. The High Priestess – Dorothy obviously. The Tower – a disaster, a new beginning? The Star – another baby? God forbid, although Star was a nice name. How long had Dominic been gone? He was a good swimmer but not so good that he could stay out there this long.

The sun glared down brightly. For Magick you needed the night, a glittering candle guttering in the dark, not this over-exposure. Viola threw away the stick and sighed at the heat. She had so far removed her boots, jacket and skirt and headscarf and was still wearing more clothes than anyone else on the beach. She was down to an antique petticoat and a mismatched long-sleeved bodice, fussy ribboned things trimmed with broderie anglaise which she had found in a second-hand shop. Unknown to Viola, the petticoat had originally belonged to a shop girl who had died of consumption and who would have been shocked and not at all pleased to see her under-garments on display on a beach in Devon.

Viola gave up on her sea-watch and rolled another cigarette. She loathed the seaside. Every summer when she was small, when they were still a proper family, they had gone to cold, wet beaches for their obligatory summer holiday. Purgatory as far as Viola was concerned. It must have been her father's idea. Her mother had probably wanted to go somewhere warm and sunny where they could *enjoy* themselves, but her father had the kind of Puritan streak that would consider a beach by the North Sea to be *good* for a child. She sucked furiously on the roll-up. Her childhood had been *warped* by his reasonableness. She lay back on the sand and stared at the cloudless sky while contemplating the unbearable tedium of her life. This in itself soon grew tedious and she sat up and pulled a book out of the bottomless rucksack.

She had never been without a book for as long as she could remember. An only child never is. Literature had fuelled her childhood fantasies and convinced her that one day she would be the heroine of her own narrative. Throughout her teens she inhabited the nineteenth century, roaming the moors with the Brontës, feeling vexed at the constraint of Austen's drawing rooms. Dickens was her – rather sentimental – friend, George Eliot her more rigorous one. Viola was currently rereading an old copy of *Cranford*. Mrs Gaskell did not feel at home in Adam's Acre, where the reading matter ran from Hunter S. Thompson to Patanjali's Sutras with not much in between. Viola sat on the hot sand, twirling a lock of hair around her finger, a long-time habit that annoyed everyone except Viola herself, and wondered why she hadn't worked harder at university instead of being led astray by Dominic and lying around smoking dope. She could have been a lecturer herself by now. A professor even. The sun flared on Mrs Gaskell's bright white pages and Viola suspected that she was about to get a headache. Her mother had, basically, died of a headache.

This short entente was broken by Sunny reversing his decision about the satsuma, but instead of eating it he threw it at Bertie, an action which led to a violent shouting match between the two of them, halted only by the diversionary tactic of giving them money to go and buy ice-creams. There was a van up on the promenade and Viola watched them tramping along towards it until she couldn't make them out any longer. She closed her eyes. Five minutes' peace, was that too much to ask?

Viola was in her first year at a brutalist concrete-and-glass university when she met Dominic Villiers, an art-school drop-out still hanging around the fringes of academic life. He was the scion (Viola had to look the word up) of a semi-aristocratic family. His legendary drug use, his public-school background and the wealthy parents he had rejected in order to live in painterly squalor all gave him a certain cachet. Viola, desperate to rebel and throw off her provincial middle-class chains, by proxy if nothing else, was attracted to his infamy.

Dominic was also very good-looking and she was flattered when, after circling around her for several weeks, he finally pounced (albeit lethargically, if one can pounce lethargically) and said, 'Come back to mine?' No etchings on offer in his squalid flat, but plenty of large canvases that looked as if they'd had primary colours simply thrown at them. 'You can tell?' he said, impressed that she understood his technique. Viola, philistine that she was, couldn't help thinking, But I could do that.

'Do they sell?' she asked innocently and received a patient lecture about 'subverting the exchange relationship between producer and consumer'.

'You mean by giving stuff away?' she said, baffled. As an only child she never gave anything away.

'Hey,' he said laconically when he turned round from appreciating his own art and saw her lying naked on his grubby sheets.

He lived off benefits, which was cool, he said, because it meant the 'Stalinist state' was paying for him to produce art.

'The taxpayer, you mean?' Teddy said. Viola had delayed taking her 'beau' (Teddy's word, he had searched for something innocuous) home for a long time, afraid that her father's quietly conservative views and the orderly restraint of his house in York would reflect badly on her. She thought with distaste of her father's garden, neat rows of salvia, alyssum and lobelia in red, white and blue. Why not just plant a Union Jack? 'It's not patriotism,' he protested. 'I happen to think that those colours go nicely together.'

'Gardens,' Dominic said.

Teddy waited for the rest of the sentence but it never came. 'You like them?' he prompted.

'Yeah, they're great. My people have a maze.'

'A maze?'

'Yeah.' Dominic, to his credit, prided himself on his egalitarianism. 'Dukes or dustmen,' he said, 'it's all the same to me,' although Viola suspected that he knew more dukes than dustmen. His 'people', as he referred to them, lived in the depths of Norfolk and were of the hunting, shooting, fishing tribe, vaguely related to royalty 'on the wrong side of the blanket'. Viola had never met them, the estrangement still firmly in place even after the birth of Sunny and Bertie. 'They don't want to meet their grand-children?' Teddy said. 'That's very sad.'

Viola had been relieved. She suspected that she would never measure up in the eyes of his 'people'. Why exactly was he alienated from them, Teddy asked? 'Oh, you know, the usual – drugs, art, politics. They think I'm a waster, I think they're fascists.'

'Well, he's a good-looking chap at any rate,' Teddy said, searching for something complimentary to say as he and Viola washed the pots together after a ham salad and an apple crumble that he'd made that morning. Teddy was 'handy' in the kitchen ('Even though I say so myself'). Dominic was having 'forty winks' in the living room. 'Tired, is he?' Teddy said. Viola had never seen her father asleep, not even a catnap or a deckchair snooze.

When Dominic woke up, Teddy, unable to think of anything else (somehow he couldn't imagine Dominic playing board games), got out the photo albums in which his daughter's awkwardness was displayed at various ages and in varying degrees. Viola was never good in front of a camera. 'She's much prettier in real life,' Teddy said.

'Yeah, very sexy,' Dominic said, leered even. Viola preened a little. Her father, she noticed, grimaced at Dominic's remark and all that it implied. Get used to it, she thought. I'm a grown woman now. ('I screw therefore

I am,' she had written in the front of her Penguin Classics copy of Descartes's *Discourse on Method*, pleased with her iconoclasm.)

She was the next in a long line of girlfriends and she was never sure why Dominic had stopped at her. Not stopped – merely paused, it turned out. 'But you're the one I always come home to,' he said. Like a dog, she thought, but not without satisfaction.

They were both, essentially, very lazy people and it was easier to stay together than it was to pull themselves apart.

Viola managed to struggle her way through her finals and came away with an undistinguished third, a mashed-up degree of philosophy, American studies and English literature. 'It's an irrelevance anyway,' she said. 'Life's about living, not about paper qualifications.' She told no one how wretchedly disappointed she was at her results and chose not to attend her graduation ceremony, it being 'meaningless lip-service to the established hierarchy'.

'You might regret it in the future,' Teddy said.

'You just want a photograph of me in a cap and gown to put on the wall and show off,' she said irritably.

Well, what would be so wrong with that, Teddy wondered?

'You're not going to get married then?' Teddy asked tentatively when Viola told him she was pregnant with Sunny.

'No one gets married any more,' she said dismissively. 'It's an outmoded bourgeois convention. Why would I want to be handcuffed to someone for the rest of my life just because an authoritarian society demands it?'

'Oh, it's not so bad,' Teddy said. 'You grow used to the "handcuffs", as you put it.'

When Sunny was born they were living in a squat in London with ten other people. They shared the kitchen and bathroom and had one room they could call their own, which was crammed with Dominic's paintings as well as all the baby paraphernalia that Teddy had funded when he realized that no one else was going to buy it. He was alarmed that Viola seemed to have no idea what having a baby involved. 'You're going to need a cot,' he told her, 'and a little baby bath.'

'It can sleep in a drawer,' Viola said, 'and I can wash it in the sink.' ('Yeah,' Dominic concurred, 'that's how poor people have always done it.') Keep it in a drawer? It? Teddy dug into his savings and sent them a cot and a pram and a bath.

Dominic hardly ever finished a painting. Occasionally, despite his avowed rejection of the capitalist economy, he tried to sell one, but he couldn't even give his art away. Viola wondered if one day they would be found buried beneath a mound of his canvases. The result was that they had no money. Dominic refused to ask his family for anything. 'It's very noble of him, sticking to his principles like that,' she told her father. 'Very,' Teddy agreed.

Squatting was the logical thing to do, she explained to her father. 'Regarding the earth as a commodity that you can own when it's something that we all share in common . . .' The argument – someone else's, not hers – ran out. She hadn't slept properly in weeks. Sunny caterwauled through the small hours as if in paroxysms of grief for his lost clouds of glory. (He never would truly recover from this theft.) Her father turned up on the doorstep of the squat one day, saying, 'I didn't wait for an invitation. Otherwise I didn't know when I would get introduced to the little chap,' which was obviously a criticism of her for not hauling the baby and his retinue of stuff on to a train when she could hardly put one foot in front of the other.

Teddy had brought a bunch of flowers, a box of chocolates and a pack of Babygros. 'Mothercare,' he said. 'It's new, have you been? I wish we'd had clothes like this when you were a baby. It was all fiddly matinée jackets and bootees. A layette, that's what we used to call it. Are you going to keep me on the doorstep?

'So this is a "squat", eh?' he said as they squeezed their way past bicycles, mostly broken, and cardboard boxes in the hallway. ('Oh, I was a radical, an anarchist even,' Viola declared in later years. 'Lived in a squat in London – exciting times,' when in fact she was cold and miserable and lonely a lot of the time, not to mention being paralysed by motherhood.)

Teddy took the train back north the same day and lay awake all night worrying about his only child and her only child. Viola had been a lovely baby, just perfect. But then all babies were perfect, he supposed. Even Hitler.

'A rural commune?' Teddy said, when Viola had told him about the next arrangement.

'Yes. Communal living. That means avoiding the destructive effects of the capitalist system and trying to find a new way of being,' she said, parroting Dominic. 'And anti-establishmentarianism,' she added for good measure. It was the longest word she knew and she had heard it bandied around at university, although its meaning remained vague to her. ('The Church?' Teddy puzzled.) 'Straight society is morally and financially bankrupt. We live off the land,' she said proudly.

'"True freedom lies where a man receives his nourishment and preservation, and that is in the use of the earth,"' Teddy said.

'What?' (*Pardon*, Teddy thought. That was what she had been taught as a child.) 'Gerrard Winstanley,' he said. 'The True Levellers. The Diggers. No?'

He wondered what else Viola had managed not to learn. Teddy was intrigued by all those radical idealistic movements that sprang up around the Civil War, wondered if he would have joined one if he'd been alive then. *You see the world turned upside down.* ('A lament, not a rejoicing,' Ursula had chided him, long ago.) They probably all spouted the same kind of nonsense that Viola did. The Kibbo Kift were their natural heirs, he supposed. 'The peaceable kingdom and all that,' he said to Viola. 'The desire for the restoration of paradise on earth,' he persisted. 'Millenarianism.'

'Oh, *that*,' she said, finally hearing something she recognized. She had seen *The Pursuit of the Millennium* on someone's bookshelf. She resented how much stuff her father knew. 'We're interested in cosmic evolutionary development,' she said airily. She had no idea what that meant.

'But you've never liked the countryside,' Teddy puzzled.

'I still don't,' Viola said. She wasn't exactly thrilled about these new living arrangements, but then anything had to be better than the shambles that was the squat.

The commune occupied a rambling old farmhouse in Devon, most of the acreage sold off but enough left for them to grow their own food and keep goats and chickens. That was the theory anyway. Since the Middle Ages it had been called Long Grove Farm, but when Dorothy bought it at auction, 'for a song', mainly because that remaining acreage was swamp, the good land having been bought by a neighbouring farmer (yes, he of the Morris Minor and the yard full of geese), Dorothy renamed it Adam's Acre. A hand-painted sign in rainbow colours declaring this new name was nailed to the gate at the entrance to the farmyard. No one, not one single person in the locality, used this new title.

The commune had been going for five years when they arrived, joining three other couples all in their twenties – Hilary and Matthew, Thelma and Dave (Scottish) and Theresa and Willem (Dutch). Viola had trouble remembering their names. As well as Dorothy there were three other single people – an American woman in her thirties called Jeanette and Brian, a teenager who seemed to have run away from home. ('Cool,' Dominic said.)

And finally there was Bill, an old guy in his fifties. He'd been a mechanic in the RAF and Viola said, 'Yeah, my dad was in the RAF during the war,' and he said, 'Oh, really? Which squadron?'

'No idea,' she shrugged. She had never talked to her

father about the war and anyway it was *years* ago. Her indifference seemed to disappoint Bill. 'I'm a pacifist,' she told him.

'We all are, dear,' he said.

She really *was*, she thought crossly. She'd gone to a Quaker school, for heaven's sake, and had taken part in an anti-Vietnam war demonstration in the course of which she had tried hard to get arrested. Her glory years were still ahead of her – Greenham, Upper Heyford – but she had long been treading the path of righteous indignation. Her father had flown planes, dropped bombs on people. He'd probably been responsible for the fire-bombing of Dresden – *Slaughterhouse-Five* had been on her syllabus at university. ('It was only the Lancasters who bombed Dresden,' Teddy said. 'So? So?' his daughter said. 'You think that absolves you?' 'I'm not asking for absolution,' Teddy said.) War was evil, Viola thought, but was rather cowed by Bill's lack of interest in her opinion. Apparently he didn't want absolution either.

Dominic was happy because he had a studio, an old whitewashed cowshed out the back, and Viola was relieved that she no longer had to co-exist with his paintings.

Their numbers were augmented by a continual stream of visitors coming mostly from London for the weekend. There were always complete strangers sleeping on floors and sofas or sitting around smoking dope and talking. And talking. And talking. And talking. They were supposed to 'contribute' by helping with gardening or general maintenance but that rarely seemed to happen.

Dorothy was the queen bee, of course. Everything was supposed to be shared and held in common but she still retained the deeds to the farmhouse, and owned the van, their only means of transport, plus the whole enterprise had been her idea. She was in her sixties, wore kaftans and wrapped her hair in long silk headscarves, and went around with a beatific smile on her face that could be very irritating if you yourself weren't feeling beatific. She was an old crone as far as Viola was concerned, almost as old as her father. She had been an unsuccessful actress but then had 'followed a man' to India and came back without him, bringing back 'enlightenment' instead. ('How is she enlightened?' Viola muttered to Dominic. 'I don't see any sign of it. She's like everyone else, but worse.')

Dominic had been vetted for his suitability for the commune but Viola didn't meet Dorothy until she moved in. Dorothy, she noticed, liked the sound of her own voice and made Viola feel as if she was back at university. 'Adam's Acre,' Dorothy said grandiloquently, 'is a place where all that is possible is made possible. Where we can explore our artistic nature and help others find theirs. We are continually moving towards the light. Tea?' she asked in the manner of a duchess, startling Viola, who had begun to nod off, as she always did in lectures.

Dorothy passed Viola a thick mug of some sludgy bitter concoction. 'Not tea as *you* know it, I expect,' Dorothy said and Viola wondered if she was trying to drug her or poison her. ('You're so paranoid,' Dominic said.) She shook her head when Dorothy said, 'Scone?' holding out a plate to her that was piled with what looked like cobblestones. There was a hiatus while Dorothy chewed her way through a mouthful of one of these pavers. 'You will find,' she continued eventually, 'that we are a loose gestalt of powerful individuals who chance to be moving in the same direction. Towards a transcendental understanding.'

'OK,' Viola said cautiously, having no idea what the words meant that were falling from Dorothy's crumb-covered lips. There was transcendental meditation, obviously, she had done that, and she had studied the Transcendentalist movement in American literature, ploughed her way through *Walden* and Emerson's *Nature*, but they didn't seem to have much to do with Dorothy's sage-burning and unholy chanting (like a depressed gorilla).

'To make it work, we must all contribute,' Dorothy said. Must we, Viola thought wearily? She was hugely pregnant with Bertie and was still lugging Sunny around in her arms.

Lacking any special skills, she was assigned to general tasks – cooking, cleaning, baking bread, working in the garden, milking the goat 'and so on'. 'Housework, basically,' Viola said. She had marched in a Wages for Housework protest when she was at university, even though she had never done any, and she wasn't very happy about doing any now. Or doing things for other people instead of doing them for herself, which seemed to be what living in a commune meant. There were also 'light gardening duties', which meant digging over the heavy red soil that was full of thistles in the borders around the lawn at the back. She was spared 'the agricultural work', as Dorothy termed the growing of puny root vegetables and worm-eaten cabbages. The Diggers, she thought miserably when she was out in the rain, trying to slice her way through the mud with a wonky spade. She had become a Digger, if not *the* Digger, as no one else ever seemed to be involved in this particular, not inconsequential task – the borders were enormous.

And they were in the middle of *nowhere*. Viola had never liked the countryside, it was a cold, muddy place, full of endless discomforts. When she was little they had lived in an old farmhouse too, in the middle of nothing but landscape, and she could remember her father continually nagging her to go outside and 'get some fresh air', to accompany him on walks to look for birds, trees, nests, 'rock formations'. Why would anyone want to look for a rock formation? She remembered how pleased she'd been to move to York, to a semi-detached house with central heating and fitted carpets. A short-lived pleasure, of course, for what was a house without a mother?

The commune ran a stall at a monthly market in town where they sold stuff they had made – heavy loaves of bread that looked like missiles you could have hurled from catapults. Then there were the multicoloured candles that smelt rank and melted in distasteful puddles. And the pottery, of course. Willem had a kiln which was the source of the thick mugs and plates that they used. There were also the wicker baskets that they all took a hand at weaving. Like blind people, Viola thought when asked to learn. It was the life of an unpaid eighteenth-century servant, she thought, with basket-making thrown in. And she had to look after the children because, despite all the talk about shared tasks, none of them were keen on Sunny, for which she could hardly blame them. Money was held in common, in a kitty, and she couldn't remove a penny without having to justify the expenditure. One day, Viola thought, she was going to run away and take the kitty with her and spend it on Coca-Cola, chocolates, disposable nappies and all the other things that were condemned by the commune.

Dorothy herself seemed to spend a lot of time 'balancing her chakras' (all right for some, Viola thought) and having her Tarot read by Jeanette. She did precious little basket-weaving and Viola had never once seen her milk the goat, a curmudgeonly Toggenburg that despised Viola as much as Viola despised it.

The only time she got any peace at Adam's Acre was when she went out pretending to look for eggs. The chickens laid anywhere they wanted, it was ridiculous. Her father kept chickens, but they were disciplined birds, laying in their nests. Even on a fruitless egg forage she wasn't safe from Dorothy swooping in (she came from nowhere, she was like a bat). 'You're Viola Todd, aren't you?' she said rather accusingly to her one day, appearing on the path in front of her like Miss Jessel. Bertie was asleep in her Maclaren buggy, an item far too flimsy for this kind of rutted terrain (the wheels were always coming off). She had left Sunny with his father, an act that was tantamount to child neglect.

Bertie stirred in her sleep and raised a hand as if to ward off the unwelcome apparition of Dorothy. Viola, who had been wandering along the hedgerows in the midst of a potent fantasy that involved both piles of hot buttered toast and Captain Wentworth from *Persuasion*, was horribly startled.

'Yes, I'm Viola Todd,' Viola said cautiously. She had been living beneath the same roof as Dorothy for over a year and Dorothy didn't know her name? 'Guilty as charged.'

'Your mother is called Nancy? Nancy Shawcross?'

'Maybe,' Viola said even more cautiously. She didn't like her mother's name being on Dorothy's lips. Her mother was sacred.

'Well, she is or she isn't,' Dorothy said.

'Is,' Viola said, reluctant to hand over the conversational gift of her mother in the past tense.

'She's one of the Shawcross sisters?'

'She is.' Plus it was nice to be talking about her mother as if she were still alive.

'I knew it!' Dorothy exclaimed theatrically. 'I knew her sister – Millie. We trod the boards together when we were both ingénues. Been out of touch for years. How is your dear aunt?'

'Dead,' Viola said helpfully, quite happy to give up Millie to the past tense.

Dorothy's face collapsed into a kind of paroxysm of anguish. She put her hand to her forehead in a mime of despair. 'Gone!'

'I hardly knew her,' Viola said matter-of-factly. 'She always seemed to be abroad.'

'Hm,' Dorothy said, as if insulted by this news. She frowned. 'What are you doing anyway?'

'Looking for eggs,' Viola lied easily. You always had to be seen to be doing something *useful*. It was so tiring.

'Shouldn't that child (they were always 'that child' or 'those children') be wearing a sun bonnet?'

'Bonnet?' Viola said, taken by such an old-fashioned

word. Captain Wentworth beckoned. 'Must get on,' she said. 'Eggs to look for.'

When Viola was pregnant with Bertie, Dorothy had advocated a 'natural birth' for the new baby at Adam's Acre. Viola couldn't think of anything worse. Sunny had been born in a big busy London teaching hospital, Viola high as a kite on Pethidine. At night the babies were taken away to a nursery and the mothers were all given sleeping pills. It was bliss. They were kept in for a week and fed meals and snacks and milky drinks and not expected to do very much other than feed and change their babies, often without even getting out of bed. Viola wasn't about to give all that up for some torturous rite of passage orchestrated by (a childless) Dorothy. Viola couldn't help but think of *Rosemary's Baby*.

She was virtually a prisoner. There was no telephone at the farm and how would she get to hospital if no one would drive her in the van? She regretted now not persevering with driving lessons with her father when she still lived at home. She hadn't wanted to be stuck in a car with her father while he taught her stuff he knew and she didn't (which was almost everything). He was an irritatingly patient teacher. She suddenly remembered something, how her father had spent every Saturday morning for a whole year coaching her so that she could get through her Maths O level. He had used the same pencil all year, a stubby soft-leaded one. Viola couldn't keep her hands on the same pencil or pen for more than a day before she lost it. She felt sick at the thought of the algebra and equations they had worked their way through, her father persevering until she had (briefly) understood. All forgotten now, of course, so what had been the point? And all it meant was that she scraped through with a low grade, got middling results in all her A levels except for English, got a foot in the door of a mediocre university and ended up with a crap degree. And look where that had got her. Here. That was where. No money, no job, two kids, useless boyfriend. She would have been better off leaving school at fifteen and doing a hairdressing apprenticeship.

In the end, of course, she had Bertie in hospital and the devil did not come calling for his child. He had no need, he already had Sunny.

She must have fallen asleep. She woke with a start and felt her face burning uncomfortably from where the sun had progressed across it. It took her a few seconds to remember her children. How long since they went for ice-creams? She struggled to her feet and looked around the beach. No sign. Kidnapped, drowned, fallen off the cliff? Any number of scenarios had Viola in their dramatic grip, all of them indicting her as a terrible mother.

They were eventually found, waiting patiently if somewhat glumly at the Lost Children hut. Viola had no idea such a thing even existed. 'Did you do that on purpose?' she said to Sunny as they raced the incoming tide to collect their wet sandy belongings and stuff them back into bags. (This is why we don't come to the beach, she thought.)

Sunny was speechless with indignation. He had been terrified out of his mind when he realized that he couldn't find his way back from the ice-cream van. The beach was vast and almost everyone on it was taller than he was. He had imagined them being washed away by the sea or having to stay there all night on the sand in the dark on their own. The added burden of knowing he was the one who, in his mother's absence, was duty-bound to look after Bertie drove him to distraction and when a nice motherly lady came up to him and said, 'Now then, what are you two doing wandering around? Have you lost your mummy?' he was overcome with relief and broke down in tears. He loved that woman with all his heart.

'Never do that again,' Viola said.

'I didn't do anything,' he said quietly. The fight had gone out of him. He had begun the day as an overwound clock. Now he knew he was barely ticking.

'Where *is* Daddy?' Bertie asked.

'Swimming,' Viola snapped.

'He's been swimming for *hours*.'

'Yeah, he has,' Viola said. She had no watch. Teddy had given her a neat little Timex when she passed her O levels but she had lost that long ago. Please let Dominic be dead, she thought.

If he had drowned out there in the sea she could start a new life. It would be such an easy way of breaking up with him, much easier than packing up and leaving. And besides, where would she go? And then there was the money. Dominic had a trust fund. She didn't know exactly what that was, but he had 'come into it' a few weeks ago. There was some complex legal reason (he said) why he couldn't walk away from this money the way that he'd walked away from his 'people'. But had he given any to her or her children? No, he was giving the money to the commune, signing it over to Dorothy! And worse – no, not worse, slightly less bad – she'd discovered a letter from his mother, who had used a private detective to find him, and in the letter she begged him to 'heal the rift' between them and let her see her grandchildren 'and their mother, who I am sure is wonderful'.

If Dominic was dead, Viola would get the trust fund (wouldn't she?) instead of Dorothy and she could go and live in a proper house and have a normal life. If only she had married Dominic and made her right to his inheritance secure, now she would be a tragic young widow and people would have to be nice to her. She could even go and live with these unknown hunting, shooting, fishing in-laws. They thought she was wonderful, after all. Of course, once they met her they would probably revise their judgement, but, who knew, perhaps over time she could be accepted into their clan and become 'people' herself. She could adopt their name. Viola Villiers, bit of a mouthful, like an elocution exercise, but nonetheless it had a ring to it, like those eighteenth-century actresses who became mistresses to the aristocracy and often ended up as duchesses themselves.

Sunny was probably the heir to an estate or something and for a moment she allowed herself to imagine swans on lakes and peacocks on lawns. She didn't mind if they were fascists, she really didn't, not as long as they had central heating and tumble dryers, and white bread instead of rye sourdough and soft mattresses instead of futons on the floor.

* * *

Should she alert someone? All three of them were exhausted, too tired surely for all the stuff that would follow the report of a missing person. But then how would they get home? She couldn't drive. She sighed heavily.

'Mummy?' Bertie said. Bertie was finely tuned to Viola's moods.

They trudged all the way back to the Lost Children hut. The motherly woman was still there. Sunny launched himself at her, hugging her round the waist, hanging on to her for dear life.

'Lost someone else?' she said cheerfully to Viola.

Sunny, Bertie, Viola and two burly policemen were all crammed into a panda car, being driven to Adam's Acre. ('That would be Long Grove Farm, would it?' one of the policemen said.) The children, in the back with Viola, fell asleep immediately. They were slick with old suntan cream, except for their legs, which were stockinged with gritty sand. Their feet were still bare, Viola hadn't had the energy to force sandals back on them. They were beginning to smell over-ripe.

Her children would probably be better off without her. She should have left them with that farmer's wife, she thought, skilfully converting selfishness into altruism. She had a sudden memory of the geese in the yard and shuddered. She had been chased by a goose when she was small, pecked half to death, and had had a terror of them ever since. Her parents – she'd had both of them at the time – had laughed at her. Geese always sensed her fear, running towards her like a mob, crowding round her, pecking and honking. 'Don't be a silly goose, Viola,' Teddy used to say to her. Always telling her how to be, how not to be. (The Voice of Reason.) *The Goose Girl*, that was a story her mother read to her. It involved a decapitated talking horse, Viola seemed to remember.

Perhaps she could ask the police to keep on driving, all the way to York, and drop her off at her father's house. She was surprised to find that she felt homesick. Not just for the narrow streets and medieval churches, for the Bar Walls and the great Minster, but for the suburban semi-detached that she had spent half of her life deriding.

'Mrs Todd?' She had told the policemen that she was a 'Mzzz' but they ignored this new-fangled idea. And she was the mother of children so they weren't going to call her 'Miss'.

'We're here, Mrs Todd. You're home.' Not really, she thought.

Viola had told her tale of woe to the woman in the Lost Children hut, who immediately took charge, alerting the coastguard, the local lifeboat and the police and several other unidentified people, most of whom milled around on the promenade, excited by the drama but disappointed that there was nothing to see. It seemed a lot for one lone swimmer lost at sea.

Viola had related the facts. They were sparse. Dominic had said, 'I'm going for a swim,' run down to the sea, plunged in, arms and legs waving, and never come back. There was no more to be wrung out of this statement and so the two burly policemen took them back to Adam's Acre. A fractious Sunny had to be prised off the body of the woman in the Lost Children hut like a limpet from a rock. 'The poor little pet,' the woman said and Viola said, 'You can keep him if you want,' which obviously the Lost-Children-hut woman thought was a joke.

The door of the farmhouse flew open as the panda car drew up and Dorothy appeared, glared at Viola and said, 'You brought the pigs to my door?' The two policemen clearly resented being addressed in this disrespectful fashion by a woman who was, let's face it, kaftan notwithstanding, an old-age pensioner and should have known better.

'You can't come in without a warrant,' Dorothy said imperiously.

'We weren't planning on coming in,' one of the policemen said, sniffing the air ostentatiously, although the only smell was the reek of Dorothy's patchouli rather than drugs, even though drugs there were a-plenty on the premises.

Dorothy had by now moved out into the farmyard and was standing arms akimbo, defending her territory. 'You shall not pass,' she said as if she were defending a barricade.

'Oh, for goodness' sake,' Viola said. She was far too worn out for this kind of nonsense.

'Where on *earth* have you *been*, Viola? We wondered what had happened to you. Dominic's in his studio, he's been back for hours.'

'He's *back*? *Here*?' Viola said.

'Well, where else would he be?'

91

'This is Mr Villiers we're talking about?' one of the policemen intervened. 'Mr Dominic Villiers?'

'The gentleman we're conducting a massive air–sea search for?' the other one said. 'The one we've scrambled an RAF rescue helicopter for?'

'And so he came back from his dip in the sea and couldn't find you? And he just drove home?' the farmer puzzled.

'In his swimming trunks?' the farmer's wife said, shaking her head in disbelief at this fact. Viola could see that she'd pushed the pair of them to the edge of their imaginations. They would never behave like Dominic because they were normal people.

She had packed a bag, taken all the money from the kitty when no one was looking and walked over to the neighbouring farm. No one had even noticed she had gone. She had been prepared to run the gauntlet of the geese but they seemed to have gone to bed for the night.

'Oh, it's you,' the farmer said. This morning seemed a long way away to all of them.

The farmer's wife bathed the children and they emerged from the bathroom wrapped in towels looking clean and polished, like new, before being dressed in the pyjamas that the farmer's wife kept for her grandchildren when they visited. She had heated up stew and potatoes and Viola and her children came to a mute agreement that no one would mention the fact that they were vegetarians. Viola felt she had enough on her plate (ha!) without this added ethical complication (they were on a farm, she excused herself). Afterwards, the farmer's wife produced junket that she'd made with cream from the burnished red cows and Viola didn't say, 'Don't eat that! It's made with rennet which comes from an enzyme in a cow's stomach!' which was how she normally greeted cheese and instead let it quietly slip down her throat. It was delicious.

They slept there, between clean old sheets, the children in a double bed. From an early age, almost before she had words for doing it, Bertie had been a sleeptalker, mumbling her way through the night, but tonight, to Sunny's relief, she slept without a murmur. He placed a pebble beneath his pillow for comfort. When he woke next morning it was the first thing he reached for. 'Oh, for heaven's sake,' Viola said when he put it next to his breakfast plate.

They ate scrambled eggs as yellow as the sun and then were dressed again by the farmer's wife in more clothes from her cache. Sunny sported clean short trousers and a little Aertex shirt while Bertie wore a print dress with a smocked bodice and a white Peter Pan collar. They looked like someone else's children.

The farmer drove them to the station, where they took a train to London, and from King's Cross they took another train to York.

'Hello,' Teddy said when he opened his front door and saw the little group of refugees standing on the doorstep. 'This is a nice surprise.'

1947

This Unforgiving Winter

February
> *The Snowdrop in purest white array*
> *First rears her head on Candlemas Day*

'I almost missed the small clump by a hedgerow ditch. The water in the ditch is still "like a stone", as is every pond and rural waterway on this island, and so I was not expecting Wordsworth's "venturous harbinger of spring" to appear on time this year. Traditionally, snowdrops are flowering by Candlemas (2nd February) and are indeed known in some parts as "Candlemas Bells" but in the midst of this bleakest, longest of winters we would surely excuse them if they were a little tardy in their arrival.'

Nancy stifled a yawn which Teddy caught but didn't comment on. She was peering at her knitting, the lamp by her side inadequate. The dreadful weather had meant cuts to the electricity all over the country, but not for them as the cottage had none to begin with. Oil and paraffin lamps downstairs, candles upstairs. They were huddled around the fire which, apart from each other, was their only source of warmth. Teddy leaned over to give the log on the fire an encouraging prod with the poker and glanced up at Nancy and thought, she'll ruin her eyes in this light. She was knitting a complex Fair Isle, a sleeveless pullover for him. There were mathematics in the pattern, she said. There were patterns in everything. Maths was 'the one true thing', according to Nancy.

'Not love?' Teddy said.

'Oh, love, of course,' Nancy said, in an offhanded way. 'Love is crucial, but it's an abstract and numbers are absolute. Numbers can't be manipulated.' An unsatisfactory answer, surely, Teddy thought. It seemed to him that love should be the absolute, trumping everything. Did it? For him?

They had married in the autumn of '45, in Chelsea Register Office with no guests other than a sister each – Ursula and Bea – who acted as their witnesses. Teddy had worn his uniform, but not his medals, and Ursula had begged one of Izzie's pre-war Paris gowns off her without telling her why and Bea had helped Nancy to alter it so it was less glamorous and more suited to austerity. Bea had been to Covent Garden that morning and bought some big mop-headed, rust-coloured chrysanthemums that she'd tied up artfully for a bouquet. The flowers went beautifully with the oyster silk of the dress. Bea had been a student at St Martin's before the war and out of all the

Shawcross girls she was the one with the most artistic nature, although Millie would have contested that furiously. Teddy still thought of them as girls, even though Winnie, the eldest, was forty now.

Neither Teddy nor Nancy had been able to contemplate a big wedding so soon after the war. 'And who would give me away?' Nancy said. 'It would be so sad not to be on my father's arm.' Major Shawcross had died, not unexpectedly, a few weeks previously.

Teddy thought he knew Nancy – before the war he *did* know her – but now she was a continual surprise. He had imagined that in marriage he and Nancy would cleave to each other and become one – in some vague biblical sense of the word – whereas in fact he was constantly aware of the difference between them and she frequently unbalanced him when he had expected – hoped – her to root him.

They had been childhood sweethearts, or so everyone told them. 'How I dislike that expression,' Nancy said on the eve of their modest wedding. They were having a drink in a rather shoddy, near-deserted pub off Piccadilly, chosen because of its proximity to the college where they were both doing an accelerated teaching qualification.

Teaching had formed part of their vision of a wholesome life after the war. It was Nancy's vision really, Teddy had simply gone along with it, unable to think of anything else. He had no intention of returning to banking – his insufferable occupation before the war – and he could no longer be a pilot. The RAF had no call for the dozens of men – hundreds, probably – who wanted to stay on after the war and continue to fly. The country was done with them. They had given everything and then they were suddenly set adrift. Gratitude was no longer the order of the day. In this atmosphere teaching seemed as good an option as anything to him. Poetry, drama, the classic novels, it was a field that he had loved once. Surely he could rekindle that love and communicating it would be a good deed, wouldn't it?

'I should say,' Nancy said enthusiastically. 'And the world needs art now more than ever. It can teach us when man clearly cannot.' Not maths then? 'No, maths can't teach us anything. It is *itself*.'

Teddy didn't believe art ('Art,' he thought, acknowledging his mother) should be didactic, it should be a source of joy and comfort, of sublimation and of understanding. ('Itself,' in fact.) It had been all these things to him once. Nancy, however, tended towards pedagogy.

The honest schoolteacher imparting knowledge, Nancy said, brightly entertained by the idea. They were the very people who would, in their own small way, be making a better future for the world. She had joined the Labour Party and steadfastly attended earnest, dreary meetings. The Kibbo Kift had prepared her well.

They were in the pub because Nancy said she wanted to make sure that Teddy wasn't suffering from 'pre-wedding jitters' and that he was 'completely certain' that he wanted to go ahead with the wedding. He wondered if it might be the other way round and that she was hoping he would set her free at the eleventh hour. They were drinking an unexpectedly good cognac that, when he discovered that they were to be married the next day, the landlord had procured from beneath the counter for the 'lovebirds'. It seemed unlikely to have had a legal provenance. Sometimes Teddy wondered if everyone had done well out of the war except for those who had fought in it.

'*Courage, mon ami*,' Nancy toasted, in honour of the brandy's homeland. Did she feel that they needed courage?

'The future,' he answered, chinking her glass. For a long time, during the war, he hadn't believed in a future – it had seemed like an absurd proposition – and now that he was living in this 'afterward', as he had thought of it during the war, it somehow seemed like an even more absurd proposition. 'And to happiness,' he added as an afterthought, because it was the kind of thing one should say, if only for luck.

'It's rather like "he married the girl next door",' Nancy continued to grumble. 'As if we had no choice in the matter, as if we were *destined*.'

'But you *were* the girl next door,' he said, 'and I *am* marrying you.'

'Yes,' she said patiently, 'but we're making a *choice*. That's important. We're not just sleepwalking into something.' Teddy thought perhaps he was.

They had known each other from childhood, if not as sweethearts then certainly as the closest of friends. When he left Fox Corner for boarding school Nancy was the only person who wasn't family that was in Teddy's prayers every night. *Please keep my mother and father safe* (he learned that no one called their parents 'Mummy' and 'Daddy' at boarding school, even in their silent prayers) *and Ursula and Pamela and Jimmy and Nancy and Trixie.*

After Trixie's death and her replacement by Jock this was amended to *and Jock and keep Trixie safe in heaven*. And, yes, dogs were family. Maurice usually made the list as a guilty afterthought, if at all.

'You don't have to go through with it,' he said to her. 'I wouldn't hold you to anything. After all, everyone got engaged during the war.'

'Oh, what a goose you are,' she said. 'Of course I want to marry you. Are you sure that *you* want to marry *me*? That's the question. And only "yes" or "no" will do for an answer. No fudging the issue.'

'Yes,' he said, quickly and quite loudly so that the pub's two other patrons – an old man and his even older-looking dog – were startled out of their torpor.

The war had been a great chasm and there could be no going back to the other side, to the lives they had before, to the people they were before. It was as true for them as it was for the whole of poor, ruined Europe. 'One thinks,' his sister Ursula said, 'of the great spires and towers that have been toppled, the *Altstadts* with their little narrow cobbled streets, the medieval buildings, the *Rathauses* and cathedrals, the great seats of learning, all reduced to mounds of rubble.'

'By me,' Teddy said.

'No, by Hitler,' Ursula said. She was always keen to lay blame at Adolf's feet, rather than the Germans in general. She had known the country before the war, had friends there, was still trying to trace some of them. 'The Germans were victims of the Nazis too, but one can't say that too loudly, of course.'

Ursula had flown on a 'Cook's tour' at the end of the

war and had witnessed at first hand the desolation, the still-smouldering ruins of Germany. 'But then one thinks of the crematoria,' she said. 'One thinks of poor Hannie. The argument always seems to end at the concentration camps, doesn't it? Auschwitz, Treblinka. The terrible evil. We *had* to fight. Yet we must move on. And there can never be any going back anyway, war or not.' (She was the family philosopher.) 'We can only ever be walking into our future, best foot forward and all that.' This was when people still believed in the dependable nature of time – a past, a present, a future – the tenses that Western civiliz-ation was constructed on. Over the coming years Teddy tried, in the manner of a simple layman, to keep up with theoretical physics, via articles in the *Telegraph* and an heroic struggle with Stephen Hawking in 1996, but admitted defeat when he came across string theory. From then on he took every day as it came, hour by hour.

Ursula had been dead for decades by then, subtracted from time altogether. But in 1947 time was still a fourth dimension that could be relied upon to shape everyday life and for Ursula that meant working in the civil service, as she would for the next twenty years, leading the decent, quiet life of a single professional woman in post-war London. Theatre, concerts, exhibitions. Teddy had always thought his sister would have a great passion of some kind – a vocational calling, a man, certainly a baby. He had looked forward to being an uncle to Ursula's child almost more than he had to his own potential fatherhood (which, if he was honest, he faced with some trepidation), but his sister was nearly forty and so he supposed she would never be a mother now.

Teddy thought of his wife and his sister as two sides of the same shining coin. Nancy was an idealist, Ursula a realist; Nancy an optimist with a lively heart, while Ursula's spirit was freighted with the grief of history. Ursula was forever cast out of Eden and making the best of it while Nancy, cheerful and undaunted, was sure her search for the gate back into the garden would be successful.

Teddy sought out involved imagery, like 'a hound looking for a fox', to quote Bill Morrison.

Nancy looked up from her Fair Isle and said, 'Go on. Carry on with your snowdrops.'

'Are you sure?' he said, sensing a certain lack of enthusiasm.

'Yes.' Said with determination, possibly grim.

> 'My friends in the south of England have yet to spy one, but here, perversely, in these hardy northern climes, Keble's "first-born of the year's delight" have begun to poke their frail heads through the blanket of snow. (*Perce-neige*, the French aptly call them.) But perhaps my favourite name for this little spring flower is the pretty "February fairmaids".'

He was Agrestis, his *nom de plume*, and these were his monthly Nature Notes, a short column for the *North Yorkshire Monthly Recorder*. Known by everyone simply as the *Recorder*, it was a small magazine, both in format and aspiration, with a strictly local circulation, apart from the few copies that were sent abroad every month, all to

Commonwealth countries and (so he was led to believe) one war bride living in Milwaukee. They were all emigrants, Teddy supposed, people who found themselves in exile from this part of the world with its sheep-auction tallies and reports from WI meetings. How long, he wondered, before the bride in Milwaukee began to feel that her native county was as alien as the moon?

A woman in Northallerton – no one at the magazine had ever met her – posted in recipes as well as the Handy Hints and the occasional knitting pattern. There was a crossword (not cryptic, not at all), readers' letters and articles about the area's beauty spots and places of historical interest, and pages of dull advertisements for local businesses. It was the kind of publication that hung around in the waiting rooms of doctors and dentists until it was months, occasionally years, out of date. Not including the woman in Northallerton, the *Recorder* had a staff of precisely four – a part-time photographer, a woman who dealt with all the administration including Notices and Advertisements and subscriptions, the editor, Bill Morrison, and now Teddy, who did everything else, including the Nature Notes.

They had moved to Yorkshire because Nancy thought it would be a place where they could lead a good, simple life, a country life, surrounded by nature, which was how man – and woman – was meant to live. Again, the Kibbo Kift had done its work. Neither of them could abide the grim, battle-scarred face of the capital, and Yorkshire, Nancy said, seemed a long way away, less affected by mechanization and war. 'Well . . .' Teddy said, thinking of the bombing of Hull and Sheffield, of the monolithic soot-blackened factories of the West Riding and, most of all, the brutal windswept airfields on which he had been stationed during the war and where the better part – perhaps the best part – of his life had been lived inside the freezing noisy shell of a Halifax bomber.

'You liked it in Yorkshire, didn't you?' Nancy said, in the casual way someone might say, 'Shall we go to the Lakes this year? You like it there, don't you?'

'Like' was hardly the word that Teddy would have used for a time in his life when every day was fragile and seemed as if it might be his last on earth and the only tense was the present one because the future had ceased to exist even though they were fighting so desperately for it. They had thrown themselves wholesale at the enemy, every day a new kind of Thermopylae. ('"Sacrifice",' Sylvie said, 'is a word that makes people feel noble about slaughter.')

But, yes, it was true, he had liked Yorkshire.

They had talked for a while about emigrating. Australia or Canada. Teddy had done his initial pilot training in Canada and had enjoyed the friendly people, the easy-going ways they had. He still remembered a trip they had gone on to pick peaches, like a dream now in this winter. He had travelled around France before the war too, even more evanescent than any dream, but France had been a young man's fancy, not a place for a married Englishman in 1947. In the end, they concluded, they had fought the war for England ('Britain,' Nancy corrected him), and it seemed wrong to abandon the country in this new hour of her need. It was perhaps a mistake, he thought in later years. They should have taken the five-pound passage and left, joined all those other disgruntled ex-servicemen who realized that Britain in the gloomy aftermath of war felt more like a defeated country than a victorious one.

Nancy found an old farm cottage to rent in a dale that was on the cusp of moorland. It was called Mouse Cottage ('How very fey,' Sylvie said), although they never found out why for they never, to their surprise, saw a single mouse the whole time they lived there. Perhaps it was called that because it was so tiny, Nancy said.

There was a cast-iron range, with a fire and oven built in, and a back boiler to provide hot water. ('Thank God,' they both said frequently, fervently, in this cold.) They often made a supper of just toast, scraped with their rationed butter, holding the bread on a brass fork in front of the fire, rather than face the icy blasts that blew through the small scullery that had been tacked on to the back of the cottage at some point in the past. On to this scullery had been attached something more like a shed than a room, in which there was a washbasin and a half-bath, its brass taps blackened and its worn enamel streaked with rust. No wireless, no telephone and an outside privy that meant in this weather an understandable reliance on the unsavoury chamber-pot. It was their first home together and Teddy thought he already understood how fondly they would think of it in the future, if not necessarily now.

They had rented it fully furnished, which was just as well as they had no furniture of their own apart from an upright piano that they had managed to cram into the downstairs room. Nancy was a good pianist although nowhere near as good as Sylvie. The previous owner had apparently died *in situ* and so they were now availing themselves of some poor old biddy's cups and saucers, cushions and lamps, not to mention the brass toasting fork. They presumed a woman because although the curtains and loose covers on the chairs were a worn linen in a Jacobean pattern that could have been favoured by either sex, the cottage was dotted with crocheted blankets and tatted mats and framed cross-stitch pictures of gardens and crinolined ladies that all spoke of an old woman. They thought of her as an invisible benefactor. Their bedding, at least, had not last embraced a corpse as Mrs Shawcross had raided her laundry cupboard for 'spares'.

They had taken on the lease in May, in blossom time, bamboozled by balmy skies. ('That's a lot of "b"s, lad,' Bill Morrison said. 'I bet there's a word for that.' ' "Alliteration",' Teddy said and Bill Morrison said, 'Well, try not to.') 'Goodness,' Sylvie said when she visited. 'Quite primitive, isn't it?' They made corned beef sandwiches and Sylvie had brought eggs from her chickens and cucumber pickles and they hardboiled the eggs and made quite a good picnic, sitting on an old rug, flattening the overgrown grass of the garden. 'You're going backwards,' Sylvie said. 'Soon you'll be living in a cave and bathing in the stream.'

'Would that be so bad?' Nancy said, peeling an egg. 'We could live like gypsies. I could grub around in hedgerows for berries and sell pegs and lucky charms from door to door and Teddy could catch fish and shoot rabbits and hares.'

'Teddy won't shoot anything,' Sylvie said decisively. 'He doesn't kill.'

'He would if he had to,' Nancy said. 'Can you pass the salt, please?'

He has killed, Teddy thought. Many people. Innocent people. He had personally helped to ruin poor Europe. 'I am here, you know,' he said, 'sitting next to you.'

'And,' Nancy continued, visibly warming to the idea, 'our hair would smell of woodsmoke and our babies would run around naked.'

She said it to annoy Sylvie, of course. Sylvie, duly annoyed, said, 'You used to be such a bluestocking, Nancy. Married life has quite changed something in you.'

'No, the war changed something in me,' Nancy said. There was a brief silence as the three of them contemplated what that 'something' might be.

He had lost Nancy to the Official Secrets Act during the war. She had been unable to tell him what she was doing and he had been incapable of telling her what he was doing (because he didn't want to) and their relationship foundered on ignorance. She had vowed to tell him when the war finished ('Afterwards, I'll tell you everything. I promise'), but by then he wasn't terribly interested. 'Cryptology and codes and so on,' she confessed, although of course he had guessed this long ago, for what else could she have been doing?

No one else who had worked at Bletchley during the war talked about what they had done and yet Nancy was quite prepared to break her oath so that there would be 'nothing between us'. Secrets had the power to kill a marriage, she said. Nonsense, Sylvie said, it was secrets that could save a marriage.

Nancy was willing to unpack her whole heart to him,

but Teddy had chambers that he never opened. He was not so honest about his own war – the horror and the violence, not to mention the fear, seemed an immensely private thing. And there was his own infidelity, too. Nancy admitted to having 'had sex' (a crude phrase to Teddy's ears) with other men when she thought he was dead, rather than in a POW camp, whereas he had been unfaithful without the excuse of thinking her dead.

She never asked, he supposed that was the beauty of her. And he couldn't see what good could come from confession. He had considered it, in that shoddy little pub the night before their wedding. He could have made a clean breast of his sins and shortcomings, but really in the end it was nothing and Nancy, too, would consider it nothing and that might be the worst of it.

Sylvie had brought cake too, a rather solid affair with caraway seeds that stuck in their teeth. She had made it herself. Having learned to cook late in life Sylvie was still baffled by the science of it. Nancy sliced the cake and served it on the old biddy's mismatched plates.

'Now if you had had had a proper wedding,' Sylvie said, 'you would have wedding presents – a china tea service, for example – so that you didn't have to serve your guests from such a rum assortment of crockery. Not to mention all the other necessities of married life.'

'Oh, we get by just fine without the necessities,' Nancy said.

'You're becoming more like your mother,' Sylvie said and Nancy replied, 'Thank you. I'll take that as a compliment,' which riled Sylvie even more. Sylvie, of course, had never quite got over being denied a wedding by Teddy and Nancy. They had 'sneaked away', in her words. 'Not exactly the kind of photographs you can put in a silver frame, are they?' she sighed, when she scrutinized the tiny snaps Bea had taken on the day on her old box Brownie.

'The cake is delicious,' Nancy said in an effort to mollify Sylvie, but was distracted by a large bee that dropped from exhaustion on to the rug and became entangled in the fibres of wool. Nancy encouraged it on to the palm of her hand and carried it over to the hedge, where she sought out a shady patch for it.

'It will die,' Sylvie said to Teddy. 'They never recover. They're worn out by hard work, they're the Methodists of the insect world.'

'Yet the instinct is to save,' Teddy said, regarding Nancy fondly as she tended to the bee, insignificant in the greater order of things.

'Perhaps sometimes we shouldn't,' Sylvie said. 'It's so hot,' she added, fanning herself with a napkin. 'I'm going inside. And the cake is *not* delicious. Nancy was always a good liar.'

They had had no suspicions of winter when they moved into Mouse Cottage. They were still talking of getting a flock of leghorns and learning beekeeping, of digging over the neglected garden and planting potatoes 'the first year' to turn over the soil. 'Eden raised,' Nancy laughed. There had even been talk of a goat. None of these things had come to pass by the time the long dark nights closed in on them. They had been too taken up with each other, grasshoppers enjoying the summer, rather than ants preparing for the winter. They were both immensely relieved that they had never got as far as the goat.

It was difficult now to remember those first summer evenings – the stored heat of the day beneath the eaves, the worn cotton curtains billowing idly at the wide-open casement. They made love when it was still light, fell into an ecstasy of sleep and woke to make love again at dawn. They never saw the dark. Now they had an old grey horse blanket tacked up at the window and lived in terror of draughts. There was ice on the window panes, both inside and out.

'It's no better here,' Ursula wrote from London. They picked up their post from a makeshift box at the end of the track. They had left for work by the time the post was delivered and, never having witnessed the heroics of their postman, could only imagine them. Their own efforts seemed epic enough. They had bought an old Army Land Rover at auction with some of Izzie's (very generous) wedding-present money. Her standard gift for family weddings was a set of fish knives and forks, but she handed Teddy a large cheque over afternoon tea at Brown's. 'Augustus owes you,' she said. Augustus, who had never grown as Teddy had, who had remained irresponsible and endlessly culpable. Teddy occasionally wondered what Augustus would be doing if he *had* grown. He imagined that this fictional doppelgänger – Gus – would now be hanging around Soho in the grimy aftermath of war, frequenting disreputable pubs and clubs. A more interesting story surely than *Augustus and the Disappearing Act*, the latest offering in the Augustus *oeuvre* which had made it through the snow two days ago and was sitting unread on top of Nancy's piano. 'In which Augustus joins a local magic circle and wreaks his usual mischief,' it said on the back of the jacket.

'Even this eternal winter must end,' Nancy said. 'And we have the snowdrops as proof. You did see them, didn't you? You weren't just making it up for your column?'

He was surprised that she would think such a thing. 'Of course not,' he said. He was beginning to wish he had never seen the dratted snowdrops, let alone chosen them as his subject. He was looking forward to March with its abundance of birds and buds. There would be no shortage of topics for Agrestis in the spring. He took a log from the basket and placed it on the fire. It spat out a glittering shower of sparks on to the hearth rug. They both watched with interest to see if any of them would catch but they sputtered harmlessly and died.

'Why don't you go on?' Nancy said.

'Sure?'

'Yes.' Her eyes firmly on her knitting. (*Nancy was always a good liar.*)

'Some say the snowdrop was first brought to these lands by the Romans, others say that they were first cultivated by monks (or perhaps nuns), and indeed in many of Shakespeare's "bare, ruined choirs" they can be found carpeting the ground in profusion in Spring. Yet somehow it feels like a flower that is native, that has been here since the dawn of time, the very essence of Englishness.

'One legend of the snowdrop's origins tells how when Adam and Eve were expelled from the Garden they were sent into what seemed to them to be the punishment of eternal Winter and that an angel, taking pity on them, turned a snowflake into a snowdrop as a sign that Spring would return to the world.'

A yawn again from Nancy, perhaps less well concealed.

'I'm only looking for corrections to mistakes,' Teddy said. 'You don't have to *like* it.'

She looked up from her knitting and said, 'I do like it! Don't be such a sensitive soul. I'm just tired, that's all.'

'Those of us enduring this unforgiving Winter can perhaps sympathize only too readily with our biblical forebears. Candlemas in the Catholic calendar is the Feast of the Purification of Mary—'

'It's quite wordy, isn't it? Don't you think?'

'Wordy?' Teddy said

Before the war he had fancied himself as something of a poet and had a couple of poems published in obscure literary magazines, but on a visit home to Fox Corner during the war he had looked through these antebellum offerings, kept in a shoebox beneath his childhood bed, and saw them for what they were – the amateur scribblings of an immature mind. In style they relied on vague, tortuous metaphors, nearly always in an attempt to describe his response to nature. He was drawn to the grand Wordsworthian sweep of hill and vale and water. 'You have a pagan soul,' Nancy had once told him but he didn't agree. He had the soul of a country parson who had lost his faith. But it didn't matter now, for the great god Pan was indeed dead and war had long ago killed Teddy's desire to make poetry.

After graduating from Oxford he had applied to stay on and do an MPhil, putting off the time when he would have to find a career. In his heart of hearts he still wanted to be a train driver but he supposed that was out of the question. He would have been very surprised (and thrilled too) if someone had told him that five years later he would be training to be a pilot.

He had settled on Blake's poetry for his research, for what he thought of as his 'opaque simplicity' ('What on earth does *that* mean?' Sylvie said), but when it came to it he was too restless and abandoned Blake after a term and went home to Fox Corner. He was tired of the analysis and dissection of literature, 'like an autopsy', he said to Hugh, who had invited him into the growlery for a glass of malt and a 'little chat' about his future.

'I would like,' Teddy said thoughtfully, 'to travel around a bit, to see the country. And perhaps a little of Europe too.' By 'the country' he meant England rather than the whole of Britain, and by 'Europe' he meant France, but refrained from saying so as Hugh had a rather baffling prejudice against the French. Teddy tried to explain to his father that he wanted to respond *directly* to the world. '"A life of the senses," as you might say. To work on the land and write poetry. The two are not contradictory.' No, no, not at all, Hugh said, Virgil and *The Georgics* and so on. A 'farmer poet'. Or a 'poet farmer'. Hugh had been a banker all his life, which was most certainly not a life of the senses.

From the age of twelve Teddy had worked on Ettringham Hall Farm in the holidays, not for the money – he was often unpaid – but for the pleasure of hard labour in the fresh air. ('I can't think of anything worse,' Izzie said. She had found him helping out in the milking-shed on a visit to Fox Corner and had almost got herself crushed by a cow.) 'In my heart I'm not an intellectual,' he said to his father, knowing this was a stance that would appeal to Hugh, who did indeed nod in sympathy. And to be connected to the land, Teddy said, isn't that the most profound relationship of all? And out of this would come writing that wasn't just the dry product of the intellect (another nod from Hugh) but was *felt*, on the pulses. Perhaps even a novel. (How callow he had been!)

'A novel?' Hugh said, unable to stop his eyebrows from rising. 'Fiction?' Sylvie was the novel reader, not Hugh. Hugh was a man of his time. He liked facts. But Teddy was one of Hugh's favourite children. Both Hugh and Sylvie had secret listings for their children, not so secret in Sylvie's case. They were similar – Pamela came in the middle, Maurice at the bottom, but it was Ursula, low on Sylvie's list, who was closest to Hugh's heart. Sylvie's favourite, of course, was Teddy, her best boy. Teddy wondered who she had preferred before he came along. None of them, he suspected.

'Well, you don't want to get *stuck*,' Hugh said. Did his father feel stuck? Is that why he offered Teddy twenty pounds and told him to go and 'live life a little'? Teddy refused the money – it was important that he make his own way, wherever that was – but he felt enormously grateful for this show of support from his father.

Not surprisingly, his mother did not give her blessing. 'You want to do *what*?' Sylvie said. 'You have a degree from Oxford and you want to wander around like a troubadour?'

'A minstrel,' Hugh said. 'A thing of shreds and patches.' He was a great Gilbert and Sullivan fan.

'Exactly,' Sylvie said. 'Tramps go from farm to farm looking to be hired for work. Not the Beresfords.'

'He's a Todd, actually,' Hugh said (unhelpfully). 'You've become a tremendous snob, Sylvie,' he added, even more unhelpfully.

'I'm not thinking of doing it for ever,' Teddy said. 'A year perhaps and then I'll settle on something.' He was still thinking about Sylvie's word 'troubadour' and how attracted he was to that (very unsettled) idea.

And so he went. He sowed cabbage seed in Lincolnshire, spent the lambing season in Northumberland, helped bring in the wheat harvest in Lancashire, picked strawberries in Kent. He was fed by farmers' wives at big farmhouse kitchen tables and slept in barns and sheds and dilapidated cottages as the year turned and, during the warm summer nights, in his old canvas tent, somewhat mildewed, that had seen him through Cubs and Kibbo Kift. Its most memorable adventure was yet to take place when in 1938 the tent accompanied Teddy and Nancy on a camping holiday to the Peak District, during which they (finally) ceased to be friends and became lovers.

'Not both?' Teddy puzzled.

'Well, of course,' Nancy said and Teddy realized that he had known Nancy too long and was too familiar with her to suddenly 'fall in love' with her. He loved her, of course, but he wasn't *in* love and never had been. Would he ever be, he wondered?

But that was in the future. Now he was in a sheep barn on lambing watch, reading Housman and Clare by the light of a Tilley lamp. He had been attempting poems, almost entirely about landscape and weather (the shoebox poems) that even he found tedious. There was no poetry to be had in sheep, or even lambs for that matter. ('The little shivering gaping things' – he had always been repelled by Rossetti's 'The Lambs of Grasmere'.) Cows yielded nothing but milk. Not for Teddy, Hopkins's 'skies of couple-colour as a brinded cow'. 'I worship Hopkins,' he wrote to Nancy from somewhere south of Hadrian's Wall. 'If only I could write like him!' He was always cheerful in letters, it seemed like good manners, when in fact he was in despair at his own cloddish verse.

Izzie came to visit him, briefly, staying in a hotel on Lake Windermere where she stood him an expensive dinner and plied him with alcohol and questions to 'lend some authenticity' to *Augustus Becomes a Farmer*.

The year turned quickly. The early apple harvest in Kent gave birth to an ode to autumn that would have shamed Keats ('The apples, the apples, rosy and fair / not yet touched by the fingers of frost . . .'). He was not yet ready to renounce either poetry or husbandry and boarded a ferry at Dover, a new unsullied thick notebook in his bag.

Disembarking on the foreign soil of France he headed due south, for the vineyards and the grape harvest, thinking of Keats's beaker of blushful Hippocrene, although the Hippocrene was in Greece, not France, wasn't it? He hadn't considered Greece. He rebuked himself for the (large) omission from his itinerary of the cradle of civilization. He rebuked himself again later for having missed the wonders of Venice, Florence and Rome, but at the time he had been happy to sidestep the rest of Europe. In 1936 it was a troubled land and Teddy felt no need to experience its political upheavals. In later years he wondered if he had been wrong, if he shouldn't have faced up to the evil that was brewing. Sometimes it takes just one good man, Ursula said to him during the war. Neither of them could think of an example from history, 'except the Buddha perhaps', Ursula offered. 'I'm not convinced by the reality of Christ.' There were plenty of instances where it had taken just one bad man, Teddy said gloomily.

Perhaps there would be time for Greece. After all, his deadline ('a year perhaps') was self-imposed.

By the time a late Sauternes harvest had finished he was 'as brown and strong as a peasant', he reported in a letter to Nancy. His French, too, had gained the coarse fluency of the peasant. After a day's picking he was ravenous and gorged on the huge evening meals that the domain provided for their workers. At night he pitched the old canvas tent in a field. For the first time since his childhood at Fox Corner he slept the dreamless sleep of the dead or the innocent, helped by the copious amounts of wine that accompanied meals. Sometimes there was a woman. He never wrote a word.

For the rest of his life he would be able to close his eyes and conjure up the sight and smell of the food he had eaten in France – he had relished the oily garlickyness of the stews, the artichoke leaves dipped in butter, the *oeufs en cocotte* – eggs baked in the oven inside huge beef tomatoes. A saddle of roasted lamb quilted with cloves of garlic and sprigs of rosemary, a work of art. These were tastes that were foreign – in every way – to the bland English palate. Cheese, sour and strong; the desserts: *flaugnarde* with peaches, *clafouti* with cherries, *tarte aux noix* and *tarte aux pommes* and a *Far Breton* – a kind of prune custard tart that to the end of his life he dreamed about eating again and never did. 'Prunes and custard?' Mrs Glover said doubtfully when he returned.

Mrs Glover left Fox Corner soon after Teddy's return, driven away perhaps by his requests for French regional cooking. 'Don't be silly,' Sylvie said. 'She's retired to live with her sister.'

Then there was breakfast, of course, taken at the big table in the domain kitchen. Not the gruel-like porridge ladled out at boarding school or the unsurprising egg and bacon of Fox Corner. Instead he sliced open half a freshly baked baguette, wadded the inside with Camembert and dipped it into a bowl of scalding strong coffee. He forgot all about this way of greeting the day when he returned home and then, decades later, when he was living in sheltered accommodation at Fanning Court, it came back to him suddenly and, inspired by the richness of the memory, he bought a baguette from Tesco's ('baked on the premises' – yes, but from what?) and a small round of unripe Camembert, and poured his morning coffee into a cereal bowl rather than the usual mug. It was not the same. Not at all.

As winter approached he moved on south – 'I'm like the swallow,' he wrote to Ursula – until he was stopped by the sea and rented a room above a café in a little fishing village, unspoilt, as yet, by visitors. Every day he sat at a table in the one and only café, a jacket and a scarf all he needed to defend himself against the Riviera winter, and smoked Gitanes and drank espresso from thick little white cups, his notebook on the table in front of him. By lunchtime he had moved on to wine, with bread and fish straight from the sea and grilled over wood, and by the time the sleepy afternoons had taken hold he was ready for an aperitif. He was living a life of the senses, he told himself, but deep down he suspected he was shirking his life and felt accordingly guilty. (He was English, after all.)

'L'Ecrivain Anglais', the villagers called him, rather fondly as he was the first poet to visit them, although artists were ten a penny in that part of the world. They were impressed by his colloquial French and his dedication to his notebook. He was glad that they couldn't read his paltry offerings. They might have lost some of their admiration for him.

He decided to be more methodical in his approach to Art (Sylvie's capital letter). Poems were constructs, not simply words that flowed willy-nilly from the brain. 'Observations' he had written as a heading at the beginning of the notebook, and the pages were filled with pedestrian images – 'The sea is particularly blue today – Sapphire? Azure? Ultramarine?' And 'The sun glints off the sea like a thousand diamonds' or 'The coastline seems composed of solid blocks of colour and hot slices of sunshine.' (He was rather pleased with that.) And '*Madame la propriétaire* is wearing her funny little green jacket today.' Was there a poem to be had from *Madame la propriétaire*, he wondered? He thought of the fields of lavender and sunflowers he had seen on his sojourn, all harvested now, and sought out images – the 'imperial spikes' and 'golden discs of Helios turning to worship their god'. If only he was an artist – paint seemed less demanding than words. He felt sure that Van Gogh's sunflowers hadn't given him as much trouble.

'Gulls wheeling and screeching overhead, excited by the fishing boats returning home,' he wrote carefully, before lighting up another Gitane. The sun was below the yardarm (almost) as his father would have said if he were here (how could he not like France?) and it was time for a *pastis*. He began to think of himself as a loafer, a lotus eater. He had enough money saved to winter on the Côte d'Azur and then perhaps head north and see Paris. 'One can't die without seeing Paris,' Izzie said. Although he did.

Shortly before Christmas a telegram arrived. His mother was in hospital. 'Pneumonia, rather poorly, best come home,' his father had written sparely. 'Her mother's lungs,' Hugh said on Teddy's return. Teddy had never known this grandmother and the legendary lungs that, according to Sylvie, had killed her. Sylvie recovered surprisingly quickly and was home before the year was out. She had not been so very ill, Teddy wasn't sure it had merited a telegram and for a while suspected some kind of family conspiracy, but 'She kept asking for you,' Hugh said, rather apologetically. 'The prodigal son,' his father said fondly when he picked him up from the station.

To tell the truth, Teddy was rather relieved to give up the pretence of poetry and after the familiarity of Christmas at Fox Corner it seemed faintly absurd to journey all the way back to France. (And for what? To be a loafer?) So instead, when his father found him a position in his bank he took it. The first day, as he entered the hushed halls of polished mahogany panelling he felt like a prisoner embarking on a life sentence. A bird with its wings clipped, earthbound for ever. Was this it? His life over?

'There, Ted,' Hugh said, 'I knew you'd settle to something eventually.'

The war, when it came, was an immense relief for Teddy.

'Penny for them?' Nancy said, taking a tape measure from her knitting basket and placing it against his shoulder.

'Not worth it,' he said. Back to the wretched snow-drop.

> 'The "drop" in snowdrop does not, as many think, refer to a snow flake but to an earring, and one can picture this delicate flower trembling in the ear of some Elizabethan beauty.'

'Strictly speaking, can an earring tremble *in* an ear?' Nancy said, laying down her needles in her lap and frowning at her knitting. She pulled on her own delicate earlobe to demonstrate the fixity of the small grey pearl therein. 'If it were *dangling* it could tremble.'

She was forensic. She would make a fine High Court judge. She could deliver an opinion that bore no weight of emotion and in the most pleasant fashion. 'How cruel you are to me,' she said, laughing. She had hinted before at what she considered the rather 'flat' quality of these pieces. It was journalism, Teddy thought defensively, an inert form of writing. Nancy always wanted everyone to find the best in everything.

When they moved to Yorkshire Teddy found himself in an indifferent boys' grammar school in a smallish woollen mill town, soot-soiled and shoddy, that was quietly dying, and knew from the very first lesson – *Romeo and Juliet*, 'Women, being the weaker vessels, are ever thrust to the wall' – to a class of sniggering thirteen-year-olds that it had been a mistake. He saw the future unravelling before him, day after dismal day. Saw himself dutifully earning money to support Nancy and their as-yet-unborn children who were already weighting him down with responsibility. Saw himself, too, on the day he finally retired, a disappointed man. It was the bank all over again. He was a stoic, it had been beaten into him at school, and he was as loyal as a dog, and he knew he would stick it out, no matter how great the sacrifice of self.

'You fought the war for those boys,' Ursula said when she visited, 'for their freedom. Are they worth it?'

'No, not at all,' Teddy said and they both laughed because it was a cliché that they were already tired of hearing and they knew that freedom, like love, was an absolute and not to be parcelled out on a whim or a favour.

Nancy, on the other hand, loved her profession. She was a maths teacher in a grammar school for well-behaved, clever girls, in a pleasant spa town. She enjoyed making them even cleverer, even better-behaved, and they loved her in return. She had lied on application, told the school that she was unmarried (not even a widow), erasing Teddy efficiently from her history. She was Miss Shawcross again. 'They don't like married teachers,' she explained to Teddy. 'They leave to have babies, or they are distracted by their domestic life, by their husbands.' Distracted? Of course, the plan was to give up teaching when they started a family, but that was in the lap of the gods and the gods didn't appear to be in a hurry.

She knew how miserable Teddy was teaching. One of the many good things about Nancy was that she didn't believe that people should suffer unnecessarily. (It always surprised Teddy how many people did.) She encouraged him to take up writing again – 'A novel this time,' she said. She had read the shoebox poems and Teddy supposed her opinion of them was pretty much the same as his. 'A novel,' she said. 'A novel for the new world, something fresh and different that tells us who we are and what we should be.' The world didn't seem very new to Teddy, but rather old and weary (as he suspected himself to be), and he wasn't sure he had anything to say that was worth writing about, but Nancy seemed determined that he would have talent. 'At least have a go,' she said. 'You won't know if you can do it until you try.'

And so he allowed Nancy to cajole him into sitting down in the evenings and at the weekends in front of the little Remington that she had found in a second-hand shop. No more 'Observations', he thought. No more thick notebooks. Just get on with it.

He found a title first, calling his debut upon the literary stage *A Bower Quiet for Us*, taken from Keats's 'Endymion':

> *A thing of beauty is a joy for ever:*
> *Its loveliness increases; it will never*
> *Pass into nothingness; but still will keep*
> *A bower quiet for us, and a sleep*
> *Full of sweet dreams, and health, and*
> *quiet breathing.*

'Oh, how he must have longed for "health, and quiet breathing",' Ursula said. 'And perhaps by imagining it he hoped it would come true.' His sister always spoke sadly of Keats, as if he had only just died. It was an awkward title though, not exactly catchy. 'It will do,' Nancy said, 'for now at any rate.' He knew her thinking. She believed he needed to be healed and writing might be the physic that did the trick. 'Art as therapy,' he had overheard her say to Mrs Shawcross. His own mother would have derided such a notion. The opening line of 'Endymion', 'A thing of beauty is a joy for ever', was more Sylvie's creed. Perhaps that would have made a better title. *A Thing of Beauty*.

Unfortunately Teddy discovered that every character

introduced or plot wrestled with was bland or common-
place. The great authors of the past had set standards that
made his own attempts at artifice look puny. He could
find no engagement with the one-dimensional lives he
had created. If an author was a god, then he was a very
poor second-rate one, scrabbling around on the foothills
of Olympus. You had to care, he supposed, and there was
nothing he cared to write about. 'But what about the war?'
Nancy said. The war? he thought, secretly amazed that
she could think that something so shattering in its reality
could be rendered so quickly into fiction. 'Life then,' she
said. 'Your life. A *Bildungsroman*.'

'I think I would rather just *live* my life,' Teddy said, 'not
make an artifice of it.' And what on earth would he write
about? If you excluded the war (an enormous exclusion,
he acknowledged) then nothing had happened to him. A
boyhood at Fox Corner, the brief, rather lonely and pointless life of a wandering poet-cum-farmhand and now the
quotidian of married life – the log on the fire, the choice
between Ovaltine or cocoa, and Nancy's neat, contained
self bundled up in sweaters against the cold. He was not
complaining about the latter, he knew he should feel
lucky to have it when so many he had known did not.

'Oh, teach me how I should forget to think,' a boy whose
name he would never remember read out in lifeless tones,
and the bell rang, causing the whole class to rise up like a
flock of sparrows and jostle their way out of the classroom door before he had dismissed them. ('Discipline
doesn't seem to be your forte,' the disappointed headmaster said. 'I thought being an RAF officer . . .')

Teddy sat at his desk in the empty classroom, waiting for a second-year English class to make its appearance. He looked around the dingy room with its scents of India rubber and unwashed necks. The morning sun was shining softly through the windows, the dust of chalk and of boys caught in a beam of sunlight. There was a world outside these walls.

He stood up abruptly and marched out of the classroom, squeezing his way past a gaggle of eleven-year-olds coming reluctantly through the door. 'Sir?' one of them said, alarmed by this dereliction of duty.

He was AWOL, driving home on the high back road, thinking he might stop somewhere and go for a long hike to give himself time to think. He was in danger of becoming a drifter, a man who couldn't stick to anything. His brothers were doing well for themselves. Jimmy was in America, leading a fast, glossy life, 'earning big bucks', while Maurice was a Whitehall mandarin, a pillar of respectability. And here he was, unable even to be a lowly teacher. He had made a vow during the war that if he survived he would lead a steady, uncomplaining life. The vow seemed doomed to be unfulfilled. Was there something wrong with him, he wondered?

He was saved by a motorist who had broken down by the side of the road. Teddy stopped the Land Rover and went to see if he could help. The old Humber Pullman had its bonnet propped up and the man was staring at the engine in the helpless way of the unmechanical, as if through the power of his thoughts alone he might get it working again. 'Ah, a gentleman of the road,' the man said, doffing his hat, when Teddy drew up in the Land Rover. 'This darn thing's worn out. Like me. Bill Morrison,' he said, extending a meaty hand.

While Teddy fiddled with the alternator they chatted about the hawthorn trees, in full glorious flush, that lined this particular stretch of road. 'The May', Bill Morrison called it. It lifted his heart to see it, he said. Afterwards, Teddy couldn't clearly recall this conversation but it had roamed 'all over the shop', as Bill put it, from the place of the hawthorn in English folklore – the Glastonbury thorn and so on – to the Queen of the May and the maypole, and Teddy had told him how for the Celts the tree marked the entrance to the otherworld and that the ancient Greeks had carried it in wedding processions.

'University man, I take it?' Bill Morrison said. Admiring rather than sardonic, although perhaps just a smidgeon of the latter. 'Ever tried your hand at writing?'

'Well . . .' Teddy demurred.

'How about lunch then, lad? My treat,' Bill Morrison said as the old Humber coughed back into life. And so Teddy found himself in a convoy of two on the way to a hotel in Skipton for what turned out to be a rather boozy roast beef affair, during the course of which he had his life examined from every angle by Bill Morrison.

He was a large bluff man with a high unhealthy colour who had 'cut his teeth' on the *Yorkshire Post*, a long time ago, and was now a blunt old-fashioned Tory. 'Avuncular but sharp,' Teddy reported to Nancy later. His God was a robust Anglican, a Yorkshireman who probably played cricket for the county when he wasn't sending laws down from the mountain. As time went by, Teddy learned more of Bill's generous heart and gruff kindness. He liked the fact that Teddy was married ('the natural state for a man') and teased his war out of him. Bill himself had 'survived the Somme'.

He was the editor of the *Recorder*. It was a surprisingly long time afterwards that Teddy learned that he also owned the *Recorder*. 'Do you know it, Ted?'

'Yes,' Teddy said politely. Did he? A vague recollection, in the dentist's waiting room, distracting himself from the imminent removal of a rotten tooth, dental care not having been a priority in the POW camp.

'Because I'm looking for someone to write the Nature Notes,' Bill Morrison said. 'It's just a few lines every week – it won't keep you in bread, let alone bacon, even if you could get your hands on any. We used to have a man did the Nature Notes, went by the by-line Agrestis. That's Latin. Know what it means?'

'A rustic, a countryman.'

'Well, there you are.'

'What happened to the old one?' Teddy asked, while digesting this unexpected offer.

'Old age took him off. He was an old-style countryman. He was a difficult bugger,' he said affectionately.

Rather shyly Teddy mentioned his own agricultural curriculum vitae, the Northumberland lambs, the Kentish apples, his love of hill and vale and water. The pleasure to be had from the cup and saucer of an acorn, the unfurling frond of a fern, the pattern on the feather of a hawk. The transcendent beauty of the dawn chorus in an English bluebell wood. He omitted France, the solid blocks of colour, the hot slices of sunshine. They would not be to the taste of a man who had fought on the Somme.

Teddy was judged sound, even though he was a southerner.

'There were two men,' Bill Morrison said as they dug into the Stilton. It took Teddy a moment to realize that this was the rather ponderous introduction to some sort of witticism. 'One of them was from Yorkshire, God's own country. The other one wasn't a Yorkshireman. The one not from Yorkshire said to the other' (Teddy began to lose track at this point), '"I met a Yorkshireman t'other day," and the one from Yorkshire said, "How'd' tha know he were from Yorkshire?" And the one not from Yorkshire' (now Teddy began to lose the will to live) 'said, "Because of his accent," and the Yorkshireman said, "Nah, lad, if he'd been from Yorkshire it would have been the first thing he told you."'

'Try putting that in a Christmas cracker,' Nancy said when Teddy attempted to relate it to her that evening after rolling home, somewhat foxed. ('Oh, my, you reek of beer. I quite like it.') 'And you have a new job, on a newspaper?'

'No, not a newspaper,' Teddy said. 'Not a job either really,' he added. 'Just a few shillings a week.'

'What about the school? You'll still teach?'

The school, Teddy thought. This morning was already the past. (*Oh, teach me how I should forget to think.*) He had absconded, he said. 'Oh, you poor darling,' Nancy laughed. 'And this will lead to more, I know it will, I can feel it in my waters.'

It did. October with its autumn colours, mushrooms

and chestnuts and a late Indian summer. November brought 'Mother Nature tucking in her charges' for the oncoming struggle, and December was of necessity holly and robins. 'Find something heart-warming,' Bill said and so he wrote about how the robin got his red breast.

They were pedestrian pieces but that was fine by Bill Morrison, who wasn't 'looking for erudition'.

Another boozy lunch just before Christmas and he was offered the job of 'roving reporter'. The previous incumbent of the post had died during the war. 'Arctic convoys,' Bill Morrison said briskly, not wanting to dwell, and he too would be dead soon, he said, if he kept racing around doing the job of two men.

'Are you happy now?' Nancy asked as they hung up the holly and mistletoe they had picked in the woods.

'Yes,' Teddy said, giving the answer perhaps more consideration than the question had demanded.

The blasted snowdrops.

> 'There are some who consider it bad luck to pick these brave little heralds of Spring and will not let them in the house. Perhaps this is due to their profusion in churchyards.'

Sylvie always picked the first snowdrops at Fox Corner. It was a shame because they wilted and died so quickly.

> 'The white of the snowdrop and its association with untaintedness has always given this humble

flower an aura of innocence (who remembers now the "Snowdrop Band" of young girls of the previous century?)

'There is a German legend—'

'Oh, lord,' Nancy muttered under her breath.

'What?'

'I dropped a stitch. Go on.'

'—which relates that when God created all things he told the snow to go and ask the flowers for some colour. All but the kindly snowdrop refused and in reward the snow allowed it to be the first flower of Spring.

'Great music has the power to heal. Germany is no longer our enemy and it is salutary for us to remember her rich store of myth and legend and fairy tale, not to mention her cultural heritage, the music of Mozart—'

'Mozart was Austrian.'

'Yes, of course,' Teddy said. 'I don't know why I forgot that. Beethoven then. Brahms, Bach, Schubert. Schubert was German, wasn't he?'

'No, another Austrian.'

'Haydn?' he hazarded.

'Austrian.'

'There's a lot of them, aren't there? So – "her cultural heritage of Bach, Brahms, Beethoven—"'

Nancy nodded silently, like a schoolteacher approving a pupil's corrections. She could just have been counting stitches, of course.

'"Of these Beethoven is—"'

'We have rather left the snowdrop behind. Why all this talk of Germans?'

'Because it was a German legend I was referring to,' Teddy said.

'This seems to be about forgiving the Germans though. Have *you*? Forgiven them?'

Had he? Theoretically perhaps, but not in his heart, where truth resided. He thought of all the men he knew who had been killed. The dead, like demons and angels, were legion.

It was three years since his own war had ended. He had spent the last year *hors de combat* in a POW camp near the Polish border. He had parachuted out of a burning aircraft over Germany and had been unable to evade capture because of a broken ankle. His aircraft had been coned and shot down by flak on the dreadful raid to Nuremberg. He hadn't known it at the time but it was the worst night of the war for Bomber Command – ninety-six aircraft lost, five hundred and forty-five men killed, more than in the whole Battle of Britain. But by the time he made it home this was all old, cold news, Nuremberg all but forgotten. 'You were very brave,' Nancy said, with the same encouraging indifference – to Teddy's ears anyway – that she might have afforded him if he had done well in a maths test.

The war now for him was a jumble of random images that haunted his sleeping self – the Alps in moonlight, a propeller blade flying through the air, a face, pale in the water. *Well, good luck to you then.* Sometimes the overwhelming stench of lilacs, at other times a sweetly held dance tune. And always at the end of the nightmare there was the inescapable end itself, the fire and the sickening hurtle of the fall to earth. In nightmares we wake ourselves before the awful end, before the fall, but Teddy had to be woken by Nancy's shushing, by her cradle hand soothing him, and he would stare into the darkness for a long time wondering what would happen to him if she failed to wake him one night.

He had been reconciled to death during the war and then suddenly the war was over and there was a next day and a next day and a next day. Part of him never adjusted to having a future.

'"Beethoven,"' he began again doggedly. You could hardly hold Beethoven responsible for the war. He had a sudden memory – himself and Ursula in the Royal Albert Hall – when was that, 1943? – listening to Beethoven's Ninth Symphony, the Choral, Ursula almost vibrating with the emotional power of the music. He had felt it too, the power of something beyond, something outwith the petty everyday pace. He shook himself, a wet dog.

'Are you all right, darling?'

An affirmative. Just dislodging the war, the awfulness of it all, the overwhelming sadness. Nothing he could convey in words to her.

'And, you know,' Nancy continued, a blithe spirit, 'I don't think people necessarily want to be reminded about the war when they're reading Agrestis's Nature Notes. In fact quite the opposite, I imagine.'

'Shall I make cocoa?' he offered, to escape the subject. 'Or would you rather have Ovaltine?'

'Ovaltine, please.'

'You'll ruin your eyes,' he said as he poured the half-frozen milk into a pan and placed it on the trivet over the fire.

'I'm stopping now,' she said, efficiently winding up her different-coloured balls of wool.

The milk rose up suddenly in the pan and Teddy snatched it away from the fire before it could boil over. His face, hot from the flames, made him aware of the burn tissue on his neck. It was just visible above his collar, the skin shiny and puckered pink, a promise of other scars in less visible places.

'Well, Wing Commander Todd,' Nancy said, 'time for bed, I think.'

She never used his wartime rank without a kind of mild irony, as if he had pretended to something. He had no idea why she did that, but it made him shrink inside a little.

They retired to Ultima Thule, as they called it, the ice-box that was their attic bedroom. Teddy shivered as he stripped himself of his layers and jumped into bed as if he was plunging into the icy waters of the North Sea.

They soon warmed each other up after the initial shock of polar sheets and frosty air. Lovemaking was vigorous rather than romantic in this kind of weather. ('One is never cold with a husband,' Nancy's sister Millie wrote from the arid heat of Arizona. 'Especially a handsome one like yours!')

A blizzard had started up and it sounded as if someone was pelting the windows with snowballs. They were a new Adam and Eve, exiled into eternal winter.

Nancy kissed him on the cheek and said, 'Goodnight, dear heart,' but Teddy was already asleep.

Nancy blew out the candle by the side of the bed and waited for Teddy's nightmares to begin.

They must have a baby, she thought. They must have a child to heal Teddy, to heal the world.

1939
Teddy's War

Innocence

He didn't hear Chamberlain make his sombre declaration on the wireless because he had chosen instead to take the Shawcrosses' old dog, Harry, for a walk in the lane. An amble, slow and arthritic, all that the Golden Retriever was capable of nowadays. His eyes were clouded with cataracts and a once large frame was now gaunt, the flesh shrunk against the bones. Deaf too, like Major Shawcross himself. The two of them, man and dog, had snoozed companionably through the long summer afternoons of 1939, locked together in their silent world – Major Shawcross in his old wickerwork chair and Harry melted on the lawn at his feet.

'It breaks my heart to see him like that,' Nancy said. She meant Harry, although the sentiment extended to her father. Teddy understood the particular poignancy of seeing a dog you had known as a puppy approaching the end of its life. 'Intimations of mortality, as Wordsworth didn't write,' Ursula said. 'Oh, if only dogs lived longer lives. We've mourned so many.'

The Shawcross girls were all enormously fond of their 'old Pa', an affection that was more than reciprocated by Major Shawcross. Hugh was close to Pamela and Ursula, of course, but Teddy was always rather surprised at the way that Major Shawcross was so free with his feelings, kissing and cuddling 'my girls' and often reduced to tears merely by the sight of them. ('The Great War,' Mrs Shawcross said. 'It changed him.') Hugh tended to reticence, a temperament that, if anything, the war had reinforced. Had Major Shawcross wished for a son? Surely he must have done, didn't all men? Did Teddy?

He intended to propose to Nancy. Today perhaps. A day of high historical drama so that in the future Nancy would say to their children (for they would surely have them), 'You know, your father proposed to me on the day that war broke out.' Teddy felt as if he had been waiting for a long time, too long perhaps. First, so that Nancy, at Newnham, could complete her Maths Tripos, and now for her to study for her PhD. Her doctoral topic was something to do with 'natural numbers'. They didn't seem at all natural to Teddy. He didn't want to find himself waiting for the war to be over as well, for who knew how long that would be?

Teddy was twenty-five, almost 'too long in the tooth' for marriage, as far as his mother was concerned. She was keen for grandchildren, keener than she had been for the ones she already had, courtesy of Pamela, who had 'three boys and counting', and Maurice, who had one of each. 'Like fish and chips,' Ursula said. Teddy barely knew

Maurice's offspring and Sylvie reported them to be 'rather dull'.

Marrying Nancy seemed inevitable. Why *wouldn't* he marry her? 'Childhood sweethearts,' Mrs Shawcross said, affected by the idea of romance. His own mother was less affected.

Everyone presumed it, even Sylvie, who thought Nancy 'too clever' for marriage. ('Marriage blunts one so.')

'And who else could there possibly *be* apart from Nancy anyway?' Teddy puzzled to Ursula. 'She's by far and away the best person I know. The nicest one too.'

'And you *do* love her. And you know that *we* all do.'

'Of course I love her,' Teddy said. (Had it been a question?) Did he know what love was? The love for a father, a sister, for a dog even, yes, but between a husband and wife? Two lives knitted inextricably together. Or yoked and harnessed. ('That's the point,' Sylvie said, 'otherwise we would all run wild.')

He thought of Adam and Eve, he thought of Sylvie and Hugh themselves. Neither seemed like terribly good examples. 'Nancy's parents' marriage,' Ursula said. 'Isn't that a good pattern? Major and Mrs Shawcross are happy. To all appearances, anyway.' But appearance and reality were different things, weren't they? And who knew the secrets of a marriage?

He had loved Nancy when they were young but that was a different kind of thing, high and clear but childishly innocent. *For now we see through a glass darkly.*

'Perhaps more to the point,' Ursula said, 'how would you feel if you *didn't* marry her?' So, yes, he thought, of course he would marry Nancy. They would move to a pleasant suburb, have those inevitable children, and he would work his way up in the bank until one day the staff would perhaps be as deferential to him as they were to his father. Or perhaps not.

It wouldn't just be the sharp knife of his wife who would be blunted. The future was a cage closing around him. Wasn't life itself a great trap, its jaws waiting to snap? He should never have returned from France. He should have ceased being indolent, stopped pretending he had a poet's soul, embraced the adventurer in himself instead, and pushed on eastwards, explored the extremities of Empire – Australia, perhaps. Somewhere raw and unsettled where a man could make himself rather than being made by those around him. Too late for that. Now it would not be the geography of Empire that would make him, it would be the architecture of war.

They had reached the dairy herd's field by now and Teddy pulled some stalks of long grass from the hedgerow and cried, 'Cush-cow, cush-cow,' but the cows, after the briefest of glances in his direction, remained placidly indifferent. He lit a cigarette and leaned on the gate while he smoked it. Harry had collapsed awkwardly on the ground, his scrawny sides heaving with exertion. 'Poor old boy,' Teddy said, reaching down and scratching behind the old dog's soft ear. He thought about Hugh. Their paths never crossed at the bank but his father would occasionally invite Teddy to lunch at his club on Pall Mall. The stolid world of finance suited Hugh, but for Teddy it was stultifying tedium and, occasionally, downright misery.

His father would retire soon, of course, potter around the garden, doze over the open pages of his *Wisden* in the garden or the growlery, get on Sylvie's nerves. That was indeed how Hugh was found, just over a year later, in a garden deckchair, a copy of *Wisden* open on his lap. Asleep for ever. Even this, the least troublesome of deaths, seemed to exasperate Sylvie. 'He just slipped away without a word!' she complained, as if he had owed her more. Perhaps he had.

'Dad was never one to make a fuss,' Ursula wrote to Teddy in Canada on flimsy blue, the ink smudged irrevocably where a tear must have dropped.

Teddy ground out the cigarette stub beneath his foot and said, 'Come on then, Harry, we're going to miss lunch if we don't get a move on.' The dog couldn't hear him but he didn't shift even when Teddy gave him a gentle prod and he feared that he had worn him out completely. He might be a bag of bones but he was still heavy and Teddy wasn't sure that he could carry the dead weight of the dog all the way home, although he supposed he would have to manage if there was no alternative – needs must. But luckily Harry hauled himself heroically on to four legs and they wended their way slowly back to Nancy's house.

'Oh, stay away, do,' Mrs Shawcross implored when she caught sight of him at the back door of Jackdaws. She flapped a tea-towel at him as if he were a fly.

Nancy, at home for the long vacation, was in bed, with what had turned out to be whooping cough ('At my age!'), being nursed assiduously by Mrs Shawcross, who knew that Teddy had also missed out on the illness as a child. 'You mustn't catch it,' she said. 'It's quite horrible in an adult.'

'Don't go near that girl,' Sylvie warned when he told her that he had offered, in the current absence of a resident dog at Fox Corner, to take Harry for a walk. Too late, he thought.

'That girl' was the girl he was going to propose to, but not today after all, perhaps. 'She's really rather poorly,' Mrs Shawcross said. 'But I'll give her your love, of course.'

'Please do.'

The various smells of Sunday lunch wafted out of Mrs Shawcross's kitchen. Mrs Shawcross, hair straggling from an untidy bun, looked rather flushed and not a little flustered, but in Teddy's experience that was the effect that cooking Sunday lunch had on women. Jackdaws, like Fox Corner, had recently lost its cook and Mrs Shawcross seemed even less suited to the culinary arts than Sylvie. Of Major Shawcross there was no sign. Mrs Shawcross herself was a vegetarian and Teddy wondered what she would eat while Major Shawcross was enjoying his beef. An egg, perhaps. 'Oh, lord, no,' Mrs Shawcross said, 'the whole idea of eating an egg makes me feel quite squeamish.'

Teddy spotted an open bottle of Madeira on the kitchen table and a little glass, half full of the brown liquor. 'War,' Mrs Shawcross said, her eyes filling with tears, and, infection forgotten, she pulled Teddy towards her in a warm, rather damp embrace. She smelt of the Madeira and of Coal Tar soap, an unlikely, rather unsettling combination. Mrs Shawcross was large and soft and always a little sad. Sylvie was annoyed by the misbehaviour of the world but Mrs Shawcross carried the burden of it patiently, as you would for a child. He supposed the war would make that burden heavier.

Mrs Shawcross placed a hand against her temple and said, 'Oh dear, I think I have one of my heads coming on.' She sighed and added, 'Thank goodness we have girls. Neville would never be able to face sending a son into battle.'

It seemed more than probable to Teddy that he was already incubating the whooping cough. Mrs Shawcross didn't know that Nancy had travelled up to London last week to see him, sneaking into his lodgings beneath the gimlet eye of his landlady and staying the night, the two of them squeezed together in his narrow bed, convulsing with laughter at the noise that the creaking bedsprings were making. They were still novices at that kind of thing. 'Rank amateurs,' Nancy said cheerfully. There was passion between them, but it was of the orderly, good-humoured kind. (Of course, one might argue that, by its definition, this was not passion.) There had been a girl or two at Oxford and a couple in France, but sex with them had been more like a bodily function, one that had left him discontented and not a little abashed. The sex act was perhaps not bestial but it was certainly animalistic and he supposed he was grateful to Nancy for domesticating it. Savage desire and yearning romance were probably best kept between the pages of a book. He was his father's son, he suspected. The war changed this, as it changed everything, introducing him to less civilized encounters. However, Teddy would never be comfortable with terms for describing sex. Prudery or reservation, he wasn't sure. His daughter had no problem with the vocabulary. Viola screwed, she got laid, she did indeed fuck, and made a point of articulating this fact. It was something of a relief to Teddy when she declared herself celibate at the age of fifty-five.

His lodgings were quite close to the British Museum, a bit of a ramshackle place but he liked it, despite the landlady, who could have given Genghis Khan a run for his money. Teddy had no idea that his furtive night with Nancy would, due to the unforgiving constraints of war and circumstances, be one of the few occasions when they would manage to be intimate with each other until the hostilities were over.

'How is poor Nancy?' Hugh enquired when Teddy returned to Fox Corner.

'Bearing up, I suppose,' Teddy said, 'although I didn't actually see her. We're at war then?'

'I'm afraid so. Come into the growlery, Ted, and have a drink with me.' The growlery was Hugh's hermitage, a place of safety into which one came only by invitation. 'Best be quick,' he added, 'before your mother catches sight of you. She'll be hysterical, I expect. She didn't take it well, even though we knew it was coming.'

Teddy wasn't sure why he had decided not to hear war being declared. Perhaps simply because taking a dog for a stroll on a sunny Sunday morning before lunch was a better calling.

Hugh poured two tumblers of malt whisky from the heavy cut-glass decanter he kept in the growlery. They chinked glasses and Hugh said, 'To peace,' when Teddy had expected him to say, 'To victory.' 'What will you do, do you suppose?' Hugh asked him.

'I don't know.' Teddy shrugged. 'Join up, I expect.'

His father frowned and said, 'Not in the Army though,' the unspoken horror of the trenches flashing momentarily across his features.

'The RAF, I thought,' Teddy said. He hadn't actually thought about it at all until this moment, but now he realized that the cage doors were opening, the prison bars falling away. He was about to be freed from the shackles of banking. Freed too, he realized, from the prospect of suburbia, of the children who might turn out to be 'rather dull'. Freedom even from the yoke and harness of marriage. He thought of the fields of golden sunflowers. The solid blocks of colour. The hot slices of sunshine.

Would France fall under Hitler's evil spell, he worried? Surely not.

'A pilot,' he said to his father. 'I should like to fly.'

The declaration of war delayed Sunday lunch. Sylvie was still plucking mint from the garden for the lamb when Teddy went to look for her. She didn't seem at all hysterical to him, merely rather grim. 'You missed Chamberlain,' she said, straightening up from her labours and rubbing the small of her back. His mother too, he thought, getting old. 'And I suppose you will have to fight,' she said, addressing the bunch of mint that she was crushing in her hand.

'I suppose I will,' he said.

Sylvie turned on her heel and stalked back inside the house, leaving the aromatic trail of mint in her wake. She paused at the back door and addressed him over her shoulder. 'Lunch is late,' she said, rather unnecessarily.

'Is she very cross?' Ursula asked him on the phone later that afternoon.

'Very,' he said and they both laughed. Sylvie had been ferocious about the need for appeasement.

There had been a flurry of phone calls between various permutations of the family all afternoon and Teddy, if he was honest, was getting rather weary of being asked what he intended to do, as if the future of the conflict was on his shoulders alone.

'But you're the family's only warrior,' Ursula said. 'What *will* you do?'

'Join the RAF,' he said promptly. The more he had been asked this question over the course of the day, the more certain his answer had become. (What would Augustus do, he wondered? The grown-up one, his counterpart, not the Peter Pan of Izzie's books.) 'And I'm not the only warrior anyway, what about Maurice and Jimmy?'

'Maurice will avoid any danger, you'll see,' Ursula said. 'But Jimmy, I suppose . . . oh dear. I still think of him as the baby, I can't imagine him with a weapon in his hand.'

'He's almost twenty,' Teddy felt it necessary to point out.

Lunch was a subdued affair. There were only the three of them – four if you counted Bridget, in the kitchen, which they didn't. They ate the lamb with potatoes and some rather stringy runner beans from the garden and afterwards Bridget plonked down an oval dish of rice pudding on the table and said, 'It's dried up, thanks to those ruddy Germans.'

'At least now Bridget will have someone other than Mother to blame for the woes of her world,' Ursula said when Teddy reported this remark to her on the phone. 'It's going to be bloody, you know,' she added sadly. Ursula seemed privy to a lot of information. She 'knew' people, of course, including a senior man in the Admiralty.

'How is your Commodore?' he asked her, rather cautiously as Sylvie was about.

'Oh, you know – married,' Ursula said lightly. 'Judge not that ye be not judged,' she had said when she confided in him about this affair. Teddy had been startled at the idea of his sister as a scarlet woman, as the *other* woman. By the end of the war there was nothing about men and women that surprised him. Nothing about anything really. The whole edifice of civilization turned out to be constructed from an unstable mix of quicksand and imagination.

There was another large whisky after lunch and then another before supper and both Teddy and Hugh, neither of whom were drinkers, were a little worse for wear by the time Teddy left for London. Back to the bank in the morning, he thought, but in his lunch hour he would find a recruitment office and sign up and the world would turn perhaps not upside down, as the old Civil War ballad would have it, but certainly a few notches in easement.

'That "ballad" was a lament, not a rejoicing,' Ursula said. She could be almost as particular as Nancy sometimes. '*Christmas was killed at Naseby fight.*' His sister was not yet a puritan – the war would make her one.

Sylvie kissed him goodbye on the cheek, very cool, and turned away, saying that she wouldn't say goodbye because it was 'too final', and Teddy thought how histrionic his mother could be if she set her mind to it. 'I'm catching the seven twenty to Marylebone,' he said to her, 'not going off to die.'

'Not yet.'

Hugh gave him a paternal pat on the shoulder and said, 'Don't pay any attention to your mother. Take care of yourself now, Ted, won't you?' It was the last time he would be touched by his father.

He made his way along the lane to the station through the twilight and by the time he had taken his seat in a second-class carriage Teddy realized that it was not Hugh's whisky that was making him feel so woozy and feverish but Nancy's whooping cough. The disease delayed his attempt to enter the war for several wretched weeks and even then when he tried to register he was sent away and told to wait. It was well into the spring of 1940 before he picked up an envelope from the hall table of his lodgings, which, when opened, proved to be a buff-coloured directive from the Air Ministry telling him to report to Lord's Cricket Ground for an interview. The summer before he went up to Oxford, his father had taken him to Lord's to see the first All-India test match. It seemed strange that this, of all places, was to be where he would be admitted into war. 'England won by one hundred and fifty-eight runs,' his father recalled when he told him of the venue. And how many runs would it take to win this war, Teddy wondered? – even at this stage of his life inclined to mutilate metaphor. Although in fact it took exactly seventy-two runs not out – the number of sorties he had flown by the end of March 1944.

There was a new lightness to his step as he walked to work. He paused to stroke a cat sunning itself on a wall. He tipped his hat to an elegant woman who, clearly charmed, smiled in response (rather invitingly, especially for this time of day). He stopped to smell a late lilac hanging over the railings around the gardens of Lincoln's Inn Fields. Wordsworth's 'glory and the dream' were not entirely forgotten, he thought.

The familiar scent of polished wood and brass assailed him as he entered the bank. No more, he thought, no more.

Nearly two years later, a pair of wings on his uniform, and his training with the British Commonwealth Air Training Plan in Canada behind him, Teddy had returned, sailing back from New York on the *Queen Mary*. 'How lovely,' Izzie said, when informed of this. 'I've had some marvellous times on board that ship.' Teddy didn't bother to inform her that the liner was now a troopship for the American forces that he had been squeezed on to ('down with the bilge water') and that the men – half of whom were seasick for the entire voyage – were packed tighter than the proverbial sardines in a tin. They felt as vulnerable, too, as they made the Atlantic crossing in foul weather without a convoy, the liner being considered fast enough to outrun German U-boats, something that Teddy was not convinced about. 'Yes, the food was wonderful,' he said sardonically to her (although it was when compared to the meagreness of rationing). He didn't know whether or not she had caught his tone. It wasn't always easy to tell with Izzie.

He had had a couple of days' leave between returning from Canada and joining an Operational Training Unit. His sister had managed to get away from London to Fox Corner for lunch. Izzie herself was 'loitering' there, uninvited, according to Sylvie. The tally for the autumn of '42: Pamela had evacuated herself to the middle of nowhere although she would soon return; Maurice spent most of his time in a Whitehall bunker; Jimmy was training with the Army in Scotland. Hugh was dead. How could that be? How could his father be dead?

Compassionate leave had been arranged for Teddy and the Navy (in the person of Ursula's man at the Admiralty, although Teddy never knew this) had found him a berth on a merchant ship sailing in convoy, but at the last minute the order was rescinded. 'You would have missed the funeral anyway,' Sylvie said, 'so there wouldn't have been much point.'

'I'm surprised,' Maurice said, 'that in the midst of war someone would have considered it a significant request.' 'Maurice,' Ursula said, 'is one of those people who rubber-stamp dockets – or not – and draw red crosses through application forms. Exactly the kind of person who would rescind a compassionate-leave request.' Maurice would have been very annoyed to be considered junior enough to rubber-stamp anything. He signed. A fluid, careless signature from his silver Sheaffer. But not in this case.

Whoever had done the rescinding was to be thanked. The convoy had been attacked by U-boats and the ship that Teddy had been designated to sail in had gone down with all hands. 'Saved for a higher purpose,' Ursula said.

'You don't believe that, do you?' Teddy asked, alarmed that his sister might have caught religion.

'No,' she said. 'Life and death are completely random, that much I have learned.'

'Completely. One learned that in the *last* war,' Izzie said, lighting a cigarette even though she had eaten hardly any of the stewed chicken that Sylvie had cooked for lunch. Sylvie had killed the bird this morning to 'celebrate' the return of 'the prodigal son'. (Again, he thought. Was this to be his role in life? The eternal prodigal?) 'Hardly prodigal,' Teddy said defensively. 'I've been learning to fight a war.'

'Yet, lo, we have killed the fatted chicken to welcome you back,' Ursula said.

'More like an old boiler,' Izzie said.

'Takes one to know one.' From Sylvie, of course.

Izzie pushed her plate away and Sylvie said, 'I hope you're going to finish that. That chicken died for you.' Ursula gave a little yelp of derision and Teddy winked at her. Yet it seemed wrong to be happy without Hugh here.

Izzie had decamped across the pond the minute war was declared but had returned by the time Teddy sailed back into port in Liverpool, claiming 'patriotism' as a higher moral duty than safety. 'Patriotism,' Sylvie said witheringly, 'contains the word "rot" within it. You came home because your marriage was a disaster.' Izzie's famous playwright husband was 'having affairs left, right and centre in Hollywood', Sylvie said. At the word 'affairs'

Teddy glanced across the Regency Revival dining-room table at Ursula, but she was keeping her eyes on the plate of sacrificial chicken in front of her.

Sylvie had quite a flock of hens now and did a good bartering trade in the village with her eggs. The spent birds usually ended up on Fox Corner's dining table when they had stopped pulling their weight on the egg-laying front. 'LMF,' Ursula said, and when Sylvie looked blank added, 'Lack of Moral Fibre. Waverers. When the nerves get the better of men in the services, but they call it cowardice.'

'I saw a lot of that in the trenches,' Izzie said.

'You weren't *in* the *trenches*,' Sylvie said, always irritated when Izzie referred to her experiences in the last war. As they all were, to some extent. Only Hugh, surprisingly, had had some tolerance for 'Izzie's war', as he referred to it. He had come across her once, during the horror of the Somme, at an advanced dressing station not very far behind the firing line. He was confused at the sight of her. She seemed to be in the wrong place – she belonged in the drawing room at Hampstead or in an evening gown, flirting and teasing some helpless man. The memory of her 'indiscretion', as he preferred to think of it – her scandalous affair with an older married man and the subsequent birth of an illegitimate baby – had been all but blotted from his mind by the mud. And anyway, that was a different Izzie to this one. This Izzie was dressed in some kind of uniform beneath a dirty apron, blood smeared across one cheek, carrying something foul in an enamel pail, and when she caught sight of him she gasped and said, 'Oh, look at you, you're alive, how wonderful! I won't kiss you, I'm awfully filthy, I'm afraid.' She had tears in her eyes and at that moment Hugh forgave his sister for many future, as yet unmade, mistakes.

'What are you doing here?' he asked, full of gentle concern. 'Oh, I'm a FANY,' she said carelessly. 'Just helping out, you know.'

'The *men* were in the trenches,' Sylvie persisted, 'not a few genteel lady volunteers.'

'The First Aid Nursing Yeomanry were not genteel ladies,' Izzie said, unruffled. 'We got our hands very dirty. And it's a terrible thing to label a man a coward,' she added quietly.

'Yes, it is,' Ursula agreed. 'Not so bad for a chicken though.' Teddy laughed, finding refuge in humour. He was terrified of being found wanting in the coming fight. 'She chickened out,' he said, indicating the chicken on Izzie's plate, and both he and Ursula tilted towards hysteria. 'What children you are,' Sylvie said crossly. Not really, Teddy thought. They were the ones who were going to have to stand fast to defend Sylvie and her chickens, Fox Corner, the last remaining freedoms.

The contents of his sister's letters to him in Canada had been sparse ('the Official Secrets Act, and so on'), but reading between the lines he gathered that she had had a pretty awful time of it. Teddy had not yet been tested in battle, but his sister had.

She had been right about the war, of course, it had indeed been 'bloody'. In the luxuriously warm safety of plush Canadian cinemas he had eaten his way through bags of popcorn while he watched, in horror, newsreels of the Blitz attacks on Britain. And Rotterdam. And Warsaw.

And France had indeed fallen. Teddy imagined the fields of sunflowers ploughed into mud by tanks. (They weren't, they were still there.)

'Yes, you've missed a lot,' Sylvie said, as if he had entered a theatre late for a play. His mother was now apparently very au fait with the events of the war and surprisingly bellicose, which was easy, Teddy supposed, from the relative comfort of Fox Corner. 'She's been seduced by the propaganda,' Ursula said, as if Sylvie wasn't there.

'And you haven't?' Teddy said.

'I prefer facts.'

'What a Gradgrind you've become,' Sylvie said.

'Hardly.'

'And what do the facts say?' Izzie asked, and Ursula, who knew a girl in the Air Ministry, didn't say that Teddy's chances of surviving his first operational sortie were, at best, slim, and that his chances of surviving his first tour were almost non-existent, but instead said brightly, 'That it's a *just* war.'

'Oh, good,' Izzie said, 'one would so hate to be fighting an unjust one. You will be on the side of the angels, darling boy.'

'Angels are British then?' Teddy said.

'Indubitably.'

'Has it been very bad?' he had asked Ursula when he met her off the train that morning. She looked pale and drawn, someone who had been indoors too long, or in combat perhaps. Was she was still seeing her man from the Admiralty, he wondered?

'Let's not talk about the war just now. But yes, it has been pretty awful.'

They made a detour to visit the churchyard where Hugh was buried. From within the church they could hear the thin voices of the Sunday-morning congregation straining over 'Praise My Soul, the King of Heaven'.

Hugh's grey headstone with its seemingly bland inscription – *Beloved father and husband* – was still harsh in its newness. The last time Teddy saw his father he had been tangible flesh and now that flesh was rotting in a hole beneath his feet. 'Best to avoid morbid thoughts,' Ursula counselled, advice that would stand him in good stead for the next three years. For the rest of his life, in fact. Teddy found himself thinking what a decent human being his father had been, the best of all the family really. The grief caught him unawares.

Beloved father and husband – it's so sad, not bland at all,' Bertie said. It was 1999, nearly sixty years by then since his father had died. Teddy's own life already felt like history. Bertie had asked him what he would like to do for his eighty-fifth birthday and he said he would like to have a little expedition around 'old haunts', so she hired a car and they took off from Fanning Court on what Bertie called a 'road trip' and what Teddy called a 'farewell tour'. He did not expect to survive much beyond the millennium and thought this would be a good way to round off a life and a century. He would have been surprised to know that he still had another decade and more ahead of him. It had been a strange and lovely trip, full of feeling ('We ran the gamut,' Bertie said afterwards) and genuine sentiment rather than just nostalgia, always a bit of a cheap emotion in Teddy's opinion.

By then, Hugh's headstone had been softened by lichen and the inscription was growing quietly less legible. Sylvie was buried elsewhere in the same churchyard, as were Nancy and her parents. Teddy had no idea where Winnie and Gertie were but Millie was here, home to roost at last after a lifetime of never settling long in one place. All these people, he thought, tied to Bertie by a thin red thread, yet she would never know them.

Pamela and Ursula, like Bea, had opted for cremation. Teddy had waited for the bluebells in the wood to flower before scattering Ursula's ashes amongst them. The dead were legion.

'Best to avoid morbid thoughts,' he said to Bertie.

'What would you like on *your* headstone?' she asked, despite this admonishment. Teddy thought of the endless white acres of the war cemeteries. Name, rank, number. He thought of Keats, 'Here lies one whose name was writ in water,' an epitaph that Ursula had always found so tragic. Or Hugh himself, who had once said, 'Oh, you can just put me out with the dustbin, I won't mind.' And written in stone on the war memorial at Runnymede, the names of the dead who had no grave at all.

Something had changed. What? Of course – the big unruly horse chestnuts that used to shade the dead on one side of the churchyard were all gone now and small flowering cherries had been planted tamely in their stead. The old stone wall that had previously been obscured by the horse chestnuts was visible now, cleaned and newly repointed.

'A woodland burial,' he said. 'No name, nothing, just a tree. An oak if you can, but anything will do. Don't let your mother be in charge.'

Death was the end. Sometimes it took a whole lifetime to understand that. He thought of Sunny, journeying restlessly in search of the thing he had left behind. 'Promise me you'll make the most of your life,' he said to Bertie.

'I promise,' Bertie said, already at twenty-four knowing it was unlikely she would be able to do so.

'Love Divine, All Loves Excelling' announced that the Sunday service was reaching its end. Teddy wandered amongst the graves. Most of the people in them had died long before his time. Ursula was picking up conkers from the stand of magnificent horse chestnuts at the far end of the churchyard. They were enormous trees and Teddy wondered if their roots had intertwined with the bones of the dead, imagined them curling a path through ribcages and braceleting ankles and fettering wrists.

When he walked over to Ursula he found her examining a conker. The spiky green shell had split, revealing the gleaming, polished nut inside. 'Fruit of the tree,' she said, handing it to him. '*Media vita in morte sumus*. In the midst of life we are in death. Or is it the other way round? There's something magical, isn't there, about seeing something brand new, something just entering the world, like a calf being born or a bud opening?' They had seen calves being born at the Home Farm when they were children. Teddy remembered feeling queasy at the sight of the slippery membrane, the cauled calf looking like something that had already been parcelled up by a butcher.

The morning-service congregation began to spill out of the church into the sunshine. Ursula said, 'You used to love playing conkers. There's something quite medieval about little boys and their conkers. Flails – is that what those spiky weapons on sticks were called? Or is it morning stars? What a nice name for something horrible.' She rambled on. Teddy could tell she was in a mood for diversion, as a remedy against the awfulness of the war, he supposed. Ursula, he thought, knew what happened on the ground during a bombing raid. Teddy could only imagine and imagination was going to have no place in his world from now on.

Of course, he had seen some pretty gruesome things too, in accidents during training, but they were not topics that you mentioned at the Regency Revival table over stewed chicken.

He ferried the dirty dishes through to the kitchen ('Bridget will do that,' Sylvie said sharply, but Teddy ignored her) and caught sight of the chicken carcass sitting on the kitchen table, denuded of its meat. His stomach heaved, taking him off guard.

At his flying training school in Ontario Teddy had witnessed an Anson coming in for an emergency landing. It had gone out on a cross-country exercise but had returned almost immediately with engine problems. Teddy had watched as it approached the airfield far too fast, wobbling all over the place before pancaking on the runway. Its fuel tanks were still almost full and the impact created a tremendous explosion. Most people had run for some kind of shelter at the sight of it. Teddy had thrown himself behind a hangar.

Everyone on the ground appeared unscathed and the fire engines and blood wagons raced out to the flaming Anson.

It was reported that one member of the crew had escaped the pyre, blown out of the aircraft when it exploded, so Teddy joined in the search with a couple of his fellow trainee pilots. They found the lone, lost soul amongst the lilac trees that bordered the perimeter fence. Later they learned it was the instructor who had been on board, an experienced pilot in the RCAF whom Teddy had flown with only yesterday. Now he presented a ghoulish sight – already a skeleton, his flesh almost entirely stripped off his bones from the force of the explosion. ('Flensed,' Teddy had thought, in one part of his brain.) The instructor's entrails, still warm, were festooning the lilacs. The lilacs were in full bloom, their scent still discernible beneath the noisome stink of butchery.

One of the men searching with Teddy fled, screaming and cursing blue murder. He washed out as a pilot, never flew again. LMF, it was declared, and he left in disgrace to go who knew where. The other trainee pilot with Teddy, a Welshman, stared at the remains and said simply, 'Poor bugger.' Teddy supposed his own reaction fell somewhere in between. Aghast at the macabre nature of the sight, relieved he hadn't been in that Anson. It was his first experience of the obscenities that could be wreaked upon frail human bodies by the mechanics of war, something he supposed his sister already knew.

'That's for the stockpot,' Bridget said when she noticed him staring at the chicken carcass, as if he might have been planning on stealing it. She was doing the wash-ing-up, standing at the big stone Belfast sink in the kitchen, elbow-deep in suds. Teddy took a tea-towel from a hook and said, 'Let me dry.'

'Go away,' Bridget said, which was, Teddy knew, her way of expressing gratitude. How old was Bridget? He couldn't even take a guess. In his lifetime she had traversed the best of her own, from naivety and even giddiness ('Fresh off the ferry,' as Sylvie always had it) to a weary resignation. She had 'lost her chance' in the last war, she said, and Sylvie scoffed and said, 'Lost your chance of what? The drudgery of marriage, the constant worry of children? You have been better off here with us.'

'I'm going home,' she said to Teddy, reluctantly relinquishing a dripping dinner plate to him. 'When all this is over.'

'Home?' Teddy said, confused for a moment. She turned and stared at him and he realized that he never really looked at Bridget. Or he looked and never saw her.

'Ireland,' she said as if he was stupid, which he supposed he was. 'Go and sit down. I have to fetch the pudding.'

And Nancy? What of Nancy? Where is she, we ask? Plucked suddenly from the arcane world of natural numbers a year ago and tucked away in a secret location. When people asked what she was doing she said she was working for a division of the Board of Trade that had moved from London to rural safety. She made it sound so boring ('rationing of home-produced scarce materials') that no one asked anything further. Teddy had been expecting to see her but she telephoned at the last minute and said, 'I can't get away, I'm *so* sorry.'

Nearly eighteen months and she was 'sorry'? He felt bruised but he was quick to forgive. 'She's so tight-lipped. I don't know when I'm going to see her again,' he said to Ursula as they 'dawdled' in the lane. ('I love that word, I do so little of it these days,' she said.) They stopped and lit cigarettes before they reached Fox Corner. Sylvie objected to smoking in the house. Ursula inhaled deeply and said, 'It's a filthy habit, but not as filthy as war, I suppose.'

'Her letters are extraordinarily bland,' Teddy said, still pursuing the elusive topic of Nancy. 'As if the censor was standing at her elbow while she was writing them. It all seems incredibly hush-hush. What do you suppose she's really doing?'

'Well, something abstrusely mathematical, no doubt,' Ursula said, determinedly vague herself. Her man from the Admiralty was inclined to pillow talk. 'I expect it's easier for her if you don't ask anything.'

'German codes, I'll bet,' Teddy said.

'Well, don't say that to anyone,' Ursula said, thereby confirming his suspicions.

After lunch, Teddy suggested to Ursula that they have a whisky in the growlery. It seemed a good way of marking their father's passing, something he didn't feel he had done.

'The growlery?' Ursula said. 'I'm afraid the growlery is no more.'

Sylvie, he discovered when he put his head round the door of the little back room, had transformed Hugh's snug into what she referred to as a 'sewing room'. 'Lovely and light and airy now,' she said. 'It was so gloomy before.' The walls had been painted a pale green, the floor covered by an Aubusson-type carpet, and the heavy velvet curtains had been done away with in favour of some kind of pale open-weave linen. A dainty Victorian sewing-table, previously neglected and relegated to Bridget's spartan room, now sat conveniently next to a button-back chaise longue that Sylvie had 'picked up for a song in a little shop in Beaconsfield'.

'Does she sew in here?' Teddy asked Ursula, picking out a cotton reel from the sewing-basket and contemplating it.

'What do *you* think?'

They went for a stroll around the garden instead, much of it now given over to vegetables as well as the large chicken coops. Sylvie's birds were kept under strict lock and key as there was always a fox on the prowl somewhere. The grand old beech tree still stood imperturbably in the middle of the lawn but the rest of the garden, apart from Sylvie's roses, was beginning to suffer neglect. 'I can't get a decent gardener for love nor money,' Sylvie said crossly. 'Oh, war is terribly inconvenient,' Izzie said sarcastically, smirking at Teddy, who didn't respond as it felt wrong to conspire with her against his mother, even when his mother was at her most annoying.

'I lost my last one to the Home Guard,' Sylvie said, ignoring Izzie. 'God help us if old Mr Mortimer is all that stands between us and the invading hordes.'

'She's getting a pig,' Ursula said to Teddy as they

regarded the incarcerated chickens, purring and crooning with broodiness.

'Who?'

'Mother.'

'A pig?' He couldn't imagine Sylvie as a pig keeper somehow.

'I know, she's full of surprises,' Ursula said. 'Who knew she had the soul of a black-market racketeer? She'll be hawking bacon and sausages round back doors. We should applaud her enterprise, I suppose.'

At the bottom of the garden they came across a large clump of dog-daisies – ox-eyes that must have emigrated there from the meadow. 'Another invading horde,' Ursula said. 'I think I shall take some back to London with me.' She surprised Teddy by producing a large penknife from her coat pocket and began to cut several of the spindly stems. 'You would be amazed at what I carry with me,' she laughed. 'Be prepared. It's the Girl Guides' motto as well as the Scouts', you know – "You have to be prepared at any moment to face difficulties and even dangers by knowing what to do and how to do it."'

'It's different in the Scouts,' Teddy said. 'Longer, more detailed in its demands.' More was expected of men, he supposed, although all the women of his acquaintance would have disagreed with that thought.

Ursula always forgot that he had never graduated from Cubs to Scouts. She, of course, had never had to suffer the indignities of the Kibbo Kift.

He elected to go back to London with Ursula, even though he knew it would disappoint his mother, who had hoped to hang on to him for another day. There was a hollow heart to Fox Corner without his father that was dispiriting.

'If we leave now we can catch the next train,' Ursula said, harrying him out of the door, 'not that it will bear any relationship to the timetable.'

'We've got bags of time actually,' she said when they had said their farewells and had stepped into the lane, 'I just wanted to get away. Mother's difficult to take at the best of times, Izzie's worse, so the two of them together are insufferable.'

'Are you going to stay at my flat?' Ursula asked when the train pulled in to Marylebone and he said, no, he was going to look up an old pal, 'Have a night on the town.' He wasn't sure why he lied, or indeed why he didn't want to stay with his sister. A nagging need to be unfettered perhaps for one last time.

When they were in the midst of their goodbyes, Ursula suddenly said, 'Oh, I nearly forgot,' and after searching through the contents of her handbag she retrieved a small object, silver but dirty with age.

'A rabbit?' he said.

'No, a hare, I think, although it's not easy to tell. Do you recognize it?' He didn't. The hare – or rabbit – sat to attention in a little basket. Its fur was chased, its ears sharp and pointed. Yes, a hare, Teddy thought. 'It hung from your pram hood,' Ursula said, 'when you were a baby. Ours too. I think it came originally from a rattle that belonged to Mother.' The hare had indeed once provided the finial to the infant Sylvie's rattle, a pretty thing, hung with bells and an ivory teething ring. She had once nearly poked her own mother's eye out with it.

'And?' Teddy puzzled.

'A good-luck charm.'

'Really?' he said sceptically.

'A talisman. Instead of a rabbit's foot, I give you a whole hare to keep you safe.'

'Thank you,' he said, amused. Ursula wasn't usually one for superstition and charms. He took the hare and slipped it casually into his pocket, where it joined the conker she had given him earlier and which had already lost its glossy newness. He noticed that Ursula's ox-eye daisies, wrapped in damp newspaper, were drooping, almost dead. Nothing could be *kept*, he thought, everything ran through one's fingers like sand or water. Or time. Perhaps nothing *should* be kept. A monkish thought that he dismissed.

'We're dying from the moment we're born,' Sylvie had said, apropos of nothing, as she watched Bridget slouching into the dining room with a dish of stewed apples. 'Nothing but windfalls,' Bridget announced. Since Mrs Glover had retired – to live with a sister in Manchester – Bridget had felt obliged to take on her mantle of disapproval. Apparently, Sylvie had sold the best of the orchard's abundant apple crop – a fruit, the only fruit, that Bridget didn't harbour suspicions about. ('She grew up in Ireland,' Sylvie said, 'they don't have fruit there.') Before he left, Bridget had pressed a small, gnarled, rather worm-eaten apple into his hand 'for the journey', and it now nestled warmly in his overcrowded pocket.

Instead of meeting up with his imaginary friend, Teddy

made a round of London pubs and got pretty drunk, being stood free drinks by a host of well-wishers. He discovered how attractive an RAF uniform was to girls, although he had tried to avoid the 'Piccadilly flak', which, he knew from his Atlantic crossing with them, was the GIs' term for the prostitutes who were to be found around the West End. They were bold, brash girls and he wondered if this had been their trade before or if they had sprung up as part of the inevitable baggage train of war.

Eventually, he found himself wandering around Mayfair wondering where he was going to spend the night. He bumped into a girl, 'Ivy, pleased to meet you,' who was also lost in the blackout and they made their way arm in arm, until by chance they came across a hotel, Flemings, in Half Moon Street. There had been much leering from the night-porter that they had laughed about as they lay on top of the covers, propped up on pillows, sharing two large bottles of beer that Ivy had procured from somewhere. 'Fancy place,' she said, 'you must be a rich bloke.' He was tonight, Izzie had given him twenty pounds – blood money for Augustus – and he felt inclined to blow as much of it as possible while he could. No pockets in shrouds, as spendthrift Izzie was wont to say.

Ivy turned out to be a happy-go-lucky ATS girl on an anti-aircraft battery, on leave from a posting in Portsmouth. ('Oops, probably shouldn't tell you where I'm stationed.')

The air-raid siren started up but they didn't go to a shelter. Instead they watched the fireworks provided free of charge by the Luftwaffe. Teddy was glad that he had caught the tail end of the Blitz.

'Bastards,' Ivy said cheerfully as the raiders flew

overhead. She was on 'the Predictor', she said. 'Operator number three.' ('Oops, there I go again!') He had no idea what that was. 'Get 'em, boys!' she shouted at one point as shells streaked red across the sky. They spotted a bomber caught in a searchlight. This was what it was like to be on the other end of it, Teddy thought, holding his breath, wondering about the pilot in that bomber. In a few weeks it would be him up there, he thought.

The aircraft slipped out of the searchlight and Teddy breathed again.

'No funny business now,' Ivy said, stripping down to her petticoat before they finally climbed into the cold bed. 'I'm a good girl,' she said primly. She was plain with buck teeth and had a fiancé in the Navy and Teddy considered her safe from his advances, especially as he was quite drunk, but somewhere in the now peaceful night they rolled towards each other in the middle of the sagging mattress and she manoeuvred herself skilfully so that he slipped inside her, still dopey with sleep, and it seemed ungentlemanly to protest. It was brief, the briefest. At best carnal, at worst sleazy. When they woke, both bleary-eyed from the beer, he expected her to be penitent, but instead she stretched and yawned and wriggled around, expecting more. In the grey morning light she looked rough and if she hadn't known so much about real anti-aircraft fire he might have mistaken her for one of the Piccadilly flak. He berated himself – she was a pleasant girl, good company even, and he was being a snob – but he made his excuses and left.

He paid for the room and asked a man at the reception

desk to see about taking a breakfast tray up to 'my wife', slipping a hefty tip across the desk.

'Certainly, sir,' the man said, sneering despite the tip.

Later that day he boarded a train at King's Cross, bound for an OTU. Operational Training Unit. After that an HCU, Heavy Conversion Unit. 'War's all about acronyms,' Ursula said.

He felt relief when the overcrowded train finally pulled slowly away from the platform, glad to be leaving behind the dirty wreckage of London. There was a war on, after all, and he was supposed to be fighting it. He discovered the little wrinkled apple in his pocket and ate it in two bites. It tasted sour when he had expected it to be sweet.

1993

We That Are Left

'There, that box is done,' Viola said, as if completing something distasteful, like picking up someone else's dirty litter, when all she had been doing was filling a cardboard box with clean glassware. She was wielding a parcel-tape dispenser as if it were a weapon. She caught sight of Sunny shaking a cigarette out of a packet and before he could strike a match yelled at him, 'Don't light that!' as if he were about to put the match to a fuse on a bomb rather than a Silk Cut. 'I'm nineteen,' Sunny muttered. 'I can vote, get married and die for my country (would he do any of those things, Teddy wondered?) but I can't have a quick fag?'

'It's a disgusting habit.'

Teddy thought about saying, 'You used to smoke,' to Viola, but could see that would just light another kind of fuse. Instead, he put the kettle on to make tea for the removal men.

Sunny collapsed on to the sofa. The sofa, like most of Teddy's furniture, was being disposed of as it was too big for the flat that he was moving to. It was being replaced by a cheap little two-seater, 'for guests', Viola said, ordering it for him from a catalogue. For himself he had something called a 'rise and recline' chair ('suitable for the elderly') that he had to admit, albeit reluctantly, was wonderfully comfortable. He didn't like the word 'elderly', it invited prejudice in the same way that 'young' had once done.

The majority of Teddy's possessions were due to be offloaded on charity shops. He was leaving behind more than he was taking. A life accrued and what was it worth? Not much apparently. 'Granddad's got so much *crap*,' Teddy had overheard Sunny say to Viola earlier, as if it were a moral affront to have hung on to a decade's worth of bank statements or a calendar from five years ago – reproductions of Japanese bird prints that he'd kept because they were so pretty. 'You can take hardly *any* of this stuff with you, you know that, don't you?' Viola had said, as if he were a toddler with too many toys. 'Do you ever throw *anything* away?'

It was true, in the last year or two he had begun to lose the thrifty habits he had once had, growing tired of the relentless culling and resolution that the material world demanded. Easier to let it pile up, waiting for the great winnowing of goods that his death would bring. 'This is good,' he had overheard his daughter say to Sunny. 'It means there'll be less to clear out when he finally goes.'

Wait until Viola was old, he thought ('old*er*', Bertie

said), and it was her children's turn to clear out their mother's 'crap' – the dream-catchers and light-up Madonnas ('ironic'), the decapitated dolls' heads (also 'ironic'), the witch balls that 'prevent evil from entering the house'.

Sunny appeared to have fallen asleep, as if exhausted, as if he had been involved in hard labour rather than moving a few boxes around. The removal men had done all the brute work while Sunny merely riffled through papers and files, saying to Teddy every five minutes, 'Do you want to keep this? Do you want to keep this? Do you want to keep this?' like a linguistically challenged parrot, until Teddy had to say, 'Just leave it to me, Sunny, I'll go through it all myself. But thank you.'

Teddy put a plate of biscuits and two mugs of tea on a tray. Plate, mugs and tray were all destined later for Oxfam. 'You have four trays! Four!' Viola said, as if Teddy was personally responsible for a capitalist glut of tea-trays. 'No one needs *four* trays. You can only take one with you.' He chose the oldest tray, a scratched and worn tin thing that he'd had since the year dot. It had belonged to the anonymous old lady who had lived and died in the cottage he had lived in when he was first married. 'The old biddy' they used to call her, as if she were a friendly ghost.

'That old thing?' Viola said, regarding the tray with horror. 'What about that nice bamboo one I bought for you?'

'Sentimental value,' Teddy said resolutely.

He took the tea outside to where the removal men were on a break. They were sitting on the tailgate, smoking and enjoying a bit of sunshine, and welcomed the tea.

* * *

Sunny opened his eyes slowly like a cat returning from sleep and said, 'Didn't you make me anything? I could murder a drink of something.' Teddy supposed Sunny got his self-absorption from his parents. Both Viola and Dominic had always put themselves first. Even the way Dominic had died had been selfish. Sunny needed to be coaxed into standing on his own feet, taking his place in the wider world, and understand that it was full of other people, not just him.

'The kettle's in the kitchen,' Teddy said to him.

'I know that,' Sunny said sarcastically.

'Don't use that tone,' Viola said (her own tone, Teddy noted). She had her arms folded in a combative way, glaring out of the window at the removal men. 'Look at them, what a pair of layabouts, being paid to drink tea.' As long as Teddy could remember, even before they lost Nancy, Viola had resented other people's pleasure, as if it subtracted something from the world rather than adding to it.

'You used to be on the side of the workers, I seem to remember,' Teddy said mildly. 'And anyway, it's me that's paying them. They're nice chaps, I'm happy to pay them to drink tea for ten minutes.'

'Well, *I'm* getting back to the endless task of sorting out all this stuff. Do you *know* how many glasses you've got? I've counted *eight* brandy glasses alone so far. When have you *ever* needed eight brandy glasses?' Viola led a sloppy kind of life. She had lurched from one disaster to the next. Perhaps having authority over tea-trays and brandy glasses gave her the illusion of control. Teddy suspected he was entering into the unsafe territory of cod psychology.

'And you certainly won't need them where you're going,' she pressed on. It sounded as if she were referring to the afterlife, rather than his move to sheltered housing, although he supposed that was a kind of afterlife. 'The odds against eight people being in your new flat and all wanting brandy at the same time are astronomical,' Viola said. Perhaps, Teddy thought, he could organize some kind of brandy-tasting soirée after he moved, for eight people, obviously. Take photographs as evidence to show Viola.

'At least you don't have a dog to get rid of,' she said.

'"Get rid of"?'

'Well, they don't allow pets where you're going. You would have to give it away.'

'Or you could take it in.'

'Oh, I couldn't manage, not with the cats.'

Why on earth were they talking about an imaginary, non-existent dog, Teddy wondered?

'Just as well that Tinker's dead,' she said. How harsh she could be.

Teddy hadn't considered it before, but now he realized that Tinker had been the last dog he would have. He supposed he had presumed there would be another one – not a puppy, he didn't have the energy for a puppy, but an older, unwanted dog perhaps, from the dogs' home. They could have lived out their last days together. It was three years since Tinker had died. Cancer. The vet had come to the house to put him down before it grew painful. He was a good dog, perhaps his best one. A foxhound, very sensible in his outlook. Teddy had cradled him in his arms while the vet injected him, looked steadfastly into the dog's eyes until the life had gone from them. He had done the same for a man once. His friend.

'I liked Tinker, Grandpa Ted,' Sunny interjected unexpectedly, suddenly six years old again. 'I miss him.'

'I know you do. So do I,' Teddy said, patting his grandson on the shoulder. 'Would you like a cup of tea, Sunny?'

'What about me? Am I included in that?' Viola said in that faux-chirpy way that she had when she was trying to pretend they were all one happy family. ('The family that put the "fun" in dysfunctional,' Bertie said.)

'Of course you are,' Teddy said.

They had moved to this house in York in 1960. Mouse Cottage had been superseded by a rented farmhouse (Ayswick), which was where Viola spent her first years. When they moved to York the loss of the countryside had felt like a wound to Teddy, but then greater wounds had been inflicted and he had soldiered on in York until he grew to like it.

The house was a semi-detached in the suburbs that looked like thousands of others across the land – pebble-dash, mock-Tudor accents, little diamond panes in the bowed bay windows, big gardens back and front. It had been Viola's home for half of her childhood – the worst half undoubtedly – although she always behaved as if it meant nothing to her. Perhaps it didn't. She had spent her sulking teenage years champing on the bit to escape its confines ('dull', 'conventional', 'little boxes' and so on). When she had finally left to go to university it had felt as if a great darkness had left the house. Teddy knew he had failed Viola but he wasn't sure how. ('Do you ever think it might be the other way round?' Bertie said. 'That she might have failed you?' 'It doesn't work like that,' Teddy said.)

He was going to a place called Fanning Court. 'A sheltered retirement housing complex.' 'Sheltered' made it sound like it was somewhere for a dog or a horse. 'Don't be silly,' Viola said. 'It's a much safer place for you to be.' He had trouble remembering a time when she didn't treat him as a nuisance. It would only get worse, he suspected, the older he grew. She had been nagging him to move for a while, so that someone could 'keep an eye on you'.

'I'm only seventy-nine,' Teddy said, 'I can keep an eye on myself. I'm not in my dotage yet.'

'Not *yet*,' Viola said. 'But you'll have to move sooner or later, so it may as well be sooner. You can't manage the stairs and you certainly can't manage the garden any more.' He managed the garden rather well, he thought, with a little help from a man who came in once a week to do any heavy work and to mow the grass in summer. There were fruit trees at the bottom of the garden and there was once a large vegetable plot. Teddy used to grow everything – potatoes, peas, carrots, onions, beans, raspberries, blackcurrants. Tomatoes and cucumbers in the greenhouse. He had built a little run for a couple of chickens and had even kept a hive of bees for a few satisfying years. These days most of the garden was given over to lawn, with easy-going shrubs and flowers – roses, mainly. He still planted sweet peas in the summer and dahlias for the autumn, although that was becoming a bit of a chore.

Losing the garden was going to be hard. When he moved here he thought the garden would be a poor consolation for the loss of the wild countryside that he had left behind, but he had been proved wrong. Now what would be his consolation? A couple of pots on a balcony, a window box perhaps. His heart sank.

For years now Viola had been going on about organic food and what a healthy diet she had fed her children, yet she seemed incapable of understanding him when he said that he had brought her up on organic food – 'straight out of the garden'. How could it be organic, she said, as if there was no manure and hard work before her time. When she was a child she hadn't been interested in learning about beekeeping, was reluctant to feed the hens or collect eggs and said the garden gave her hay fever. Did she still have hay fever in the summer?

'Do you still have allergies?' he asked.

'I would let you live with me,' she carried on as if he hadn't spoken ('let', Teddy thought?) 'but there's so little room and, of course, you would never be able to get up and down the stairs. They're simply not suitable for an elderly person.'

Viola had left York for Leeds several years ago. In York she had worked in a Welfare Benefits Unit (Teddy had no idea what that was), but then she got a job in 'Family Mediation' in Leeds. That, too, seemed a vague kind of occupation and, from the name of it, hardly something that Viola sounded suited for. Of course, the move was prompted by her marriage to Wilf Romaine. ('We eloped,' she says rather giddily in a *Woman and Home* interview in 1999. Teddy wasn't sure that 'elope' was quite the right word when you were over thirty and had two small children.)

Now she was in Whitby, living off welfare benefits herself as far as he could tell, although they didn't talk about it. She had bought an old fisherman's cottage with the proceeds of her divorce from Wilf Romaine. She was forty-one and had spent most of her life living off money given to her by other people – Teddy, Dominic's family ('a pittance') and then the disastrous marriage to Wilf. 'If I'd realized,' she said crossly, as if it were someone else's fault, 'I would have sidestepped motherhood and men and gone straight into a profession when I graduated. I would probably be a controller at the BBC by now, or something in MI5.' Teddy made a non-committal noise.

The cottage in Whitby was just four rooms, piled crookedly, one on top of another. Teddy wouldn't have been surprised if Viola had gone out of her way to find somewhere unsuitable for an 'elderly person'. As if he would ever have contemplated living with her. ('Fate worse than death,' Bertie agreed.)

Viola was 'writing', she said. Teddy wasn't too sure what this meant and didn't like to ask too closely, not because he wasn't interested but because Viola got very snappish if you asked her to go into detail about anything. Sunny was the same, exasperated by even the most inoffensive questions. 'So what are you up to these days?' Teddy had asked his grandson when he arrived – reluctantly – this morning to help with the move. Any question about Sunny's plans for the future elicited a shrug and a sigh and the answer, 'Stuff.'

'He's so like his father,' Viola said. (No, Teddy thought, just like his mother.) 'I despair of him. He hasn't grown up, he's just got bigger. Of course, if he were a child nowadays he'd probably be diagnosed with dyslexia, and some kind of hyperactivity thing as well. And dyspraxia probably. Autistic even.'

'Autistic?' Teddy said. It was funny how she always managed to wash her hands of responsibility. 'He always seemed a pretty normal little chap to me.' This wasn't entirely true, Sunny had stumbled and faltered his way through his life so far, but someone had to come to the poor boy's defence. If Teddy had been forced to 'diagnose' him with anything it would have been unhappiness. Teddy loved Sunny in a way that made his heart ache. He feared for him, for his future. Teddy's love for Bertie was more straightforward, more optimistic. Bertie had a bright-eyed intelligence that reminded him of Nancy sometimes (in a way that Viola never had). Something of the same quicksilver nature too, a merry soul, although in death, in memory – which was the same thing now – Nancy had perhaps grown more mercurial than she had been in life.

'What *is* this?' Viola sounded outraged, as if the small rectangular cardboard box contained evidence of some terrible transgression. There was a picture of a coffee grinder on the unopened box.

'It's a coffee grinder,' Teddy said reasonably.

'It's the coffee grinder I gave you for Christmas. You haven't used it.'

'No, I haven't.'

'Yours was ancient. You said you needed a new one.' She started opening doors and looking in his kitchen cabinets, finally producing – 'A coffee grinder. You bought *yourself* one? I spent money I didn't have on a *present* for you. Oh, wait.' She put a hand out as if trying to stop a tank. 'Wait. Oh, of course . . . '

Sunny wandered into the kitchen and groaned. 'What's the drama queen ranting about now?' Viola showed him the box containing the unused coffee grinder. '*German!*' she pronounced, as if she was in court and had just produced the deciding evidence.

'So?' Sunny said.

'Krups,' Teddy said.

'So?' Sunny said.

'He doesn't buy German things,' Viola said. 'Because of the *war*.' She said the word 'war' sarcastically as if she was arguing with her father about the length of her skirt or the amount of eye make-up she was wearing or the smell of tobacco on her breath – all hotly debated topics in her teenage years.

'The Krupp family supported the Nazis,' Teddy said to Sunny.

'Oh, here comes the history lesson,' Viola said.

'Their factories produced steel,' Teddy continued, ignoring her. 'Steel is at the heart of all war.' He had bombed (or tried to bomb) the Krupps' works in Essen several times. 'They used slave labour. And Jews from the concentration camps.'

'It's not the same Krup!' Viola shouted at him. 'They're completely different! And anyway, the war ended nearly fifty years ago. Don't you think it's about time you got over it? Plus' – there was always a plus with Viola – 'a lot of the workers in those factories you were bombing were slave labourers, Jews too. There's an irony for you,' she said triumphantly. Case closed. Jury convinced.

Viola's first car after her 'emancipation' from Dominic (and four attempts at passing her driving test) had been an old VW Beetle and when Teddy had murmured something about 'buying British' she had erupted with accusations of xenophobia. Later, after he'd been living in Fanning Court for several years, the cheap built-in oven that came with the flat gave up the ghost and Viola ordered a new Siemens one from Currys, without any consultation with Teddy. When the delivery men turned up with the oven he asked them (very politely) to put it back on the van and return it to the store.

'I suppose you bombed them too?' Viola said.

'Yes.'

He remembered Nuremberg (he could never forget), the last raid of his war, and in the briefing the intelligence officer – a woman – telling them that the Siemens factory there produced searchlights, electric motors 'and so on'. He learned after the war that they had manufactured the ovens for the concentration camp crematoria and wondered if that was the 'and so on'. During the war he had been introduced to a friend of Bea's called Hannie, a refugee, and, although he knew it could mean nothing to Hannie now, it was for her that he made this rather paltry gesture towards Currys. Six million was just a number but Hannie had a face, a pretty one, little emerald earrings ('Costume!'), and she played the flute and wore Soir de

Paris and had a family who had been left behind in Germany. There was a suggestion that Hannie was still alive when she was shovelled into the ovens at Auschwitz. ('One so wants to forgive them,' Ursula had said long ago, 'and then one thinks about poor Hannie.') So he didn't really feel that he needed an excuse for not buying a German oven. Or for having bombed the living daylights out of them for that matter either. That wasn't entirely true and he might have admitted it if he hadn't been in an argument with someone as intransigent as his daughter. He had killed women and children and old people, the very ones that society's mores demanded he protect. At the twisted heart of every war were the innocents. 'Collateral damage' they called it these days, but those civilians hadn't been collateral, they had been the targets. That was what war had become. It was no longer warrior killing warrior, it was people killing other people. Any people.

He didn't offer this reductionist viewpoint to Viola, she would have agreed with it too easily, wouldn't have understood the dreadful moral compromise that war imposed on you. Scruples had no place in the middle of a battle where the outcome was unknown. They had been on the right side, the side of right – of that he was still convinced. After all, what was the alternative? The awful consequence of Auschwitz, Treblinka? Hannie thrown into an oven?

Teddy looked at Sunny, slouched against the kitchen sink, and knew he could never communicate any of this to him.

What a pair of old farts, Sunny thought as the row in

the kitchen continued, backwards and forwards like a game of table-tennis. He had enjoyed table-tennis (once, anyway) when he was a child, although Sunny wasn't entirely convinced that he had ever been a child. They'd had a summer holiday – himself, Bertie and Grandpa Ted – in a big old dilapidated house somewhere, with a table-tennis table in a garage or a shed. It had been the best holiday of his life. There'd been horses ('Donkeys,' Bertie corrected) and a lake ('a pond').

The argument in the kitchen ground on. Ha ha.

'So you bought a Philips coffee grinder instead?' Viola said. 'And you're going to tell me that *their* hands were clean during the war? No one's hands are clean in a war.'

'Philips's hands were pretty clean,' Teddy said. 'Frits Philips was declared "Righteous Amongst the Nations" after the war. That means he helped the Jews,' he explained to Sunny.

'Pah,' Viola said dismissively, indicating she was losing the argument.

Sunny yawned and wandered back out of the kitchen.

Viola escaped to the garden. It wasn't as neat as it used to be but it still betrayed the fact that her father was anally retentive. Beans grew straight on their canes, roses remained unspotted and uneaten. On her mother's coffin her father had placed not a florist's wreath but a bunch of roses from the garden. Viola remembered thinking that her mother deserved something opulent and fancy from a less amateurish hand. Home-made was nicer, her father said. Quite the opposite, Viola thought.

He disliked profligacy, whereas Viola failed to see why

it was such a sin. There was no need to throw things out if they were still working. (The Voice of Reason.) You could re-use yoghurt tubs and tin cans for seedlings, make stale bread and cake into puddings, mince leftover scraps of meat. (Who had a mincer any more?) Old woollen jumpers were cut up and used to stuff cushions. Anything that moved was made into jam or chutney. When you left a room you had to turn off the light and close the door. Not that Viola did. She never had paper to draw on as a child but was always given the unused bits of wallpaper rolls. ('Just turn it over, it's perfectly good.') Vinegar and newspapers were used to clean windows. Everything else went out to the compost bin or the birds. Her father removed the hair from hairbrushes and combs and put it out for the birds to line their nests with. He was overly preoccupied with garden birds.

He wasn't mean, she would give him that. The house was always warm – too warm, the central heating cranked up high. And he gave her generous pocket money and let her choose her own clothes. Food was plentiful. She used to despise the fact that nearly everything came from the garden: fruit, eggs, vegetables, honey. Not the chickens, chickens came from the butcher. He couldn't kill a chicken. He let them die of old age, which was ridiculous because he became overrun with old chickens.

She had spent endless summer hours in the garden like a peasant in the fields, hands sticky from picking redcurrants, blackcurrants, raspberries. Scratched by gooseberry bushes, stung by wasps, bitten by grass mites, disgusted by slugs and worms. Why couldn't they shop in brightly lit supermarkets, choose colourful packets of ingredients, shiny fruit and vegetables that came from far away and were picked by other people?

Nowadays, if she was honest with herself – which she rarely was, she knew – she missed all those meals she had hated at the time. Her father had commandeered Nancy's old cookbooks and made Sunday roasts and apple pies, hot-pots and rhubarb crumbles. 'Your dad's fantastic,' everyone used to tell her. Her teachers loved him, partly because they had loved Nancy, but also because of the way he'd taken over the role of mother. She didn't want him to be her mother, she wanted Nancy to be her mother.

('We were early adopters of the Green movement. I was brought up in a self-sufficient household, very ecologically minded. We grew our own produce, we recycled everything, we were really ahead of the times when it came to respecting the planet.' Teddy was very surprised to read this in a Sunday-colour-supplement interview not long before he left Fanning Court for the nursing home.)

Her father read *Silent Spring* when it was first published, just after her mother's death. A library copy, of course. (Had he ever actually *bought* a book? 'But we should support the public libraries or they'll cease to exist.') He used to bore her rigid by reading out passages aloud. That was when he became obsessed with garden birds. There were several of them now on the bird feeder, different kinds. Viola had no idea what any of them were.

She returned to the kitchen – now empty of everyone, thank goodness – and started hauling dishes out of the cupboards and putting them in boxes, dividing things between the boxes destined for Fanning Court and those for the charity shop. (Who needed four covered vegetable dishes or even one soup tureen?)

Everything in the kitchen seemed to bring back memories. The Pyrex dishes reminded her of the cottage pies and rice puddings that had been cooked in them. The horrible tumblers, in a crinkly green glass that had made everything they held look contaminated, had contained the milk she had drunk every night before bed – accompanied by two Rich Tea biscuits, as basic a biscuit as it was possible to devise, when she had craved something more interesting – a Club, a Penguin. Her father's insistence on an unadorned bedtime biscuit seemed to say everything about his austere morality. ('I'm thinking of your teeth.') Oh, and that Midwinter-pattern crockery brought on a fit of melancholy. A whole life could be contained in a dinner-service pattern. (A good phrase. She tucked it away.) One day this would all be 'vintage' and Viola would be very annoyed that she had packed it off to Oxfam without a backward glance.

Her father seemed so old-fashioned, but he must have been like new once. That was a nice phrase. She tucked that away for later use as well. She was writing a novel. It was about a young girl, brilliant and precocious, and her troubled relationship with her single-parent father. Like all writing, it was a secretive act. An unspeakable practice. Viola sensed there was a better person inside her than the one who wanted to punish the world for its bad behaviour all the time (when her own was so reproachable). Perhaps writing would be a way of letting that person out into the daylight.

She dropped a Midwinter milk jug and it broke into several pieces. 'Fuck,' she said, more quietly than she'd intended.

Teddy had let Viola arrange for a couple of the bulkier pieces in his house to be shipped off to auction, where they had fetched, in her words, 'a pittance'. Nancy's piano, Gertie's sideboard. Precious objects. The piano was out of tune and neglected, played by no one now. Viola gave up her lessons (she had little aptitude) after Nancy died.

When Teddy thought about Nancy he often pictured her sitting at the piano. He thought about her every day, as he thought about so many others. The dead were legion and remembrance was a kind of duty, he supposed. Not always related to love.

He recalled – near the end – walking into this room and seeing Nancy playing the piano. Chopin. He had been reminded of Vermeer, one of his paintings in the National Gallery – a woman in a room, a virginal – he couldn't remember exactly, it was years since he had been up to London. *Woman Interrupted at the Piano*, he thought when he saw Nancy. He could imagine her living in one of Vermeer's cool, uncluttered interiors. The reading of the letter, the pouring of the milk. Order and purpose. She had looked up from the piano as he entered the room, surprised, as if she had forgotten his existence, and wearing that cryptic expression she had sometimes as though she had been lost inside herself. The secret Nancy.

He had felt an awful wrench when the removal men had taken the piano. He had loved Nancy, but perhaps not in a way that suited her. There had probably been someone else out there in the world who would have made her happier. But he *had* loved her. Not the high romance of passion or chivalry, but something more robust and dependable.

And Gertie's sideboard, he was sad to see that go too. It had belonged to the Shawcrosses originally, had lived in the dining room at Jackdaws. It was a Liberty Arts and Crafts piece, out of fashion for many years but coming back now, although not soon enough for Viola, who had always regarded it as ugly and 'depressing'. Fifteen years later, in 2008, she saw the twin of Gertie's sideboard – perhaps the sideboard itself – on the *Antiques Roadshow* and was furious that she hadn't 'hung on to it' given the price it was valued at. 'I would have kept it,' she said to Bertie, 'but *he* insisted on getting rid of it.' The older Teddy got the more Viola simply referred to him as 'he', as if he was a patriarchal god who had blighted her life.

'Where's that old carriage clock of yours?' she asked suddenly, casting her eye around the now almost denuded living room. 'I don't remember seeing it when we were packing.' The clock had been Sylvie's, and her mother's before that. It had gone to Ursula on Sylvie's death and Ursula had left it to Teddy, and so it had zigzagged its way down the family tree. 'You know,' Viola said with a faux nonchalance, 'if you don't want it I'll take it off your hands.' She was the worst kind of liar – transparently untruthful and yet completely convinced of her ability to deceive. If she needed money why didn't she just *ask* him? She was always looking to be given things, a cuckoo rather than a predator. It was as if there was something hungry inside her that could never be filled up. It made her greedy.

The clock was a good one, made by Frodsham and worth quite a bit, but Teddy knew that if he gave it to Viola she would sell it or misplace it or break it and it seemed important to him that it stayed in the family. An heirloom. ('Lovely word,' Bertie said.) He liked to think that the little golden key that wound it, a key that would almost certainly be lost by Viola, would continue to be turned by the hand of someone who was part of the family, part of his blood. The red thread. To this end, he had given the clock to Bertie the last time she visited him. He should have given her Gertie's sideboard too, it would have suited the Arts and Crafts cottage where she lived with her twins and the good man she married – a doctor whom she met by chance on Westminster Bridge, the week of the Queen's Diamond Jubilee. Years later, after Bertie married and moved to this cottage in East Sussex, she had the clock valued for insurance and discovered that it was worth a whopping thirty thousand pounds. Every time Viola came to visit, Bertie had to hide her little golden nest-egg and muffle its chime. Teddy had been in the earth for two years by then and never saw Bertie's Arts and Crafts cottage, never saw the clock continuing to count down time on her mantelpiece.

'Have you already packed the clock?' Viola asked accusingly.

Teddy shrugged innocently and said, 'Probably. It'll be at the bottom of a box somewhere.' He loved Viola as only a parent can love a child, but it was hard work.

* * *

'We'll probably have to give this place a lick of paint before it can go on the market,' Viola said. 'But the estate agent said it should sell quite easily.' (She had talked to his estate agent? Behind his back?) 'And then you'll have a bit of an income to live out your days on.' That's what he was doing from now on, wasn't it? Living out his days. That's what he'd always done, of course, what everyone did, if you were lucky.

'New home,' Viola said. 'A fresh start. It will be . . .' she sought a word out of the air.

'Challenging?' Teddy offered. 'Distressing?'

'I was going to say energizing.'

He had no desire for a fresh start, and he doubted that Fanning Court was ever going to feel like a home. It was still a new building, still smelling of paint and fire-proofed furnishings. The flat that Teddy had bought was one of the last in the complex to be sold. ('You were very lucky to get it,' Viola said.) At least he wasn't moving into a flat where someone had just died and been shipped out. These places were 'one out, one in', weren't they? 'No, this is just a staging post, Teddy,' one of his (few remaining) friends, Paddy, said. 'The stations of the cross.' Teddy had tipped the balance, he knew more dead than living now. He wondered who'd be the last man standing. He hoped it wasn't himself. 'Next stop's the nursing home,' Paddy said. 'Me, I'd rather be put down like a dog than go to one of them.' 'Me too,' Teddy agreed.

The public spaces of Fanning Court were decorated in a bland palette of pinks and magnolias and the walls of the corridors were hung with inoffensive Impressionist prints. It seemed doubtful that anyone ever looked at them. Art as wallpaper. 'Lovely, isn't it, Dad?' Viola said to him with a forced kind of optimism when they were first shown round. 'It feels a bit like a hotel, doesn't it? Or a cruise ship?' When had Viola ever been on a cruise ship? She was grimly determined that he was going to like Fanning Court.

The tour was conducted by the warden, a woman called Ann Schofield, who said, 'Call me Ann, Ted.' (Call *me* Mr Todd, Teddy thought.) 'The Warden', like something from Trollope. And now he was to be a bedesman in Fanning Court – an almshouse for a new age. Not that Ann Schofield bore any relationship to Septimus Harding. Busty and bustling, her slow Midlands accent ('a Brummie and proud of it') belied a determined kind of energy. 'We're a happy family here,' she said, rather pointedly, as if Teddy might turn out to be the black sheep.

She led from the front. She had an enormous backside and Teddy chided himself for his lack of gallantry but you couldn't help but notice. 'The Fat Controller', Bertie called her when she first visited him in Fanning Court. She had loved the *Thomas the Tank Engine* books, loved all books. She was in her first year up at Oxford, at the same college that Teddy had attended – co-educational now. Studying the same subject too. She was his legacy, his message to the world.

They went first to the residents' lounge, where a little knot of people were playing Bridge. 'See, Dad,' Viola whispered. 'You like playing cards, don't you?' ('Well . . .' Teddy said.)

'Oh, we have every kind of activity here,' Ann Schofield said. 'Bridge – as you can see – dominoes, Scrabble, carpet bowls, amateur dramatics, concerts, a coffee morning every Wednesday . . .' Teddy tuned out. His leg was getting crampy, he wanted to get home, have a cup of tea and watch *Countdown*. He wasn't a big TV watcher but he liked quizzes – decent ones with quiet, middle-aged audiences. He found them comforting and challenging at the same time, which at his age was more than enough.

The tour wasn't over. Next stop was a hot, damp laundry room full of huge machines and then the (rather smelly) 'refuse store', with its industrial-sized bins that could have swallowed an 'elderly person' whole if they weren't careful. 'Lovely,' Viola murmured. Teddy glanced at her. *Lovely*, he thought? She looked slightly manic. Then a 'kitchenette' where they could make themselves 'hot beverages' when they were 'socializing together' in the residents' lounge. Wherever they went people smiled and said 'Hello' or asked him when he was moving in. 'New friends for you,' Viola said brightly.

'There's nothing wrong with my old ones,' Teddy said, his feet beginning to drag.

'Well, apart from the fact that most of them are dead.'

'Thanks for reminding me.'

'All right?' Ann Schofield said, glancing back at them, sensing dissension in the ranks.

A woman hirpled along the corridor towards them with the aid of a walking frame. 'Hello, coming to join us, are you?' she said cheerfully to Teddy. It was a bit like a cult. Teddy was reminded of that television programme from the Sixties that Viola had liked to watch. *The Prisoner*. His heart sank. This was to be his prison, wasn't it? A prison with a warden.

More women – everywhere, in fact. Once he had moved in he realized that nearly all of the 'residents' were women. They liked him, women always did. Of course he was still pretty spry then, and competent, and the women belonged to a generation that could be impressed if a man simply knew how to flick a switch on a kettle. He set quite a few frail hearts a-flutter in Fanning Court but had done his best to neatly sidestep romance and intrigue, for although it was all pleasantries on the surface, beneath the magnolia paint the place seethed with gossip and cattiness. Teddy, still a good-looking man in his eighties (especially if you were a woman in your seventies), unintentionally provoked all kinds of heightened emotions.

'I suppose men are in short supply at my age,' he said, excusing some incident of spiteful behaviour.

'At my age too,' Bertie said.

'Come along, Ted,' Ann Schofield said. 'Plenty more to see.' 'Plenty more' was a bit of garden, planted in municipal style. Some benches. A car park.

'Oh, I don't think he'll be bringing his car,' Viola said.

'Oh, I think he will,' Teddy said.

'Really, Dad, you're getting on a bit for driving.' (She wanted his car, he supposed. Hers was always breaking down.) Viola liked having this kind of argument in a public arena with an audience who could see how reasonable she was being and how unreasonable her other family members were. She used to do it with Sunny all the time. Drove the poor boy mad. Still did.

'Oh, lots of residents have cars,' Ann Schofield said, letting Viola down.

*   *   *

The flat itself would have fitted into his grandmother's drawing room in Hampstead. Teddy hadn't thought about Adelaide in a long time and surprised himself with a vivid memory of her, dressed in long Victorian black even in the Twenties, complaining about her boisterous grandchildren. What a long, long way they had come from those days.

Once, he remembered, on a particularly tedious visit, he and Jimmy had crept upstairs to investigate her bedroom, a place that was strictly off limits to them. He remembered her wardrobe, an immense contraption, lined inside with pleated silk and reeking with the competing scents of camphor and lavender, underpinned by the perfume of decay. The two of them had climbed inside, their faces brushing rather unpleasantly against Adelaide's strange outmoded clothes. 'I don't like it in here,' Jimmy whispered. Neither did Teddy and he stepped out first and accidentally knocked the door so that it swung shut. It took a while to get it open again as the handle had a rather odd mechanism.

When Jimmy finally tumbled out his shrieks of terror summoned the whole household. Adelaide was furious ('Wicked, wicked boys'), but he remembered Sylvie holding her hand over her mouth so that Adelaide couldn't see that she was laughing. Poor Jimmy had never liked confined spaces after that. He had been a Commando during the war, had landed on Sword Beach and skirmished his way across the ravaged remains of Europe after D-Day before slogging out the endgame, attached to the 63rd Anti-Tank Regiment. How he must have hated the cramped insides of tank destroyers. He had been with the 63rd when they liberated Bergen-Belsen, but he and Teddy had never spoken about that, had barely spoken about the war. He wished they had.

Until he found out about Jimmy, one unexpected day just after the war had ended, Teddy's picture of queers had been the fairies and pansies he saw about Soho. He hadn't considered such men capable of the kind of brutal courage that Jimmy must have had.

Jimmy was long gone, to a fast-growing lymphoma in his fifties. When he was given the diagnosis he drove his car off the road and over a precipice. Flamboyant in life, flamboyant in death. He lived in America, of course. Teddy hadn't gone to the funeral, but he went to a local church and sat silently with his thoughts at the same time that Jimmy was being buried on the other side of the Atlantic. A few days later a flimsy blue airmail letter had drifted through his letter-box like a rare leaf. In it Jimmy had made his farewells. He wrote that he had always loved and admired Teddy and what a good brother he had been. Teddy didn't think this was true at all. If anything he had been quite derelict in his fraternal duties. He had never asked about Jimmy's homosexual life (hadn't wanted to know, really) and had always thought (condescendingly, he was ready to admit now) that his profession – in advertising – was rather trivial. He had felt similarly disappointed when Bertie took a job in advertising, which as far as he could tell was just encouraging people to spend money they didn't have on things they didn't need. ('It is,' Bertie agreed.)

'Well, Jimmy had a terrible war,' Ursula said at the time.

'I think triviality is as good an antidote as anything.'

'We all had a terrible war,' Teddy said.

'Not everyone,' Ursula said. 'You did, I know.'

'So did you.'

'There was a job to do,' Ursula said. 'And we did it.'

Oh, how he missed his sister. Out of everyone, the legions of the dead, the numberless infinities of souls who had gone before, it was the loss of Ursula that had left him with the sorest heart. She had a stroke, nearly thirty years ago now. A swift death, thank goodness, but she was too young. And now Teddy was too old.

'Dad?'

'Yes, sorry, miles away.'

'The warden – Ann – is explaining the emergency cords.'

Oh joy, Teddy thought.

Thin red cords dangled from the ceiling in every room. 'So if you have a fall,' Ann Schofield said, 'you can pull on one and summon help.' Teddy didn't bother asking what would happen if he wasn't near a cord when he fell. He imagined Ann Schofield waddling at speed towards him along the pink and magnolia corridors, and thought he might prefer to lie where he had dropped and slowly expire with some dignity remaining.

Ann Schofield referred to the complex as 'the Fanning' so that it sounded to Teddy's ears like a hotel in Mayfair, one he had stayed the night in once with a girl. He couldn't remember the name of the hotel (Hannings? Channings?) but he was pretty sure the girl had been called Ivy. They had bumped into each other in the blackout, both looking for somewhere to lay their head that night. She had been looking for the Catholic Club in Chester Street and now

Teddy couldn't remember what, if anything, he had been looking for. He had been drunk and she had been fairly tipsy and they had stumbled (literally) across the hotel.

The present was a rather dim, unfocused place – he supposed that could only get worse – but the past was increasingly bright. He could see the grubby steps of that London hotel, the white portico and the narrow stairway up to the fourth-floor attic bedroom. He could almost taste the beer they had drunk. There was a shelter in the cellar but when the siren sounded they didn't go down to it, instead they hung out of the window, in the freezing night air, watching the raid, the ack-ack battery in Hyde Park making a frightful racket. He was on leave after returning from training in Canada, a pilot who had not yet been blooded in battle.

She had been engaged to a sailor. He wondered what had happened to her. What had happened to her sailor.

He had thought about her once, on an op to Mannheim, as they crossed the heavy belt of searchlights that defended the Ruhr. He had thought how down there on the ground, on enemy soil, there were probably hundreds of Ivys, nice Fräuleins with buck teeth and fiancés on U-boats, manning the German ack-ack, all united in an effort to kill him.

'Dad? Dad? Really. Pay attention, will you?' Viola rolled her eyes at Ann Schofield, trying to display amusement and affection at the same time, although Teddy doubted that she was feeling either. You'll be old too, one day, he thought. Thank goodness he wouldn't be around to see that. And Bertie too, how sad to think that one day she might be an old lady with a walking frame, shuffling along uninspiring corridors. *It is the blight man was born for.* That was Hopkins, wasn't it? *It is Margaret you mourn for.* Those lines had always moved him, he remembered—

'Dad!'

It was his own fault, he supposed. He had slipped on a patch of black ice near his house and knew straight away that it was bad. He heard himself howling with the pain, surprised that he could make such a noise, surprised that it was himself making it. He had ended up half sitting, half sprawled on the pavement. He had been shot down in flames during the war, you would think that there wasn't anything worse that could happen to you. But this felt unbearable.

Several people, perfect strangers, rushed to his aid. Someone called an ambulance and a lady who told him she was a nurse draped her coat over his shoulders. She crouched down next to him and took his pulse and then gently patted his back, as if he were an infant. 'Don't move,' she said. 'I won't,' he said meekly, rather glad for once to be told what to do. She held his hand while they waited for the ambulance to arrive. Such a simple thing and yet he was overwhelmed with gratitude. 'Thank you,' he murmured when he was finally loaded into the ambulance. 'You're welcome,' she said. He had never learned her name. He would have liked to have sent her a card or some flowers perhaps.

He had broken his hip and needed an operation. The hospital insisted on notifying his 'next of kin', even though Teddy asked them not to. He wanted to crawl away and heal his wounds in peace, like a fox or a dog, but as he came round from the anaesthetic he could hear Viola muttering, 'It's the beginning of the end.'

'You're nearly eighty,' she said, using her 'reasonable' voice. 'You can't go gallivanting around like you used to.'

'I was on my way to the local shop to buy milk,' Teddy said. 'I would hardly call that "gallivanting".'

'Even so. It's only going to get more difficult for you. I can't keep rushing over every time you do something silly.'

Teddy sighed and said, 'I didn't ask you to come over.'

'Oh, and I wouldn't?' she said self-righteously. 'Not come and help my own father when he'd had an accident?'

He endured her presence for three days after he was discharged. She fretted the whole time about leaving her cats in order to look after him. Also, she 'hated being in this house', she said. 'Look at it, you haven't done a thing to it for decades. It's so *old-fashioned*.'

'*I'm* old-fashioned,' Teddy said. 'I don't think that's a bad thing.'

'You're impossible,' Viola said, twirling a strand of her heavily hennaed hair around a finger (an irritating habit he had forgotten about).

Viola phoned Sunny and told him he would have 'to put in some time' looking after his grandfather. Whenever Viola thought about Sunny she was gripped with panic. He'd already made a half-hearted attempt at suicide. He was too apathetic to actually kill himself though. Wasn't he? What if he did? The panic tightened its grip on her heart. She thought she was going to pass out. She had failed Sunny and had no idea what to do about it.

Terror made her callous. 'It's not as if you've got anything else to do,' she said to him.

Sunny, for his part, liked the respite of being back in Grandpa Ted's house. It was the only place he'd ever been happy.

Teddy slept on the sofa downstairs while Sunny took the pleasant back bedroom upstairs that had once been his mother's and then had been Bertie's during the year in which she had lived here. Sunny had lived here too, of course, although not for quite as long, as he had been forced to endure that terrible long summer at Jordan Manor. He wondered if he would ever get over it.

He liked this little back bedroom. It was where his sister had slept. At some point in the night he had always made his way through to Bertie's room. His sister had saved him in some fundamental way – warmth and light – but she was gone now. To Oxford, a foreign world. 'We're pinning our hopes on that one!' Viola used to say to her friends, pointing at Bertie. As if it was funny. It didn't help that they all thought that women were 'the superior species' (all that 'fish on a bicycle' crap). Sunny was apparently the living proof of this.

The harsh smell of burning vegetation drifted out of Sunny's bedroom and down the stairs every night when Teddy was dropping off to sleep. Marijuana, he supposed, although he knew little about it.

Sunny still lived in Leeds, left behind by Viola when

she moved to Whitby. He was currently living in a sordidly unruly flat with several members of his peer group, all too self-centred to qualify as friends.

He had dropped out of college (Communication Studies – 'Oh, the irony,' Viola said), and now didn't seem to be doing much of anything. The boy was all awkward corners. He didn't seem to have any of the skills that were necessary to negotiate the simple challenges of everyday life. He played guitar in a band, he said, shouting from the kitchen where he was heating up a tin of baked beans for their tea.

'Good for you!' Teddy shouted back from the living room. He was pretty sure he could smell the baked beans burning.

They had tinned beans and spaghetti hoops quite often. Fish and chips too, Sunny actually making the effort to go and pick them up from the local chip shop. Otherwise their dinners were delivered from restaurants all over town, indeed all over the world – Indian, Chinese. Pizzas, plenty of those. Teddy hadn't realized, he thought it was just the women from the WRVS who did meals on wheels. 'Eh?' Sunny said.

'Joke,' Teddy said.

'Eh?'

It all cost Teddy a fortune. (Needs must, his mother's voice said in his brain.) The boy couldn't cook at all. Viola was a rotten cook too, stodgy dishes made from brown rice and beans. Viola had brought both her children up as vegetarian, Bertie still was, but Sunny now seemed happy to eat anything going. Teddy thought if he could get back on his feet a bit he could teach him some simple dishes

– lentil soup, hot-pot, a Madeira cake. The boy just needed a bit of encouragement.

It transpired that Sunny had a provisional driving licence. Teddy tried not to show surprise, he was so used to Viola telling him about Sunny's incompetence and general lack of initiative. 'Right then,' Teddy said, 'my car's just sitting in the garage feeling neglected, let's take her for a spin. Viola's old L-plates are in there somewhere.' Viola had been very resistant to instruction.

'Really?' Sunny said doubtfully. 'Mum won't get in the car with me any more. She says she wants to die of old age.' Teddy didn't think that getting in a car with Sunny in the driving seat could measure up to flying night after dark night into the heart of an enemy whose only desire was to kill him and said, 'You'll never learn if you don't do it, come on.' Someone had to have some confidence in the boy, Teddy thought. They packed the wheelchair that the NHS had loaned him into the boot of the car and set off.

They ended up in Harrogate, a town Teddy was fond of. He had gone there often, both during the war and since. They parked the car in the town centre, although it took a very long time to slot it into a space as Sunny didn't seem to understand the difference between left and right, backwards and forwards. He wasn't a bad driver though – slow and hesitant, but his nerves grew stronger when he realized that Teddy, unlike Viola, wasn't going to shout at him all the time. 'Practice makes perfect,' Teddy said encouragingly.

They had a nice lunch in Bettys and then went into the

Valley Gardens. Here and there the first shoots of spring were making a reassuring reappearance in the damp earth. Sunny tended to push the wheelchair a little too fast and Teddy rather wished that they could swap places for a while so that Sunny could experience how uncomfortable it was when you went over bumps and kerbs, but on the whole Teddy was rather pleased with how this outing was going. 'Do you know what I'd like to do before we go back?' he said as they did a (somewhat alarming) U-turn and headed back towards town.

'A cemetery?' Sunny said. He'd never been in a cemetery, it turned out. He hadn't been to his father's funeral and he didn't know anyone else who had died.

'Stonefall,' Teddy told him. 'Commonwealth War Graves Commission. It's mainly Canadians buried here. A few of the Aussies and Kiwis, a handful of Americans and Brits.'

'Oh,' Sunny said. It was hard to engage the boy's interest.

An acreage of the dead. Neat rows of white gravestones – hard pillows for their green beds. Crews buried next to each other, kept together in the next life as they had been in this one. Pilots, engineers, navigators, wireless operators, gunners, bomb-aimers. Twenty years old, twenty-one, nineteen. Sunny's age. Teddy had known a boy who had lied magnificently about his age and had been the qualified pilot of a Halifax by the age of eighteen. Dead by the time he was nineteen. Could Sunny have done what he did? What they all did? Thank goodness he didn't have to.

'They were just boys,' Teddy said to Sunny. But they had seemed like men, had done the job of men. They had grown younger as Teddy had grown older. They'd sacrificed their lives so that Sunny could live his – did he understand that? Teddy supposed you shouldn't expect gratitude. Sacrifice, by its nature, was predicated on giving, not receiving. 'Sacrifice,' he remembered Sylvie saying, 'is a word that makes people feel noble about slaughter.'

'These aren't the crews of aircraft that were shot down over enemy territory,' Teddy said to Sunny. 'These are just (*just!*) the ones who died on training flights – over eight thousand altogether.' (*Here comes the history lesson*, he heard Viola say.) 'Or quite a few of these boys will have been killed when they crash-landed on return, or died later in Harrogate hospital from wounds they received on a raid.' But Sunny had ambled off along the rows of the dead. Shoulders up, head down, he never seemed to really *look* at anything. Perhaps he didn't want to see.

'At least they *have* a grave, that's something, I suppose,' Teddy said, continuing to talk to Sunny even though he was apparently out of earshot. It was a trick he learned when Sunny was little. He might not look as if he was listening but he had the hearing of a dog and Teddy had always hoped that he would absorb knowledge, more by osmosis than an intellectual process. 'Over twenty thousand bomber crew don't have a grave,' he said. 'There's a memorial at Runnymede.' For the ones who had no stone pillow to rest their heads on, whose names were written on water, scorched into the earth, atomized into the air. Legion.

Teddy had been to see the memorial, shortly after it

was unveiled in '53 by the young Queen. 'Why don't I come with you?' Nancy had said. 'We can make a weekend of it. Stay in Windsor or go up to London.' It was a pilgrimage, not a holiday, he tried to explain, and when he did go on his own, Nancy had been sparing in her farewells. He had 'shut her out' from his war, she said, which he found ironic for someone whose own war had been so clandestine and who on the rare occasions when they had met during it had spent a good deal of time urging him to forget the hostilities so that they could enjoy their time together. He was sorry now. Why shouldn't they have made a weekend of it?

' "Safe in their Alabaster Chambers",' he said to Sunny, when he sauntered back.

'Eh?' Sunny said.

' "Untouched by morning and untouched by noon, sleep the meek members of the Resurrection, rafter of satin and roof of stone." Emily Dickinson. It was your mother, funnily enough, who introduced me to her. She was a poet,' he added when Sunny looked puzzled, as if he was mentally riffling through a list of Viola's acquaintances to find an Emily Dickinson. 'Dead. American,' Teddy added. 'Quite morbid, you might like her. "I heard a fly buzz when I died".' Sunny perked up.

'I'll walk for a little bit,' Teddy said. Sunny helped him heave himself out of the wheelchair and gave him his arm so they could hobble slowly along the ranks of the dead.

He would have liked to have talked to his grandson about these men. How they were betrayed by that wily fox, Churchill, who never even mentioned them in his Victory Day speech, how they were given neither medal nor memorial, how Harris was pilloried for a policy he hadn't devised, although God knows he had carried it out with wretched zeal towards the end. But what good would it do? (*Here comes the history lesson.*)

'So . . .' Sunny said, scuffing the toe of his boot against a gravestone. The boots were ugly, unpolished things that looked as if they belonged on the feet of a paratrooper. 'So did you see, like, really bad things?'

'Bad things?'

Sunny shrugged. 'Grisly.' He shrugged again. 'Awful.'

Teddy didn't really understand the attraction of the dark side for the young these days. Perhaps because they had never experienced it. They had been brought up without shadows and seemed determined to create their own. Sunny had confessed yesterday that he'd 'quite like' to be a vampire.

'Ghoulish,' he added, as if Teddy might not have understood 'grisly' and 'awful'. Teddy thought about the Canadian flight instructor who had been stripped of his flesh and of everything 'awful' that had happened afterwards. *Good luck to you then.* A propeller flying through the air. What was that WAAF's name? Hilda? Yes, Hilda. She was tall with a round face, plump features. Often drove them out to dispersal. She had been a good pal of Stella's. Stella was an R/T girl whose plummy drawl provided a welcome voice for exhausted crews returning from ops. He had liked Stella, thought that there might be something between them, but there never was.

Hilda was the cheerful sort. 'Good luck, boys!' He could see her saying it now. Always hungry. If they came back with any rations left over they gave them to Hilda.

Sandwiches, sweets, anything. Teddy laughed. It seemed such an odd thing to be remembered for.

'Grandpa?'

It had been just before the end, before Nuremberg. He had been out at dispersal, talking to one of the fitters about *F-Fox*, his aircraft at the time. They had watched together as another aircraft approached, a very late returner from the previous night's op. It looked wounded, certainly looked like it was heading for a shaky landing. And there was Hilda, cycling sedately along the perimeter path. It was a huge airfield, everyone cycled. Even Teddy had an old boneshaker of a bike, although as a wing commander he had access to an RAF car as well. He had wondered what Hilda was doing out there. He would never know the answer to that. The damaged kite roared towards the runway, but Hilda barely gave it a glance. She caught sight of Teddy and waved. She never saw the propeller coming off, one of the blades breaking free, shearing through the air with astonishing speed, a huge sycamore seed spinning and spinning so fast that there was no time for Teddy or his fitter to react. No time to yell, 'Watch out!' She didn't see it coming, that was something, Teddy supposed. It was just bad luck, a case of inches and seconds. 'Shame she was so tall,' the fitter said afterwards, practical to a fault.

'Grandpa?'

Decapitated. Her head cleaved off by the blade. He heard the shrill scream of a WAAF, louder than the ungodly sound of the wounded aircraft tearing the runway up. The bomb-aimer was killed in the crash, the navigator aboard already dead, hit by flak somewhere over the Ruhr. It seemed secondary. WAAFs were running towards

Hilda, screaming and crying, and Teddy ordered them to go away, to get back to the Waafery and stay there, and he went out and picked up the head. It seemed wrong to expect anyone else to do it. The wheel of her bicycle was still spinning.

That's what it was, a head, not Hilda any more. You couldn't think of it as having anything to do with plump, cheerful Hilda. The next night he took Stella to a dance at a neighbouring squadron, but nothing ever came of it.

'Grandpa?'

'Lots of awful things happen in a war, Sunny. It doesn't help to remember them. Best to avoid morbid thoughts.'

'Are you looking for someone?' Sunny asked.

'Yes.'

'Don't they have, like, a map?'

'Probably,' Teddy said. 'But look, I've found him.'

He stopped in front of a headstone that read *Flight Sergeant Keith Marshall RAAF. Bomb-Aimer* and said, 'Hello, Keith.'

'He's not buried with his crew,' Sunny said, embarrassed to be with a man talking to the dead, even though they were the only people in the cemetery.

'No. The rest of us were OK. He was killed when we were attacked on our way back to the airfield from the Big City – that's what we used to call Berlin. Sometimes intruders – Germans – hid in the bomber stream on the way home. That was a mean trick. He was my friend, one of the best I ever had.'

'Any others you want to look for?' Sunny asked after a few minutes of heroically repressed impatience.

'No, not really,' Teddy said. 'I just wanted to let Keith know that someone's thinking about him.' He smiled at his grandson and said, 'Home, James. And don't spare the horses.'

'Eh?'

It was growing winter-dark by now and Sunny said, 'I've never driven at night.'

'Always a first time for everything,' Teddy said. Of course, sometimes the first time was the last time too. The journey back was a bit hairy but Teddy was determined to remain calm to bolster Sunny's confidence. To Teddy's surprise, Sunny asked, 'So what was it you did? You flew a bomber? You were the pilot?'

'Yes,' Teddy said. 'I was the pilot of a Halifax bomber. The bombers were named after British towns – Manchester, Stirling, Wellington, Lancaster. Halifax. Of course, it was the Lancasters who got all the glory. They could fly higher and carry heavier bomb loads, but actually by the end of the war when the Halifaxes had their Bristol engines fitted they could match the Lancasters. We loved the old "Halibag". The Lancasters were the celebrities after the war and we turned out to be the bridesmaids. And you were more likely to survive in a Halifax if you had to get out in a hurry. The Lancasters had this ruddy big spar in the middle and—' Sunny suddenly swerved across two lanes of traffic. Luckily the road was almost empty. ('Oops.') Teddy didn't know whether he was trying to avoid something or whether he had nodded off to sleep. Teddy supposed he'd better shut up. Nancy's voice came back to him from long ago. *Let's talk about something more interesting than the mechanics of bombing.* He sighed and murmured, 'Thermopylae,' to himself.

'Eh?'

When they finally got home Teddy said, 'You did very well, Sunny. You're going to make a very good driver.' Best always to praise rather than criticize. And he had done well, after all. Sunny made bacon sandwiches (he was showing definite signs of improvement on the kitchen front) and they ate them in front of the television, with a glass of beer each to celebrate their safe return. For the first time in decades Teddy thought that he needed a cigarette. He resisted the temptation. He was exhausted and fell asleep on the sofa before either the beer or *Noel's House Party* had finished.

Perhaps he should have moved back to the countryside when Viola fledged and left for university. Not far, the Hambledon Hills maybe. A little cottage. (He thought fondly of Mouse Cottage.) But instead he had stayed and plodded on, because something told him that this was the life that had to be lived out. And he liked York, liked his garden. He had friends, he belonged to a few clubs. He was a member of an archaeological society and went on digs with them. A ramblers' club, an ornithological group. He preferred solitary pursuits, and being a member of a group seemed rather dutiful, but he could do dutiful and somebody had to or the world would fall apart. He hadn't considered that working on a provincial newspaper was the most taxing job in the world, but nonetheless was surprised by how much time he suddenly had free when he retired. Perhaps too much.

* * *

'What about these?' Viola asked, indicating the bookcase that held *The Adventures of Augustus*. 'Do you think there's some second-hand value in them? I mean they went out of fashion years ago. They're all dedicated to you – I suppose that detracts from their value. There's a full set though, so someone might be interested in them.'

'I'm interested in them,' Teddy said.

'But you've never liked them,' Viola said. 'You haven't even read them.'

'Yes, I have.'

'They're in pristine condition.'

'That's because I was taught to take care of books,' Teddy said. So had Viola been, of course, but she was a filthy reader. Food and drink, cat sick, heaven knows what else all over the pages of her books. She was always dropping them in the bath or leaving them out in the rain. When she was a child she used to hurl them like missiles whenever she was angry. Teddy had been clipped on the forehead more than once by Enid Blyton when Viola was small. *The Land of Far-Beyond* had almost broken his nose. He wouldn't be surprised if she still threw things. Teddy supposed she had so much anger because she had lost her mother. There he went with the cod psychology again. ('I'm angry because I *have* a mother,' Bertie said.) Sylvie had never subscribed much to theories of childhood trauma. People came as they were, she said, all packeted up, complete, waiting to be unwrapped. His mother's generation seemed wonderfully free of guilt.

Teddy fetched an empty box and started putting Augustus into it. Years since he'd opened one. Izzie wrote the last one in 1958. They hadn't sold for a long time, not since the war really. Augustus's heyday had been between the wars. Augustus Edward Swift *floruit* 1926–1939. Of course, poor old Augustus was finished long before Izzie died in 1974. Teddy's version of him lingered on, rearing his head occasionally. Was he an old man now, being dragged, kicking and screaming, into sheltered housing, a fag hanging out of the corner of his mouth? Stained trousers and whiskery chin?

Teddy went to visit Izzie a few days before she died. She was pretty doolally by then. It was hard to conjure her up now, she was an impression, the greedy red mouth, the perfume, the affectations. She had wanted to adopt him at one point. Would his life have turned out very differently or would it have developed in much the same way?

In her will Izzie left the copyright for Augustus to Teddy. It was worth virtually nothing. The rest of the estate, which mainly comprised the house in Holland Park, went to 'my granddaughter', a woman in Germany whom they had never heard of. 'For reparation,' it had said in the will.

Pamela and Teddy and Pamela's daughter, Sarah, had sifted through everything in the house after Izzie's funeral. A nightmare of a job. They had found a Croix de Guerre at the bottom of her jewellery box. It seemed so unlikely. These twin mysteries, the German granddaughter and the Croix de Guerre, summed up the impenetrable nature of Izzie. If Ursula, with her detective soul, had still been alive she would have got to the bottom of both. Teddy had been uninterested (he felt guilty about that now) and it wasn't long before Pamela was showing the signs of early-onset Alzheimer's. Poor Pammy, she spent years living a grey half-life. So the ambivalence that was Izzie was never solved, which was exactly how she would have liked it.

He packed the studio portrait that Cecil Beaton had taken of Izzie after her first flush of success. It made Izzie look like a film star, artificial and full of manipulation. 'But glamorous,' Bertie said. 'Yes, I suppose so,' Teddy said. He gave her the photograph the first time she visited him in Fanning Court. 'But it was my mother who was the beauty,' he said. Sylvie's corpse, he remembered, in the open coffin for viewing. The years had fallen from her face and Bea had clutched his arm, just the two of them, as if they were at a private exhibition (they were, he supposed). Why Bea? Where was Nancy that day? He couldn't remember. Bea gone too now, of course. She had been close to his heart, perhaps closer than she knew. Dear God, Teddy thought, stop thinking about dead people. He packed the Beaton in with the Augustuses ('Augusti' perhaps) and taped the box shut. 'They're coming with me,' he said decisively to Viola.

'Where's Sunny?' Viola puzzled.

Yes, where *is* Sunny?

> I have seen a large dog fox several times recently but it was a hot afternoon and no doubt, like most creatures, it was lying low in the shade. The fox has an unfortunate reputation. A crafty thief, often a charming one in fable and fairy story, its name is a byword for low (and occasionally high) cunning. A moral outlaw, a trickster and

sometimes downright malevolent. The Christian
Church often equated the fox with the devil. In
many churches across the land you will find
images of the fox in priestly robes preaching to
a flock of geese. (There is a fine woodcut in the
Cathedral at Ely.) The fox is a subtle outlaw, a
devilish predator without conscience, and the
geese a flock of innocents . . .

He was in the attic, where, unbelievably, there were
even more boxes of crap. The atmosphere up here was
thick with neglect. There was a box full of this stuff –
mouldy, flimsy paper, crammed with single-space faded
typing. Some of it was incomprehensible so probably
poetry, Sunny concluded.

It was like a neglected museum in the attic, all dust and
rust. Sunny didn't like the atmosphere in museums but
he liked the idea of collecting, liked all those trays of
butterflies and insects, cabinets of rocks. He liked the
Augustus books, although he wouldn't have said so. Not
the insides so much, just the uniform outsides. They each
had a number on their spines so that if you lined them up
they counted from one to forty-two. When he was little
he collected stones, pebbles, bits of gravel from the road,
anything. Sometimes, still, he felt the urge to pick up a
stone and put it in his pocket.

A fine dust, like grey talcum, was dislodged every time
he took the papers out. He read slowly, his lips forming
each word as if he was deciphering a foreign language.

The stable where the Holy Family were taking
refuge for the night had but a small fire which

was on the verge of going out. A robin – one of the many small creatures who had come to rejoice at the advent of the Messiah – seeing how cold the infant was, placed himself in front of the weak fire and fanned the flames with his wings. In doing so he burnt his breast which for evermore would be red as a sign of gratitude.

There were lots of these. At the end of each one was typed 'Agrestis'. Whatever that meant. Different topics each time – 'truffling for primroses', 'the welcome return of spring', 'the golden pomp of daffodils', 'an otter and her kits, sleek with water', 'the snowdrop in purest white array'. Hares – 'the Celtic messengers of Eostre, the goddess of spring' – that were boxing in a field. Hares boxed, Sunny puzzled? Competitively?

Another fusty box full of buttons and old coins. A shoebox with photographs. He recognized hardly anyone in the photographs. A lot of them were small black-and-white ones dating from pre-history as far as Sunny was concerned. In the Seventies they changed to colour. Some little square snaps of him and Bertie in Grandpa Ted's garden, fading to yellow. They were dressed in primary-coloured outfits that made them look like clowns. Thanks, Viola, he thought bitterly. No wonder he was bullied as a child. Himself and Bertie standing in front of a flower-bed with Tinker seated between them. His heart gave a little twitch. He had cried when his grandfather told him that Tinker had been put down. He took the photo and put it in his pocket.

There was another box, small and rusty, and when he

opened it he found medals inside. His grandfather's presumably, from the war. Also a small gold caterpillar. A caterpillar? A little card, soft with age – a 'Caterpillar Club membership', it said, made out for 'W/C E. B. Todd'. Another membership card, different, for the 'Goldfish Club' for 'P/O E. B. Todd'. What did all these mysterious letters mean? What were all these weird clubs that Grandpa Ted was a member of? He could just make out the typed lettering on the Goldfish Club membership card, 'escaping death by use of his emergency dinghy, February 1943'.

Sunny thought about the outing they'd had to Harrogate when Grandpa Ted was laid up with his hip. He hadn't said so, but Sunny had enjoyed it. He had appreciated the orderliness of the gravestones in the cemetery. He had had to walk away at one point and leave Grandpa Ted in his wheelchair because he had felt tears starting. All those dead guys, it was so sad. They were his own age, doing something noble, something heroic. They were lucky. They'd been given history. It wasn't going to happen to him. He was never going to be given the chance to be noble and heroic.

It made him feel angry. He took the medals out of the tin and slipped them in his pocket along with the purloined photograph.

The war was interesting actually, all that stuff about the bombers. Perhaps Sunny would read a book about the war. Maybe then he could talk to Grandpa Ted about it without feeling like an idiot. His grandfather was a hero too, wasn't he? He'd had a life. Sunny wondered how you went about getting one of those.

He climbed awkwardly down the ladder from the attic

and dropped a box on the floor. Viola made a great show of choking on the dust. 'You know I'm allergic,' she said crossly.

'There's a whole load more stuff up there,' Sunny said.

'Oh, for God's sake,' Viola said to Teddy. 'You're a *hoarder*, Dad.'

Teddy ignored her and said to Sunny, 'You didn't come across a box that had my medals in it when you were up there, did you?'

'Medals?'

'From the war. I haven't set eyes on them in years. I was thinking of going to an RAF reunion dinner, thought I could take them along.'

Sunny shrugged and said, 'Dunno.'

'Can we get on, please?' Viola said.

'That's everything loaded on to the van,' Viola said. 'You just need to do an idiot check before it leaves.'

'A what?' Teddy said.

'An idiot check,' Viola repeated. 'You know, look round, make sure you haven't left anything behind.'

Only my life, Teddy thought.

1951

The Invisible Worm

Viola delayed her appearance on the world's stage. Teddy and Nancy had been married for five years with no sign of a baby and had almost given up hope. They considered adopting. They would soon be too old, a humourless woman at the council-run adoption agency said, and babies were scarce at the moment (as if they were seasonal). Did they want to put their names down?

'Yes,' Nancy said, more eagerly than Teddy had expected. The humourless woman, a Mrs Taylor-Scott, was sitting behind a cheap government-issue desk. Teddy and Nancy sat on uncomfortable chairs in front of her, being grilled. ('Rather like naughty pupils,' Nancy said.)

'If there's a "shortage",' Nancy said, 'then we don't mind if it's a coloured baby.' She turned to Teddy and said, 'We don't, do we?'

'No,' he said, caught on the hop. This wasn't something they had ever discussed. It had never even crossed his mind that their baby wouldn't be white. On one op in the war he'd taken an odd bod, a rear-gunner who was from Jamaica, black as coal. Couldn't remember his name, only that he'd been nineteen years old and hopping with life until he was hosed out of the rear-turret on a return from the Ruhr.

'I don't mind,' Teddy said, 'although I might draw the line at green.' It was, he knew, a feeble attempt at humour. He imagined not telling Sylvie of this plan, of watching her expression the first time she peered in the crib and saw a little black face looking back at her. He laughed and Mrs Taylor-Scott gave him a doubtful look. Nancy reached across and gave his hand an encouraging squeeze. Or perhaps a warning. They did not want to appear mentally unhinged.

'Accommodation?' Mrs Taylor-Scott said, writing something illegible on their application form in her cramped hand.

They had left Mouse Cottage behind now and were living a few miles further into the dale, in a rented farmhouse called Ayswick, on the outskirts of a small village that had a little school, a pub, a shop, a village hall and a Methodist chapel, but no church. 'Everything we need,' Nancy said, 'although perhaps not the chapel.' Half a century later the pub was a 'gastro pub', the school had turned into a pottery, the shop was a café ('all home-made on the premises'), the village hall was an art gallery that also sold the usual tourist bric-a-brac of tapestry kits, calendars, 'spoon rests' and sheep-themed ornaments, and the Methodist chapel was a private house. Most of the remaining cottages were second homes. The tourists came, in coachloads sometimes, because the village had been used as the backdrop of a television series that was set in the nostalgic past.

Teddy knew all this because he returned with Bertie in 1999 on his 'farewell tour'. They found that Mouse Cottage had disappeared altogether, not a stone remained, but Ayswick was still where it had been, looking much the same on the outside. It was a B&B now, renamed Fairview, run by a couple in their fifties 'escaping the urban rat race'.

They decided on a whim to stay the night there. Teddy was assigned the bedroom he had once shared with Nancy and asked to be moved, and instead slept in a small room at the back that only when he woke up the next morning did he realize had once been Viola's room, and he wondered how he could have forgotten that. In here had been her cradle and then her cot, and finally her little single bed. Under Nancy's direction he had nailed painted plywood cut-out figures on the wall – Jack, Jill, the well and a bucket. ('No, further over to the left – make the bucket look as if it's tumbling over.') There had been a small nightlight by her bed, a little house, the warm light glowing through the windows. He had built a bookcase for Viola's childhood reading – *The Wind in the Willows*, *The Secret Garden*, *Alice in Wonderland* – and now here he was on the other side of the looking glass gazing at a Toile de Jouy wallpaper, a large, amateurish painting of the dale in winter, and a bedside lamp with a cheap white paper shade. And no going back, ever, to the other side.

The house was much warmer than it had been when he had lived here with Nancy, although he was sad to see that the Georgian panelling had gone from the walls, a victim of the Sixties, Teddy supposed, and now the place was decorated in fresh florals and stripes, pale rugs and 'en-suites' in every room. Ayswick was transformed into something unrecognizable – into Fairview, in fact – and nothing remained of himself or his past. No one now but Teddy would ever know that once he and Nancy had huddled by the great Aga in the kitchen while the wind blew up the hill and whistled through every room, competing with Beniamino Gigli and Maria Caniglia singing *Tosca* on their cherished gramophone. No one would know that their black-and-white collie had been called Moss and slept contentedly on a rag-rug in front of that great Aga while Teddy drafted his Nature Notes in a reporter's notebook and Nancy, a ripe seed-pod about to burst, knitted little lacy things for the baby they were about to meet.

It would all die with him, he realized, as he buttered toast in Fairview's breakfast room – once a dusty and unused back parlour and now, he had to admit, rather nice with three round tables dressed in white tablecloths, a little posy of flowers on each. He was the first of the guests to come down and had already eaten a plate of bacon, egg and sausage (he still had 'a good appetite', according to Viola, who made it sound like a criticism) and chatted affably to the proprietress before anyone else put in an appearance. He didn't mention to her that he had once lived here. It would seem odd, he decided. And the conversation would run on predictable lines. She would express surprise and say, 'It must have changed a lot since your day,' and he would say, 'Yes it certainly has!'

and none of it would convey the cawing of the rooks in the evening hurrying to roost in the stand of trees behind the farmhouse or the Blakean magnificence of the sunset from the top of the hill.

'Ayswick,' Nancy said. 'It's a farmhouse.' Mrs Taylor-Scott raised an eyebrow as if she disapproved of farmhouses. 'In a village,' Nancy added hastily. 'Or at any rate on the edge of it. All the necessary amenities and so on.'

They were able to rent Ayswick because the farmer who owned it had built himself a modern brick house 'with all mod cons' and regarded the old farmhouse as a 'white elephant' and was only too glad to have tenants willing to take on its draughty, stone-flagged passages and rattling windows. 'But so much character!' Nancy said, delighted when they signed the lease.

Where Mouse Cottage was tiny, the farmhouse was vast, far too big for two people. It dated from the mid-eighteenth century and the weathered grey stone of the exterior gave away little, but inside it revealed a certain elegance in its broad oak floorboards, the painted Georgian panelling in the living room, the swag and drop cornices and, best of all, the huge farmhouse kitchen with an old cream Aga 'like a big comforting animal', according to Nancy. They still had no furniture of their own apart from Nancy's piano and no old biddy to lend them her goods and chattels post-mortem, so they were grateful to the farmer and his wife for leaving behind their enormous kitchen table, meant for feeding breakfast to a herd of hungry farm workers.

The farmer's wife had insisted on plain new-fashioned

Ercol in her small spare dining room. 'Lovely,' Nancy said politely when she visited. She had taken flowers to say 'thank you' and sat at the simple elmwood table and drank Camp coffee that had been boiled up with evaporated milk. Both Teddy and Nancy were rather particular about their coffee. They had the beans, an Italian roast, sent in the post from Border's in York. The postman always looked taken aback by the aroma escaping from the brown paper packet. They ground the beans themselves in a hand grinder that they left permanently clamped on to the kitchen table and made their coffee in an old percolator that Teddy had brought back with him from France, before the war.

'The new farmhouse is quite soulless,' Nancy reported back to Teddy. 'No character.' No spiders or mice either. No dust, no cracks creeping across the ceiling or damp inching its way up the walls that would one day give their hard-won daughter a croupy cough and winter catarrh. And the new farmhouse nestled in the sheltering lee of a hill, whereas Ayswick looked down the length of the dale, taking the brunt of the wind's brute force. They could stand at their front door and watch the weather coming towards them, like an approaching foe. It lived with them, it had a personality – 'the sun's trying to come out', 'I think it wants to rain', 'the snow's keeping itself off'.

It was a Saturday and Nancy found Teddy in pastoral mode when she returned from the new farmhouse.

> The woods are full of foxgloves at the moment. The Latin name – given to this humble native flower by sixteenth-century German botanist

Leonhart Fuchs – is *digitalis*, which translates as 'of the finger', and indeed here in Yorkshire they are sometimes referred to as 'Witches' fingers'. (It is perhaps an odd coincidence that 'Fuchs' is the German for 'fox'.) The foxglove goes by many other names – fairy gloves, fairy bells, fox bells, tod-tails – but most of us are most familiar with 'foxglove'. The word most likely comes from the Anglo-Saxon *Foxes glófa*.

'I never thought about where the word came from before,' Nancy said. She stood behind him, resting her hands on his shoulders while she read.

It is a flower without pretension and was used for centuries as folk medicine to cure a multitude of ailments before its efficacy in treating heart problems was discovered. During the war some of you may remember or have been a member of one of the County Herb Committees, tasked with picking foxgloves for the manufacturing of the medical *digitalis* when we were unable to import from our usual source.

'You got that from my mother,' Nancy said.

'I did. She was the chairwoman of the County Herb Committee.'

'Your mother thinks my mother's a witch,' Nancy said. 'She would have had her ducked and drowned three hundred years ago.' Their own garden, Ayswick's garden, was full of foxgloves and little else. They made a rough lawn by borrowing a pair of scythes from the farmer and left the rest to nature. There seemed little point in creating a garden to have it dwarfed by the magnificence of the landscape. Teddy was surprised when they moved to York to discover how much enjoyment there was to be had from a suburban quarter-acre.

Nancy kissed the top of his head and said, 'I have marking to do.' She no longer taught her keen grammar-school girls, eventually drawn by conscience to go where she was 'really needed'. She drove every day to Leeds, where she was head of maths in a grateful secondary modern. Nancy went by her married name now, having left 'Miss Shawcross' behind at the grammar school. The new school, full of 'disadvantaged' pupils, was not so ambivalent about married women. They would not have minded, Nancy said, if she had been a headless horse as long as she could rescue their maths department.

Teddy himself had slowly become the de facto editor of the *Recorder* as Bill Morrison had taken more and more of 'a back seat'. Teddy employed a school leaver to do some of the more tedious leg-work but still found himself writing most of the contents.

At weekends, as reported to Mrs Taylor-Scott, they went on long tramps over hill and dale, observing nature 'in all her different raiments', as Agrestis put it, and gaining inspiration for the Nature Notes. They had a dog, Moss, a very good black-and-white collie who went to work every day with Teddy. In the evenings they did the crossword or read out snippets from the *Manchester Guardian* to each other. There was the wireless and they liked to play cribbage and listen to the gramophone that had been a wedding present from Ursula.

'And friends?' the woman from the adoption agency

asked. 'Not much time, really,' Nancy said. 'We have our jobs and each other.'

'It was like an awful oral exam,' Nancy said afterwards to Teddy. 'When I said we liked to listen to opera records I swear she winced. And when I said we both came from quite large families you could see her wondering if we were constitutionally inclined towards incontinent lust or – worse – Catholicism. And I couldn't work out whether it was good to have a large social circle or just one or two friends. I faltered on that one, I think. We probably shouldn't have mentioned Moss, she wasn't a dog-lover. And the *Guardian* was a mistake, you could tell she was a *Mirror* reader.'

'Church?' Mrs Taylor-Scott had asked, staring at Teddy as if trying to force a guilty secret out of him.

'Every Sunday, C of E,' Nancy said briskly. Another quick squeeze of the hand.

'And your vicar will write a reference?'

'Of course.' ('I didn't fudge that one.' No, just an outright lie, Teddy thought.)

'We could become Methodists, join our local chapel,' Nancy said afterwards. 'I'm sure Wesley would appeal to Mrs Taylor-Scott, he was so very intent on exemplary behaviour. "God grant that I may never live to be useless!" ' Teddy quoted those words at Ursula's funeral and then regretted doing so because it made his sister sound awfully po-faced, especially in 1966 when usefulness was out of fashion. Ursula hadn't been religiously inclined at all, the war knocked that out of her, but she admired the way that Non-Conformism forged both reticence and endeavour.

Teddy had made all the arrangements for Ursula's funeral and then spent months afterwards expecting her to write and tell him all about it. ('My dearest Teddy, I hope this finds you well.')

'Are you all right, Grandpa?' Bertie asked, slipping into the chair next to him at the Fairview breakfast table and leaning over to kiss his cheek. 'Is this jaunt down memory lane getting to you?' He patted her hand and said, 'Not at all.'

Today they were setting out to explore some of the airfields where he had served out his RAF career during the war. Industrial estates now, or out-of-town shopping complexes. Houses had been built on them, and on one a prison, but where he had been stationed on his first tour was still the abandoned, melancholy place of his imagination, with the ghostly remains of accommodation blocks, the trace of the perimeter track, the outline of a grassed-over bomb dump and the hollow-eyed, broken shell of the control tower with its rusted window frames and crumbling concrete. The inside had been colonized by shabby weeds – rosebay willowherb, nettles and docks – but there remained part of the ops board, and a faded, tattered piece of a map of Western Europe still adhered to the wall, long out of date.

'And this too shall pass,' Teddy said to Bertie as they surveyed the map and Bertie said, 'Don't. We'll start to cry. Let's find somewhere to have a cup of tea.'

They found a pub called the Black Swan where they had tea and scones and it was only as they were paying the bill that Teddy remembered that this was the place on his first tour that they used to call the Mucky

Duck and where they had gone on many a crew binge.

'Do you think we passed Mrs Taylor-Scott's catechism?' Nancy fretted.

'I don't know. She was keeping her cards close to her chest.'

But before a baby of any colour was found, Nancy came down to breakfast one morning and said, 'I think I have been visited by an angel.'

'I'm sorry?' Teddy said. He was toasting bread on the Aga, his mind on Agrestis, not annunciation. He had seen hares boxing in the field yesterday and was trying to phrase something that conveyed the pleasure he had felt.

'An angel?' he said, wrenching his mind away from *Lepus europaeus* ('the Celtic messengers of Eostre, the goddess of spring').

Nancy smiled beatifically at him. 'You're burning the toast,' she said. And then, 'Blessed am I among women. I *think* that I'm having a baby. We. We are having a baby, my love. A new heart beating. Inside me. A miracle.' Nancy may have rejected Christianity a long time ago, but sometimes Teddy caught a glimpse of the sublime *religieuse* who dwelled within.

There was a moment, near the end of Nancy's harrowing two-day labour, when Teddy was taken aside by a doctor and warned that he might have to make a choice between saving Nancy and saving the baby. 'Nancy,' he said, without any hesitation. 'Save my wife.'

Teddy had been unprepared. With the end of the war he was supposed to have moved out of the valley of the shadow of death into the sunlit uplands. He had become unready for battle.

'They asked you to choose,' Nancy said when mother and child were both safely gathered in. (Who had told her, he wondered?) She was lying in bed, white from the blood loss, her lips dry and cracked, her hair still limp with sweat. He thought she looked beautiful, a martyr who had survived the flames. The baby in her arms seemed strangely untouched by their trial by ordeal. 'I would have chosen the baby, you know that, don't you?' Nancy said, tenderly kissing this new creature on the forehead. 'If it had been a choice between saving you or the baby, I would have had to choose the baby.'

'I know,' he said. 'I was being selfish. You were responding to a maternal imperative' (a paternal one did not apply apparently). In later years Teddy wondered if Viola somehow knew that, in theory if not in practice, he had been willing to condemn her to die without a second thought. When, during her pregnancy, she was asked what she was hoping for – a boy or a girl – Nancy always laughed and said, 'I'll just be happy if it turns out to be a baby,' but when Viola was born and they learned she was to be their only child, she said, 'I'm glad it's a girl. A boy grows and marries and leaves. He belongs to another woman, but a girl always belongs to her mother.'

There would be no more babies, the doctor said. Nancy was one of five children, as was Teddy. It was strange to be reduced to this singularity, this fat pupa in its cradle cocoon. Sugar and spice. (More spice than sugar, it turned out.) They had already discussed names – Viola for a girl.

Nancy, thinking of her own four sisters, imagined daughters, adding a Rosalind, a Helena and perhaps a Portia or a Miranda. Resourceful girls. 'No tragedies,' she said. 'No Ophelias and Juliets.' And a son, she had thought, for Teddy, and they would call him Hugh. The boy that would never be.

Shakespeare had seemed an obvious choice for a name. It was 1952 and they were still considering what it meant to be English. To help them there was a new young queen, Gloriana risen. On their treasured gramophone they listened to Kathleen Ferrier singing British folk songs. They had journeyed to hear her sing with the Hallé at the reopening of the Free Trade Hall in Manchester. It had been blitzed in 1940 and Nancy said 1940 seemed so long ago. 'What silly patriots we are,' she said, wiping a tear away as the audience stamped and cheered their approval of Elgar and 'Land of Hope and Glory'. When the following year Kathleen Ferrier died, too young, Bill Morrison said, 'A grand lass,' claiming her for the north, even though she was from the wrong side of the Pennines, and wrote her obituary for the *Recorder*.

Nancy fell in love with Viola at first sight of her. A *coup de foudre*, she said, more intense and overwhelming than any form of romantic love. Mother and daughter were each a world to the other, complete and unassailable. Teddy knew he could never be so consumed by another person. He loved his wife and daughter. It was perhaps a stalwart affection rather than a magnificent obsession, but nonetheless he didn't doubt that if called upon to do so he would sacrifice his own life in a heartbeat for them. And he also knew that there would be no more hankering for something else, something beyond, for the hot slices of colour or the intensity of war or romance. That was all behind him, he had a different kind of duty now, not to himself, not to his country, but to this small knot of a family.

Was it simply love on Nancy's part? Or something more febrile? Their shared experience of being in the place between life and death, perhaps. His own experience of motherhood was based on Sylvie, of course. He knew that she had loved him hugely when he was a boy (all his life probably), but she had never invested her happiness in him. (Had she?) Of course, he had never understood his mother, he doubted that anyone ever had, certainly not his father.

Nancy, the easy-going atheist, decided that Viola should be christened.

'I believe that's called hypocrisy,' Sylvie said to Teddy, out of earshot of Nancy (which was where many of her conversations with Teddy took place).

'Well then that makes two of you,' Teddy said. 'You still go to church but I know you don't believe.'

'What a good husband you are,' Nancy said afterwards, 'always taking your wife's side rather than your mother's.'

'It's the side of reason that I'm on,' Teddy said. 'It just so happens that that's where you're always to be found and my mother rarely.'

'I'm not taking any chances,' Nancy told Sylvie at the christening. 'I'm hedging my bets, in the manner of Pascal.' Sylvie was not mollified by references to philosophical French mathematicians. If only Teddy had married someone less educated, she thought.

They went 'home' to have Viola christened. 'Why do we still call it that when we have a perfectly good home of our own?' Nancy mused. 'I don't know,' Teddy said, although he knew that in his heart Fox Corner would always be home.

The godmothers – aunts Bea and Ursula – pledged to reject the devil and all rebellion against God and afterwards they celebrated at Jackdaws with cream sherry and a Dundee cake, Sylvie, needless to say, very put out that they weren't next door at Fox Corner.

Teddy gave Nancy a ring, a small diamond solitaire, to mark Viola's safe passage into the world. 'The engagement ring I never gave you,' he said.

Viola grew, the pupa fattened but not yet turned into a butterfly. Nancy returned to work when Viola herself started at the village primary school, taking a part-time job in a nearby expensive private Church of England boarding school for girls who had failed their Eleven Plus but whose parents couldn't countenance the social humiliation of a secondary modern.

The farmer had offered to sell them Ayswick and they had applied for a mortgage to buy the old farmhouse. Life seemed as if it would go on in much the same way for ever, Teddy was not ambitious and Nancy seemed contented until one day in the summer of 1960, when Viola was eight years old, she decided she wanted to upheave them.

Living in the country was all very well, she said, but Viola would soon need more, a good secondary school that wasn't an hour's bus ride away, friends, a social life, and it was hard to find those 'in the middle of nowhere'. And the farmhouse was too big, impossible to keep clean, it cost a fortune to heat, the plumbing was from the Dark Ages. And so on.

'I don't think they had plumbing in the Dark Ages,' Teddy said. 'I thought you loved it because it had character.'

'You can have too much character.'

This ambush had been a complete surprise. They were sitting up in bed at the time, both reading their library books, a sedate conclusion to what had been, for Teddy at any rate, a rather tedious day, covering a local agricultural show for the *Recorder*. There were only so many well-groomed sheep and intricate vegetable displays that a man could take an interest in. Rather to his despair, he had been dragooned into adjudicating the Victoria sponges in the WI tent (feeling rather like a novelty judge at a beauty contest). 'As light as a feather,' he declared the winner, falling gratefully back on cliché.

It was the school holidays and Nancy had wanted to visit an optician for a check-up and as it was such good weather Teddy said he would take Viola along to the agricultural show with him. Viola, of course, didn't really like farm animals. She was nervous around cows and pigs, even sheep made her anxious, and she screeched if a goose came anywhere near (an unfortunate incident when she was smaller). 'But there'll be other things going on,' Teddy said hopefully, and there was indeed a flower show that Viola said was 'nice', although – despite Teddy's warnings – thrusting her nose into vase after vase of sweet peas brought on her hay fever. The sheepdog trials, however, were 'boring' (Teddy had to agree on that one) but the Young Farmers' coconut shy was a success and she spent a lot of money at it for little return, throwing wildly and with no aim. Eventually Teddy had to step in and lob a few balls and win a goldfish so that she didn't come away empty-handed. There was also a pony show which, despite an avowed aversion to horses, she enjoyed watching, clapping enthusiastically whenever anyone managed to hop over the small jumps.

In the WI tent Viola was treated like a pet – all the WI women knew Teddy well and fed her far too much cake. Fed Teddy far too much cake as well. Viola was like Bobby, their yellow Labrador – she would keep on eating until someone told her to stop. Like Bobby, too, she was a little on the plump side. 'Puppy fat,' Nancy said. For Viola perhaps, but not for Bobby, long past puppyhood now. Moss, their excellent collie, died not long after Viola was born and placid Bobby had been chosen to be the faithful and uncomplaining companion of Viola's childhood.

By the end of the afternoon Viola was crotchety with heat and tiredness. That, mixed with the cake and the copious amounts of orange squash she had drunk, made for a lethal combination and Teddy had to stop the car twice on the way home so that Viola could be sick on the grass verge. 'You poor thing,' he said, trying to give her a cuddle, but she squirmed out of his arms. Teddy had hoped for a relationship with his daughter that would be like the one that Major Shawcross had had with his daughters, or perhaps the slightly more restrained one that Pamela and Ursula had enjoyed with Hugh, but Viola had no space left in her heart for him, Nancy occupied it all. After they lost her, Nancy occupied even more space in Viola's heart. His daughter was consumed with bitterness towards a universe that had taken her mother and left her with the poor substitute of her father.

Viola slept the rest of the way home, leaving Teddy to worry about the goldfish (already named Goldie by Viola) in the suffocating heat of its plastic prison.

'I want a pony,' Viola declared to Nancy when they got home, and when Teddy said quite reasonably, 'But you don't like horses,' Viola burst into tears and shouted at him that ponies weren't horses. He didn't argue the point. 'She's over-tired,' Nancy said as Viola flung herself down on the sofa in a fit of – rather histrionic – sobbing. 'Whither the famous Todd stoicism?' Nancy murmured. 'Sensitive' was how she described their thin-skinned daughter. 'Over-indulged,' Sylvie would have said. Teddy rescued the goldfish from being squashed beneath Viola's puppy fat. 'It's all right, darling,' Nancy said to Viola. 'Come on, let's get you a little bit of chocolate, that will cheer you up, won't it?' It would and it did.

Teddy took the goldfish through to the kitchen and set it free from the bag, watching it slither into a washing-up bowl of tap water. 'Not much of a life, is it, Goldie?' he said to it. Teddy was an early member of the Goldfish Club, although he rarely gave this fact much thought. There was a little cloth badge somewhere, a fish with wings, a result of having ditched in the North Sea. It was during his first tour and sometimes he wondered if he couldn't have made a better job of it, made those last few miles to land instead of thudding his Halifax on to the sea. It had been a horrible affair. *Well, good luck to you then.*

He made a mental note to go to a pet shop tomorrow and buy a bowl for Goldie so that the fish could spend the rest of its life swimming round and round in solitary confinement. He could, he supposed, buy a companion for it but that would simply be doubling the misery.

Lying in bed that night, Teddy could feel that he was paying the price for all that WI cake – stuck uncomfortably somewhere beneath his ribs.

'Poor you,' Nancy said. 'Shall I get you some Milk of Magnesia?' She used the same tone of voice, he noticed, that she employed to quell Viola's pain and distress (*a little bit of chocolate*). He declined her offer of the Milk of Magnesia and returned to his book. He was reading *Born Free*, Nancy was reading Iris Murdoch's *The Bell*. He wondered if their books said something about themselves.

He couldn't concentrate, however, and snapped the book shut rather more forcefully than he had intended. 'So you want us to move?' he puzzled.

'Yes, I think I do.'

When Viola was born Teddy and Nancy had enthusiastically discussed the robust rural childhood they intended for her – imagining her climbing trees and jumping ditches, rambling around the countryside with just a dog for company. ('A bit of neglect never does any harm,' Nancy said. 'You could argue it did us good when we were children.') Viola, it was revealed by the passage of time, was not a country child. She was quite happy to be sequestered inside all day, reading a book or listening to the little Dansette record player they had bought her (Cliff Richard, the Everly Brothers) with Bobby lying lazily on the carpet at her feet. Both dog and child had long since come to an agreement about not tramping and jumping. Perhaps Nancy was right. Viola would fare better in the suburbs.

And anyway, perhaps a change would be good for all of them, Nancy said. Teddy felt no need for change, he was quite content to be in 'the middle of nowhere' and had thought Nancy was too. '*Good* for us?' he said. 'In what way?'

'More stimulating. More to *do*. Cafés, theatres, cinemas, shops. *People*. We can't all be content with truffling out the first primrose of spring or listening for larks.' (She wasn't content? *The Discontented Wife*, like a Restoration comedy, Teddy thought. A rather poor one. He couldn't help but think of his mother.) 'You used to be content with "truffling primroses", as you put it,' he said. He rather liked the phrase, more poetic than was Nancy's wont, and he put it aside for Agrestis's use. As the years had gone by his alter ego had taken on shape and character in his mind – a hardy countryman, cap on head, pipe in hand, a down-to-earth man, yet nonetheless attendant upon the whims of Mother Nature. Teddy occasionally felt himself wanting in comparison to this sturdy counterpart.

There was a time when the discovery of a bird's nest or, indeed, the first primrose would have delighted his discontented wife. 'But none of us are the same people we once were,' she said.

'I am,' Teddy said.

'No, you're not.'

'Are we having an argument?'

'No!' Nancy said, laughing. 'But we're in our forties now, plodding along . . .'

'Plodding?'

'It's not an insult. I'm just saying that maybe we need to shake ourselves up a bit. You don't want life to pass you by, do you?'

'I thought this was about Viola, not us?'

'I'm not suggesting we emigrate to the other side of the world,' Nancy said. 'Just as far as York.'

'York?'

Nancy climbed out of bed, saying, 'I'm going to fetch you that Milk of Magnesia anyway. All that cake has clearly made you grumpy. That will teach you to be so charming to all those WI ladies.' As she passed by his side of the bed she ruffled his hair affectionately, as if he were a little boy, and said, 'I'm only saying we should *think* about it, not that we should necessarily *do* it.'

He smoothed his hair down and stared at the ceiling. *Plodding*, he thought. Nancy returned from the bathroom, shaking the contents of the blue glass bottle. For a moment he feared that she was going to spoon-feed him the Milk of Magnesia but instead she handed it to him, saying, 'There you go, that should do the trick.' She climbed back into bed and returned to her book, as if the subject of changing their lives had been satisfactorily debated and decided.

He took a swig of the chalky white medicine and switched off his bedside light. As was so often the case, sleep was evasive and his thoughts turned to Agrestis, who was working on a column about water voles.

> Although of the order *Rodentia* this charming
> little fellow (*Arvicola terrestris*) is often
> wrongly called a water rat. That much-loved
> character Ratty in Kenneth Grahame's *The Wind
> in the Willows* is actually a water vole. A short-
> lived creature in the wild, it has a mere handful
> of months to fulfil its time on earth, although
> it has proven to be much longer-lived when in
> captivity. There are around eight million water
> rats, living – like Grahame's Ratty – in burrows
> in the river banks, as well as ditches and streams
> and other waterways . . .

Not long before he left Fanning Court for Poplar Hill Care Home, when he was already well over ninety ('living in captivity' clearly having prolonged his life), Teddy read an article in the *Telegraph* (by then he was employing the aid of a magnifying glass to see the print). The article stated that there were barely a quarter of a million water voles left in Britain. He felt angry on their behalf and introduced the subject, rather vigorously, at the weekly coffee morning, somewhat to the disconcertion of the residents. 'Farmed mink,' he explained, 'escaped into the wild and usurped the voles. *Ate* them.'

One or two of the older female residents in the com-munal lounge had hung on grimly to their mink coats, mothballed in the flimsy melamine wardrobes of Fanning Court, and were not inclined to sympathy towards the innocent water vole. 'And, of course,' Teddy pursued, 'we've destroyed their habitat, something humans are very good at.' And so on. If they had been paying attention, and many were resolutely not, there would have been nothing that the Fanning Court residents would not have learned about the water vole (or indeed the tetchy subject of global warming) by the end of this lecture.

Teddy's crusade for a small neglected mammal did not go down well over the Nescafé and the chocolate bourbons. (Nor his feelings about the humble hedgehog and the brown hare, 'and when did you last hear a cuckoo?') 'Tree-hugger,' one of the male residents – a retired solicitor – muttered.

'Really, Dad,' Viola said, 'you can't *harangue* people.' Apparently, the Fat Controller, Ann Schofield, had asked Viola to 'have a word' with Teddy about his 'belligerent' behaviour. 'But we've lost nearly ninety per cent of the water-vole population in thirty years,' he protested to Viola. 'That's enough to make anyone feel belligerent. Although not a patch on how annoyed the water voles must feel, I imagine.' ('You don't know what you've got till it's gone,' Bertie said. 'As the song goes.' Teddy didn't know what song but he understood the sentiment.) 'Don't be silly,' Viola said. 'And I think you're a bit old to be embracing *causes*.' Wildlife took its chances in his daughter's harsh Darwinian universe. 'All this obsession with ecology isn't doing you any good,' Viola said. 'You're too old to be getting so worked up.'

Ecology, Teddy thought? 'Nature,' he said. 'We used to call it Nature.'

At the time of this 'flying visit' to Fanning Court, Viola was already campaigning for Teddy to move to a nursing home – she had brought a handful of leaflets with her. He had taken a fall a couple of days ago, not a bad one, his legs had given way and he had gone down like a collapsed concertina. 'Stuck on my bloody arse,' he said gruffly to Ann Schofield when she came in (yes, he had been near one of the red cords, and yes, he had pulled it). 'Language, please!' she reprimanded, as if he were a delinquent child, when only yesterday he had overheard her when she thought she was alone in the laundry room addressing a truculent door on a washing machine with the words, 'Why don't you behave, you little fucking shit?' An invocation made all the more scrappy somehow by her Birmingham accent.

He had managed – with minimal help from the Fat Controller ('against Health and Safety regulations, I have to call the paramedics') – to get on to his knees and from there on to the sofa and was perfectly fine apart from a couple of bruises, but this was 'proof positive' to Viola that he couldn't manage 'independent living'. She had harried him out of his house and into Fanning Court. Now she was trying to shuck him out of here and into a place called Poplar Hill. He imagined she wouldn't be satisfied until she'd badgered him into his coffin.

She fanned out the nursing-home leaflets, the one for Poplar Hill placed significantly on top of the pile, and said, 'At least take a look.' He gave them a cursory glance – photographs of happy, smiling people with full heads of grey hair and, as he pointed out to her, not a hint of shit and piss and dementia.

'Your language is terrible these days,' Viola said primly. 'What's happening to you?'

'I'll be dead soon,' he said. 'It's making me bolshie.'

'Don't be silly.' She was dressed very smartly, he noticed. 'I'm on my way somewhere.'

'Somewhere?' She had always hated *explaining*, it was part of her closed-off character. He had passed her in the street once, when she was a teenager. She was with friends from school and she had looked right through him when she passed. A son called Hugh would never have done such a thing.

'Somewhere?' he repeated, trying to needle her into elaboration.

'They're making a movie out of one of my novels. I've got a meeting with the execs.' The offhand but deliberate way she said the words 'movie' and 'execs' made them sound like she was indifferent when she clearly wasn't. There had been a film of her second novel, *The Children of Adam*. It had been an inferior sort of film – British, Viola had given him a DVD. Not that the book was much cop to begin with. Not that he would ever have said that to her. He had found it 'very good', he told her.

'Just "very good"?' she frowned.

Good lord, he thought, wasn't that enough? He would have been more than pleased with a 'very good' if he had ever finished his attempt at a novel. What had it been called? Something about sleeping and quiet breathing, it was a quote from Keats, that much he remembered, but which poem? He could sense the clouds gathering in his brain. Perhaps Viola was right, perhaps it was time to give up, check into God's waiting room.

Her first novel, *Sparrows at Dawn* (what a terrible title!), had been about a 'clever' (or annoyingly arrogant) young girl being brought up by her father. It was clearly meant to be autobiographical, a message of some sort to him from Viola. The girl was relentlessly badly done by and the father was a doltish martinet. Not what Sylvie would have called Art.

'Which one?' he asked, gathering his thoughts, pushing the clouds out of the way. 'Which novel are they making into a film?'

'*The End of Twilight*.' And then, impatiently when she caught him looking blankly at her, 'It's the one about the mother who has to give up her baby.' ('Wishful thinking on her part,' Bertie said.) She made a show of looking at the heavy gold watch on her wrist. ('Rolex. It's an investment really.') He was unsure whether this ostentatious gesture was meant to remind him of her busy life or her success. Both, he supposed. She was a more streamlined version of herself these days, dieted and coiffed, her hair ten different shades of blonde that Teddy had never seen before. No more henna, no more droopy clothing. All the velvets and sequins she'd held on to into middle age had gone and now whenever he saw her she was dressed in tailored suits and neutral colours. '*The Children of Adam* changed my life,' he read in a copy of *Woman's Weekly* left in the communal lounge that he had been idly leafing through, looking for recipes promised on the cover for 'Cheap and Easy Suppers'. 'Prize-winning author Viola Romaine talks about her bestselling early novel. "It's never too late to pursue your dream," she tells us in this exclusive interview.' And so on.

'I have to go,' she said, standing up abruptly, swinging her handbag on its heavy gilt chain. 'You have to start considering a nursing home, Dad. "Care home" – that's what they're called these days. Money's not an issue. I'll help out, of course. This one here—' she tapped the Poplar Hill brochure with a pink-varnished fingernail, 'is supposed to be excellent. Think about it. Think where you would like to go.'

Fox Corner, he thought. That's where I'd like to go.

Teddy didn't fight Nancy's sudden desire to move and when the job came up on the *Yorkshire Evening Press* he applied and a few weeks later they moved to York. (It was swift, like an incision.) Nancy easily found part-time work in the maths department at the Mount, a Quaker school, and returned to the relief of educating clever, well-behaved girls. Viola took up a place in the junior school. Nancy liked the Society of Friends, she said, it was the nearest Christianity could get to agnosticism.

Teddy knew York from the war. Then, it had been a mysterious maze of dark, narrow streets and snickets. It had been a place to go drinking and dancing, carousing in Bettys Bar or shuffling girls around the De Grey rooms, a place of fumbled kisses with willing girls in the tenebrous blackout. In the light of peace York was a less veiled city, its history on show everywhere. He liked it more in the daylight yet it remained a place of secrets, as if whenever one layer had been unearthed another one was waiting to be discovered. One's own life seemed puny against the background of so much history. It was a strange comfort to think of how many had gone before, how many had been forgotten. It was the natural order of things.

The house they bought – a solid semi in the suburbs – wasn't the kind that Teddy had ever imagined living in.

Unlike Mouse Cottage and Ayswick, it had no name, only a number, which suited its bland anonymity. No 'character' at all. The new Nancy, the one who didn't go about truffling primroses, embraced it – 'sensible and practical', she called it. They installed central heating, fitted carpets and modernized both kitchen and bathroom. It had no aesthetic virtues whatsoever in Teddy's eyes. Sylvie would have been appalled, but she had already been dead for two years by then, felled by a stroke while she was pruning her roses. They always used the possessive pronoun – the roses belonged to no one but their mother. Now they didn't even exist – 'dug up', according to Pamela, by the new owners of Fox Corner. 'The trick, I suppose,' Ursula said, 'is not to mind.' But he did. And so did she.

For months after they moved to York, Teddy would wake in the morning and feel a pang of sorrow as he listened to a subdued suburban dawn chorus competing with the low rumble of traffic from somewhere – the A64, he guessed. He missed having a wild green world on his doorstep – no rabbits or pheasants or badgers in York, only peacocks in the Museum Gardens. He didn't see another fox until the mangy urban species started raiding the bins around the back of Fanning Court. Teddy sneaked leftovers out to them, covert charity that left Ann Schofield reeling with horror. They were vermin, she said. ('She's the vermin,' Bertie said. Sometimes Bertie reminded him of Sylvie – the best of her, at any rate.)

The new house had a generous back garden and he bought a Reader's Digest book on gardening. A garden, as far as Teddy could see, was nature tamed and constrained by artifice. His wings had been clipped, like Tweetie, the blue budgerigar that Viola had insisted on for her birthday. 'A robin redbreast in a cage,' Teddy murmured when Nancy returned home from the pet shop with the bird. 'I know, I know,' she said, 'puts all heaven in a rage. But budgerigars are *bred* for captivity. It's a shame, but they don't know anything else.'

'That must be a great consolation to them,' Teddy said.

Their other little POW, the hapless Goldie, did not survive the house move. In Blake's litany of wrongdoing there was nothing about a goldfish in a bowl, but he would surely not have approved. Viola was upset at the sight of the pale, floating corpse and Teddy rooted out his old Goldfish Club badge and showed it to her. 'Imagine him with wings,' he advised, 'rising up to heaven.'

Tweetie proved to be a misnamed bird, never uttering a single chirp in his whole short life, most of which he spent either pecking listlessly at his cuttlefish bone or paddling from one foot to another on his wooden perch. Better perhaps, Teddy thought, in a fleeting moment of identification with the morose creature, to be Icarus and embrace the fall.

'Away? Again?' he said, making an effort to sound casual.

'Yes, again,' she said lightly. 'That's all right with you, isn't it?'

'Yes, of course,' Teddy said. 'It's just . . .' He hesitated, not sure how to give voice to his misgivings.

This would be the third time Nancy had been away in as many months, each time to visit one of her sisters. Firstly, she had gone down to Dorset to help Gertie move house, and this was quickly followed by a trip to the Lakes with Millie. ('Wordsworth's cottage and so on.') Millie was leading a rather rackety life in Brighton and was 'between husbands' at the moment. 'She probably needs a sympathetic ear,' Nancy said.

Nancy claimed to be 'a homebody', not even keen on decamping for their annual seaside holiday. Every summer, the three of them, 'the family triumvirate' as Nancy called it – according Viola equal power with her parents, Teddy noted, although really they were not so much a triumvirate as a tiny tyrant and her two dedicated attendants – took a dutiful holiday on the east coast – Bridlington, Scarborough, Filey. This was for Viola's benefit rather than their own. 'Bucket and spade,' Nancy said, that was all a small child needed, and persisted heroically in this belief as the triumvirate sheltered, shivering, in the lee of hired windbreaks or took refuge in damp and steamy tea-shops after eating the liver-sausage sandwiches that their boarding-house landlady packed up for them every morning.

It was less of a holiday and more of an endurance test. 'Can we go home yet?' was Viola's constant refrain, echoed silently by Teddy. They stayed in boarding houses from which their dog was exiled and so it was at these times that Viola's stark status as an only child was most apparent. She wasn't very good at playing by herself and even less so with others.

A wind-whipped Yorkshire coast wasn't Teddy's idea of a holiday. The North Sea was the graveyard of many of the incorporeal dead at Runnymede, the sea-bed littered with the rich and strange. Two of the worst nights of his war had been spent helplessly floating on its uncharitable waves. (*Well, good luck to you then.*) When Viola was a bit older, Nancy said, they would go further afield – Wales, Cornwall. 'Europe,' Teddy said. The solid blocks of colour. The hot slices of sunshine.

Yet now Nancy was proposing a visit to Bea in London. ('Just a couple of nights, take in a show, maybe an exhibition.') It was late, nearly bedtime, and she was still marking homework. Teddy could see columns of fractions that were meaningless to him. 'Show me your workings,' Nancy wrote in neat red pen and then paused and looked up at him. She always wore such a frank, guileless expression, it invited confession, promised absolution. He imagined her pupils adored her.

'Well, anyway,' Nancy said, 'I thought I would leave for London on Wednesday evening and be back on Friday. Viola will be at school while you're at work and after school she can go home with her friend – Sheila – and wait for you to pick her up.' (How detailed this scheme was, Teddy thought. Wouldn't it be easier for everyone if she simply visited Bea at the weekend?) 'You don't mind holding the fort, do you? And Viola will love spending some time alone with you.'

'Will she?' Teddy said, somewhat ruefully. Viola, nearly nine now, still doted on her mother, while Teddy seemed to be merely a parental necessity.

'I won't go if you don't want me to,' Nancy said. What a polite conversation this was, Teddy thought. What if he said, 'No, don't go,' what would she say then? Instead he said, 'Don't be silly, why wouldn't I want you to? Of course you should go, no earthly reason why not. And I can reach you at Bea's if there are any problems.'

'I'm sure you won't need to,' Nancy said and added casually, 'and we'll be out a lot, I expect.'

When Nancy had been in the Lakes there had been no telephone in the cottage that Millie had rented. When she had helped Gertie move house the new telephone had not yet been connected. 'If there's a dreadful emergency,' Nancy said breezily, 'or some terrible accident occurs' (it was tempting fate to refer to such things so glibly, Teddy thought), 'you can put out one of those announcements you hear on the radio. You know – *the police are trying to contact – whoever – believed to be in the Westmorland area. Please get in touch*, and so on.' Forty years later, when he was living in Fanning Court, Viola gave him a mobile phone and said, 'There, now you'll never be out of touch. If you have another accident' (she meant the broken hip, she never let him forget this mishap, as if it had exposed a great flaw in his character) 'or get lost or something.'

'Lost?'

He never learned how to use the phone. The buttons were too small, the instructions too complicated. 'Old dog, new tricks,' he said to Bertie. 'And anyway why would I want to be "in touch" all the time?'

'There's nowhere for anyone to hide these days,' she said.

'In the imagination,' he offered.

'Even there,' Bertie said grimly, 'you're not safe.'

'Good,' Nancy said. 'I'll go on Wednesday then. That's settled.' She started stacking the homework jotters tidily on top of each other. 'All finished. Why don't you heat up the milk for some cocoa?' She gave him a quizzical smile and said, 'Is everything all right? We don't have to bother with cocoa, if you don't want.'

'No,' he said, 'it's fine. I'll do it.' Show me your workings, Nancy, he thought.

When Nancy had been unreachable in Dorset, helping Gertie to move house, Teddy had been surprised when the phone rang and it was Gertie herself (although her phone was supposedly not yet connected). A woman not given to preamble, she said, 'You know that big oak sideboard in my dining room, the Arts and Crafts one that used to be in the dining room at Jackdaws?'

'The one with copper hinges and the De Morgan tiles?' Teddy said. Clearly, he did know it.

'That's the one. There's no room for it in this new house – no room for hardly anything,' she added cheerfully and Teddy remembered how much he liked Gertie and why. 'Anyway,' she carried on, 'I know you've always admired it and so I thought you might like to have it. I can stick it on a van, one of those part-load ones, it shouldn't cost too much. Otherwise I'm afraid it might have to go into a sale.'

'That's very kind of you. I'd love it, but,' he added doubtfully, 'I'm not sure that we have room.' He thought wistfully of Ayswick and how handsome the sideboard would have looked in the big farmhouse kitchen, but here, within the blandly ordinary walls of the York semi, it would surely look quite out of place. He was surprised by a sudden pang of desire – it was a piece of furniture that he remembered well from the Shawcrosses' house. From the past. 'What does Nancy say about it?'

'I've no idea,' Gertie said. 'Why don't you ask her yourself?'

'Can you put her on?'

'Put her on?' Gertie said. 'What do you mean?'

'Put her on the phone.'

'Can *I* put her on the phone?' Gertie sounded baffled.

'She's there with you,' Teddy said, wondering how they had achieved such a cross-purpose with each other.

'No, she's not,' Gertie said.

'She's not in Lyme Regis? With you? Helping you move?'

There was an awkward silence before Gertie said cautiously, 'No, not here.' Teddy sensed that she was anxious that she might have betrayed Nancy in some way and his first instinct (curiously) was to save Gertie from the flap she was getting into, so he said genially, 'Oh, don't worry, I've got mixed up. I'll chase her down and get back to you. The sideboard is a lovely offer, by the way. Thank you, Gertie.' He got off the phone quickly, needing to review this odd information. *I'm going down to Lyme to give Gertie a hand with her house move.* It was hardly a statement that was open to misinterpretation.

If there had been something that Nancy had not wanted him to know, something that had necessitated her pretending to be in Dorset with Gertie, then surely she must have a reason? He knew she could lie with grace when necessary but Nancy was not *furtive*, in fact quite the opposite. Sometimes he felt that the intimacy of their marriage had been based on her breaching the Official Secrets Act. When she returned from 'Dorset' he asked her nothing, other than 'How was the move?' to which she replied, 'Good, all went well.'

'Gertie's new house is nice, is it?'

'Mm. Very nice,' she said rather vaguely and he left it at that, not wishing to seem as if he were interrogating her. Instead he would wait and see if something developed from this omission. Adultery was not high on his list of suspects, he found it almost impossible to consider Nancy as the sort of wife who would hoodwink a husband. He had always thought of her – still thought of her – as irreproachable, scrupulous in both thinking and doing the right thing. Nancy was not the sort to feign innocence. But then nor was she the sort to misdirect. If she had lied to him it must be a lie based on utilitarian principles. Perhaps there was a surprise hidden at the heart of this sleight of hand – a birthday treat or a family reunion? With Sylvie dead and Fox Corner sold it seemed there was nothing left to shepherd the whole Todd family together any more. Teddy and his more stalwart siblings – Ursula and Pamela – never seemed to be together in the same place at the same time, except at funerals. No weddings – there didn't seem to be weddings any more, why was that? 'It's because we're between generations,' Nancy said. 'It'll be Viola's turn soon enough.'

Viola was the solitary arrow they had shot blindly into the future, not knowing where she would land. They should have aimed better, Teddy thought as he watched her (having sidestepped marriage to Dominic, the father of her children) finally tying the knot in Leeds Town Hall to Wilf Romaine – a botched-up job of a marriage if ever there was one. 'He enjoys a drink, doesn't he?' Teddy said cautiously the first time Viola introduced him to 'my new man'. 'If that's a criticism,' Viola said, '– and when have you ever done anything but find fault with me? – you can go and shove it where the sun doesn't shine.' Oh, Viola.

When Nancy left next, to meet up with Millie in the Lake District, Teddy vowed to himself not to check up on her like some tawdry private detective. No birthday treat or family reunion had revealed itself since her return from Dorset but that was not proof of anything underhand. He resisted picking up the phone and calling Millie's flat to see if Millie was there, but his unease must have infected Viola, who spent the whole fretful time that Nancy was absent nagging, 'When is Mummy coming back?' It gave him a legitimate reason, he argued rather speciously with himself, for chasing up his discontented wife.

'Oh, hello there, Teddy,' Millie drawled carelessly. 'Haven't spoken to you in ages.'

'You're not in the Lakes with Nancy then?' he said baldly, finding himself suddenly angry. Justifiably, surely? There were a couple of beats of silence before Millie said, 'Just got back. In fact I've just seen her on the train home to you.' She was an actress, never so good on the stage as she was now, he thought. It made no sense that Nancy would have gone all the way down to Brighton before returning home, but he had no way of proving that this was what she had done. Or not done. Teddy had never experienced jealousy before, he realized, as the tawdry private detective reared his ugly head and said, 'And so how *were* the Lakes, Millie? What did you do exactly?'

'Oh, you know,' she said easily. 'Wordsworth's cottage and so on.'

* * *

Did Millie not relate this conversation to Nancy? She certainly seemed blithely unaware that he had doubted her when she declared her intention to visit Bea. (Were *all* of her sisters conspirators in deception? Even good-hearted Gertie and solid, matronly Winnie?)

Teddy felt not forbearance but paralysis. He couldn't ask Nancy what was going on (the obvious thing to do) because the answer would either be a lie or a truth he didn't want to hear. So he 'plodded' along (the word seemed to haunt him), although now he found everything sullied by suspicion. He brooded forensically on every nuance in Nancy's behaviour. There was, for example, something decidedly clandestine about discovering her in the hallway one evening, leaning against the Anaglypta-papered wall, murmuring into the phone and then cutting the conversation short when she caught sight of him. 'Who was that?' he asked, as if it was a matter of indifferent interest to him. 'Just Bea, just idle gossip,' she said. Or the way that she was eager to be the first to pick up the post in the morning before she cycled off to school with Viola. Was she expecting something? No, not at all.

He had come across her on more than one occasion wearing a preoccupied frown on her face or staring into the middle distance when she was stirring a sauce or making a lesson plan. 'Sorry, miles away,' or 'Bit of a headache,' she would say – she had become a victim of migraines in the past few months. Sometimes, too, he caught a fleeting expression of pain on her face when she looked at Viola. Torn between feelings for lover and child, he supposed. Betraying one's husband was bad enough, but to betray one's child was a different matter.

He didn't believe that she was intending to visit either London or Bea. In his imagination – by now quite lurid – his scarlet wife was conducting her debauched trysts somewhere nearby, holed up perhaps in a sordid hotel on Micklegate. (A wartime memory of his. A local girl. A regretfully dissipated encounter.)

After she had left to catch the train to King's Cross he phoned Ursula and unburdened himself, but instead of sympathy she was sharp and said, 'Don't be silly, Teddy, Nancy would never be unfaithful.'

Et tu, Brute? he thought, for once disappointed in his sister.

As planned, on Friday evening his errant wife was brought promptly back from the station by a taxi. Teddy caught sight of it pulling up and watched as Nancy paid and the taxi driver took her small case out of the boot. She looked weary as she walked up the gravel path to the house. Worn out by passion probably or distraught at having to leave her lover.

He opened the door while she was still fumbling for her key. 'Oh, thanks,' she said, walking past him into the hall without looking at him. She reeked of tobacco and of alcohol too. 'You've been smoking?' he said. 'No, of course not' – her lover must be a smoker, leaving his scent all over her. His *spoor*. 'And drinking,' he said, feeling revulsion.

'Everyone was smoking in my carriage,' she said dispassionately, 'and yes, I had a whisky on the train. Does it matter? I'm sorry, but I'm dog-tired.'

'It must be all those museums and exhibitions,' he said sarcastically.

'What?' She put her case down and turned to stare at him, her expression unreadable.

'I know what's going on,' he said.

'Do you?'

'You're having an affair. You're using all these little jaunts as cover.'

'Jaunts?'

'You must think I really am slow to catch on. Poor old *plodding* Teddy.'

'Plodding?'

'I know what you've been up to,' he repeated, growing irritable that she wasn't responding to his needling. If she confessed, declared that her affair was over, he would forgive her, he decided magnanimously. But if she continued to lie he feared he might do or say something that there would be no going back from. ('I was never "in love" with you, you know.')

It didn't help when she simply turned away from him and walked off into the kitchen, where she drew a glass of water from the tap. She drank it down slowly and then placed the empty glass carefully on the draining board.

'I *know*,' he said furiously, yet still trying to keep his voice low as Viola was asleep upstairs.

Nancy looked at him sadly and said, 'No, Teddy. You don't know. You don't know anything.'

1942–43
Teddy's War

Experience

'*Twenty minutes to the run in to the target, skipper.*'

'*OK, navigator.*'

They had ploughed their way through the flak put up by the coastal defences and dog-legged faithfully along the flight plan over occupied territory before making it through the thick belt of searchlights that girdled the Ruhr. There had been very little cloud on the run in and they had occasionally been able to make out lights below – a factory at work or a blackout not being strictly observed. More than once, torches or lamps had flashed up at them and, over Holland, Norman Best, their quiet flight engineer, had read out loud the Morse code from a well-wisher below, *dit-dit-dit-dah*. V for victory. It was a message of both faith and comfort that they saw frequently.

'Thanks, pal, whoever you are,' Teddy heard the rear-gunner say. The rear-gunner was a scrawny, red-headed

Scot, eighteen years old and the talkative sort, but he made an effort to keep his volubility for when they were on the ground. Teddy's crew knew that he favoured silence on the intercom unless there was something that needed saying. It was too easy to start chattering, especially on the way back when everyone was more relaxed, but even a moment's distraction, especially for the gunners, and that was it. End of the story.

Teddy felt the same as his rear-gunner did about the anonymous Dutchman – or woman – down there. It was good to know that they were appreciated up here. They were so cut off from the ground – even when they were destroying it with their bombs (especially when they were destroying it with their bombs, perhaps) – that you could sometimes forget that there were entire nations for whom you were the last hope.

'I can see the target markers going down, skipper, twenty miles ahead cherry-red.'

'OK, bomb-aimer.'

It was the final op of their tour and they were edgy with foreboding. They had beaten the odds to get to tonight and were all wondering if fate could be so cruel as to bring them this far and then give them the chop. (It could. They knew.) 'Just one more, Jesus, just one more,' he had heard his godless Australian bomb-aimer murmuring as they waited on the runway for the green Aldis light.

It had been a terrific slog to reach the requisite thirty. Some of their sorties only counted as a third of an op. 'Gardening' runs – mine-laying in the Dutch shipping channels or off the Frisian coast – or attacking targets in

France only chalked up a third of an op. Occupied France was considered a 'friendly' country, but friendly or not it was still full of Germans trying to shoot them down. It was true you were more likely to be killed on a raid over Germany ('Four times more likely,' according to Ursula's girl at the Air Ministry), but you were still risking your life. It was rather iniquitous, Teddy thought. Or, in the more straightforward language of his bomb-aimer, 'Bloody unfair.' Keith was the first person that Teddy crewed up with at the OTU.

Crewing up was an unexpected affair that had taken them largely by surprise. All the components – pilots, navigators, wireless operators, bomb-aimers and gunners – were simply emptied in a jumble into a hangar and told by the station commander, 'Right, chaps, sort yourselves out best as you can,' as if some mysterious law of attraction would form a better bomber crew than any military procedure. And, strangely, that seemed to be true, as far as Teddy could see anyway.

They had all milled about aimlessly for a while like a flock of geese in a farmyard at feeding time, somewhat abashed by what was being asked of them. 'It's like a bloody dance hall, waiting to catch some girl's eye,' Keith said, approaching Teddy and introducing himself, 'Keith Marshall, I'm a bomb-aimer,' his dark-blue uniform marking him out as Australian.

Teddy's first port of call had been a navigator but he liked the look of Keith and if the war was teaching Teddy anything it was that you could often tell a man's character from the way he looked, an expression in the eyes, a glance here and there, but mostly something indefinable, and he wondered if it had been this elusive quality that had made him warm immediately to Keith. And the fact, of course, that he had overheard an instructor saying that he was a 'good bloke, who knows his stuff'. Turned out this was true. Keith may have washed out as a pilot ('Couldn't land the bloody thing') but had graduated top of his class on his bombing course.

Australians had a reputation for being rambunctious but Keith seemed steady, his blue eyes thoughtful. He was twenty, brought up on a sheep station, and had spent a good deal of his life, Teddy supposed, gazing at a distant horizon under a harsh sun, unlike the soft green fields of Teddy's own childhood. It must form your perception of life, he supposed.

He was looking forward to seeing something of the world, Keith said, 'even if it's only the Third Reich on fire'.

They shook hands, like gentlemen, and Keith said, 'Well, skipper, best get a move on, we don't want to be left with just the wallflowers.' This was the first time, Teddy thought, that a member of his crew (his crew!) had called him 'skipper'. He felt as though he had finally stepped into his own shoes.

They scanned the hangar together and Keith said, 'See that bloke over there, by the wall, laughing at something? He's a wireless operator. I had a drink with him last night and he seemed like a straight sort.'

'OK,' Teddy said. It seemed as good a recommendation as any.

The spark was a nineteen-year-old from Burnley called George Carr. Teddy had already witnessed George Carr offering to mend someone's bicycle, enthusiastically taking it to pieces and putting it back together again before presenting it to its owner, saying, 'There, better than when it was new, I'll bet.' He liked fiddling with things, he said, which seemed a useful trait in a wireless operator.

George in turn pointed out an air-gunner for them, again an acquaintance based on a night drinking in the mess. He was called Vic Bennett and he was from Canvey Island and had a toothy grin (he had the worst teeth of anyone Teddy had ever seen), and after he was introduced he hailed 'a mate' who he'd been on his gunnery course with. 'Sharp as a tack,' he said. 'Reflexes of a rat. Looks a bit like one too. A ginger rat.' This was their talkative young Scot, 'Kenneth Nielson, but everyone calls me Kenny.'

Still no navigator, Teddy thought, bemused at how quickly he'd lost any control of this process. It was a little like a game of Consequences, or perhaps Blind Man's Bluff.

How do you tell a good navigator, he wondered, looking round the room. Someone unflappable, but then that was a quality they all needed, wasn't it? Nose to the table, focused on nothing but the job. From somewhere behind him he heard the slow, imperturbable notes of a Canadian accent. He turned around and, identifying the owner of the voice, caught sight of his navigator's brevet and said, 'Ted Todd. I'm a pilot in the market for a good navigator.'

'I'm good,' the Canadian said with a shrug. 'Good enough anyway.' He was called Donald McLintock. Mac, naturally. Teddy liked Canadians, in his time over there he had found them to be reliable and not given to neuroses or over-active imaginations, neither of which were good qualifications for a navigator. And just hearing the accent had brought back fond memories of the big open skies where he had learned to fly on Tiger Moths and Fleet Finches, fluttering above the great patchwork of Ontario. They were fragile little things compared to the Ansons and Harvards he had graduated on to, to say nothing of the hulking Wellingtons that they were going to be doing their training on at the OTU. 'Bus drivers' was how fighter pilots referred derisively to bomber pilots, but it had seemed to Teddy that it was going to be the buses that won the war.

'Welcome on board, navigator,' Teddy said. More gentlemanly handshaking all round. They were a mixed bag, all right, Teddy thought. He rather liked that. 'We just need a Kiwi for a flight engineer,' Keith said, echoing his thoughts, 'and it'll be like the bloody League of Nations.' They didn't get a Kiwi, they got Norman Best, from Derby, a rather shy, earnest ex-grammar-school boy with a degree in languages and a firm Christian faith, but not until they reached their Heavy Conversion Unit, so that was that for now. They were a crew. Just like that. From now on they drank together, they ate together, they flew together and their lives were in each other's pockets.

That first night after crewing up they went on the obligatory crew binge. The egalitarian spirit meant that everyone must take their turn to buy a round, so seven pints later they staggered back to their sleeping quarters as drunk as lords and declaring their undying friendship.

Teddy had never been so inebriated in his life, and he realized as he lay on top of his bunk that night, the room revolving around him, that he had never been as elated either. Or at least not for a long time, not since he was a boy perhaps. He was about to have an adventure.

They were all NCOs apart from Teddy. He had been given a commission, for no other reason, as far as he could tell, than that he had been to the right school and the right university and that, when asked, he had said that, yes, he liked cricket, which he didn't that much actually but he could see to say so would be the wrong answer. And that was why he was here now, months later, en route to Duisburg, a leader of men, the master of his fate, the captain of his soul and of a bloody big four-engined Halifax with an unnerving tendency to swing to the right on take-off and landing.

'Ten minutes to target, skipper.'

'OK, navigator. Ten minutes to target, bomb-aimer.'

'OK, skipper.'

In the air they addressed each other by their roles but on the ground they were defined by themselves – Ted, Norman, Keith, Mac, George, Vic and Kenny. Like play-mates in a storybook adventure, Teddy thought. Two of Augustus's 'pals' were called Norman and George, but Izzie's Augustus and his cohorts were still eleven years old, forever young, and occupied with their catapults, with catching minnows and raiding the larder for jars of jam, which for some reason they seemed to regard as the holy grail of foodstuffs. Izzie's creation and his band of merry boys were currently 'doing their bit' in *Augustus and the War* – scavenging for paper by taking the newspaper from people's letter-boxes and collecting scrap metal for salvage by stealing pots and pans from the Swifts' out-raged neighbours. ('"The frying-pan isn't scrap," an exasperated Mrs Swift said. "But it's for the war," Augustus protested. "You're always sayin' we have to give up things. I'm givin' up people's pans."') Izzie's Augustus, Teddy thought rather resentfully, didn't have to deal with flak or worry about a Messerschmitt descending on him like a hungry bird of prey.

His own Augustus – his grown-up double, as he imagined him – was almost certainly dodging life in the services. He was probably a spiv, a war profiteer, selling spirits and fags and anything else he could get his mucky hands on. ('There you go, guv, that'll be ten bob. Remember, mum's the word.')

They were toiling through flak – continual shell flashes and oily grey puffs of smoke buffeting them – although the noise of the explosions was drowned out by the air-craft's own deafening Merlin engines.

'Keep a sharp lookout, everyone,' Teddy said.

In the distance he could see a shower of incendiaries coming down, being jettisoned probably by an aircraft trying to gain more height. All it did was provide helpful illumination for the German fighters flying above the bomber stream who were dropping marker flares – pretty, like chandeliers – that seemed to hang in the air, pro-viding a well-lit corridor for the unfortunate bomber to fly along. Seconds later the bomber erupted into a blood-red fireball, belching black smoke.

'Log that, navigator,' Teddy said.

'OK, skipper.'

They had taken off late. As an experienced crew they would normally have been near the front of the bomber stream, but there had been trouble with the port inner engine and they became the last rather than the first aircraft to take off from their station and were right at the tail of the skein when they reached the rendezvous point over Flamborough Head. 'Well, someone has to bring up the rear,' Teddy said, in a rather futile attempt to encourage his downhearted crew. They all knew that being a straggler made them an easier target for the fighters to pick off – a distinct little blip on the German radar rather than part of a protective flock.

A crowded bomber stream presented its own terrors, of course. Earlier in their tour they had been part of Harris's first thousand-bomber raid on Cologne. In a great Armada like that you found yourself wallowing in someone else's slipstream, wondering all the time where everyone else was. It had seemed to Teddy that the greatest danger came not from the German fighters or flak but from their own side. They had been stacked in layers, the slow Stirlings at the bottom, the high-flying Lancs at the top, the Halifaxes providing the filling in the sandwich. The exact speed, height and position for each aircraft was predetermined, but that didn't mean that everyone was where they were supposed to be.

At one point on the route another Halifax had passed right over the top of them with only twenty or so feet clearance, a great dark shape like a whale, one with red-hot exhausts. And later, on the track to the target, Vic Bennett, in the mid-upper turret, had started yelling blue murder because there was a Lancaster above them that had just opened its bomb doors and Teddy had to jink away from it, worrying that they in turn would slam into another aircraft.

They had witnessed a collision too close for their own comfort when a Halifax on their port beam crossed the bomber stream and a Lancaster flew smack into it. Their own aircraft – *J-Jig*, before they lost her – was rocked by the massive explosion. Bright white sheets of flame shot up from the petrol tanks in the wings of the Lanc and Teddy shouted at his gunners not to look in case they lost their night vision.

There had been no trouble finding Cologne. By the time they reached the target it was ablaze, filthy red flames and smoke everywhere that had already hidden the marker flares, so they headed for the centre of the largest fire and dropped their bombs and banked away. Looking back, despite the colossal size of the enterprise, it seemed like an uneventful raid, and to tell the truth, Teddy could barely remember the details of it now. It felt as if he had lived many lifetimes. Or perhaps just the one endless night that, according to Blake, some were born to.

And time itself had a different quality. Before it had been like a vast map – seemingly endless – that had been unrolled before him and on which he could choose in which direction to go. Now the map only unrolled beneath his feet a step ahead at a time and might at any moment disappear. 'I felt the same at the height of the attacks on London,' Ursula said, attempting to decode this tortuous metaphor when he saw her on his first leave – they had six days off every six weeks, and he had chosen to spend them in London rather than Fox Corner. He didn't even tell Sylvie he had leave.

'Before the war,' Ursula said, 'every day was much the same, wasn't it? Home, the office, home again. Routine dulls the senses so. And then suddenly it feels as if one's living on the forward edge of one's life, as if one never knows if one is about to fall or fly.' Neither extreme seemed to involve a soft landing, Teddy noticed.

'I suppose so,' he agreed, realizing he had no real idea what he was talking about and didn't much care. He lived his life in the face of death. It was a simple enough reduction without hedging it around with figurative language.

'Eight minutes to target, skipper.'
  'OK, navigator.'
  'Stay alert, gunners.'
  'Yes, skipper.'
  'OK, skip.'
The gunners didn't need reminding, it was just a way of keeping everyone in touch. He knew they were swinging their guns around the sky, ever vigilant. They had hardly fired their guns in the whole of the tour. As soon as you started shooting you marked yourself as a target. A fighter could easily miss you in the dark, but if you were laying a thread of red tracer fire right to your door he would soon find you. And his big cannons would do a lot more damage than their own puny Browning machine guns could. Gunners were – essentially – your look-outs. There

were gunners who went through a whole tour without ever firing off a round.

Teddy's sister Pamela was married to a doctor who told him that he had read some data about experiments in oxygen chambers and that oxygen would help the gunners' eyesight, which was also the first thing that would go if they started to suffer from oxygen deprivation. After that Teddy had started keeping his gunners on oxygen from take-off to landing.

They were in the thick of a heavily defended area. A grey curtain of smoke from the flak barrage lay dead ahead of them, a curtain of explosive that they had to get through.

Compared to those big thousand-bomber raids, tonight was a relatively modest one, some two hundred or so aircraft – twelve from their own squadron – all heading in their loose gaggle towards the Ruhr, the Happy Valley.

They had seen a Lancaster go down, hit in the wing by a fighter, seen it turn into a falling leaf of fire, and they had seen, too, a fellow Halifax being coned as it came through the Ruhr's defences. It was caught in the blue master beam and they watched without comment as the slave beams turned, like soulless automata, towards their prey, trapping it in blinding white light and pumping their shells remorselessly up at it. The aircraft dived desperately into a corkscrew, but the beams were locked relentlessly on it and the heavy flak must have found it because they saw it explode in a great ball of flame.

'Log that, navigator,' Teddy said in a dispassionate voice. 'Did anyone see any parachutes?'

A murmuring of 'no's on the intercom, a 'poor

bastards' from Keith, settled flat out on his front in the nose of the aircraft, ready for the run in. It was always a shocking thing to see an aircraft going down but there wasn't time to think about it. It wasn't you, that was the important thing.

If we go, Teddy prayed, let us go instantly, the fireball not the fall. There would be no soft landing, whichever way. He was fatalistic rather than morbid. The last thing his crew needed at the moment – at any moment – was a despondent captain. Especially tonight when they were so jittery. They looked exhausted too, Teddy thought, a weariness that went beyond mere tiredness. What they looked was old, Teddy realized. And yet Keith had only just celebrated his twenty-first birthday, with a raucous party held in the sergeants' mess. There was an innocence in all their celebrations, like naughty boys at a noisy children's party. The sooty footprints on the ceiling, the unseemly lyrics of the sing-songs around the piano after the WAAFs had decorously retired for the night (a bolder one or two sometimes remaining). Not so very different from Augustus and his little pals, after all.

Sylvie, rather inclined to indolent timekeeping, kept the clocks at Fox Corner running ten minutes ahead (a practice that tended to lead to confusion rather than punctuality). Teddy thought now how much better it would have been if someone had pushed their clock backward, if they had been led to think that this was their twenty-ninth sortie rather than their thirtieth, freeing them from their gloomy premonitions.

To make matters worse, they had a second dickey on board. He was a novice pilot being blooded on his first trip. It was customary to send a tyro up with an experienced crew for a 'look-see' before he took his own crew on operations, but for some reason a green second pilot was regarded as a jinx. There was no rhyme or reason to this belief as far as Teddy could see. His own first blood was drawn on a flight to bomb the docks at Wilhelmshaven with *C-Charlie*, a crew on their twelfth op, and they had barely acknowledged his existence, as if by ignoring him they could pretend he wasn't sitting there in the dickey seat. *C-Charlie* came back with hardly any damage – some holes from flak and one engine out – but even after they had landed the crew still avoided him as if he might taint them somehow. Unlike his own crew, who were overjoyed to have him back 'safe and sound' on the earth, and they all went on a mighty crew binge at a local pub, ground crew included, to celebrate this fact. The Black Swan, known by everyone as the Mucky Duck, had a very accommodating landlord who let the aircrews have running tabs knowing that many of them would never be paid. The dead reckoning.

On Teddy's second tour there was a sprog crew – *W-William* was their aircraft – who lost their pilot when he took his flight with another crew. They were immediately given a replacement, who duly took his dickey flight and also didn't come back. (Perhaps they were bad luck, after all.) The pilotless sprog crew were beside themselves at this point, like anxious dogs, and so when they were given a third (understandably nervous) pilot Teddy took the whole crew up on their first op together, the new pilot in the dickey seat of *W-William*, his own aircraft. It was a testing maximum-effort raid to Berlin and they more than held their nerve.

When they landed they were filled with jubilation. 'Well done, boys,' he said. They *were* boys, not one over twenty. They invited him to have a drink with them in the sergeants' mess – he was, after all, part of their crew, they said. He went but bowed out early, 'Discretion being the better part of valour,' he wrote to Ursula, as it was one of her favourite aphorisms.

'Not always,' she wrote back.

W-William was on the battle order next day, a relatively safe mine-laying trip to drop 'veg' off Langeoog in the east Frisians. Teddy felt more than usually sad when reading the familiar entry in the operations log the next day. *This aircraft took off at 16.20 hours and failed to return. It has therefore been reported as missing.* He found it difficult after the war to look at the North Sea without thinking of it as one enormous, watery graveyard, full of the rust and bones of aircraft and youthful bodies.

On their next sortie the crew of *C-Charlie,* who had so reluctantly taken Teddy as their second dickey, ran out of fuel looking for somewhere to land in fog and crashed on the moors near Helmsley. 'Their thirteenth,' Vic Bennett said, as if that explained it. He was the most superstitious of all of them. When they flew their own thirteenth op, to Stuttgart – on a Friday, no less – he asked the chaplain to put a special blessing on poor old *J-Jig,* which the chaplain, a jolly, obliging sort, did quite happily.

The first five ops and the last five ops were believed by crews to be the most dangerous, although as far as Teddy could see the laws of probability applied every time. Only one in six aircrew made it through their first tour. (Never before or since, he thought, would so many be so obsessed with statistics.) He hadn't needed Ursula's girl in the Air Ministry to tell him that the odds were stacked against them. At the beginning of this tour, if Teddy had been a gambling man, which he wasn't, he wouldn't have laid bets on them living to see their grandchildren. Or their children, for that matter, as they hadn't even reached that stage in their lives yet. None of them were married and according to Teddy's reckoning at least half of them had been virgins when he first met them. Were any of them now? He didn't know. Not Vic Bennett, he was engaged to a girl called Lillian (Lil) who he never stopped talking about, including everything they 'got up to'.

Vic was getting married to Lillian next week, they were all invited. Teddy didn't think Vic should have made plans. He didn't make plans himself any more. There was now and it was followed by another now. If you were lucky. ('What a fine Buddhist monk you would make,' Ursula said.)

'If you look at the percentage loss,' Ursula's girl from the Air Ministry said, sipping primly on a pink gin, 'then, mathematically speaking, death is inevitable.' There were other ways of looking at the figures, she added hastily when Ursula glared at her. Teddy met her when he was on leave the following May. The three of them went for a drink together and then on to dancing at the Hammersmith Palais. Teddy didn't enjoy himself, he had the uncomfortable feeling that every time the girl from the Air Ministry looked at him she was seeing a set of actuarial tables.

Did Nancy know the cold calculus of death in Bomber Command? Probably not. She was cocooned somewhere in the clinical safety of an intellectual post. She was trying to make arrangements to see him in London as soon as the tour finished. She had written, 'Perhaps I could come to your colleague's wedding? Can you wangle an invitation or are girlfriends considered surplus to requirements?!' The tone of this letter felt all wrong to him. The unfortunate use of the word 'colleague', for one. Vic Bennett wasn't a 'colleague'. He was *part* of Teddy, like an arm or a leg. He was a pal, a mate, a comrade. If civilization survived – and it was currently hanging in the balance – would it be as a society of equals? A new Jerusalem full of Levellers and Diggers? And it wasn't just the RAF, surely, where class barriers had broken down as everyone was forced to muck in together. Teddy rubbed shoulders with men – and women – he would never have come across in a world of public school, Oxbridge, banking. He might be their captain, he might be responsible for them, but he wasn't their superior.

He had burnt Nancy's letter in the stove in his hut. They were always short of fuel.

'Four minutes to target, skipper.'

'OK, navigator.'

'Four minutes to target, bomb-aimer.'

'OK, skipper.'

'That ruddy port inner's still not happy, skipper,' Norman Best said. The light on the fuel pressure gauge had been flicking on and off for the whole flight, seemingly living a life of its own. It was the same engine that had delayed their take-off and Norman had been monitoring it suspiciously for some time now. It was just as well they'd been late getting off, Vic Bennett said. He, of all people, had somehow or other managed to forget his good-luck charm and had persuaded the WAAF driver who had brought them out to dispersal to race him back to the crew room to retrieve this item while the ground crew worked on the misbehaving engine. They were the unsung heroes of the 'spanner brigade' – the riggers and fitters and mechanics. NCOs or lowly erks, they worked all day and night in every kind of weather. They waved them off when they left and greeted them when they returned. They might stay out all night in their huts on bleak dispersals waiting for 'their' aircraft to return safely. No good-luck charms for them, just civil handshakes all round on departure and 'See you in the morning then.'

Vic Bennett's own particular fetish was a pair of red satin knickers belonging to his fiancée, the aforesaid Lil. These 'unmentionables', as Vic called them, were carried, neatly folded, in the pocket of his battledress on every trip. 'If we make it to his wedding,' Keith said, 'I know what we'll all be thinking about when the blushing bride walks down the aisle.'

'It'll be me that's blushing,' Kenny Nielson said.

Luck was everything. 'No lady,' according to Keith, 'just a bloody tart.' Superstition was rampant on the station. Everyone in the squadron seemed to have their own voodoo – a lock of hair, a St Christopher, a playing card, the ubiquitous rabbit foot. There was a flight sergeant who always sang 'La Donna è Mobile' in the crew room when they were getting dressed in their flying clothes and another who had to put his left boot on before his right. If he forgot he had to take all his kit off and start again. He survived the war. The flight sergeant who sang 'La

Donna è Mobile' did not. Nor the other hundreds with their weird rites and sacraments. The dead were legion and the gods had their own secret agenda.

Keith did not have a mascot, claiming that his whole family was 'widdershins', their luck back-to-front, and he could probably have walked under a ladder with a dozen black cats crossing in front of him and he would be 'just fine'. His convict antecedents were Irish gypsies, deported to Australia for vagrancy. 'Not proper gypsies, probably,' he said. 'Rogues and tramps, I expect.'

Kenny Nielson was the youngest in a family of ten, 'the bairn', and his lucky mascot was a shabby little black cat – just the one – made of pieces of felt sewn together rather ham-fistedly by one of his many nieces. It was a deplorable creature that looked as if it had spent most of its life in the mouth of a dog.

And, yes, Teddy's ju-ju was the silver hare that Ursula had given him, which he had initially treated with careless disregard but which now flew every op cradled snugly in his battledress pocket, lodged above his heart. He had unconsciously developed his own ritual, touching the hare like a relic before take-off and after landing, a silent prayer and thank-you. Not that he could feel the little inanimate creature through the thick layers of his sheepskin flying jacket and Mae West. But he knew it was there, silently doing its best to keep him safe.

They mooched morosely around as they waited for the WAAF to bring Vic back. George Carr ate his chocolate ration as usual. Everyone else saved theirs for later, but George reasoned that he might die during the raid and 'never get to enjoy it'. Chocolate had been in short supply in his Lancashire childhood, he said.

They smoked their last cigarette for the next six hours or so, emptied their bladders against *S-Sugar*'s tail and stared glumly at the ground. Even their normally chirpy little Scot was silenced. The poor second dickey was beginning to look as if he was on the way to his execution. 'Are they always like this?' he muttered to Teddy, and Teddy, who could hardly say to the poor boy, 'They think they're for the chop tonight,' instead betrayed the collective character of his crew and said, 'No, they're just a miserable bunch of so-and-sos.'

That morning Teddy had received a letter from Ursula. Inconsequential stuff, but at the end she had written, 'How are you?' and the emotion compressed into those three laconic monosyllables seemed to rise off the page and unfold into something so much larger and more heartfelt. 'All is well here,' he wrote back, with equal compression. 'Don't worry about me,' he added, giving her the reassuring gift of a disyllable.

He asked a WAAF, a parachute packer called Nellie Jordan who was sweet on him, to post the letter. The WAAFs were all sweet on Teddy. He suspected this was simply because he had been around longer than most crew members. It was a letter to be sent, not one to be kept in his locker in the event of him not coming back. Teddy had three of those, one for his mother, one for Ursula, one for Nancy. They all said much the same thing, that he loved them and that they mustn't mourn him too much because he died doing something he believed in and they should get on with their lives because that was what he would want. And so on. He didn't think this one-sided, final correspondence was a place for soul-searching or philosophical introspection. Or for truth, for that matter. It had felt strange to write about himself in a future where he didn't exist, a kind of metaphysical conundrum.

If he were to die, someone from the committee of adjustment – a ridiculous euphemism – would come and swiftly clear away his kit. Anything that would give a mother or a wife pause for thought – smutty photos, letters to other women or French letters – would be put in a different bag. Not that Teddy had any indiscretions to hide, none that would leave tangible evidence anyway. He sometimes wondered what happened to these bene-volently censored items – were they simply thrown away or was there a store somewhere full of unwanted secrets? He never did find out the answer to this question.

The following year, during his second tour, he inadvertently opened the door to a storeroom on the station and found it full of aircrew uniforms on hangers. He thought they must be replacement issue until he looked more closely and saw the brevets and stripes and ribbon medals and realized they had come off the bodies of the dead and injured. The empty uniforms would have provided a poetic image if he hadn't more or less relinquished poetry by then.

Sometimes when a new crew arrived at a station they found that the belongings of the previous occupants of their Nissan huts were still strewn around the place as if they were about to walk back in. The committee of adjust-ment would shoo them out while they 'cleared up', packing away the dead crew's belongings as WAAFs or orderlies stripped the beds and made them up anew. And sometimes those same sprogs would go up on a sortie that night and not come back and never even sleep in those newly made beds. They could come and go without anyone even knowing who they were. Their names written on water. Or scorched into the earth. Or atomized into the air. Legion.

Vic Bennett arrived back, bearing aloft the unmentionables ('And yet mentioned so often,' Mac said sardonically), and they climbed into *S-Sugar*, *J-Jig*'s replacement. *J-Jig* had been an unwieldy beast. Like a lot of the Mark IIs she had seemed reluctant to leave the ground. If she'd been a horse she would be the kind that you had to encourage to start the race, let alone finish, and if you hadn't known about her, if you hadn't been warned about her foibles, particularly her suicidal desire to swerve to the right, then it could have been the end of you before you had even begun.

Tonight was only the second op they had flown in *S-Sugar*. It was a new kite, straight from the factory floor, as fresh as her crew had once been. They had all wanted to finish their tour in *J-Jig*, already an object of fond reminiscence. She had brought them luck, she had kept them safe and they were still resentful at her loss and convinced it was yet another sign that they weren't going to make it to thirty. She had had twenty-six bombs stencilled on her fuselage, one for every mission flown, a key for her twenty-first mission and an ice-cream cornet that some joker had given her for a raid on Italy. *S-Sugar*'s only op so far, to Dusseldorf, hadn't yet been commemorated and despite her newness none of them trusted her. The over-heating port engine was just one of many niggles.

Their CO had hitched a ride out to dispersal with Vic and was fretting now at the time. 'Ten minutes,' he said, tapping his watch. Ten minutes to get off or they would be out of time and would have to be scrubbed.

The truck with the WAAF and the CO aboard followed them along the perimeter track and parked by the flying-control caravan, where they climbed out and joined a rather ragged-looking farewell party that was waiting patiently to wave them off. Teddy suspected some of them had given up hope that they were ever going to go and had abandoned them.

They lumbered along the runway, everyone waving enthusiastically at them, particularly the CO, who made a point of always being there at every take-off and often gave the impression that he believed that if he waved vigorously enough – with both arms aloft, running along the flare path beside them – he would help them lift their wheels successfully and drag their full bellies of bombs into the air. Crashing on take-off accounted for so much loss of life that it was always a moment of supreme reprieve for Teddy when he had managed to haul the Halifax off the concrete and above the hedges and trees.

If you turned back from the target – and it happened all the time because of weather or technical problems with the aircraft – then those runs also didn't count as an op, no matter how hair-raising. 'Bloody unfair,' Teddy said. 'Iniquitous, old chap,' Keith said in an atrocious attempt at a posh English accent. They were uproariously drunk at the time, on the forty-eight-hour stand-down after Turin. They should have turned back from Turin, Teddy realized that now, but he was one of those pilots who 'pressed on'. Some didn't.

The first time they ever turned back – only their second sortie – was because their starboard engine started leaking coolant over the North Sea and then the spark's intercom packed up and so Teddy made what he thought was the sensible decision to turn for home, jettisoning their bombs harmlessly into the North Sea. Their CO – a different one from now – wasn't impressed. He frowned upon early returns and he interrogated them for a long time about why they had thought they shouldn't press on to the target. Teddy thought it was fairly obvious why – the engine was going to overheat and catch fire (in those early days they were less sanguine about such things) and they needed to be able to communicate with the spark. '*Do* you?' the CO said. 'In an extremity you would manage surely? And a good pilot wouldn't think twice about flying on only three engines.'

It was then that Teddy realized that they were not so much warriors as sacrifices for the greater good. Birds thrown against a wall, in the hope that eventually, if there were enough birds, they would break that wall. Statistics in one of Maurice's great War Office ledgers. ('What a pompous ass he has become,' Ursula wrote crossly.)

And that was when Teddy resolved that he would not have their courage questioned again, they would not be Harris's 'weaker brethren', but would 'press on' to the target every time unless it was absolutely impossible, but that he would also do everything he could to keep them all alive. Over the rest of the first tour whenever they weren't on ops he had them constantly doing parachute and ditching drills – unrealistic perhaps with neither air nor water to practise with, but if they knew what to do, if it literally was drilled into them, then they would – might – beat those overshadowing odds. When they had first crewed up at the OTU, Vic and Kenny had done more air-gunnery practice than anyone else. They had gone on dummy bombing runs to Immingham harbour and done countless fighter affiliation exercises, practising evasive manoeuvres. Teddy still took them up on as many cross-country exercises as he could and did fighter affiliation with the Spitfires from the nearest fighter station. He coaxed the whole crew into being proficient in Morse code and having an understanding of each other's jobs so that in that unsympathetic CO's 'extremity' they might be able to understudy for one another. In theory, Keith, who had trained initially as a pilot, would be the best person to take over if something happened to Teddy, but Teddy had also trained Norman Best in the rudimentaries of flying, 'because that bloody Aussie shearer might be able to fly the kite but he won't be able to land the bloody thing'. Teddy swore a lot these days, blasphemy was infectious, but he still tried to avoid the worst words. Of course, if something happened to Teddy they were prob-ably all doomed already anyway.

Teddy knew that Mac always worked out the route to the nearest neutral territory – Switzerland or Sweden or Portugal – and whenever it was a clear night he would hone his astro-navigational skills. And the shy and retiring Norman Best wore an entire set of French clothing, right down to the underwear, beneath his battledress, the clothes acquired in Paris when he was a student. An authentic French beret in his pocket too. A Boy Scout if ever there was one, Teddy thought. 'Be prepared in mind by having thought out beforehand any accident or situation that might occur.' Somehow it seemed unlikely that his own Kibbo Kift training with a bow and arrow was going to be much of a help if he was on the run in France.

Norman did bail out over France, as it happened, flying with another crew on a second tour of duty in '43, but his preparation for evading was all for nought as his parachute was already on fire when he exited the aircraft and he fell to earth like a fiery plumb bob, his body never recovered. Norman carried no good-luck charm, had no compulsive rite like George Carr, who had to turn round three times to the right, like a dog settling, before entering the aircraft and thought that no one noticed.

The wretched second dickey stood next to Teddy for take-off. He was called Guy – an old Etonian, he said, hoping to form some kind of bond with Teddy. 'I didn't go to Eton,' Teddy said rather dismissively. Guy had a lot to learn. If he lived long enough. ('What a mug,' Vic said.)

Of course, he wasn't the first second dickey they had carried and they had flown with a couple of odd bods when various members of the crew hadn't been able to go on ops. George Carr had been given leave to go to his father's funeral. Mac had missed an op because of stomach 'flu and Kenny had a sprained ankle that put him out of action for a raid on Bremen (the result of one of Teddy's parachute drills). Vic Bennett had missed *J-Jig*'s final eventful op to Turin last week because of a debilitating cold.

Mac had made up his numbers flying with another crew but that still left both their gunners an op short of a full tour. They would have to fly as odd bods in someone else's crew. Unlucky mascots.

On the Turin raid they had flown with a replacement air-gunner in Vic's position in the mid-upper turret. He had a soft West Country burr ('Zummerzet') and spoke no more than a few words on the whole trip.

They had flown over the snowy peaks of the Alps by the light of a brightly full moon. 'Not many people have seen that, eh, skipper?' Kenny Nielson piped up on the intercom. Even Mac came out from behind his curtain to 'take in the view'. 'Almost as good as the Rockies,' he said and Kenny said, 'Aye, but you haven't seen the Rockies from *above*, have you?' and Keith started muttering something about the Blue Mountains until Teddy said, 'OK, everyone,' before a full-blown discussion about the relative merits of the world's mountain ranges took hold.

The odd bod had nothing to say about mountains. Teddy supposed they didn't have many in Somerset. Apart from a few seaside holidays in Cornwall when they were children the south-west was not a part of the country that he had explored. If he survived the war, he thought, he would rather like to go on a grand tour of England, all the highways and byways, the hidden villages, the grand monuments, the meadows, moors and lakes. Everything they were fighting for.

They were 'privileged', Norman said, to see the world in a way that few people ever had. A privilege they were paying a terrible price for, Teddy thought.

They had been awestruck not only at the sight of the

Alps by moonlight but by the depthless inky-black skies, pricked with thousands upon thousands of stars – bright seed broadcast by some generous god, Teddy thought, drifting dangerously close to the forsaken realm of poetry. There were sunsets and dawns of thrilling grandeur and once, on a run to Bochum, a spectacular show that the Northern Lights put on for them – a vibrating curtain of colours draped in the sky that had left them searching for superlatives.

In his isolated position at the back Kenny Nielson claimed that he had 'the best seat in the house'. Sunsets in particular left him wonderstruck. From the tail of the aircraft he could see the sun going down long after the rest of the crew had flown into the darkness. 'The sky's on fire,' he reported excitedly one time after Teddy had lugged the Halifax off the runway and into the air. Teddy had a moment of terror – a vision of Armageddon being wreaked on them by the enemy, but then Vic Bennett in the mid-upper turret said, 'That's the best sunset I've ever seen.'

'Aye, like God's painted the sky,' Kenny said, and Teddy said, 'Can we have some peace and quiet?' relieved that the end of the world was not nigh and shocked at himself for having thought that it might be. 'It *is* braw,' Kenny persisted, not quite able to let the beauty go. Or 'Beauty' as Sylvie might have said.

As a rear-gunner, Kenny was the least likely of all of them to live to see a sunset in peacetime. Only a one-in-four chance of staying alive until then, Ursula's girl said. In the end, of course, it was the girl from the Air Ministry who was living without a future, killed by the Aldwych V-1 rocket in June of '44. She had been on the roof of

Adastral House, where the Air Ministry was housed, sun-bathing whilst eating her lunchtime sandwiches. (What were the odds against *that*, Teddy wondered?)

Other Air Ministry girls were sucked out of the shattered windows of the building and fell to their deaths in the street. One man was sliced in half by a sheet of falling glass, Ursula said. Teddy supposed for some people Ursula was a girl too – the girl from Civil Defence.

She was called Anne. The girl from the Air Ministry. And when they parted at the end of the evening they had spent in each other's company at the Hammersmith Palais (she danced a neat foxtrot) she said to Teddy, 'Well, good luck,' and didn't look him in the eye.

There hadn't been much in the way of flak on the run in to Turin, the Italian ack-ack guns always seemed half-hearted. They bombed the target from sixteen thousand feet, on the red markers. The weather had started to close in on the approach. The Alps were no longer beautiful – no longer visible, in fact – and as they turned for home they found themselves confronted by a huge dark tower of cumulus, looming high above them. Inside this monster there were flashes and sparks as if small explosions were going off and at first they thought it must be something to do with the bombing – or even some new kind of weapon that was being tried out on them – and it took a few moments before they understood that they were flying into an enormous, sinister thunderhead.

The turbulence was atrocious, rocking *J-Jig* around as if it were a toy aircraft. As flies to wanton boys. Or wanton gods. Zeus throwing his thunderbolts, Thor wielding his hammer. The fairies moving their furniture, Bridget used to say, a less vengeful interpretation for a kinder time. Some fairies, Teddy thought. On the intercom he could hear the curses ranging from Norman's terrified Christian restraint – 'Oh, dear lord' – to Keith's bitter 'Fuck, fuck, fuck, get us the fuck out of this, skip.'

They were all agreed afterwards that it was worse than any flak they had ever encountered. Flak they understood, but this was something more primeval. Occasionally the lightning illuminated malevolent fissures and caverns within the dark mass. The turbulent air currents were random – bucking and bucketing them up and down or sideways – and Teddy wondered if the aircraft might simply break up from stress.

The outside temperature dropped dramatically and ice started to form on the wings. Ice was a fierce enemy, it could appear rapidly and sometimes without warning – several tons of it, freezing the engines and the controls and covering the wings in thick white slabs. It could make an aircraft so heavy that it simply fell out of the sky or broke into pieces in the air.

The intercom was alive now with involuntary 'Jesus's and 'Christ's and 'Fuck's as they were thrown around and, too, the murmur of Psalm 23, 'Yea, though I walk through the valley of the shadow of death,' which was interrupted by several gasps of astonishment as *J-Jig* was abruptly ejected from the thunderhead only to find herself possessed by a phantom.

Touched everywhere by St Elmo's fire, bright blue and unearthly – an eerie luminescence that flared along the edges of the wings and even whirled round with the propellers, spinning off them and making strange feathery trails in the darkness, like ghostly Catherine wheels. It was 'dancing' between the tips of his guns, Kenny reported from the rear. 'Up here too,' from the mid-upper.

The strange phenomenon made Teddy think of the Willis in *Giselle*. He had seen a performance of the ballet when he was at school, a trip to the Royal Opera House organized by the music master. The dancers had been lit by the same rather sinister and otherworldly blue light that was now attracted to *J-Jig*. Looking back, it had been an odd choice for a class of boisterous thirteen-year-old public-school boys. His father, when told, had raised an eyebrow and asked the master's name ('An admirer of Wilde, I expect') and even Sylvie, with her love of Art, had questioned them being exposed to this rather 'fey' choice, as she put it, when usually the only time they left the school grounds was to go to an away rugby match. Afterwards Teddy had nightmares, dreaming that the spectral women had their hands on him and were trying to drag him down into some dark, unknown place.

The blue fire finally flickered and died and the starboard outer engine began to start and stutter with vibration before running wild. Teddy had just feathered it when the troublesome port inner also began to vibrate. It sounded as if it was going to shake itself free from the aircraft altogether. They would probably be better off without it.

Teddy told Mac to draw up a new flight plan that would take them the quickest way home. The storm had left their magnetic instruments useless and Mac had to use dead reckoning to plot a new course, but not before the port inner decided to catch fire. Give me a break, Teddy thought, pushing the throttles forward to take them into a steep dive ('Hang on, everyone!') that had the welcome effect of not only extinguishing the flames but also dislodging the ice on the wings. Every cloud had a silver lining, he thought. Conversely, every silver lining was in a cloud.

The starboard outer was now smoking and a few minutes later Keith reported seeing flames and then without warning the engine exploded, the force almost flipping the aircraft over. A spate of 'Jesus Christ's and 'Fucking hell's on the intercom and Teddy said, 'It's OK.' What a ridiculous thing to say, he thought. They were flying on two engines, fighting a headwind, still icing up, with no wireless and only dead reckoning to get them home. They were not OK at all.

Teddy was considering giving the order to abandon the aircraft when something even more alarming happened. Mac started singing. Mac! And not some ditty from the Canadian backwoods but a cacophonous performance of 'Boogie Woogie Bugle Boy'. Even allowing for the intercom it was a pretty dreadful rendition, particularly when he imitated the bugle, like an elephant in pain. This was followed, even more shockingly, by their dour Canadian laughing, rather in the manner of Charles Penrose singing 'The Laughing Policeman'. Teddy asked Norman to find out what was happening behind Mac's curtain.

It transpired that his oxygen tube had become frozen. Norman tried to defrost it with the coffee from his flask but the coffee was only lukewarm by now. They dragged Mac out from his seat and managed to hook him up to the central oxygen tank and hoped for the best. Hypoxia tended to make you do the oddest things and then it tended to kill you.

After the war, Mac worked for a big insurance company in Toronto. He married and had three children and had taken early retirement ('made some canny investments') by the time Teddy met him at a squadron reunion dinner, the only one Teddy ever attended. He hadn't seemed familiar in any way and it struck Teddy that perhaps he had never really known him. Perhaps he had never known any of them. It had just seemed so because of the circumstances they had found themselves in. This older version of Mac seemed rather self-satisfied to Teddy's eyes. The awfulness of the time they had shared didn't seem to have left a mark on him. He supposed that old men had reminisced about old wars since time began. Jericho, Thermopylae, Nuremberg. He didn't really want to be one of them. Teddy left the reunion early, saying, 'Sorry, have to give you the chop, chaps,' slipping back easily into that 'lingo' that people now made fun of.

Yet even then, all those years later, he found that in the long dark watches of the night, plagued by insomnia, he would recite those names. *Essen Bremen Wilhelmshaven Duisburg Vegesak Hamburg Saarbrucken Dusseldorf Osnabruck Flensburg Frankfurt Kassel Krefeld Aachen Genoa Milan Turin Mainz Karlsruhe Kiel Cologne Gelsenkirchen Bochum Stuttgart Berlin Nuremberg*. Some might count sheep. Teddy counted the towns and cities he had tried to destroy, that had tried to destroy him. Perhaps they had succeeded.

*   *   *

On the return from Turin they were caught by flak as they approached the French coast. An ack-ack shell blasted through the fuselage, almost jolting *J-Jig* out of the skies. They were flying through thick cloud and for a disorientating moment Teddy thought they were flying upside down. The aircraft reeked of cordite and there was smoke coming from somewhere, although no sign of flames.

Teddy did a crew check. 'Everyone OK?' he asked. 'Rear-gunner? Mid-upper? Bomb-aimer?' Teddy always worried most about his rear-gunner, stuck out there at the back, far away from them. It surprised him that someone as garrulous and sociable as little Kenny Nielson was so cheerful in his cold and lonely nest. Teddy knew he couldn't have tolerated that cramped, claustrophobic space.

Everyone reported themselves variously 'OK,' 'Fine,' 'Still here,' and so on. Norman went back to check for damage. Some holes in the fuselage and the lower escape hatch blown off. And the hydraulics must be severed, he said, because he'd been sloshing around in fluid, but there was nothing on fire. They were flying lower and slower with every mile. They were below five thousand feet and took off their oxygen masks. Mac had rallied by now and lay down on the crew rest.

Teddy decided that they couldn't limp on like this much longer and told everyone to prepare to abandon the aircraft, but they were already out over the sea and they all agreed they would prefer to press on than ditch. Their faith in Teddy's abilities to get them to the target and home again had become unshakeable as the tour had progressed. Possibly a misplaced faith, Teddy thought ruefully.

By the time the English coast came into view ('Thank you, Lord,' he heard Norman say) they were almost running on empty and there wasn't much more fuel to be coaxed out of the tanks. George had spent the last few hours fixing the wireless and managed to put out a 'darkie' call for an emergency landing but everywhere seemed to have closed up shop for the night. They were so low over land now that when they flew over a railway line they could see a train snaking below, the red-hot glow from the firebox of the engine escaping from its blackout shields. He didn't fancy their chances of parachuting successfully from this height and told them to assume crash positions, which meant not much more than bracing themselves against anything handy, but then at the last minute a coolly competent female voice at Scampton gave them permission to land and Norman said, 'We can do it, skipper,' and they did, more, Teddy thought, by wishing it to be so than by any skill on his part. If seven minds working as one could fly an aircraft on willpower alone then they did. Six minds, it turned out.

They didn't quite manage to make it to the runway. Lacking hydraulics Teddy couldn't use the flaps and the undercarriage wouldn't come down so they made a wheels-up landing at 150mph, overshooting the runway, smashing through the perimeter hedge, careering into a field, bouncing over a road, almost clipping the gable-end of a row of farm cottages before slewing through another hedge and ploughing up a field in which they finally slithered to a juddering, bone-shaking stop. Several of the crew were propelled into the forward bulkhead so that, bruised and battered, it took them a while to clamber up the ladder out of the upper escape hatch. The aircraft had immediately filled with acrid smoke and Teddy, standing at the foot of the ladder to shepherd them out, urged them to be 'as quick as you can, lads'. He counted them out. Two missing, one of whom was Kenny. No sign of the mid-upper either.

When Teddy finally got out he could see that the rear-turret was still attached but the rest of the aircraft was pretty much in pieces. *J-Jig* had left a trail behind her – wheels, wings, engines, fuel tanks, like a wanton woman divesting herself of clothing. What was left of the fuselage was on fire and he found his dazed crew gathered around the rear-turret where Kenny seemed to be trapped, Keith yelling at him, 'Get out, you stupid bugger!' although he clearly couldn't as the doors of the turret were jammed and wouldn't rotate.

Oh, ye gods, Teddy thought, was there to be no end to this nightmare op? Would it be just one horror followed by another? Yes, he supposed, for wasn't that what war was?

The fuselage was burning fiercely now behind Kenny and Teddy thought with horror of the belts of ammunition that fed the guns and wondered how long before the fire found them. Kenny was screaming his head off, expletives that later even Keith said he had never heard before. Were they all going to have to watch him burn to death?

There was a small panel in the turret where the Perspex had been removed to give the rear-gunner a clearer view (as well as freezing him half to death) and they began to exhort Kenny to try to climb through this tiny aperture. He had already managed to divest himself of his bulky heated suit but was still encumbered by uniform.

Once, on a trip to the zoo in London, Teddy had seen an octopus squeeze itself through an impossibly small hole, a party trick that the keeper was keen to demonstrate to small boys. But the octopus had not been hampered by a battledress jacket and bulky flying boots and neither was it in possession of a skeleton. But if anyone could perform this Houdini-like trick it was their little rat-like rear-gunner.

He managed to get his head out and started to wriggle his shoulders through. Teddy imagined it was rather like being born, although he was hazy about the mechanics of that act. Once Kenny had manoeuvred his shoulders through the gap they grabbed hold of him and pulled and pulled, everyone yelling their heads off, until suddenly he simply popped out like a cork from a bottle or Jonah being vomited up by the whale. But then, to their alarm, instead of immediately jumping down he disentangled himself from their grasp and reached his head and an arm back through the hole into the turret, emerging triumphantly a second later, bearing aloft one tatty and very lucky black cat.

Then they all ran like hell to get away from the remains of the aircraft, which a minute later exploded, bright tongues of white flame licking the dawn sky, thanks to the oxygen bottles, followed by a nasty popping and spattering from the ammunition belts.

And that was the end of poor *J-Jig* who, workhorse that

she was, had carried them to hell and back in her stinking, oily belly.

'She was a good kite,' Keith said, performing the eulogy. She was, they all agreed.

'RIP,' Kenny said.

The occupants of the cottages had had a rude awakening, but a nice motherly woman brought out a tray with mugs of tea on it. The farmer appeared and castigated them for destroying his cabbages and was himself chastised by the motherly woman, by which time a truck from Scampton had pulled up to give them a lift back to the station, where they were given breakfast and then had to wait for transport back to their own squadron.

All they wanted was sleep and the journey back seemed interminable. Even when they arrived back they still had to go through the usual routine of reporting to an intelligence officer. They were grey with fatigue, their faces still creased from their oxygen masks, almost deaf from the din of *J-Jig*'s engines. Teddy had a pounding headache, which was usual at the end of a trip.

It was almost lunchtime by then, although they were still awarded their customary mugs of tea laced with tots of rum and the chaplain did the rounds with cigarettes and biscuits and said, 'Good to see you back, boys.' The ground crew had waited up for them until they heard from Scampton that they were safe and the CO hadn't been to sleep at all and sat in on their debriefing with the intelligence officer. They were his longest-serving crew and he was paternally fond of them. Turin had been their twenty-eighth op.

They had landed without the odd bod. They worked out that he must have bailed out pretty sharpish when Teddy first ordered them to abandon *J-Jig*. That had been over France. Hadn't it? Or over the North Sea. Teddy was so tired he could barely remember his own name, let alone the finer details of the harrowing return. He certainly couldn't remember the odd bod's name.

'Fred, I think,' George Carr said. 'Frank,' according to Norman. 'Definitely something beginning with an "F",' they agreed and the intelligence officer had to riffle through her paperwork before saying, 'An "H" actually. Harold Wilkinson.'

'Close,' George Carr said.

Mac had no memory at all of the anoxia, said he didn't even know the words to 'Boogie Woogie Bugle Boy', although they never stopped singing it to him on the crew binge that followed Turin. They had forty-eight hours' leave and they slept for half of that and then got blind drunk in Bettys Bar in York for the other half.

After the war, a long time after the war, Teddy did a bit of investigating to see if he could find out what happened to the odd bod. There were no reports of him parachuting successfully, of evading or of being taken prisoner. He was one of the missing and eventually his name appeared on the Runnymede memorial for the men who had no known grave, where he was remembered as Harold Wilkinson, not 'the odd bod'. 'Silly clot,' Vic Bennett said. 'He should have had more faith in his pilot, shouldn't he? Can't believe I missed the excitement.'

They weren't as late returning as the crew of *A-Able*, who

had been on the same raid as them to Turin but had diverted on the way home to Algiers when two of their engines were knocked out. They had been posted as officially missing by the time they got back to the station. Their Halifax, much to everyone's delight, was loaded down with crates of oranges, which were distributed around the squadron, some going to the local primary school. Teddy ate his orange very slowly, savouring every segment and thinking about hot slices of Mediterranean sun he never expected to see again. He didn't. After the war Teddy never went abroad again, never took a foreign holiday, never stepped on board a modern aircraft or took a boat on the sea. Viola told him that this 'isolationist policy' was 'pathetic' and he said it wasn't a *policy*, it was just the way things had happened. Nor was it 'jingoistic' and 'xenophobic' – another two words in her arsenal. She accused him of having 'no sense of adventure', and he thought that the war had provided enough 'adventure' for several lifetimes and a man could nurture himself just as well in his own garden. *'Il faut cultiver notre jardin,'* he said to her, but she had never heard of *Candide*. He wasn't sure she'd even heard of Voltaire.

'*Bomb doors open, skipper.*'
'*OK, bomb-aimer.*'
'*Steady, skipper. Left. Left. Steady. Right a bit. Steady, steady. Bombs gone.*'

S-Sugar bounced up in the air, relieved of her burden of bombs. No escape yet for them though as they had to carry on flying over the target, straight and level for another thirty seconds or so while the photo-flash flare dropped and the camera in the bomb-bay shuttered and took the photograph. It was their proof that they had been on the bombing-run – without it, it might not count as an op – but God knows what anyone would see when they scrutinized the results, Teddy thought. There was complete cloud cover over the target and add to that the sooty industrial miasma that permanently cloaked the Ruhr and it could have been the surface of the moon down there for all they knew. They had bombed on sky markers laid down by the newly formed Pathfinder force and hoped for the best.

Later, much later, after the war, when all the history books and memoirs and biographies started to come out and people stopped wanting to forget the war and started wanting to remember it, Teddy had looked into this raid and discovered that a large part of the force had bombed a place ten miles west of the target, and, on balance, probably more damage had been suffered by the bombers than by anyone on the ground. The more he read, the more he discovered how inaccurate their bombing had been in those earlier years. He had talked about this with Mac at the reunion dinner. 'What a waste,' Teddy said. 'A waste of bombs,' Mac said. Teddy supposed that as a navigator Mac felt personally slighted. 'Well, that wasn't really what I meant,' Teddy demurred. 'So many men and aircraft lost for so little result. We thought we were crippling their economy but a lot of the time we were killing women and children.'

'Can't believe you've joined the hand-wringers, Ted.'

'I haven't,' he protested.

'They started it, Ted,' Mac said.

And we finished it, Teddy thought. He was glad that he had sat out the last eighteen months of the war in a POW camp, hadn't witnessed Bomber Command trying to remove Germany from the map of Europe.

It was the backstop of every argument. They started it. They sowed the wind. They asked for it. The clichés thrown up by war. 'An eye for an eye,' Mac said. 'And you can say what you like, Ted, but a good German is still a dead German.' (All of them, Teddy wondered? Even now?)

'I know. I'm not saying we shouldn't have bombed them,' Teddy said, 'but with hindsight— '

'The question is, Ted, with all your so-called "hindsight" would you do it again, if asked?'

He would. Of course he would (Auschwitz, Treblinka), but he didn't give Mac the satisfaction of an answer.

The camera shuttered and Teddy banked *S-Sugar* away and Mac set the course for the homeward leg. 'That wasn't so bad,' the second dickey said. (Guy, wasn't it? Teddy wasn't sure. He seemed like a Guy. Or was it Giles?) Two or three voices groaned on the intercom. It was considered particularly bad luck to say a thing like that. 'Long way to go yet,' Teddy said. And indeed the flak was as bad, if not worse, on the way out as it had been on the way in. They could feel the blast from the ack-ack shells bursting all around them and the jar and thud as splinters of flak hit the fuselage.

There was a sudden blinding flash on the port side as a Lancaster was hit in the wing. The wing was blown off and sheared through the air under its own volition until it hurtled into another Lancaster, slicing off its mid-upper turret. Both Lancasters then spiralled down to earth, almost balletic in their fiery fall.

'Fuck,' a horrified voice said over the intercom. Vic or George, Teddy wasn't sure. Fuck, indeed, he thought silently. He sent Norman back to assess the flak damage. 'Bloody big hole,' he said. They hardly needed telling this, there was an Arctic gale blowing through S-Sugar. Guy seemed to have changed his mind about how bad it was and he indicated to Teddy that he was going to the back of the aircraft to acquaint himself with the unsavoury Elsan. Guy. Went to Eton. Must remember, Teddy berated himself. The lost odd bod from Somerset had left him feeling guilty, derelict in his duty. Everyone on the aircraft was his responsibility, after all. The least he could do was to remember their names, for heaven's sake. Guy never came back because at that moment both gunners started yelling down the intercom at once, 'Fighter port quarter, corkscrew port, go!' and Teddy rammed the control column forward, but not before they were hit by cannon fire from a fighter, a great rattling like some sky god throwing stones at the fuselage. The stink of cordite fumes filled the aircraft.

Teddy had thrown S-Sugar into a steep dive but by the time he had banked to starboard and started to climb back up the fighter had gone without Teddy ever having seen it. It didn't come back, disappearing as mysteriously as it had appeared. Mac set a direct course for home, avoiding the heavily defended areas around Rotterdam and Amsterdam, but by the time they reached the Dutch coast they were down to two thousand feet. The fighter had done its work. The port and starboard inners were out, the starboard aileron gone, and five wing tanks were perforated. There was also a big gash in the fuselage. Teddy feathered the useless engines and they persevered, too late to turn back as they had been flying through cloud and when they finally came out of it they were well over the North Sea.

For a while another straggling Halifax formatted with them, but they were flying so low and slow that their companion gave up on them and climbed away with a farewell waggle of her wings. They were alone.

At fifteen hundred feet Teddy told his crew to prepare for ditching. Ten miles to the English coast, he reported calmly. 'Get us a bit closer, skipper,' someone said. The idea of ditching was bad enough but to go down in the drink and be picked up by Germans was unthinkable. 'Keep going,' Norman pleaded. 'We made it back from Turin, remember.'

At one thousand feet they could see the white horses on the crests of the waves. Fifteen, perhaps twenty foot high. Tempest-tossed, Teddy thought.

By now they had jettisoned everything they could – the navigator's table, cushions, flasks, oxygen bottles. Keith attacked the seats with the axe to break them up and Vic dismantled the mid-upper guns and threw them out of the aircraft, followed by the turret itself. Anything to keep them going that little bit longer. 'Four miles to the English coast,' Mac reported, his voice as calm as ever. His papers and maps had flown all over the place when they had gone into the dive to evade the fighter and now he was gathering them all together as if he was shutting down an office for the weekend. It was one thing not to panic,

Teddy thought, but another to have no sense of urgency. He recalled how, when they were trying to extricate Kenny from the rear-turret, Mac had stood back commenting while the others worked themselves into a frenzy.

'Keep going, skipper,' another voice said. At five hundred feet George Carr clamped the Morse key down, set the IFF on the international distress frequency and collected the dinghy wireless.

At four hundred feet the fuel gauges read zero. They opened the escape hatches and Teddy told everyone to assume ditching positions. Mac lay down in the starboard rest position, Norman on the port side, their feet braced against the front spar. The gunners had their backs to the rear spar and George and Keith sat between their legs. They all placed their hands behind their necks or rested them on their parachute packs to absorb the shock. Teddy had drilled them well.

They hit the water at 110mph. The bomb-aimer's compartment broke on impact and a huge wave of oily water swept inside *S-Sugar*, immersing them up to their necks almost before they had time to inflate their Mae Wests. George had been knocked out on impact and they man-handled him awkwardly through the escape hatch. It turned out that Kenny couldn't swim, and furthermore was terrified of water, and Mac had to secure him with one hand by the scruff and drag him through the water that had filled the fuselage while he thrashed about, squawking with fear. Teddy brought up the rear. A captain was always the last off the ship.

The dinghy that was stowed in the wing had been inflated and was now blocking the overhead escape hatch.

S-Sugar was almost completely full of water and beginning to roll to port, and for a moment Teddy thought, this is it then, but then he kicked down into the water and swam through the gaping hole in the fuselage.

They all made it out and somehow or other they scrambled on to the dinghy. Norman cut the painter and they floated away from *S-Sugar*. She was still afloat, bobbing lopsidedly in the unforgiving grey, but within minutes she was sucked down and lost to the world for ever.

Somewhere out in the dark they could hear an engine. Mac grabbed for the Verey pistol and tried to fire off a cartridge but his fingers were so swollen and numb with cold that he couldn't do it. How many hours had they been in the water? They had all lost track of time. This was their second night, they were all sure of that. It had quickly become apparent to them that the ditching was only the beginning of their problems. There had been a huge swell on the sea and no sooner had they successfully made it into the dinghy than they were all pitched back into the sea again by an enormous wave. At least the dinghy had stayed the right way up (small mercies), but it had taken a tremendous, almost superhuman effort for them all to clamber back in again, not to mention having to haul the insensate George back as well.

Vic had lost his boots somewhere along the way and was in agony with the cold. They all took it in turns to rub his feet but their own hands had grown increasingly benumbed. Their clothes were completely waterlogged and they were sodden through to the skin, intensifying their cold and misery a hundredfold.

Poor concussed George Carr was propped up awkwardly but kept slipping down into the water on the floor of the dinghy. He was semi-conscious but moaning a lot. It was hard to say whether or not he was in pain, but Mac gave him a shot of morphine anyway and he grew quiet.

The dinghy wireless had been lost when they were washed into the sea and who knew how far they had drifted from their original ditching position. The chances of an aircraft spotting them or a rescue launch finding them seemed remote.

The sound of the engine had faded altogether by the time one of them – Norman – managed to pull the trigger on the Verey pistol and Keith said, 'Too fucking late.' The cartridge served only to illuminate the vast darkness that they were adrift in and, if possible, lowered their spirits even further. Teddy wondered if they had hallucinated the aircraft engine. Perhaps it was like being lost in the desert and soon they would see mirages or become prey to all sorts of deceptions and delusions.

'I'd give anything for a coffin nail,' Keith said.

'I did have a packet of fags,' Kenny said, struggling to produce them from his pocket. They regarded the wet Woodbines with regret before they were tossed over the side. All the emergency supplies had gone, of course – cigarettes, food and anything that might have cheered or sustained them had been washed away when they had been submerged a second time. Teddy found a piece of chocolate in a pocket and Mac divided it up scrupulously with his penknife and divvied up the fragments. George had been right to eat his chocolate ration before they took off, Teddy thought – he was beyond caring now. Vic refused the chocolate, he was suffering terribly with seasickness.

'I've heard all those tales,' Keith said, 'of men drifting at sea for weeks in an open boat and how they end up eating each other, starting with the cabin boy.' They all instinctively turned to look at Kenny. 'But I just want to let you know, I'd rather eat my own foot than any of you buggers.'

'I feel personally insulted,' Mac said. 'I'd make any man a good meal.'

That set them all off talking about food, which is never a good idea when there is no possibility of any, but gradually the talk subsided and died away. They were too exhausted for conversation and one by one they fell into fitful sleep. Teddy worried that they might not wake from this cold slumber and remained awake on watch.

He occupied himself by wondering what he would choose to eat. If he could have one meal, what would it be? A grand restaurant or a nursery supper? In the end he settled on one of Mrs Glover's game pies and, to follow, a treacle sponge pudding and custard. But it was not the food that he cared about, it was for them all to be sitting at the Regency Revival table, Hugh at its head, reinstated from the dead. Jimmy sitting on Pamela's knee, the girls still in their hair ribbons and short skirts. Bridget ferrying dishes from the kitchen, Mrs Glover grumbling backstage. Sylvie graceful and light-hearted. There was even a place for Maurice. And a dog sitting beneath the table. Or two – for they existed in his imagination, not their graves, and so both Trixie and Jock lolled warmly together at his feet. Despite his best intentions he couldn't keep his eyes open and he fell into the dark pit of sleep.

*   *   *

The second morning at sea had brought a leaden kind of light that promised nothing. The sea had been calmer for a few hours but now turned suddenly squally. They were drenched continually by spray, it hit them full in the face, making it difficult to breathe. It seemed impossible that they could be any wetter and yet it turned out to be perfectly possible. To make matters even worse, they discovered that the dinghy seemed to have developed a leak and they had to pump with the emergency bellows, but after a while they gave out too and they couldn't find a way to fix them and the only way they had of bailing water was to scoop it up with their frozen hands, making them even more unserviceable.

George was in a bad way, as was Vic. Neither of them could put up a defence against the waves that were continually battering them. Teddy crawled over to George and tried to take his pulse but the motion of the waves was too violent. He thought George might be dead but didn't say anything to the others.

When he glanced over at Kenny he saw that he was staring mournfully at George. He turned his gaze to Teddy and said, 'If I'm going to die, skipper, I'd rather die with you than anyone.'

'You're not going to die,' Teddy said, rather curtly. They would all be done for if they started to despair. *Best to avoid morbid thoughts.*

'I know, but if I do . . .'

Where was their second dickey, you might be wondering? Guy. No one could remember seeing him after they had been attacked by the fighter and for a while there was much discussion in the dinghy about what might have happened to him. In the end they concluded that he had not simply disappeared into thin air but must have fallen, unseen and unheard, through the hole in the fuselage when they corkscrewed and had plummeted into the North Sea without a parachute.

Another large fateful wave hit them like concrete. They hung on as best they could, but both Vic and Kenny were tipped into the water. Teddy never knew how they had the strength to retrieve a terrified Kenny ('Because he was a runt,' Keith said later), yet retrieve him they did. But no matter how many times they tried to heave the dead weight of Vic back on to the dinghy he would slip back into the water. It was a hopeless task, they were simply too weak. They managed to loop one of his arms through the dinghy's ropes, but Teddy didn't see how he could last more than a few minutes in the water.

Teddy took up the position closest to Vic and was still trying to hang on to him when he rolled his head back and looked Teddy in the eyes and Teddy knew there was no fight left in him. 'Well, good luck to you then,' Vic whispered and let his arm slip out of the dinghy rope. He floated away, just a few yards, and then disappeared quietly beneath the waves and into his unknown grave.

George Carr was not dead, as Teddy had feared, but he died two days later in hospital, of 'shock and immersion', which Teddy supposed meant the cold.

They were found by chance by a Royal Navy boat that had been hunting for another downed aircraft. They were lugged on board and stripped of their clothing and given hot tea and rum and cigarettes, and then wrapped in blankets and laid tenderly in bunks, like babies. Teddy immediately fell into the deepest sleep he had ever known, and when he was woken an hour or so later with yet more hot tea and rum he wished that he could have been left asleep in that bunk for ever.

They spent a night in hospital in Grimsby and then caught the train back to their squadron. Except for George, of course, who was retrieved by his family and buried back in Burnley.

They were given several days' leave, but there was still the question of Kenny's missing thirtieth op. None of them could believe that after everything they had gone through he would still be expected to officially finish his tour, but the CO, who they knew to be a kindly man, said 'his hands were tied'.

So, only a week after they had been pulled like half-drowned kittens from the deep, they found themselves sitting on the runway waiting for the signal for take-off. The remaining crew – Teddy, Mac, Norman and Keith, all tour-expired – had volunteered to go up again with Kenny for one last raid. He cried when they told him and Keith said, 'You soft little bugger.'

It was a reckless, cavalier kind of affair. For some reason they felt 'proofed' by the ditching, as if nothing bad could happen to them, which, as the girl from the Air Ministry could have told them, was simply not the case. This was despite the fact that all the signs and portents were bad. (Perhaps Keith's widdershins luck was at work.) They had

borrowed an aircraft from another crew and took up two
other men needing to make up sorties, on the principle
that they were all odd bods on this trip. They even took a
second dickey with them, although the second dickey
wasn't a new pilot getting experience but their own CO,
who 'felt like' going up. Teddy expected they might be
given a gentle ride by him – a nickel op, perhaps, to drop
leaflets on France – but no, they went to the Big City on a
maximum-effort raid. They were all infected by a kind of
madness and were ridiculously high-spirited, like boys
setting out on a Scouts' expedition.

They weaved their way to Berlin and back untouched
by flak and didn't even encounter a fighter. They were one
of the first aircraft to land back at the squadron. Kenny
climbed out of the aircraft and kissed the concrete of the
runway. They all shook hands and the CO said, 'There,
that wasn't so bad, was it, lads?' He shouldn't have said
that. He flew on the fateful raid to Nuremberg and Teddy
heard afterwards that he never came back.

Lillian was quite clearly in the family way, wearing an old
printed smock already stretching at the seams. She looked
weary, dark circles beneath her eyes and veins standing
out on her skinny legs. No blooming here, Teddy thought.
It was hard to believe that this was the same Lil of the red
satin unmentionables. Look where they had got her.

'We had a wake instead of a wedding,' Mrs Bennett said.
'Sit down, Lil, take the weight off your feet.' Lillian sat
obediently while Mrs Bennett made a pot of tea.

'I've never been to Canvey Island before,' Teddy said,
and Vic's mother said, 'Why should you have?' Vic had

inherited his bad teeth from her, Teddy noticed. 'He didn't say anything about the baby,' Teddy said and Mrs Bennett said, 'Why should he have?' and Lillian raised an eyebrow and smiled at Teddy. 'Born out of wedlock,' Vic's mother said, pouring tea from a big tin pot. She was an odd mixture of disapproval and comfort.

'Won't be the first, won't be the last,' Lillian said. 'He left a letter,' she said to Teddy. 'They all do, you know.'

'Yes, I know,' Teddy said.

'Of course he knows,' Mrs Bennett said. 'He'll have left one himself.'

Teddy supposed that Vic's mother could never officially be Lillian's mother-in-law and in the future there might be some escape from her for the poor girl. Small mercies.

'He *said*,' Lillian persisted, ignoring Mrs Bennett, 'he said that when the baby was born, if it was a boy, I was to call it Edward.'

'Edward?' Teddy repeated blankly.

'After you.'

And for the first time in the whole of the war Teddy broke. He burst into tears, ugly, painful sobs, and Lillian stood up and put her arms round him and pulled him towards her swelling body and said, 'There, there,' as she would in a few months to her own child.

Vic's mother, softer now, insisted that he eat with them, as if her corned-beef fritters would somehow heal their collective grief. He was fed more tea and cigarettes and sweets that they had bought for Vic's homecoming and was allowed to escape only when his eyelids started drooping and Lillian said, 'Let the poor man go, I'll walk him to the bus stop.'

'I'll come with you,' Mrs Bennett said, cramming a hat on her head. He was all they had left of Vic, Teddy thought, and they couldn't quite bear to let him go.

'He wrote about you,' Vic's mother said, staring straight ahead as they waited at the bus stop. 'He said you were the best man he'd ever known.' Teddy noticed her lip trembling. The bus hove into view, saving Teddy from trying to think of an answer.

'I almost forgot,' he said, 'our rear-gunner – Kenny Nielson – asked me to give the baby something.'

Teddy produced the shoddy black cat that had been Kenny's lucky mascot. It had survived its dunking in the North Sea but certainly didn't look any better for it. On its very last op it had ridden proudly up in the cockpit all the way to Berlin and back.

'That's disgusting,' Mrs Bennett said at the sight of it. 'You can't give that to a baby.' But Lillian took the little cloth cat and said to Teddy, 'Thank you, I'll treasure it.'

'I'll be off then,' Teddy said, stepping on to the platform of the bus. 'It was nice to have met you. Well, good luck to you then,' he added, only later realizing that these had been Vic's last words too.

1982

The Courage of the Small
Hours

Most nights he sobbed into his pillow, wondering what he had done to deserve this. It was because something was wrong with him, wasn't it? Everyone said so – his mother, his grandmother, even his sister sometimes – but what *was* it? Because if he knew what it was that was wrong he would try to fix it, he really would. Really, really try. And then maybe this endless punishment would end and the evil witch who claimed to be his grandmother would let him go home and he would never be naughty ever again as long as he lived.

Every night when he went to bed Sunny reflected in despair at the catalogue of bewildering rules, questions and general dissatisfaction (on all sides) that had filled his day at Jordan Manor (*stand up straight close your mouth when you eat not in the house thank you very much wash <u>inside</u> your ears are you trying to grow potatoes in them what's* *that in your hand what's <u>wrong</u> with you*). It didn't matter what he did, it was never right. It was making him a nervous wreck. And why could he *never* remember to say 'please' and 'thank you', his grandmother scolded.

He had to muffle his crying because if she heard him she stomped up the stairs and barged into his room and told him to be quiet and go to sleep. 'And don't make me come up here again,' she always added. 'These stairs will be the death of me one day.' Oh, if only, Sunny thought. And why had she put him up here if the stairs were so difficult for her?

It was a cell, although she said it was the 'nursery' – a horrible room in the attic on what she called 'the servants' floor', although they no longer had 'proper' servants, she said. The ones they did have – Mrs Kerrich and Thomas – never came up here anyway. They were living in 'reduced circumstances', his grandmother said, which was why there was only Mrs Kerrich, who came in every day to cook and clean, and Thomas, who lived in a cottage at the gates of Jordan Manor and who lifted and carried and repaired and 'attempted' the garden. Sunny didn't like Thomas. He was always saying things to him like 'Alroyt? Dew yew want to come and see moy woodshed, young bor?' and then laughing as if this was the greatest joke ever, showing the gaping black holes where his teeth were missing. Both Thomas and Mrs Kerrich had peculiar accents, flat and sing-song at the same time. ('Norfolk,' Mrs Kerrich explained.) 'They're peasants really,' his grandmother said. 'Good sort of people though. More or less.'

Both Thomas and Mrs Kerrich spent a lot of time grumbling to each other about being 'at her ladyship's beck and call', and even more time grumbling about Sunny and the 'extra work' he was causing them. They talked about him right in front of him as if he wasn't there, sitting at the kitchen table with them, Thomas smoking his Woodbines and Mrs Kerrich drinking tea. He felt like saying, 'Where's Mr Manners today?' to them, which is what his mother would have said to *him* if he was being rude to people to their faces. In fact Mr Manners would have been kept very busy if he had lived at Jordan Manor. Sunny would never be rude again to anyone as long as he lived if they would just *let him go home*.

Still, it was better in the kitchen than the rest of the house. It was the warmest room and there was always the chance of food. If he hung about the kitchen long enough Mrs Kerrich fed him, in the same casual way she occasionally tossed a tidbit to the dogs. His grandparents were frugal in their eating habits and he was always hungry. He was a growing boy, he was supposed to eat. Even his mother said so. To make matters worse, meal-times were accompanied by a barrage of instructions – *chew with your mouth closed sit up straight use your knife and fork properly were you brought up in a barn?* His table manners were 'appalling', his grandmother said, perhaps they should feed him pig swill seeing as he ate like one. 'They don't keep pigs any more,' Mrs Kerrich said, 'or she'd probably feed *yew* to *them*.' Not so much a threat as a statement of fact really.

Mrs Kerrich sighed and said to Thomas, 'Well, better get her ladyship's "morning corfy",' these last two words heavy with sarcasm, indicating Mrs Kerrich's peasant status as a proud drinker of strong, sweet tea rather than pretentious upper-class coffee. Sunny's grandmother wasn't a 'ladyship', she was just a regular 'Mrs'. Mrs Villiers. Mrs Antonia Villiers. 'Grandmama' – which was a word he stumbled over almost every time he tried to say it (not least because he found it hard to believe he was actually related to her). Why couldn't he just call her Gran or Granny? He had tried it once. She had been standing at the French windows in the 'drawing room', watching Thomas, who was mowing the grass ('Incompetent!'), while Sunny was playing on the carpet with an old Meccano set of his father's that had been 'lent' reluctantly to him ('Be careful with it!') by his grandmother when he said, 'Can I have a glass of milk, Gran?' and she had whipped round and stared at him as if she had never seen him before and then she said, 'I'm *sorry*?' a bit like his mother did only ten times nastier, like she wanted to bite you with the words. 'Grandmama,' he amended hastily. 'Please,' he added. (Mr Manners nodded approval.) His grandmother just carried on staring at him until he thought one of them would turn to stone, but eventually she murmured to herself, '*Can I have a glass of milk, Gran*,' as if it were the most puzzling thing she'd ever heard. And then she returned to watching Thomas. ('You'd think he'd never seen a lawn before!')

'Milk?' Mrs Kerrich laughed. 'Yew never sa'isfied, bor, that's your trouble.' Growing boys were *supposed* to drink milk, Sunny knew that, everyone knew that! What was *wrong* with these people? And eat biscuits and bananas and bread-and-butter-and-jam and all the other things that were considered indulgences at Jordan Manor but which his real grandfather – Grandpa Ted – saw as

311

necessary punctuation marks during the day. Sunny was accustomed to being with grown-ups who seemed to know nothing about children – Adam's Acre, his mother's 'women's peace group', his class at school – but in all these places he got fed, sooner or later.

'Oh, man, yeah,' his father, Dominic, said. 'It's like living in a Dickens novel. *Please, sir, can I have more?* I remember. And then when you leave to go to boarding school you'll have to eat the shit that they feed you there.' Boarding school, Sunny thought? He wasn't going to boarding school, he was going home at the end of the summer holidays, back to the school in York that he hadn't liked much but now was beginning to feel like a lost paradise. 'Oh, don't be so sure,' his father said. 'Now she's got her claws in you she won't let you go.'

Dominic was living above the stable block ('my garret') and was usually to be found lying on a battered old sofa, surrounded by unfinished canvases. All that remained of the horses was the lingering smell of manure as you walked up the external stone steps to his room. Sunny's father was in exile ('self-imposed') from the main house.

Dominic didn't seem to eat much either, although he usually had a chocolate bar somewhere that he portioned out between them. He hadn't been well, he said, 'hospital and all that shit', but now he was a lot better. Every time Sunny went to see him he seemed to be asleep although he claimed to be thinking. There was no use in complaining about anything to him. He was on 'heavy-duty prescription drugs', he said. The little bottles were lined up on the window-sill. 'He's like a sloth,' Sunny's grandmother said to his grandfather ('Grandpapa' – another mouthful) and although Sunny felt he ought to defend his father there was no getting away from the fact that his grandmother was right. In fact, sloths would get impatient with Dominic. (Sunny had watched a nature programme about sloths with Grandpa Ted.) Grandpapa had no opinion about Dominic. This was because he was 'ga-ga', according to Mrs Kerrich. 'Scrambled eggs for brains.'

'How can Dominic possibly inherit in that condition?' Sunny's grandmother rattled on, unperturbed by the one-sided nature of all conversations with her husband – possibly she preferred it that way. 'What if he doesn't pull himself together? That child will be our only hope, God help us.' 'That child' wondered at the meaning of these words. He didn't really feel up to being anyone's only hope. He was the 'last Villiers' apparently. But what about Bertie? 'She's a *girl*,' his grandmother said dismissively. '"The line ended in daughters." That's what it will say in *Debrett's*.' It seemed a good enough place to end to Sunny, but they needed a male heir, his grandmother said, even an illegitimate one. ('He's a little baaarstard, isn't he?' Mrs Kerrich said to Thomas, 'in more than one way.') 'We'll make a Villiers of him yet,' his grandmother said, 'but it's uphill work.'

The 'condition' his father was in was Sunny's fault apparently. How? Why?

'Jus 'cos yew exist,' Mrs Kerrich explained, handing him a dry Rich Tea biscuit. 'If young Dominic 'an't got 'iself involved with drugs an' your mother and so orn,' she said, 'then 'e could have gorn riding every day and married a bootful girl 'oo wore pearls and a twinset, like 'is kind o' people are s'posed to. 'Stead 'e became' – she made rabbit ears – '"an aaartist". And then 'e 'ad the strain orv 'avin' a child like yew.' Mrs Kerrich was a bottomless source of information, most of it false or misleading, unfortunately.

The dogs, divining biscuits, surged into the kitchen and boiled around their legs beneath the table. There were three of them, slobbery things, some kind of spaniel, interested in no one but themselves. Snuffy, Pippy and Loppy. Stupid names. Grandpa Ted had a proper dog called Tinker. Grandpa Ted said Tinker was as 'steady as a rock'. His grandmother's dogs were always giving Sunny secret little nips with their nasty teeth and when he complained to her she said, 'What did you do to them? You must have done something to them, they wouldn't bite for no reason,' when that was exactly what they did.

'Orf yew go, yew 'orrible 'ounds,' Mrs Kerrich said to them, words that had no effect on them at all. They weren't even properly house-trained and left what his grandmother indulgently called 'little sausages' all over the Persian rugs, which had 'seen better days'. ('Disgustin',' Mrs Kerrich said.) The whole house had seen better days. It was falling down around their ears, according to his grandmother, whose scratchy voice could be heard shouting from another part of the house, 'Snuffy! Pippy! Loppy!' and the dogs swirled out of the kitchen as fast as they'd entered. 'I'd 'ave the lot of them put down if they was mine,' Mrs Kerrich said. Sunny suspected that she didn't just mean the dogs.

Sunny was much better behaved than the dogs and yet was treated much worse. How could that be fair?

One of the servants' bells in the hallway started to ring.

The bells clanged horribly as if the person on the other end who was ringing them was furious (although, actually, they usually were). 'Oh, my giddy arnt, there's 'is lordship again,' Mrs Kerrich said, heaving herself out of her chair. 'Summoned by bells.' (She said this every time.) His lordship – again not a lord, but 'Colonel Villiers'. Sunny's grandfather (supposedly) rarely moved from his armchair by the fire. He had pale-blue rheumy eyes and tended not to speak so much as to make a sound somewhere between a bark and a cough, like a seal, that Sunny's grandmother and Mrs Kerrich seemed to have no trouble interpreting but Sunny had enormous difficulty translating into recognizable English. Whenever Sunny was anywhere near his grandfather he would grab him and hold on to him, frequently pinching him at the same time, and bay into his ear, 'Who are you?'

Sunny wasn't at all sure what the answer to this question was. He wasn't Sunny any more, apparently. His grandmother said she couldn't bring herself to call him such a silly name. 'Sun' was even more ridiculous and so she said from now on he was called Philip, which was his ga-ga grandfather's name.

'Oh, man,' his father said wearily when Sunny went to inform him that he was called Philip now. 'Just let her call you anything she wants. It's easier than fighting her. What's in a name anyway? It's just a label they hang round your neck.' It wasn't just his name, his grandmother had taken him into Norwich and kitted him out in completely new clothes so that he no longer wore his clownish stripy hand-knitted jumpers and dungarees but instead sported khaki shorts and 'smart' sweatshirts, and his jelly sandals were replaced with old-fashioned Start-Rite ones. Worst of all, she had taken him to a 'gentleman barber' who had sheared and shaved his long locks into something called a 'short back and sides' that transformed his appearance completely. He truly was no longer himself.

He didn't tell Grandpa Ted about this new identity, sensing it would lead to more questions than he was capable of answering. There was a weekly phone call. His grandmother stood next to him while he fumbled with the big awkward telephone receiver in his hand and 'had a little chat' with Grandpa Ted. Unfortunately, the strangely threatening presence of 'Grandmama' prevented Sunny from shouting out the truth about how wretchedly miserable he was. He wasn't very good at 'chatting' and so on the whole gave monosyllabic answers to Teddy's questions. Was he enjoying himself? *Yes*. Was it nice weather? *Yes*. (It was usually raining.) Was he getting enough to eat? *Yes*. (No!) And then Teddy usually finished by saying, 'Do you want to speak to Bertie? (*Yes*) and, as she was as hopeless at 'chatting' as Sunny was, there followed two minutes of silence while they listened to each other's adenoidal breathing until his grandmother said impatiently, 'Give the telephone back to me,' and ordered Bertie on the other end to return the receiver to her grandfather. Then his grandmother put on a nicer voice and said things like, 'He's so settled here now, I think he should stay a little bit longer. Yes, all the fresh country air, and being with his father. And, of course, it's what dear Viola wants.' And so on. Dear Viola? Sunny thought, unable to conceive of a scenario that contained both 'Grandmama' and 'Dear Viola' in the same room.

Sunny wished that he knew a code or had a secret language in which he could have conveyed his distress (*Help me!*) but instead he said, 'Bye bye, Grandpa,' even as he felt something horrible (grief) rising up from his (pretty empty) stomach.

'Stockholm syndrome,' Bertie said. 'You began to identify with your captors, like Patty Hearst.' This was 2011 and they were sitting at the top of Mount Batur, watching the sunrise. They had hiked up here by flashlight before dawn. Sunny had been living on Bali for two years by then. Before that he had been in Australia and before that in India for years. Bertie had visited him several times, Viola never.

Bertie would have fared better at Jordan Manor. She knew how to please but she also knew when to rebel. Sunny had never really learned how to do either properly.

'They were like vampires,' Sunny said to Bertie. 'They needed an infusion of fresh blood. No matter how tainted.'

'Do you suppose they were as bad as you remember?' Bertie asked.

'Worse, much worse,' Sunny laughed.

They had, basically, kidnapped him and now they were holding him prisoner against his will. 'Do you fancy a little holiday with your dad?' Grandpa Ted had asked him. It was the summer holidays. It seemed a lifetime since they had left Devon and the commune at Adam's Acre. Devon had grown into a golden memory, undoubtedly fed by his sister's infant utopian fantasies of geese and red cows and cake. Sunny had hoped they might all live with Grandpa Ted when they moved to York but his mother said, 'Not likely,' and after a couple of weeks she had rented a dingy little terraced house and put him in 'the Steiner school', which he hadn't liked but would willingly go back to now.

'You can get to know your other grandparents,' Grandpa Ted said, with what was clearly a hearty, false kind of enthusiasm. 'They live in a big house in the country, dogs and horses and so on. It might be nice to visit them for a couple of weeks, what do you say?' The horses had been got rid of a long time ago and the dogs would eat him if they got the chance. 'They've a maze as well,' Teddy said. Sunny thought he said that these previously unknown grandparents were 'amazed', which didn't surprise him. He was pretty amazed too, to find himself being packed off to stay with them. He had no free will, he knew that. Viola had inculcated that into him – 'You don't get to say what you want to do,' 'You'll do what I say, not what you want,' 'Because I *say* so!'

'Not my idea,' Sunny overheard his grandfather say on the phone to some invisible caller, 'but his mother's very keen on it.' This was after his mother had abandoned them, of course, 'to stand up for her beliefs', she said. What did that mean? Weren't her children as important as her beliefs? Weren't they the same thing? She had gone to Greenham Common. Bertie said it sounded like a fairy-tale place (until Bertie went there herself). Bertie thought everything sounded like a fairy-tale place. Viola was 'embracing the base' there, whatever that meant. 'She could try embracing her children,' Sunny heard Teddy grumble.

His grandmother and Dominic had arrived in a big old car and as they climbed out Grandpa Ted whispered in Sunny's ear, 'That's your grandmother, Sunny,' although he hadn't met her before either. His grandmother was wearing a shabby fur coat that looked as if it were made from rat skins and her teeth were as yellow as the daffodils in his grandfather's garden. She seemed ancient, but looking back later Sunny reckoned she couldn't have been much more than seventy. ('People were older in the past,' Bertie said.)

'Daddy!' Bertie shouted, barrelling past Sunny and throwing herself into their father's arms, surprising Sunny, not to mention Dominic, with her puppy-like eagerness. 'Hey,' their father said, taking a step backward as if his daughter might be attacking him.

'Hi, Ted,' Dominic said to Teddy once he'd identified Bertie for who she was. 'How's it going?'

Teddy invited them in for a cup of tea. 'And I've made a cake, a Victoria sandwich,' he said, and their new grandmother frowned at the idea not only of cake but of a man making it.

And then that was it. Tea drunk, cake eaten – or not – and Sunny was bundled into the back of the car with three very resentful dogs and the next thing he knew he was in Norfolk and his supposed grandmother was telling him that he needed to start growing up. He was only seven! He didn't need to grow up for years yet! It was so unfair.

He gave a final miserable sniffle into his pillow. He had trouble getting to sleep every night and when he did sleep he would wake with a sudden start and find himself surrounded by all kinds of sinister objects that loomed out of the dark at him. In the safer light of day he could see them for what they were – the junk, piled up over the years, that a resentful Thomas had left behind when he was ordered to clear out the room for 'the boy' – a frayed basketwork cradle, a broken cot, a partnerless ski, a huge lampshade and, worst of all, a wooden tailor's dummy that Sunny could swear edged closer, inch by terrifying inch, as the night wore on, as if it were playing a malevolent game of statues. 'Oh, man, "the nursery",' Dominic said, 'what a hell-hole. If I had kids I'd give them the nicest room in the house.'

'You do have kids,' his kid said.

'Oh, yeah, well, right, you know what I mean.'

Not really, Sunny thought.

It was always cold in the nursery, even though it was summer. There were water stains on the walls and a piece of the wallpaper had peeled off and was hanging like flayed skin. The single window, speckled with black mould, was jammed shut or Sunny might have tried to climb out and escape down a drainpipe – the kind of thing that Augustus did in books.

Grandpa Ted had these books, loads of them, called *The Adventures of Augustus*, which had been written all about him apparently by his aunt. Viola had read a couple of them to Sunny. Augustus got up to all kinds of naughty things but everyone seemed to think that was all right, sort of, but if Sunny so much as dropped a pea from his plate he was the worst boy in the world as far as his grandmother was concerned. It wasn't fair.

He wished Bertie was here. She would have snuggled in bed with him and kept him warm. She was good at cuddling, so was Grandpa Ted. No one in Jordan Manor ever touched him unless it was to pinch or smack or, in the case of the dogs, bite. His grandmother favoured a wooden twelve-inch ruler on the back of his legs. 'It was good enough for Dominic,' she said. ('Yar, an look 'ow 'e tuuurned out,' Mrs Kerrich said. Not that Mrs Kerrich was against corporal punishment. Far from it.) He wet the bed quite a lot, which he'd done at home as well, but here it was Mrs Kerrich who had to deal with the bed sheets and she never stopped reminding him that he was 'a little pisser', and when she was really annoyed she made him sleep in the cold damp sheets the next night as well.

Mouldering books and Victory puzzles had also been carelessly left behind in the nursery. Sunny did his best with them. He was a terrible reader but he was very good at jigsaws, although there were only so many times that you could gain satisfaction from making 'Anne Hathaway's Cottage' or 'King Arthur on Dartmoor'.

The nursery was still littered with the debris of Dominic's childhood and Sunny was forever standing on a rogue toy soldier or skidding on a Dinky car and he gathered these little treasures into an old shoebox. He had held on to (against all the odds) the little silver hare that Grandpa Ted had given him, but he wished he had the comfort of his stones. There was some gravel on the driveway but that was hardly enough. His best pebble, the one he had found on the beach just before they left Devon, had been taken from him by his grandmother. ('Dirty thing.') If he'd had his stones he could have left a trail like Hansel and Gretel did and then found his way back home. Or Bertie, his Gretel, could follow the trail and find him and release him from his cage and push 'Grandmama' into an oven and burn her to ashes. He fell asleep with this happy thought in his head.

The 'vexed question' of educating him arose. Mrs Kerrich said to Thomas that she didn't see why he couldn't just go to the local school. 'Not good enough for a Villiers,' Thomas said. My name's Todd, Sunny thought, Sunny Todd, not Philip Villiers. How long before he forgot this? Mrs Kerrich said she thought 'the son and heir' was backward so her ladyship didn't need to get her knickers in such a twist about his education. 'I'm not backward,' Sunny muttered. Mrs Kerrich said, 'Speak when you're spoke to, young fellow my laaad.' Mr Manners shook his head in despair at Thomas and Mrs Kerrich's lack of breeding.

Mrs Kerrich was right, the local primary was out of the question for his grandmother, the very words 'state school' made her shudder. He wasn't old enough for the boarding school that Dominic had attended. 'Yet,' his grandmother said. Not until his eighth birthday. Eight seemed awfully young, even from the view of a seven-year-old. 'Yeah,' his father said. 'I was miserable there, but not *homesick*. You can't be *homesick* for somewhere like here, you can feel sick when you're *in* Jordan Manor but it's a relief to be *out* of it.' This was quite a lot of words for Dominic. He was coming 'out of hibernation', he said, throwing off his torpor. 'Stopped taking the medication and all that shit. Seeing things clearer now. Need to get away from here.'

'Me too,' Sunny said. Perhaps they could run away together. Sunny had a vision in his mind of the pair of them walking along a country road, carrying their belongings in red-and-white spotted handkerchiefs knotted on to sticks. Perhaps a little dog trotting by their side.

'They don't know anything about children,' his father said. 'You have no idea what it was like growing up here.'

I do know what it's like, Sunny thought. I *am* growing up here.

'They believe in deprivation, that's the problem, they think it's character-building when in fact it's quite the opposite. Of course, really, I was raised by a nanny. She was worse than the lot of them put together.' Sunny had no idea what a nanny was. The only nanny he knew about was the goat that he remembered from Devon. She had smelt horrible and always tried to eat your clothes if you got too close to her. It seemed unlikely that his father had been brought up by a goat, but Sunny was beyond surprise these days. 'Yeah,' Dominic said, drifting away on the memory. 'Nanny was a real cunt.'

'What's that?' Sunny asked.

'A really bad person.'

'A solution' was found by his grandmother. A local prep school, a day school – Thomas would drive him to and fro every day. ('Oh, he will, will he?' Thomas said.) 'Not a terribly good school, actually,' his grandmother said. 'But that means we won't be so embarrassed by Philip's behaviour.' What behaviour? He was as meek as a mouse these days.

'I'm going to school here,' he said to Grandpa Ted in the weekly phone call.

'I know,' Teddy said, sounding almost as miserable as Sunny felt. 'Your mother's cooked it up with Antonia. I'm going to try and do something about it, all right? Until then you're just going to have to be a stoic, Sunny.' Sunny had no idea what a stoic was but it clearly wasn't pleasant.

The few days before he was due to start school the weather was lovely, as if it had made a point of waiting until there was hardly any time to enjoy it. Sunny played in the overgrown neglected grounds all day long. It was boring on his own and he'd pretty much exhausted his capacity to be a solitary medieval jousting knight, Robin Hood or a jungle explorer. So it was a relief when his father said, 'Let's have an adventure, shall we, Phil?'

Sunny felt that he might have had enough of 'adventure'. He had accidentally wandered into the maze a few days ago – he was 'officially banned' from it by his grandmother, but as he didn't even know what it was it was hard to avoid it. It was a terrifying place, completely overgrown and he had turned back almost immediately – but too late! He was already lost, beset by thorns and hedged in by privet. It was dark by the time Thomas came looking for him, whistling for him as if he were a dog. Sunny had fallen asleep amongst the harsh roots of the hedge and was woken by Thomas flashing a torch on his face and giving him a little kick with his boot to encourage him to get up.

'Why did you do that when you were expressly told not to?' his grandmother shrieked. No care from anyone for the terror he had suffered, of course. He was pretty much used to that by now, so when his father said 'adventure' a little voice inside advised caution. It was a word that usually promised much from his father but tended to deliver little. The opposite was usually true with Grandpa Ted.

'Yes, get him out of the way for the day,' his loving grandmother said.

For several days now Dominic had been painting, working all hours, night and day, splashing paint on canvas. 'Inspired,' he said. 'Doing some brilliant shit.'

Dominic shocked them all one morning by bounding down to breakfast, a meagre meal at the best of times, and calling cheerfully for 'Your finest bacon and eggs, Mrs Kerrich!' when she sidled in with her usual pot of watery porridge. She left griping, 'Oh, gawd, 'ere we go again. 'E's on the up.' Neither bacon nor eggs appeared, which was no surprise to Sunny, who knew the state of the pantry better than most as he spent a lot of time smuggling himself in there to scavenge for food. Slim pickings, the odd pickled onion or cold potato. Sometimes he ran his finger nervously round the inside of the marmalade pot. Mrs Kerrich was like a hawk.

Dominic seemed to forget immediately about the bacon and eggs and instead lit up a cigarette. His grandmother smoked a lot as well, the whole of Jordan Manor had a faint wash of yellow to the walls. Dominic's eyes were bloodshot and he was as jumpy as a frog. 'Come on then, Phil,' he said before Sunny had a chance to spoon his porridge into his mouth. 'Let's get going.'

* * *

They had walked for hours, sustained by one messy, half-melted Mars bar that Dominic pulled apart and shared. He had taken a couple of little pink pills early in the walk, showing them in the palm of his hand to Sunny and debating with himself whether or not to give a bit of one to him. 'Like maybe just a quarter of a tab?' he mused. 'Because to trip as a kid, imagine what that would be like.' In the end he decided against it because he would just get 'a bad rap' from 'the she-wolf'.

They drank water from a rather green-looking pond that Dominic said was a magic source of water and contained, deep down, a toad with a ruby in its forehead. 'If you look closely you can see it.' Sunny couldn't, to his father's disappointment. They set off again, his father still rambling on about the toad. Sunny was exhausted by now. It didn't feel much like an adventure.

'I'm tired,' Sunny said. 'Can we stop for a bit?' He was worried about how they were going to get back to Jordan Manor. Not walk all the way surely? They had come miles and his legs were getting shaky with tiredness. If Grandpa Ted was here he would have given him a piggy back and said, 'Oof, I'm getting too old for this.'

'It's good exercise for you,' Dominic said, striding on. 'Come on.'

Sunny's face was burning. He knew he was supposed to be wearing a hat and sun cream. He was very thirsty and they hadn't passed any more ponds, green or otherwise. It struck Sunny that he wasn't with someone who was actually *responsible* for him. His father wasn't really a grown-up, was he? A little spear of fear stabbed him in his tummy. He wasn't safe out here.

They came to a wood, which was a relief because it provided a bit of shade, and Sunny found some wild raspberries which were horribly sour but at least they were food.

They had to keep stopping all the time so that Dominic could admire the leaf of a fern or rhapsodize about a bird singing. 'Can you hear that? Jesus Christ, can you *hear* that, Phil?' When he found a gigantic toadstool growing on a tree he dropped to his knees and stared at it. The toadstool kept him enraptured for what seemed like hours and Sunny said, 'Can we go, please?' because his tummy was hurting, probably from the sour raspberries, but Dominic started leaping about and shouting, 'Omigod, omigod, I can't believe I didn't see it – toadstools! *Toad* stools – the toad with the ruby in its forehead – the two are connected!'

'Because it's a stool for a toad?' Sunny hazarded.

'Because the toad is the *king* of the toadstools – that's the secret. That could change everything. We have the secret knowledge. Gnostic.'

'Nosstick?'

'Yeah. Oh, man.'

And so it went on for quite a lot longer. Sunny thought about lying down and covering himself with leaves like a small woodland animal. He could have a nap and then maybe when he woke up he'd find himself back at Jordan Manor, or, even better, Grandpa Ted's house. But no, they trudged on.

Out of the wood and back into the torture of the hot

sun. Dominic had stopped talking, in fact his whole mood seemed to have shifted and slipped into something darker. He was muttering to himself, but the words didn't really make any sense.

They were walking down a lane now, lined by big hedges, and then suddenly the lane stopped and they came out on to a small road. It was very hot on the road and Sunny's feet were so sore he didn't think he could walk any more. There were two white gates on the road. There was a big red circle in the middle of each gate and a little lamp on top of each of them that wasn't lit because it wasn't dark. They walked through the open gates and Sunny realized that they were on a railway. At last, something exciting. Was there going to be a train? Could they wait for it? 'Of course,' Dominic said. 'That's probably why we were led here.' By whom, Sunny wondered? The king of the toadstools? He didn't question this, he was just relieved that his father seemed happy again.

Sunny had never come across a level-crossing before. He loved trains. Grandpa Ted took him to the railway museum in York all the time. He said he'd loved trains too when he was a boy.

Sunny was expecting that they would cross over the tracks, but Dominic sat down right in the middle of the road between the two white gates and started to roll a cigarette. Sunny hovered uncertainly next to him. Sitting down on a road, especially one with railway tracks crossing it, didn't seem like a terribly good idea, even to a seven-year-old, but on the other hand his legs and feet couldn't take much more.

The tracks were embedded in wood where they crossed over the tarmac and his father patted the wood next to him and said, 'Relax, have a seat.' He lit his roll-up and discovered a flattened bag of completely melted chocolate buttons in his back pocket and looked at them in astonishment. 'Wow,' he said. 'Purple.'

Sunny sat, less reluctant now that he'd seen the chocolate, and the wooden part of the road wasn't too hot. He could see all the way along the railway track in both directions. 'Cool, huh?' Dominic said. 'Like a lesson in perspective. Do you know about perspective?' He didn't.

'You've got to paint something smaller the further away it is. It took people, like, thousands of years to work that out.'

Sunny's leg touched one of the metal rails and he gave a little yelp because it was so hot. 'Yeah, the sun, man,' Dominic said. 'It's hot. Like, and *you're* the sun, right?' His father wasn't really speaking sentences, Sunny thought, just jumbled thoughts. 'And toad and Todd! Can't be a coincidence that the two words are so similar, can it? Ra. Apollo. They would have been cool names too, but we called you Sun. Our Sun.' (Or perhaps he said 'son'. Sunny's name always led to confusion.)

'I'm Philip now,' Sunny reminded him. He was covered in melted chocolate, which was exactly the kind of thing that got you into trouble with 'the she-wolf' but he was too sleepy now to care. He began to nod off, leaning against his father's thin, agitated body. 'And with parallel lines, like the railway track, then you have to have a vanishing point.' Sleep seemed like the most delicious thing. Dominic's incoherent thoughts – sun worship, perspective, toadstools – faded pleasantly away.

He was woken up by bells ringing and lights flashing and saw that the two white gates were moving slowly, closing off the road. Were they going to be trapped? Finally the gates clanged noisily shut. 'Wow,' Dominic said. 'This is going to be amazing, you don't want to miss it.' Sunny suspected that he did and he tried to stand up, but Dominic pulled him back down. 'Trust me, Phil, you're going to want to see this. Oh, man – look, it's coming. See the train? See it? Unbefuckinglievable.'

Dominic stood up suddenly, yanking Sunny to his feet.

The small object that was far away – the three-thirty from Liverpool Street to Norwich, as it would be explained later at the inquest – was growing larger and larger, its perspective changing by the second. 'Stay, stay,' Dominic urged as if Sunny was a dog. 'What's wrong with you? Don't you want to experience this? It's going to be mind-blowing. *Now!* Aargh!—' No, not exactly 'aargh' – that was something Augustus would have said, not a man being hit full in the face by an express train.

'Rightio, this must be it,' Teddy said. In the back of the car Bertie slurped the dregs from her juice box and looked around with interest.

A sign affixed to one of the pillars of the arched sandstone gateway announced 'Jordan Manor' and beneath that another sign said, 'Private'. Teddy wondered if this was a biblical Jordan or if it referred to someone's name. A few years ago he would have considered Jordan to be a surname. He had known a WAAF called Nellie Jordan during the war (and, no, not in a biblical way), but apparently nowadays it was used as a Christian name – there was a Jordan (a boy) in Bertie's class at school. There was also, along with the usual clutch of Hannahs and Emmas, a Saffron and a Willow (both girls), and a Dharma (a pale, skinny child whose gender Teddy had never been able to determine). In Sunny's class there had been a girl called Squirrel. At least it was a name that couldn't be shortened, that was something that had occupied Nancy when they had named Viola. 'Will people call her "Vi", do you think? I do hope not.' As the years rolled on Teddy found himself occasionally wondering about Squirrel. Did she change her name or, somewhere in the adult world, was there a teacher or a solicitor or a housewife who answered to 'Squirrel'?

Any of the aforementioned professions seemed unlikely, given the kind of school it was. Rudolf Steiner – 'child-centred education', according to Viola, unlike Viola herself, who was not really very child-centred at all. And now she was a recusant and had approved the Villierses' choice of a local fee-paying prep school for poor Sunny. It was bad enough that she had more or less washed her hands of him but she had also separated him from his sister. Teddy could imagine only too well the pain he himself would have felt if at the tender age of seven he had been deprived of Ursula and Pamela. And what if the Villierses changed their mind about Bertie? Would Viola let them have her too?

'Dom's parents can give Sunny all kinds of advantages,' Viola said to Teddy. 'He's the Villierses' heir, after all, and Dom's been reconciled to the family. He's moved back, in fact, and he's working on his paintings.' Teddy had a tendency to forget that Dominic was an artist, perhaps because he was so spectacularly unsuccessful at it. 'And you must agree it would be good for Sunny to have a father back in his life again.' And so on, endlessly justifying her decision to abandon her child. Money, and her need for it, was at the root of it all, Teddy suspected.

Of course, the original proposal had been for 'a couple of weeks' in the school holidays and Teddy hadn't realized that there might be a longer-term plan afoot. Now it seemed that Sunny was to remain with the Villierses ('For ever?' Bertie said, a look of horror on her face). He was a sensitive child and it seemed quite wrong to Teddy's mind to uproot him like this and expect him to flourish with people who were more or less strangers to him. Without mentioning it to Viola, Teddy had been to see his solicitor and set in motion an appeal to the family courts for custody of his grandchildren. He wasn't too hopeful about the outcome, but someone had to be their champion, surely?

The impressive cast-iron gates to Jordan Manor were wide open and they drove through unimpeded. It had taken longer to drive to Norfolk than Teddy had calculated. He had never been here before, to the rump on the map of England. They had been on a single-track road for the last tortuous half-hour, stuck behind slow-moving farm vehicles and recalcitrant sheep. Their provisions were more or less used up. They had sustained themselves on the journey with cheese-and-pickle sandwiches on white bread, salt-and-vinegar crisps and KitKats – all of which were strictly forbidden by Viola, who had left 'dietary suggestions' ('nothing with a face') with Teddy for Bertie and Sunny – meals such as 'millet-and-spinach casserole' and 'noodle-and-tofu bake'. He could cope with them being vegetarians ('I don't eat dead animals, Grandpa Ted,' Bertie said), it was an admirable regime in many ways, but not with Viola's edicts from on high. 'My house, my rules,' Teddy said. 'And that means no budgerigar food.' He remembered buying sprays of millet for Viola's budgie, Tweetie. Poor bird, he thought, even all these years later.

The vegetarianism, the Steiner school, the traipse across town to Woodcraft Folk meetings, Teddy was willing to comply with all of these if it meant that Viola allowed them to stay safely beneath his roof. He had been wrong to let Sunny go to the Villierses. Viola had swanned off down south to demonstrate against cruise missiles and when Teddy had mildly suggested that her duties as a parent, and a single one at that, might trump the need for world peace, she said that was the most ridiculous thing she'd ever heard as she was trying to secure the future of all the children in the world, which seemed a bit of a tall order for one person. The last time she had gone down to protest she had taken Sunny and Bertie with her and camped at Greenham Common for several days. The children begged not to go again – 'cold' and 'hungry' seemed to be the words that summed up their experience and they had been frightened by the Thames Valley police on horseback treating women like football hooligans. Next time, Viola said, she was hoping to get arrested. Teddy said most people went through their lives hoping *not* to get arrested, and Viola said he didn't understand non-violence and did he ever think about the thousands of innocent people he had bombed during the war? She was a mistress of non sequiturs. 'That's got nothing to do with it,' Teddy said, and Viola said, 'It has *everything* to do with it.' (Did it? He no longer knew. Ursula would have had an answer.) In the end Teddy said, 'Sunny and Bertie can stay with me,' and Viola looked like Atlas might have looked if someone had said to him that it was OK, he could put the world down now.

That was several months ago and they had settled into a routine. Love had always seemed to Teddy to be a practical act as much as anything – school concerts, clean clothes, regular mealtimes. Sunny and Bertie seemed to agree. They had previously been subject to Viola's whimsical mothering ('I was a terrible mother!' she cries gaily, *Mother and Baby* magazine, 2007. 'You were,' Bertie agreed).

Teddy still had the chickens and bees at the time and the children loved both. They played outside a lot. Teddy hung a swing from the branch of one of the big pear trees at the bottom of the garden. They had expeditions into the countryside around York, to the water lilies in Pocklington, to Castle Howard and Helmsley, to the Dales in lambing time, to Fountains Abbey, to Whitby. The North Sea seemed less forlorn in the company of Bertie and Sunny. They loved hiking along ferny trails or having picnics on the purple moors. They were vigilant for adders, butterflies and hawks. (Were they really Viola's children?) Teddy was retired now and the children filled a lot of the spaces in his life. And he filled a big space in theirs.

He started to make long-term plans. Perhaps he should

move them to a state school, join them up for Cubs and Brownies rather than Woodcraft Folk, and then, out of the blue, Viola phoned and gave these new instructions for Sunny. Teddy had baulked at the idea of Sunny going to Jordan Manor, but what could he do? Viola was the one with all the rights. All this time, Viola had given the impression that she was living at the peace camp and only when she returned months later did he discover that she had gone off with Wilf Romaine after some big CND demo in Hyde Park and they had been 'shacked up', as she put it, in Leeds ever since. The first he knew of it was when she said, 'I'm getting married next week, do you want to come?'

An avenue of elms must have once provided a magnificent guard of honour for the long drive that led to Jordan Manor, but now all that was left were the stumps of the diseased trees. The same tragedy had struck at Ettringham Hall over a decade ago, but they had replanted with oaks. It seemed to Teddy that to plant an oak was an act of faith in the future. He would like to plant an oak. He had returned to Ettringham Hall many years later, in 1999, on his 'farewell tour' with Bertie. The Hall had become a 'country house hotel'. They had a drink in the 'Daunt Bar' and ate a not-bad meal in the restaurant, but stayed in a cheaper B&B in the village. It was hardly a village any more. Fox Corner and Jackdaws had been surrounded by a new estate of expensive detached houses. 'Footballers' houses,' Bertie said. They had been built on the meadow. The flax and larkspur, the buttercups and the corn poppies, red campion and ox-eye daisies. All gone.

The changes made Teddy sadder than he had expected, and Bertie too, because it was a place she had never known and never could know and yet in some way she understood that it had made her the person she was. She wanted to knock on the door of Fox Corner and ask the current owners if they could come in, but there were electronic gates with security cameras on them and when Bertie pressed the buzzer no one answered. Teddy was enormously relieved. He didn't think he would have been able to step back over the threshold.

'Dutch elm disease,' Teddy explained to Bertie as they drove towards Jordan Manor. 'It's killed all the elms.' 'Poor trees,' she said. Unlike at Ettringham Hall, the felled elms had not been replaced by any new planting and the resulting scene was dismal, as if there had been a war fought in the grounds. The air of neglect was palpable long before they reached the front door. Viola must have overestimated the Villiers' wealth. It would cost a fortune just to repair the roof on a place like this.

Perhaps, Teddy castigated himself, if he had brought Sunny here himself he would have realized how dilapidated the Villiers were in both home and character, but instead Dominic and his mother had driven to collect him one afternoon at the beginning of the school holidays.

'Antonia,' Teddy had said amicably, putting a hand out to shake, and she had given him a cold limp claw in exchange and said, 'Mr Todd,' without actually looking at him.

'Ted, please,' Teddy said.

'Antonia' was wearing a handful of diamond rings, grey and cloudy with dirt. He had given Nancy a little diamond ring when Viola was born – nothing flashy – and she said it was illogical to have an engagement ring when they were already married (*'post facto'*), but they had never been properly engaged during the war and he wanted her to have a token of his faith in their future together. Despite her scepticism she said it was a lovely gesture. She cleaned the ring every week with a brush and toothpaste so that it always sparkled. He had kept the ring for Viola and gave it to her on her twenty-first birthday but he couldn't recall ever seeing her wearing it.

And Dominic, it became apparent during the course of the afternoon, had either taken some kind of hallucinogen – LSD, Teddy supposed – or was as mad as a hatter. 'Cake!' he said, rubbing his hands together when Teddy laid out slices of the cake on a plate. 'How about that, Ma?' he said, taking three slices off the plate and wandering away, leaving Teddy and Antonia to fend for themselves in the conversation stakes.

'Tea, Antonia?' Teddy offered, not unaware how calling her by her first name riled her. It seemed important to him, however, that she reconciled herself to their equality as progenitors of the small squirming child who was reluctantly suffering their company.

Sunny and Bertie had disappeared almost as soon as their visitors had alighted from the car and Teddy had to cajole Sunny into returning to the living room. The boy was a terrible fidget and within minutes his newly introduced grandmother was saying 'Sit still' to him and 'Stop bouncing around on the sofa.' Teddy knew then that it was a mistake to let him go with her, but nonetheless he had, hadn't he?

'How do you take your tea?' he asked politely and Antonia said, 'China, weak with a little lemon,' and Teddy said, 'Sorry, I've only got Rington's English Afternoon Blend. Loose though, not tea bags.'

'I must go and see that the dogs are all right,' Antonia said, standing up abruptly and putting her cup and saucer down, tea untouched. 'They're in the back of the car,' she added when Teddy looked blankly at her. He hadn't noticed any dogs and he said, 'Dogs,' to Sunny, who perked up a bit at the idea. Sunny liked dogs. 'Why don't you go with your granny and see her dogs?' Teddy said, noticing that she flinched at the word 'granny'.

Yet still he had let the boy go with her!

'*Mea culpa*,' he murmured as he and Bertie drew up outside the front door of Jordan Manor. No sign of life, no dogs, no Antonia, no Sunny. Teddy sighed and said, 'Let's hope someone's got the kettle on, Bertie.' It was hardly likely to be Antonia.

When she had gone to see to her dogs, Teddy had gone looking for Dominic and found him in the back garden with Bertie and Tinker. The roses were in full bloom – Teddy had several splendid ones against a sunny wall – and Dominic had picked one, a wonderful cerise Belle de Crécy. A 'bed of crimson joy', Teddy had thought when he planted it, and hoped no invisible worm would eat its dark secret heart, even though he knew that was a metaphor on the part of Blake rather than some kind of horticultural caution.

Bertie glanced at the plucked rose and said to Teddy, 'Is that all right?' She seemed to be monitoring Dominic rather anxiously, her first flush of enthusiasm at seeing him having worn off. Teddy wondered if she was remembering how unpredictable her father's behaviour had been when she lived with him. Tinker was sitting alertly next to Bertie, glued to her side, as if he might be called to action at any moment.

'Yes, of course,' Teddy said. 'He's welcome to it. It's such a beautiful flower, isn't it?' he said to Dominic, who appeared to be completely captivated by the rose, which he was holding no more than an inch from his face.

'Yeah,' Dominic said, 'incredible.'

'It's called Belle de Crécy,' Teddy said helpfully.

'I mean, *look* at it, man, really look at it. Imagine if you could get inside it.'

'Inside it?'

'Yeah, 'cos it's like . . . a *universe* in there. There could be whole galaxies hiding in there. It's like when you travel through space—'

'Do you?' Teddy asked.

'Yeah, sure, we're all travelling through space. And you go down a wormhole, you know?'

'Not really.'

'The *meaning* of the rose,' Dominic said. 'It could be the clue. Wow.'

'Why don't you come back inside, Dominic?' Teddy said. Before you disappear inside that rose and we lose you for ever, he thought. It was like listening to the prattling nonsense of an idiot. And still he had let Sunny go with them! 'Come and have more cake, Dominic,' he said in the tone of voice you might bribe a rabid child with.

At that moment the patio doors opened (sliding,

double-glazed, Teddy had only recently had them installed and was very pleased with them) and three yapping dogs rushed headlong into the garden. Tinker, lulled into a false sense of security by the meaninglessness of Dominic's conversation, was caught off guard when he found himself suddenly surrounded by a trio of yipping, snarling guests.

'Snuffy! Pippy! Loppy!' Antonia shouted from the patio. Teddy and Tinker exchanged glances and Teddy said, 'It's all right, boy,' in as reassuring a voice as he could muster. He wouldn't have packed his own dog off with the Villiers, and yet he had sent his grandson.

'I don't want to go,' Sunny said when they were standing by the car, Dominic putting his small suitcase in the boot. He clutched on to Teddy's hand and Teddy had to prise himself free as gently as he could. 'I've got something for you,' he said, reaching into his pocket and producing the little silver hare that had once hung from his cradle, according to Ursula. He put it in Sunny's own pocket and said, 'That kept me safe all through the war. Now it will keep you safe, Sunny. And it's only for a couple of weeks. You'll enjoy it when you get there. Trust me.' *Trust me!* Teddy had betrayed all trust by sending him off with those people. He watched the car drive away with a heavy heart. Bertie cried and Tinker gave her hand a comforting lick. Something was wrong, but the dog had no idea what. Now they were journeying to right that wrong. They were going to rescue Sunny.

They climbed out of the car. Teddy stretched and said, 'Getting too old for this lark,' to Bertie. 'Old bones can't sit for long without seizing up.' There was a stiff bell-pull instead of a doorbell that Teddy had to yank hard for any result. They could hear a faint ringing somewhere beyond the fortress-like front door. No footsteps of anyone rushing to open it. It was a house in mourning, Teddy supposed.

Dominic had been dead for three weeks before Antonia saw fit to inform Teddy. His regular phone calls to Sunny had gone unanswered during that time and he was wondering about driving down when finally she telephoned and said there had been 'a tragedy'. For one terrible moment Teddy thought she meant Sunny, so when she said that Dominic was dead he almost laughed with relief, not quite the right response obviously, but he managed to say, 'Dominic?' Drugs, he supposed, but Antonia said 'a terrible accident' and wouldn't, 'couldn't' elaborate. 'I really can't talk about it.' Why on earth hadn't she told him sooner? 'I have lost my only child,' she said coldly. 'I have better things to do than telephone all and sundry.'

'All and sundry?' Teddy spluttered. 'Bertie's Dominic's *daughter*.' And Sunny, he thought, how on earth was poor Sunny coping?

He had fretted over how to break the news to Bertie. In the end it wasn't so much her father's death that troubled her as the existential problem of his current whereabouts. Nowhere, Teddy thought. Or perhaps he was in the mystic heart of the rose. He plumped for reincarnation as the best child-friendly answer to the conundrum. Her father might have become a tree, he suggested. Or a bird? She settled on a cat. Teddy supposed there was something cat-like about Dominic, mostly his knack for falling asleep. 'Will he be a kitten?' Bertie asked. 'Or a cat?'

'A kitten, I suppose,' Teddy said. That seemed logical.

'If we find him,' Bertie said, frowning, 'should we keep him as a pet?'

'Probably not,' Teddy said. 'Tinker might not like it.'

And what of poor Sunny all this time?

He had started school 'before his father was even cold and in the ground', as Mrs Kerrich put it. Even her lard-hardened heart was softened – slightly – by the way Sunny was expected to get on with things as if nothing had happened. He lasted three days at the school before his grandmother was asked to take him away. 'He's almost feral,' his housemaster reported to her. 'Biting, kicking, screaming, fighting everyone in sight. He took quite a chunk out of Matron's hand. You would think he was raised by wolves.'

'No, by his mother – much the same thing, I suspect. He's never been disciplined, I'm afraid.' His grandmother turned to Sunny – yes, this conversation was taking place in his presence, Mr Manners cringing at his side – and said, 'Anything to say for yourself?' What could he say? He'd been bullied horribly from the moment he stepped through the door of the school. They had made jokes about his father's death, about his accent (not posh enough), about his ignorance of 'the Three Rs', whatever they were, about anything they could find to use against him. They had harried him from pillar to post, pinching and shoving and giving him Chinese burns. They pulled his grey flannel shorts down around his ankles – twice – in the toilets, and once one of the boys had waved a ruler about and said, 'Stick it up his bum,' and was probably only prevented from doing so by Matron putting her head round the door and saying, 'Now, boys, enough fun and games.' ('That's the normal rough and tumble of a boys' school,' the housemaster said.)

And all the time his mind was swamped by what had happened on the level-crossing (he had learned that was what it was called). He had managed to wrench himself out of his father's grip at the last moment, but the rest was just a blur of overwhelming noise and speed. He had flung himself away from the engine and didn't see what happened to Dominic, although it wasn't hard to guess. From his perspective on the ground he could see down the track, see that the train, far, far in the distance, had come to a halt. He didn't think he was actually hurt, a bit of scrape and graze, but he decided just to stay there and pretend to be asleep. The consequences of what had just taken place were going to be too awful to deal with.

A policeman had picked him up and driven him to the hospital. If he closed his eyes Sunny could still feel the thick material of the policeman's uniform when he had leaned his head against his chest. 'You're all right, sonny,' the policeman said and Sunny wondered how he knew his name. He loved that policeman.

'I know it's terrible, what happened to his father,' the housemaster continued (it happened to me too, Sunny thought), 'and I believe he died a hero' (his grandmother gave a mute, restrained nod, accepting this as a compliment), 'but you know this kind of boy . . .' The sentence went unfinished, leaving Sunny wondering what kind of boy he was. Wicked, obviously, that seemed to go without saying. He had killed his father, apparently. How? How had he done that? How?

'Cors yew knows yew was with your dad when 'e died,' Mrs Kerrich said. 'An' if yew 'adn't been with 'im 'e wouldn't 'ave been there, would 'e? Orn that level-crawsin'. An' 'cos 'e saaarcrified 'iself for yew, didn't 'e? T'save yew from that darn train.'

Really? Sunny thought. This didn't tally with his own fragmented, anguished memory of events, but then what did he know? ('Nothing,' his grandmother said.) This, apparently, was the version of the accident that the inquest had settled on. His father had pushed him out of the path of the train. The traumatized train driver (who was on permanent sick leave because of the 'incident') reported that 'It all happened so fast. A man – Mr Villiers – appeared to be struggling with a small boy on the level-crossing. The man – Mr Villiers – seemed to be trying to pull them both out of the path of the train. He managed to push the boy to safety but he didn't have enough time to save himself.' Mr Villiers was to be commended for his heroic selflessness, the coroner said.

'HERO DAD DIES SAVING SON' it said in the local paper. At work, Teddy had sent a junior to look up the microfiche and found the newspaper account of the accident as well as a report on the inquest. Unmanned level-crossing, three-thirty down train to Norwich, and so on. Dominic Villiers, local artist. His son was known to have behavioural problems and was 'fascinated by trains', Thomas Darnley, local gardener and handyman at Jordan Manor, the boy's home, said.

'Dear God,' Teddy said.

The true verdict – that Dominic had killed himself while out of his mind on a cocktail of LSD and defective brain chemicals, that he had tried to take his son with him, was never proposed, although as far as Teddy was concerned this was infinitely more likely than Sunny's father being unable to move quickly enough to avoid a speeding train.

Poor Sunny, never to know the truth, to live with the burden of guilt all his life, or at least until he became a Buddhist and sloughed off the past.

('You were seven years old!' Bertie said. 'How could you possibly have been to blame?')

'We'll keep him at home,' his grandmother said to the housemaster.

'In chains, I hope,' the housemaster laughed.

He wet the bed every night now and he often wet his pants during the daytime. He seemed to have no control over his body or his mind. It was frightening. They 'engaged a tutor' – a Mr Alistair Treadwell – whose method of teaching was simply to repeat things more loudly each time until he lost his patience. Mr Treadwell spent a lot of his time talking to Sunny about 'injustice' and how 'the case against him' had been 'trumped up' by someone with a grudge. He was never even *alone* with the child, he said. But once your reputation was questioned, that was it.

They had lessons at the dining-room table, which was as big, if not bigger, than Teddy's actual dining room. Mr Treadwell ate egg sandwiches for lunch and then breathed his eggy breath all over Sunny in the afternoon. Sunny usually fell asleep and when he woke up Mr Treadwell was reading a fat book ('Tolstoy'). Sunny was 'practically unteachable', Mr Treadwell told his grandmother. 'Didn't you learn anything at your last school?' he was always asking him. 'Not *any* of the basics? The Three Rs?' Apparently not. Steiner didn't teach the basics until you were over six and Sunny had spent his days drawing with wax crayons and singing songs about dwarves and angels and blacksmiths, the mysterious trinity of the Three Rs still a distant threat on the horizon.

And then one day while they were doing what Mr Treadwell called 'simple arithmetic' but which Sunny found far from simple, Sunny realized that he needed the toilet, but Mr Treadwell said, 'Get to the end of this sum first, please,' so that by the time he got to the end of the sum – or rather by the time Mr Treadwell had given up on ever getting the correct answer out of him, it was becoming clear to Sunny that he was never going to make it. The nearest toilet was the 'downstairs cloakroom' which was still miles away, and he set off running awkwardly and almost knocked himself out when he turned a corner and ran into his grandmother.

'I need to go,' he said.

'Haven't you forgotten something?' she said. He started to panic because he couldn't think what it could be and he really, really needed the toilet. What had he forgotten? 'Please – thank you – I'm sorry, Grandmama,' he said, desperately throwing everything he could think of at the question.

'Excuse me,' she said.

'OK,' he said.

'No, excuse me.'

'Yes, OK.'

'You forgot to say "excuse me".'

But it was too late, he had to do a number two, right this second. He made a snap decision as to which would be the lesser of two evils – shorts on or off. What would Mr Manners do? Not dirtying his shorts seemed the decent thing to do, so he followed the dogs' example and squatted on the carpet.

His grandmother screamed as if she'd been confronted by a murderer. 'What are you *doing*?'

'A shit,' he said, in the frenzy of the moment reaching for the word that his mother frequently used ('call a spade a spade').

'A *what*?' She didn't seem to be able to get her breath and reached to some ornamental thing (a jardinière actually) for support, sending it crashing to the ground. The commotion brought both Mrs Kerrich and Thomas running.

'Yew filthy narsty little braaat,' Mrs Kerrich said.

But the dogs did it! 'Little sausages,' he said, appealing to his grandmother. Mr Treadwell had arrived by now. It was incredibly embarrassing having all these people gathered around in this situation.

'You are the most disgusting boy who ever lived,' his grandmother shouted at him and he shouted right back, 'And you're a cunt!'

Whump! Somebody (Thomas, it turned out later) hit him and sent him skittering across the floor and spinning into the nearest wall.

* * *

He was sent to his room. 'No supper for yew, li'ul Lord Fauntleroy,' Mrs Kerrich said. 'Yew'll be lucky if you're ever fed again.' His head was horribly sore where it had smashed into the wall. He wished he'd been run over by the train.

He *was* fed again. Mrs Kerrich brought him a bowl of porridge the next morning and advised him to stay in his room and 'lie low today', which was where he was, lying very low indeed, when Teddy and Bertie arrived at Jordan Manor.

Eventually, after much pulling on the bell, the front door of Jordan Manor creaked suspiciously open.

Mrs Kerrich led them down a long hallway. From the state of the hall, and the occasional glimpse through the open doors of the rooms that led off it, the neglect in the house was clear. 'A touch of the Miss Havishams,' Teddy murmured to Bertie. They were taken into an enormous drawing room, occupied only by the now rather shrunken figure of Antonia. The Colonel was parked in the leaking conservatory as after Dominic's death no one had the patience for him.

'Sorry to drop in unannounced, Antonia,' Teddy said.

They were all too tired to get home that night, so Teddy stopped off at a farmhouse that did B&B and then set off bright and early the next morning. 'To market, to market to buy a fat pig,' Bertie said as Teddy started the car engine. It seemed to take even longer on the way back and both Bertie and Sunny slept soundly for the last part of the journey, curled up like kittens on the back seat of Teddy's car.

Teddy had expected to have a bit of a fight on his hands with Antonia, but she'd given Sunny back without a struggle. 'Take him,' she said, 'you're welcome to him.' Sunny had a nasty bruise on the side of his head and Teddy said to her, 'I ought to call the police,' but he was really just glad to get Sunny out of that place.

Teddy put his hand out to touch Sunny and he flinched. Teddy tried again more slowly, as you would with a nervous dog, palm downward, and capped Sunny's shorn head in his hand and felt his heart break for the boy.

The Colonel died the following summer but Antonia carried on rotting away for many more years. Social Services got involved and Thomas and Mrs Kerrich were prosecuted for stealing from her. ('It were only li'ul things,' Mrs Kerrich said in her defence.) They had also tried and failed to get her to change her will in their favour (she was ga-ga too by then, as if it were catching). Her will was still made out to Dominic when she died, so Bertie and Sunny inherited everything. Probate took years – shades of *Bleak House* in more ways than one, Teddy thought. By the time Jordan Manor was sold and death duties were paid they were left with a few thousand each. Bertie bought a new car and Sunny gave his money away to an orphanage in India.

As if by some instinct both children woke up when they rounded the corner into Teddy's street. 'Home again, home again, jiggety-jig,' Bertie said sleepily as Teddy parked the car in the driveway.

He had left Tinker with a neighbour and when she opened her front door and said, 'Hello there, Ted, did you have a nice time?' Tinker nosed his way politely past her legs to greet them. Sunny's heart was so full he could hardly speak and when Teddy said, 'How about we go inside? I know I need a cup of tea and I'm sure you'd like some milk and cake, wouldn't you, Sunny? I made your favourite – chocolate,' Sunny thought his heart would burst and spill over with happiness. 'Yes please, Grandpa Ted,' Sunny said. 'Thank you, thank you very much, thank you,' and Teddy said, 'No need to thank me, Sunny.'

1943

Teddy's War

A Thing of Beauty

He caught the scent of the last of the wild roses on the warm, dusty breeze. There were already many quite large hips on the bushes that were entangled with the hedgerow, but a few late blooms still lingered in the heat of the dog days. The dog paused momentarily and raised its nose to the sky as if it too was savouring the dregs of this sweetness.

'*Rosa canina*. Dog roses,' Teddy said to the dog, as if it might appreciate the name. 'Dog days,' he added for good measure. The dog had no way of naming things for itself and so Teddy had dutifully taken it upon himself to lexiconize the world for it.

They were two old dogs out for a walk and they both had the hollow look around the eyes that went with age or ordeal. In reality, Teddy had no idea how old the dog might be, but he knew it had experienced a bad time during the Blitz and Teddy, at the age of twenty-nine, was an ancient ('the old man' he had heard himself called, affectionately) compared to the rest of the crew. The dog was called Lucky, which it was. Named by his sister ('an awful cliché, sorry') after she had rescued it from the streets of beleaguered London. 'Thought your squadron might like a mascot,' she said.

The last time he had taken a dog for a walk in the lane was before the war – Harry, the Shawcrosses' dog. Harry died when Teddy was training in Canada and Nancy had written, 'Sorry for the "radio silence". I couldn't put pen to paper for a while, just writing the words "Harry has died" made me so sad.' Her letter had arrived the same day as the telegram informing him of Hugh's death and although it was a lesser grief he nonetheless had space in his heart for sorrow at the news.

Lucky ran ahead and started barking, transfixed by something in the hedgerow – a vole or a shrew, perhaps. Or nothing at all – it was a city dog and the countryside and its inhabitants were a mystery to it. It could be spooked by a low-flying bird but remain indifferent to four Rolls-Royce Merlin engines roaring overhead. They should have had Bristol Hercules engines on the Halifaxes to begin with, that was what they were designed for, and the Merlins had never performed as they should have done. At least the Halifaxes had had their tail-fins modified, thanks in part to good old Cheshire, who had pressed the powers-that-be to change the old triangular tail-fins that could cause you to go into a lethal stall if you had to corkscrew, but unfortunately they still had the Merlins. Teddy supposed that someone – someone like Maurice in the Air Ministry – had made the decision to put the Merlins in. Economy or stupidity or both, as the two usually went hand in hand. The Hercules—

'Oh, please, darling,' Nancy said, 'let's not think about the war. I'm so tired of it. Let's talk about something more interesting than the mechanics of bombing.'

Teddy was silenced by this remark. He tried to think of something more interesting, and couldn't. Actually, the Halifax engines had been the prelude to an anecdote that he knew Nancy would want to hear, but now something cantankerous in him decided not to offer it up to her. And of *course* he wanted to talk about the war and 'the mechanics of bombing' – that was his life and was almost certainly going to be his death, but he supposed she couldn't understand that, locked away as she was in her ivory tower of secrets.

'Well, we can talk about what *you* do all day long,' he said, rather meanly, and she held his hand tighter and said, 'Oh, you *know* I can't. Afterwards, I'll tell you everything. I promise.' How odd it must be, Teddy thought, to believe in an afterwards.

This was a couple of days ago and they had been strolling along a seaside promenade. ('Sea,' he said to an ecstatic Lucky.) If you could manage to ignore the trappings of coastal defence all around them (difficult, admittedly) it might have seemed a normal activity for a couple on a summer's day. By some miracle Nancy had managed to synchronize her leave with his. 'A tryst!' she said. 'How romantic!' Teddy had gone straight from debriefing after a raid on Gelsenkirchen – and the customary bacon-and-egg reward for staying alive during an op – to the train station, from whence he had undertaken an interminable journey to King's Cross. Nancy had met him on the platform and it *had* seemed romantic, in the way of films and novels anyway (although the first thing that came to mind was *Anna Karenina*). It was only when he caught sight of her eager face that he realized he had forgotten what she looked like. He had no photo of her, which was something he thought that he really ought to rectify. She had put her arms around him and said, 'Darling, I've missed you so much. And you have a dog! You never said.'

'Yes, Lucky.' He had had the dog for a while now. He must have forgotten to mention it to her.

She crouched down and made a fuss of the dog. Perhaps slightly more of a fuss than she had made of Teddy, Teddy thought. Not that he resented that.

He had expected they would stay in London but she said it would be 'nice to get away' for the night (she seemed intent on forgetting the war) and so they had crossed town to another station and taken a train to the coast. She had booked a room in a large hotel ('guest-house landladies are far too nosy') and had come prepared with a wedding ring ('Woolworths'). They discovered that the hotel was full of naval officers and their wives, although it was mostly the landlocked wives as the officers seemed to be busy elsewhere, doing whatever it was naval officers did when they were ashore. Teddy had felt rather self-conscious in his RAF uniform.

One of the officers' wives had come up to him while he was waiting in the bar for Nancy to appear and, touching him on the forearm, said, 'I just wanted to tell you that I think you chaps are doing a splendid job. It's not all about the Senior Service, even though they think it is, of course.'

Teddy had never thought it was – as far as he could see, the bombers were the only ones taking the war to the enemy – but he smiled and nodded politely and said, 'Thanks.' He felt more pressure from her hand on his arm and smelt her gardenia scent. She took out a cigarette case and said, 'Would you like one?' and she was just leaning in to catch the flame from his lighter when Nancy appeared, looking lovely in pale blue, and the officer's wife said, 'Gosh, is this your wife, aren't you a lucky man? Just cadging a light,' she added for Nancy's benefit and drifted rather gracefully away.

'That was well done,' Nancy laughed. 'She saved herself with the manner of her exit.'

'What do you mean?'

'Oh, darling, don't be naïve, surely you understood what she was after?'

'What?'

'You, naturally.'

Yes, of course he had known that, and he wondered what would have happened if he had been on his own. He supposed he would have gone to bed with her. He was continually surprised by how forward the war had made women and he was in a state of mind that made him easy prey. She had lovely shoulders and a certain panache, as if she knew her own worth.

'She would have eaten you alive,' Nancy said. She was presuming, he noticed, that he wouldn't have liked that. Or that he wouldn't have been up to it somehow. 'I'll have a gin, please,' she added.

'You look lovely,' Teddy said.

'Why, thank you, kind sir. And you look very handsome.'

* * *

Nancy had been right, he admitted rather grudgingly to himself, it was nice to get away. He woke early and found that his arm was trapped awkwardly beneath her body. The bed sheets smelt of her lily of the valley, more wholesome than cloying gardenia.

The seagulls must have woken him. They were making a dreadful racket but he rather liked their rowdiness. He realized what an inland life he had been living since the war began (flying over the North Sea in the dark didn't really count as 'seaside'). The light had a quite different quality too, even the little that had found its way through the gap in the heavy brocade curtains. They had rather a good room, French windows opening on to a wrought-iron balcony and a sea view. Nancy said that she had paid 'a king's ransom' for the room and they had only got it because a rear admiral didn't need it for the night. She was very au fait with naval ranks, much more so than Teddy, who had an airman's contempt for the other forces. Naval codes, he thought, that must be what she was working on.

The dog, attuned to his every breath, had woken up at the same time. They had made a bed for it overnight in a drawer that they had pulled from the dressing-table and padded with a spare blanket foraged from the wardrobe. 'Gosh,' Nancy said, 'that looks more comfortable than our own bed.' Teddy – absurdly in his own eyes – felt self-conscious about making love to Nancy with the dog in the same room. He imagined it regarding them with perplexity if not downright alarm, but when he had glanced over at the drawer in the middle of the 'act' ('Is everything all right, darling?' Nancy asked) the dog appeared to be fast asleep. Discretion being the better part of valour.

He suspected that the well-appointed drawer had indeed provided a better night's sleep than the rear admiral's mattress, a lumpy horsehair thing that was almost as hard as the RAF 'biscuits'. When he woke Teddy felt as stiff and cramped as if he'd just spent nine hours in a Halifax. Nancy had been right again – she generally was – he would not have been up to the attentions of the naval officer's wife last night. He was far too exhausted to have survived her arachnoid charms.

Before Lucky could wake Nancy by jumping up on the bed, something it was allowed to do in Teddy's quarters, he extricated himself from the sheets and slid his feet noiselessly to the floor. The windows had been left wide open all night and he slipped between the curtains and out on to the balcony, stretching his arms above his head and filling his lungs with the clean air. There was a salty smack to it that felt like a relief. The dog joined him and he wondered what it made of the view. 'Sea,' he reminded it. Two nights ago his new aircraft, *Q-Queenie*, had made an emergency landing at Carnaby. Carnaby was on the coast and equipped with an extra-large runway to catch the poor crippled strays limping home across the North Sea, as well as those, like *Q-Queenie*, who were simply lost in the murk. Carnaby was equipped with 'FIDO', an acronym whose meaning Teddy had forgotten, only that it was something to do with fog. The runway was limned with fuel pipes containing thousands of gallons of petrol that could be ignited in case of fog to guide the lost and wounded home.

When he was safely returned to his own airfield Teddy had found himself telling the dog, his own Fido, about Carnaby, thinking it would be interested because of the name. That was the moment at which he realized that he had possibly become unhinged. He laughed at the memory now and scratched the top of the dog's head. What did it matter? The whole world was unhinged.

The balcony had suffered in the sea air, large spots of rust showed through the white paint. The whole country was in a state of disrepair. How long, Teddy wondered, before it became irreversible, before Britain crumbled away in rust and dust?

He didn't hear the discreet knock on the door that signalled the tray of morning tea they had ordered the night before and was surprised when Nancy stepped on to the balcony next to him and handed him a cup and saucer. She was wearing serviceable cotton pyjamas, 'not really honeymoon wear,' she said.

'Is this a honeymoon?' Teddy asked, sipping the tea, already cooling in the morning air.

'No, but we should have one, don't you think? First we would have to get married, of course. Shall we? Get married?'

'Now?' Teddy said, rather thrown. For a moment he thought perhaps she had arranged it as a surprise, a special licence in a local church, and he half expected a crowd of Todds and Shawcrosses to burst into the room, spouting congratulations. He thought of Vic Bennett who had never got to his wedding and what a knees-up it would have been, despite Lillian's condition. He felt guilty about the fact that he had not stayed in touch and knew nothing of Vic's child. Edward. Or a girl, perhaps. Lillian and the child would go on, but Vic was being slowly erased day by day until the time would come when no one would remember him. *He said you were the best man he'd ever known.* Vic should have lived longer, Teddy thought, he would have come to know many who were better.

'No. Not *now*. After the war.'

Ah, the afterward, Teddy thought. The great lie. 'Yes,' he said. 'We should, of course. Is that it? Are we engaged? Do you want me to get down on bended knee?' He laid the cup and saucer down on the balcony and dropped on to one knee, the dog a curious witness to this behaviour, and said, 'Nancy Roberta Shawcross, may I have your hand in marriage?' (Is that what one said?)

'I should be delighted,' she said.

'Do we need to buy a ring?'

She held up her ring finger and said, 'This one will do for now. One day you can buy me a diamond.' They married with the Woolworths ring. 'Sentimental value,' she said when he placed it on her finger in the Chelsea Register Office after the war.

It had been a small wedding and later Teddy wondered if they shouldn't have made more of a fuss. Ursula and Bea took on the roles of guests, bridesmaids and witnesses. Ursula brought Lucky with her, a red ribbon bow tied on his collar, and said, 'Here's your best man, Teddy.'

They never replaced the Woolworths ring with a more expensive one, even though the cheap alloy sometimes left an unattractive circle of black on Nancy's finger. Teddy did buy her a diamond though, a small one, when Viola was born.

* * *

'Betrothed,' she said as they walked arm in arm along the beach after breakfast. They had negotiated the shingle and the anti-tank traps to reach the coarse brown sand near the water's edge, exposed by the low tide. The dog was running in and out of the waves. Occasionally Teddy tossed a pebble for it, but it was too in thrall to the novelty of the sea to be interested in the mundane canine tasks of fetching and carrying. 'Plighting our troth,' Nancy persisted merrily. 'How archaic. Where does the word "troth" come from, do you suppose?'

'It's the Old English word for "truth",' Teddy said, his eyes still on the dog.

'Of course. That makes sense.' She squeezed his arm and Teddy thought of the officer's wife last night. Nancy smiled at him and said, 'Are you happy, darling?'

'Yes.' He had no idea any longer what that word meant, but if she wanted him to declare happiness then he would. ('The mistake,' Sylvie said, 'is thinking that love equates with happiness.') 'I was going to tell you,' he said, relenting and offering the Halifax anecdote that he had denied her the previous day, 'I was in the mess last week, playing cards actually. We were on ops that night, Wuppertal, and there's always this lull around mid-afternoon, after you've done all your flying checks and you're waiting for the briefing—' He felt her arm slacken slightly. He would happily have listened to the everyday details of her life if she had cared to offer them up. 'Shall I go on?'

'Of course.'

'Well, then I heard an aircraft engine – nothing unusual about that, obviously, but then Sandy Worthington – my navigator – poked his head round the door of the officers' mess and said, "Come and see, Ted, it's the new Halifax, the Mark III."'

'And it's much better, it's got a different tail,' Nancy piped up, like a keen pupil pleased with their memory for dull facts.

'No, that's not the interesting thing – although it is, to me, very interesting because it will save lives. So anyway, I borrowed a bicycle and raced along to the runway – the mess is a long way, it's a big airfield—' Nancy picked up a piece of driftwood and threw it into the sea for the dog, who seemed to consider retrieving it and then thought better of it. 'And the aircraft,' Teddy continued, 'was just taxiing along the perimeter fence to the dispersal, and guess who had flown it there?'

'Gertie?'

Now at last he had her attention. 'Yes, Gertie. It was such a surprise.'

Nancy's elder sister was in the Air Transport Auxiliary, ferrying aircraft to and fro from squadrons, factories, maintenance units. She had gained a pilot's licence before the war and Teddy remembered how envious he had been. The men in Teddy's squadron, although they didn't always admit it, had a lot of respect for the ATA girls ('women', Gertie amended). They flew anything and everything at a moment's notice – Lancs, Mosquitoes, Spitfires, even the American Fortresses – feats of aviation that would have defeated most RAF pilots.

'Yours, I think,' the CO said to Teddy as they stood at dispersal with Gertie, admiring the new aircraft.

'Mine?' Teddy said,

'Well, you are squadron leader, Ted, methinks you should have the best kite.'

'She flies well,' Gertie said to him. And so Q-Queenie became his.

Gertie was treated as an honorary officer and invited into the mess for tea ('And scones! How lovely.' They weren't). By chance, rather than her having to catch a train, there was an aircraft that needed to be flown to a maintenance unit to have its twisted fuselage straightened out. Aircraft hadn't been designed for the kind of violent manoeuvres that corkscrewing necessitated (neither had he, Teddy often thought). Gertie had not set any male hearts a-flutter during her brief sojourn – except perhaps the CO's, who remarked that she had 'guts' – for, like Winnie, she was a straightforward, rather homely type. Teddy tended to rank the Shawcross girls ('women') in terms of attractiveness – he suspected everyone did – from Winnie, the least pulchritudinous, down to Nancy and elfin Bea. In his heart he believed Bea to be the most attractive, but loyalty to Nancy usually censored that thought. 'Each Shawcross girl is smaller and prettier than the last,' Hugh had said once when they were younger. Millie, in the middle, would have been most annoyed to hear this judgement.

Gertie got a good send-off from the squadron, partly because she had delivered the very welcome new 'Halibag' and partly because of her connection to Teddy, 'like a sister-in-law' he had explained, as he supposed she would be if there were an afterward. A little huddle gathered at the control caravan for her take-off, Teddy amongst them, and they all waved as vigorously as if she was off on a raid to Essen rather than delivering a Halifax to an OMU in York. She waggled her wings in farewell and roared off into the blue. Teddy felt proud of her.

'I haven't seen her in ages,' Nancy said.

'You haven't seen anyone in ages.'

'Not by choice,' she replied, sounding rather brittle. He was being unfair, of course the war must be taking a toll on her too. He tucked her arm tighter into his and whistled to the dog. 'Come on,' he said, 'I'll buy you a sandwich in the station tea rooms. There's plenty of time before the train.'

'You certainly know how to treat a girl,' Nancy said, good humour restored.

The dog didn't reappear when Teddy whistled. He scanned the beach, the sea, a bubble of panic rising in his chest. The dog always came when he whistled. The Channel looked calm but it was a small dog and perhaps it had worn itself out by swimming too much, or it had met a treacherous current or a fishing net. He thought of Vic Bennett slipping beneath the waves. *Well, good luck to you then*. Nancy was walking up and down the beach, shouting the dog's name. He knew its senses were tuned to some higher animal frequency. His ground crew had told Teddy how Lucky would wait with them for his return and knew long before they did when his aircraft was approaching the airfield. If he was late returning or had to make an emergency landing elsewhere the dog remained resolutely at his post. When Teddy finally didn't return at all, when he was taken prisoner by the Germans, the dog remained for days, gazing steadfastly at the sky, waiting.

Eventually the dog was returned to Ursula's care and

when he came home Teddy didn't claim him back, much as he would have liked to. He had Nancy as his companion, he reasoned, but his sister had no one and loved the little dog almost as much as he did.

Not long ago the dog had stowed away on *Q-Queenie*. They had never quite been able to work out how. He was sometimes in the habit of hitching a ride in the lorry that transported them to dispersal, although no one remembered seeing him on this occasion and the first they knew of him being on board was after they had reached their rendezvous point over Hornsea when he had slunk – rather guiltily – from beneath the port rest position where he had concealed himself.

'Ay up,' Bob Booth, their wireless operator, announced over the intercom, 'we seem to have got ourselves a little second dickey.' The fact that this was against all rules, more so probably even than taking a WAAF up in the air, wasn't the problem. The problem was that they were already above five thousand feet and Teddy had just told everyone to put their oxygen masks on. The dog already looked unsteady on its feet, although that could well have been due to being inside a monstrous four-engined bomber struggling to reach operational height over the North Sea.

Teddy had suddenly remembered Mac singing 'Boogie Woogie Bugle Boy' on the journey back from Turin. He didn't think that Lucky was capable of anything so outlandish, but there was no doubt that the inevitable outcome of oxygen deprivation would be the same for both men and dogs.

Perhaps the dog had just been curious to know where

they went when they climbed inside their metal behemoths. Perhaps his loyalty to Teddy had driven him, or a desire to test his own canine courage. Who knew the mind of a dog?

Everyone but the gunners shared their masks with the dog, an awkward experience for all concerned. 'Oxygen,' Teddy said to the dog as he placed his own mask over its small snout. Luckily it was a gardening run in the Dutch shipping channels rather than a long raid to the Big City. After they had landed safely, Teddy smuggled the dog out of the aircraft, stuffed inside his flying jacket.

After that Teddy tried to remember to take a spare oxygen mask on board so that in the event of another stowaway they would be able to hook them up to the central oxygen. Although who in their right mind would want to stow away on a bomber?

He turned round and suddenly the dog was there, bounding along the beach, looking rather tired but without the vocabulary to tell him of any adventure he might have had.

Reunited, they ambled along the pier until they were stopped by a photographer and agreed to have a snap taken. Teddy paid the man and gave his squadron address and when he came back from his six days' leave, the photograph – which he had already forgotten about – was waiting for him. It was a nice one and he wondered about getting more copies – for Nancy perhaps – although he never got round to doing anything about it. He was in his uniform, of course, and Nancy was wearing a summer dress and a pretty straw hat, the cheap wedding ring invisible. They were both smiling as if they didn't have a care in the world. Lucky was with them, also looking happy with himself.

Teddy carried the photograph in his battledress pocket, beside the silver hare. It survived the war and the camp, and was thrown, rather carelessly, into a box of mementos and trophies afterwards. '*Objets de vertu*,' Bertie said, looking through this box after he moved to Fanning Court. She was always fascinated by Nancy, the grand-mother she had never known. 'And a dog!' she said, drawn immediately to the little dog's cheerful demeanour. ('Lucky,' Teddy said fondly. The dog had been dead for over forty years but he still felt a little stab of sadness to the heart when he thought of its absence from the world.)

The photograph had acquired a stain, a swathe of brown smeared across the top, and when Bertie asked its origin Teddy said, 'Tea, I think.'

When his first tour had finished Teddy had moved to an Operational Training Unit as an instructor, but asked to be put back on ops before his stint was up. 'Why, for heaven's sake?' Ursula wrote. 'When you could have had a few more months of relative safety before having to do another tour?' 'Relative' was a good word for an OTU in Teddy's opinion. When he first arrived there he had looked out over the fields surrounding the station and counted the wreckage of at least five aircraft that had not yet been cleared away. At an OTU you were given clapped-out old kites to fly – pensioned-off aircraft mostly – as if the dice weren't already loaded against green crews. Teddy didn't ask about the fate of the occupants of the aircraft that littered the fields. He decided he would really rather not know.

'Well,' he wrote back to his sister, 'the job isn't finished yet.' Nowhere near, he thought. Thousands of birds had been flung against the wall and it was still standing. 'And I'm a damned good pilot,' he added, 'so I think I can serve the war effort better by flying than by coaching sprogs.'

He reread the letter. It sounded like a reasonable justification. One that he could present to his sister, to Nancy, to the world, although he was slightly resentful that he felt the need to justify himself when they were in the midst of battle. Hadn't he been designated the family's warrior? Although he suspected that this noble mantle might now have passed to Jimmy.

The truth was there was nothing else he wanted to do, could do. Flying on bombing raids had *become* him. Who he was. The only place he cared about was the inside of a Halifax, the smells of dirt and oil, of sour sweat, of rubber and metal and the tang of oxygen. He wanted to be deafened by the thunder of her engines, he needed to be drained of every thought by the cold, the noise, and the equal amounts of boredom and adrenalin. He had believed once that he would be formed by the architecture of war, but now, he realized, he had been erased by it.

He had a new crew – gunners Tommy and Oluf, one a Geordie, the other a Norwegian. There were quite a few Norwegians in No. 4 Group as there were not enough of them to form their own squadron, like the Poles had done. The Norwegians were almost as fierce as the blood-thirsty Poles in their commitment. *They* always pressed on. They lived for the day they could fly home to a free

Poland. It didn't happen, of course. He often thought of them as Poland negotiated its way through the twentieth century.

It was another motley crew. Sandy Worthington, his navigator, was from New Zealand; Geoffrey Smythson, his flight engineer, was a Cambridge graduate. ('Mathematics,' he said solemnly, as if it was a religion.) Teddy wondered if he knew Nancy and he said he had heard of her, she had won the Fawcett Prize, hadn't she? 'Clever girl,' he said. 'Clever woman,' Teddy said. His wireless operator was Bob Booth from Leeds and his bomb-aimer was—

'G'day there, mate.'

'What the hell are you doing here?' Teddy asked.

'Well, I was instructing at an OTU when I heard that the renowned Ted Todd had come back on ops early and I thought, he's bloody well not flying without me. An Aussie squadron tried to claim me but I pulled a few strings.'

Teddy had felt almost overwhelmed at the sight of Keith – he had been the one he was closest to in the old crew and they had shared so much that they couldn't talk about with anyone else, yet on meeting again they had controlled themselves to a short manly handshake of greeting. Later, as the century wore on, Teddy observed how men seemed gradually to lose constraint where their feelings were concerned, until by the time the twentieth tipped into the twenty-first (and the advent of the unattractively named 'noughties') they gave the appearance of having lost control of their emotions altogether, perhaps their senses too. Footballers and tennis players blubbing all over the place, the ordinary man in the street embracing and kissing other men on the cheeks. 'Oh, for heaven's sake, Dad,' Viola said. 'How can you think such crap? The stiff upper lip! Do you honestly think that the world was a better place when men kept their feelings hidden?'

'Yes.'

He still sometimes remembered with horror how he had broken down in Vic Bennett's mother's kitchen. He couldn't see that it had done anyone any good, particularly him. When Nancy died he had wept quietly and privately, it had seemed the respectful way to mourn someone.

'I blame Diana,' Bertie said.

'Diana?'

'Princess. She made being hurt look heroic. Used to be the opposite in your day.' They were sitting on top of the White Horse at Kilburn eating sandwiches that a nice B&B landlady had packed for them at a stop on their farewell tour.

Like a dog, Teddy thought, he had had his day. 'I'm too old for the world,' he said.

'Me too,' Bertie said.

Nancy had only been able to get one night off and so they parted on yet another station platform barely twenty-four hours after they had met on one. He had been under the impression that they would be able to spend longer together and felt rather blue as he waved her off, but once the train had disappeared he realized that perhaps what he felt was guilt at the relief.

* * *

Keith had also come up to London on leave and they met up and made a congenial, platonic foursome in Quaglino's with Bea and her friend Hannie, a refugee. They all drank a good deal, and Keith did his best to flirt with two women at once. Hannie was very pretty but seemed uninterested and Bea was 'spoken for', engaged to a doctor, although they were both very sweet to Keith. Teddy never met Bea's doctor. He went over with the troops on D-Day and was killed on Gold beach and instead she married a surgeon after the war.

Bea was working at the BBC, producing and doing a little continuity, and some 'behind-the-scenes' things, and Hannie worked as a translator for an obscure-sounding government department. Bea had moved in a medical world during the Blitz when she had been recruited to work in a mortuary, piecing together jigsaws of body parts. Her art-college background had, for some unlikely reason, deemed her suitable for this work. 'Anatomy, I suppose,' she said. Even Teddy, who had become inured to the sight of the disintegrated bodies of men, didn't think he would have had the stomach for such work. In later years, in a different age of terrorism, Teddy read about bombs in parks and nightclubs, in sky-scrapers and passenger airliners, bodies blown to bits or falling to earth, and wondered if someone pieced them together again. Sylvie had always maintained that science was about men finding new ways to kill each other, and as the years went by (as if the war wasn't evidence enough) he grew to think that she was perhaps right.

He danced with Hannie, she was just the right height for him, and she smelt of Soir de Paris, which she said 'someone' had brought her back from France, which made him think that she must move in rather secretive circles. (Was there a woman he knew who didn't?) She was wearing emerald earrings and she hooted with laughter when he commented on them and said, 'Costume! Do I look like someone who can afford emeralds?' She had left her family behind in Germany and wanted 'every single Nazi' to die in agony. Fair enough, Teddy thought.

The four of them arranged to meet up again the following night and went to see *Arsenic and Old Lace*, which they all agreed was an excellent antidote to the war.

After the war Teddy learned from Bea that Hannie was with the SOE and had been parachuted into France before D-Day. Ursula and Bea had done their best to find out what had happened to her ('because she has no one else now'). It was the usual awful story.

It turned out those earrings weren't paste but genuine emeralds, French, *fin de siècle*, very pretty and had belonged to her mother, who was herself French. ('And I have some Hungarian blood as well as German, of course, and a little Romanian even. A European mongrel!') The earrings had begun their life in a goldsmith's *atelier* in the Marais in 1899 and, in the manner of objects, lived on long after the people who had worn them. Hannie left them with Bea for 'safekeeping'. ('You might not see me for a few weeks.')

'I think she knew she wasn't coming back,' Bea said. Bea gave them to Teddy before she died, because he was, literally, the only other person in the world who remembered Hannie, and thus it was that Bertie wore the earrings on her wedding day, a day that sadly Teddy didn't live to see. She married in winter, to the man she met by chance on Westminster Bridge, in a Saxon church in the Cotswolds, and wore antique lace and carried a bouquet of snowdrops. After some argument she allowed Viola to give her away. It was perfect.

The next day, Sunday, Keith and Teddy caught an early train to Fox Corner, where Sylvie had made a great fuss about inviting them to lunch. Keith was enthusiastic, he had visited before and charmed Sylvie. He also knew how well stocked her larder was. Ursula declined to come with them. 'Mother can have you all to herself,' she said and laughed rather wickedly.

Teddy took Keith round to Jackdaws to meet Mrs Shawcross, who was always keen – keener than Sylvie, perhaps – to meet any members of Teddy's crew who came down to Fox Corner with him. He was able to tell her that he had seen Gertie, and Mrs Shawcross said, 'How exciting, but I worry about her so. One thinks about Amy Johnson, you know.' Millie was 'briefly' in residence and flirted outrageously with Keith. 'That girl ought to be chained up,' he laughed when they finally escaped her clutches. 'Not my type,' he said. He was still rather smitten with Hannie, Bea's friend. 'Can't imagine taking her back to the sheep station though,' he said. Keith never doubted that he would be going back to Australia, and Teddy took a lot of comfort from his certainty. 'She's Jewish, you know,' Keith said.

'I know.'

'First Jewish person I've met,' Keith said, as if amazed. ('Jewess,' Sylvie would have said.) 'It must be nice to fall in love,' he added, revealing a surprisingly romantic side. 'Follow your heart and all that.'

'Steady on,' Teddy said. 'You're beginning to sound like a matinée idol' (or a woman). Months later, Teddy himself 'fell in love'. He followed his heart and it led him up a blind alley, a dead end, but he didn't mind that much.

A romantic interlude.

Julia. She was tall and fair, neither of which were attributes that Teddy usually found attractive in a woman. 'A *natural* blonde,' she pointed out. 'I don't think I've ever met one of those,' Teddy said. 'Now you have,' she said and laughed. She threw her head back when she laughed in a way that could have been crude but was actually charming. She wasn't one of those women who covered their mouths when they laughed but then she had nice teeth, creamy and very pearly. ('Good breeding,' she said. 'Good dentistry too.') She laughed a lot.

She had been to school with Stella and Stella had told Teddy to 'look Julia up' when he was in London, which was selfless of Stella. 'Don't fall in love with her,' she warned (priming the pump). 'She's broken the hearts of better men than you.' Even though Stella didn't know a better man than Teddy.

Teddy didn't want to die without falling in love and, as he expected to die at any given moment, he undoubtedly forced the hand of Cupid into giving him a taste of wartime romance. He was ripe for it.

Julia was in the ATS, working in a garage in central

London, driving Army lorries. There was always a smear of oil or grease on her and her fingernails were filthy. Nonetheless she always turned heads. It came as naturally to her as the blonde hair. She was the sort of girl who always had good restaurant tables, good theatre seats, the sort of girl who people gave things to. There was something dazzling about her, a kind of glamour that spelled people. Spelled Teddy. For one whole week.

She 'wangled' some leave after their first dinner together. First night together too. ('No point in hanging about, darling,' she said, unbuttoning his uniform jacket.) She was the kind of girl who could wangle leave. 'Pa knows everyone.' Pa was an 'adviser to the government', whatever that meant, but let his only golden child run wild and free. She was twenty-two, not a child. Mummy was dead. 'So sad.'

Julia had 'pots of money' – Pa was also a lord. Teddy had been at school with the sons of plenty of lords and wasn't put off by her breeding, although he couldn't help but be a little impressed by the enormous mansion near Regent's Park that was the family's 'London house'. They had 'an ancestral pile' in Northamptonshire and 'a place' in Ireland. 'Oh, and an apartment in Paris that some disgusting *Gauleiter* is currently occupying.' Pa had moved out, staying somewhere in Westminster, and Julia had a flat in Petty France.

The London house was shut up for the duration. Everything had simply been left where it was, shrouded in dust-sheets. The enormous chandeliers still hung from the ceilings beneath their covers, looking like awkwardly wrapped presents. Valuable paintings had cloths hung

over them as if the house was in mourning. An odd assortment of dust-sheets and old bed linen – and some not so
old – had been flung over the furniture. Teddy discovered
a Louis XV couch beneath a candlewick counterpane, a
magnificent Louis XIV Boulle commode draped in a sheet,
a writing desk that had apparently belonged to Marie
Antoinette with an eiderdown stuck on top of it. He found
a Gainsborough beneath a tea-towel. He fretted for their
safety. 'Aren't you worried about these things?'

'Worried?' (It wasn't a word in her vocabulary, she was
criminally carefree, it was what attracted him to her.)

'That someone will steal them or they'll be destroyed
by a bomb?'

Julia just shrugged and said, 'We have loads of this kind
of stuff.'

He lifted the veil on a small Rembrandt every time he
passed it on the staircase. No one would miss it, he thought.
Did such careless people even deserve such treasure? If he
took the Rembrandt his life would be quite different.
He would be a thief, for one thing. A different narrative.

There were a couple of Rubens, a Van Dyke, a Bernini
in the hall, all kinds of Italian Renaissance treasures. But it
was the little Rembrandt that stole his heart. He could have
robbed the entire house. There was a key beneath an urn at
the front door. When he chided Julia for the lack of security
she laughed and said, 'Yes, but it's a very *heavy* urn.' (It
was.)

'You can have it as far as I'm concerned, darling,' Julia
said when she caught him looking at the Rembrandt. 'It's
a murky old thing.'

'Thank you, but no.' What a pillar of moral rectitude. In

later life, he wished he had appropriated the painting. No one would have believed it was a genuine Rembrandt, it would have existed entirely for his own guilty pleasure, hanging on a suburban wall. He should have done. The London house was hit by a V-2, the Rembrandt lost for ever.

'You can keep your art as far as I'm concerned,' Julia said. 'I'm very shallow, I'm afraid.' In Teddy's experience people who claimed to be one thing were generally the opposite, although in Julia's case it was true. She was magnificently philistine.

They didn't go to Petty France. Instead they spent their romantic interlude in the London house or, on one memorable night in which sleep played no part, at a suite in the Savoy that seemed to be permanently available to her. There were 'gallons' of champagne in the cellar of the London house and they spent the week drinking it and making love on top of a variety of priceless antiques. It struck Teddy that it was possible that Julia lived her life like this all the time.

She had a perfect body, the Grecian-goddess type. He could imagine her as a goddess, cool and indifferent, quite happy to condemn some poor Actaeon to be torn to death by hounds. Nancy could never inhabit the cruel world of Olympus, she was more of a merry pagan sprite.

'Who is Nancy?'

'My fiancée.'

'Oh, darling, how sweet.'

He was rather put out by her response. The piquancy of a little jealousy would have added to the whole experience.

That's what it was, an experience, his heart was never truly engaged. He was playing at romance. This was after Hamburg, after Beethoven, after Keith died, not long before Nuremberg, when he didn't care too much about anything, particularly beautiful shallow blondes. But he appreciated the gift of having unfettered, lusty sex ('Filthy,' as Julia put it), so that in later years when he returned to the more common-or-garden type he at least knew what it was to fuck with abandon. He wasn't fond of the word but it was the only one that would do for Julia really.

On the last day of his leave he turned up at the London house and shifted the heavy urn to find no key, only a piece of paper bearing a scribbled message: 'Darling, it was lovely, see you around, Jxx.' He rather resented being locked out of the house, he had begun to feel quite at home there.

Not long afterwards Julia was posted to an Army ordnance base and was one of seventeen people who were killed when a bomb dump accidentally exploded. Teddy was already in the POW camp by then and didn't find out about this incident until years later when he read about her father's death in his own newspaper ('Peer in sex scandal falls to death').

He imagined Julia's perfect white limbs broken and scattered like ancient statuary. It was old news, too old for him really to care – Nancy had just embarked on her illness. He hadn't known about the London house either until he read it in the same newspaper article ('Many priceless works of art lost during the war'). He mourned the little Rembrandt more than he did Julia, who he hadn't thought of for a long time.

But that was in the future. Now he was returning from Jackdaws with Keith and finding Fox Corner's drawing room alive with guests. Sylvie had invited people for lunch, people Teddy had never met and in whom he had little interest.

There was a pontificating local councillor and his wife, a solicitor (a self-styled 'old-fashioned bachelor') who seemed to be lining himself up as a prospective suitor for Sylvie. There was also a widow, rather elderly, who complained a good deal, particularly about how hard the war had made her life, and finally a 'man of the cloth', as Sylvie referred to him. Not just an ordinary cleric but a bishop – a superior kind of devil-dodger. He was rather unctuous, as Teddy expected a bishop to be.

They were drinking dainty glasses of sherry – the men too – and Sylvie said to Keith and Teddy, 'I expect you would prefer beer.'

'I wouldn't say no to a jar, Mrs T,' Keith replied, at his most affably Australian.

Sylvie seemed to have assembled a cast list of characters for a banal farce. It was the kind of bourgeois society that she had little time for usually and Teddy couldn't work out why she had chosen to broaden her social circle with the great and the good of the parish. It was only when she started making a performance out of pointing out his medal ribbons and boasting about his 'brave deeds' – even though he had told her virtually nothing about his 'deeds', brave or otherwise – that he began to suspect that she was showing him off to this collection of worthies. He found he had absolutely nothing to say when they urged him to recount some of his 'feats of derring-do' and it was left to Keith to entertain them with humorous accounts of their exploits, so that the war began to sound like a series of madcap escapades, rather like one of Augustus's adventures.

'But still,' the bachelor said, in search of something more barbaric, 'it's not all fun and games. You've certainly been bombing the daylights out of Jerry.'

'Yes, well done,' the local councillor said pompously. 'A good show. Hamburg has been a great success for the RAF, hasn't it?'

'Yes, well done, lads,' the bishop said, making a slight toasting gesture with his sherry glass. 'Now let's get the rest of them.'

All of them, Teddy wondered?

'I should warn you,' Ursula had written to Teddy, 'that the pig has been killed.' Teddy had met Sylvie's pig on several occasions since its arrival as a rotund pink piglet. He had rather admired the pig. It had no pretensions to grandeur, snuffling and truffling around in its knocked-together pen, grateful for any scraps that came its way. And now, apparently, the poor creature was being packaged up as bacon and sausages and ham and all the other products that a pig was destined to be in its afterward. To be hawked around for money by spivvy Sylvie, presumably.

They were to eat roast leg of pork with vegetables from the garden and apple sauce bottled from last autumn's apples, and a Queen of Puddings provided mostly by the overworked chickens. Teddy couldn't help but think of the pig when it was alive, still in possession of four sturdy legs.

'Everything from Fox Corner,' Sylvie said proudly, 'from the pig on the table to the jam and eggs in the pudding.' Perhaps she was advertising her household economy to the bachelor. Or the bishop. Teddy couldn't imagine his mother remarrying. She had settled into a rather stout, self-satisfied middle age and enjoyed having her own way.

'That's a smell to raise a man's spirits,' the bishop said, raising his refined episcopal nose to sniff the roasting pig.

'You're very ingenious to be so self-sufficient, my dear,' the solicitor said to Sylvie, draining his sherry from the tiny glass and looking round hopefully for a decanter.

'There should be medals for women on the home front,' the councillor's wife grumbled, 'for our ingenuity, if not for everything we have to suffer,' a remark that provoked more grousing from the elderly widow. ('Suffering! Tell me about it.')

Teddy felt himself growing hot and restless. 'Excuse me for a moment,' he said, putting his glass of beer down. 'All right, mate?' Keith said as he pushed past him. 'Just need a bit of air,' Teddy said.

'Off to have a smoke,' he heard Keith say, making an excuse for him.

Teddy whistled for the dog, which he found outside, intent on studying the chickens safely interned behind the wire in their run. Lucky, obedient to the last, followed Teddy into the lane.

The dog slipped beneath the gate into the dairy herd's field and then stopped in bewilderment at the sight of the cows. 'Cows,' Teddy said. 'They won't hurt you,' he added, but the dog began barking wildly. He was both nervous and defiant, a mixture that was unsettling to the normally easy-going cows, and Teddy retrieved the dog before he could cause any trouble.

Hamburg *had* been a 'good show', he reflected. There had been perfect flying conditions in the run in over the North Sea and the Germans had jammed the wrong Gee chain so that the navigators were able to get reliable fixes on the target from the radio navigation system. (*Let's talk about something more interesting than the mechanics of bombing.*)

After the long journey over the featureless dark of the North Sea it had been a relief to reach the German coast and see the route markers dropped by the Pathfinders, golden candles of fire spilling gracefully and dripping to earth, marking their wicket gate, gathering and shepherding them towards the straight and narrow way of the bomb run. It had been emphasized to them at the briefing that the bomber stream needed to pack itself tightly, not only to concentrate the bombing but also so that Window, which they were using for the first time, could protect as many of them as possible. There had been some scepticism about the mysterious Window and in the briefing you would have thought that the boffins had come up with the Holy Grail, but in the event the crews were all as pleased as punch with it. Window was their new 'secret weapon' – a kind of aluminium chaff.

Some aircraft had already been modified with a special chute, but most, like *Q-Queenie*, were still using their flare chute to deploy Window. It was a wretched job and Teddy had sent a very resentful Keith down to the freezing fuselage where, hampered by his portable oxygen bottle as well as a torch and a stopwatch, he had to perch next to the flare chute where, every sixty seconds, he had to remove the elastic from the awkward bundles and post them out of the aircraft. But, oh, the beauty of them, those long silvery streamers that fell to earth and snowed up the German ground radar so that their fighters couldn't be vectored on to the bombers. They could see the search-lights roaming aimlessly around the sky while the blue master beams stood to helpless attention. The German ack-ack guns had nothing to aim at, so as they approached the city itself there was only a barrage of flak sent up in blind hope, like firecrackers on Bonfire Night. They had reached the target without acquiring any real damage.

And what a target – 2,300 tons of bombs and over 350,000 incendiaries in an hour. A world record. The first Target Indicators dropped over the city by the Pathfinders were fountains of red and gold, showering the earth below, and they were followed by lovely green ones, so that the overall effect was of jewelled fireworks cascading in the black sky. The coloured lights were joined by the bright quick flashes of the high explosive and the larger, slower explosions of the 4,000-lb cookies, and everywhere there was the enchanting twinkling of white lights as thousands upon thousands of incendiaries rained down on the city.

The intention was for the heavy bombs to blow open the buildings, taking the roofs off so that the incendiaries could fall and start fires, turning the buildings into fiercely burning chimneys. That's what bombers did, they set fire to whatever was on the earth below them. It was tinder dry in the city, hardly any humidity, perfect conditions for finally showing Hitler (and the British government) what Bomber Command could do.

Q-Queenie had gone in on the second wave, behind the Pathfinders and the Lancasters who had already lit up the target for them.

It was like Christmas, the glitter and sparkle of incendiaries speckling the sky. Red fires were glowing everywhere although they soon began to be obscured by a dark pall of smoke. Keith talked them in, to the centre of this pyrotechnic display, 'Left, right, right a bit more—' until Teddy heard him say 'Bombs away' and they made for home as another four waves of bombers were still making their unharried way to the target.

They went to Essen the next night, another maximum effort, and then were stood down for a much-needed twenty-four hours while the Americans took over, two daylight raids on Hamburg, one after the other, stoking the fires with incendiaries and creating more with their high explosives. Teddy felt sorry for the American fliers – travelling in tight formation in daylight they took the brunt of the German defences. Q-Queenie had made an emergency landing at Shipdham USAAF base a few weeks ago and they had been given a rousing welcome. They hardly ever came across their Allied counterparts, so it was heartening to find themselves in the midst of an American squadron whose fliers were, as Tommy, their Geordie, put it, 'Just like us.' Except shinier and newer, the gloss not quite as worn off, although it soon would be. And with much, much better food, so that when she eventually returned to her own station Q-Queenie was laden with chocolate and cigarettes, canned fruit and goodwill.

The weather on their stand-down had been good and the crews lounged in lawn chairs or set up card tables outside. Someone organized a cricket match in an adjacent field, a rough, enjoyable game, but many simply slept, worn out by war. Teddy and Keith went for a long, lazy bike ride with a couple of WAAFS, Lucky lolloping beside them. When he got tired he was put in the basket on the front of one of the WAAFs' bikes where he sat like a proud figurehead, his ears flattened by the breeze. 'In the cockpit,' the WAAF said. Edith, a chop girl you couldn't help feeling sorry for. The last three aircrew she had dated had failed to return from ops and now no one would go near her. In a darker moment Teddy had considered sleeping with her just to see what would happen to him afterwards. Perhaps he still would, he thought. She was keen on him, but then all the WAAFs were.

They ate fish-paste sandwiches and drank water from a stream and it was as if the Third Reich didn't exist and England was restored to her green and pleasant self.

He checked his watch. Three o'clock. They would have eaten lunch at Fox Corner without him. He hoped so anyway. He had left Keith in their unholy clutches long enough, he supposed.

They crossed the meadow, in full summer regalia – flax and larkspur, buttercups, corn poppies, red campion and ox-eye daisies – and skirted the edges of one of the Home Farm's big wheat fields. The wheat glimmered and undulated in the breeze. He had often worked on the harvest in these fields, punctuated by beer-and-cheese lunches with the farmhands beneath a hot sun. Hard to believe life was so simple once. He remembered it now as a romantic pre-war idyll, *You sunburnt sicklemen of August weary, come hither from the furrow and be merry*, but he supposed for the farmhands there was no Shakespearian pastoral to be found in their toiling and the harvest was just another turn of the agricultural year and its never-ending, grinding labour.

There was a scattering of poppies amongst the wheat, red spots of blood amongst the gold, and he thought of those other fields in that other war, his father's war, and felt a great fall inside himself at the memory of Hugh. He wished his father was in Fox Corner, waiting for his return with a glass of beer in the garden or a tumbler of whisky in the growlery.

The dog had bounded off into the middle of the wheat and he could no longer see it but he could hear it barking with excitement, not nervous now, so it must have found some creature less threatening than a cow – a rabbit or a harvest mouse. Teddy whistled so that the dog could keep its bearings and navigate its way out of the field.

'Time to go,' he said, when it finally scampered back.

'We thought we'd lost you,' Sylvie said crossly.

'Not yet,' Teddy said.

'All right?' Keith asked, handing him a glass of beer. Keith was sitting on the terrace, looking very at home. The great and the good appeared to have left.

* * *

He decided to spend the last night of his leave with Ursula. Keith was off on the razzle with some of his fellow countrymen.

Teddy walked through the parks and then took up a sentry post outside Ursula's office and waited to surprise her when she came out from work.

'Teddy!'

'The very same.'

'And Lucky! What a treat to see him.' Again, Teddy felt himself coming in second to the dog. Lucky was beside himself at seeing Ursula again. 'This is good timing,' she said, 'or perhaps you'll think it bad. How do you feel about chumming me along to the Proms? I've got two tickets and the friend who was coming with me has had to drop out. We can eat afterwards.'

'Splendid,' Teddy said, groaning inwardly at the idea of attending a concert, possibly the last thing he felt like doing. The sea air and his twenty-four-hour furlough with Nancy, not to mention the lunch at Fox Corner, had drained him of whatever reserve of energy he had left and he would rather have gone to a cinema and fallen asleep in the fuggy dark, or perhaps drunk the night into oblivion somewhere pleasantly unchallenging.

'Oh, good,' Ursula said.

She decided to leave the dog in her office. 'Against the rules, I expect,' she said cheerfully, but there would be a lot of people working through the night, 'and he'll be spoiled rotten'. Lucky was a pragmatic dog and immediately attached himself to one of the secretaries.

It was a beautiful evening and they enjoyed the short walk along to the Royal Albert Hall. They were early and there was still plenty of sunshine to warm them in Kensington Gardens, where they took a seat on a bench and ate the remains of Ursula's lunchtime sandwiches that she hadn't had time to finish because she'd had to 'run up and down' to Whitehall. 'All I do really is move paper around. I think it's what most people do. Not you, of course.'

'Thank goodness,' Teddy said, remembering the tedium of the bank. If by some chance he survived the war, what on earth was he going to do? The idea of an afterward filled him with dread.

His sister stood up and brushed crumbs off her skirt. 'Best get going, don't want to keep Beethoven waiting.'

They had good seats, the tickets given to Ursula by 'someone'. She had hoped to bring her friend, Miss Wolf, but she'd had to cancel. 'It's very sad,' Ursula said, 'she's just learned that her nephew in the Army has been killed in North Africa. Miss Wolf is a simply *splendid* person, a shining star, and she is a great believer in the power of music to heal. And to hear Beethoven in the midst of war, especially *this* Beethoven, would have pleased her enormously.'

Which Beethoven, Teddy wondered? He read the programme notes. The Ninth. The BBC Symphony Concert Orchestra with the Alexandra Choir, Adrian Boult conducting.

'*Alle Menschen werden Brüder,*' Ursula said. 'Do you think it's possible? One day? That all men could be brothers one day? People – by which I largely mean men – have been killing each other since time began. Since

Cain threw a rock at Abel's head or whatever it was he did to him.'

'I don't think the Bible's that specific,' Teddy said.

'We have terrifically *tribal* instincts,' Ursula said. 'We're all primitives underneath, that's why we had to invent God, to be the voice of our conscience, or we would be killing each other left, right and centre.'

'I think that's what we *are* doing.'

The auditorium was rapidly filling up, people shuffling in, and they had to move their knees to one side several times to let people pass. Down below, the promenaders were jockeying politely for good spots in the arena. 'These are rather good seats,' Teddy said. 'Whatever man gave you them must like you a lot.'

'Yes, but they're not the *best* seats,' Ursula said, seeming to find this remark very amusing. 'Those were huge raids last week,' she said unexpectedly, the non sequitur knocking him off balance.

'Yes.'

'Do you think Hamburg is finished?'

'Yes. No. I don't know. Probably. From seventeen thousand feet you can't see much. Just fire.' The choir began to take their places.

'They took a real hammering,' Ursula continued.

'They?'

'The people. In Hamburg.' Teddy didn't think of them as people. They were towns. They were factories and railway yards, fighter stations, docks. 'Do you ever have any doubts?' she persisted.

'Doubts?'

'You know, about area bombing.'

'Area bombing?' It was a term he had heard, but not one that he had given a great deal of thought to.

'Indiscriminate attacks. The civilian population considered to be a legitimate target – innocent people. It doesn't make you feel . . . uncomfortable?'

He turned and looked at her, astonished by her bluntness. (*Uncomfortable?*) 'We don't *target* civilians! Can you devise a war where no one is killed? We have to destroy their industry, their economy, if we're to win. Their housing, too, if necessary. I'm doing – we're doing – what's been asked of us to defend our country, to defend freedom. We're waging war against a deadly foe and we're risking our lives every time we fly.' He could hear himself slipping into rhetoric and grew irritated, more with himself than Ursula, for surely she of all people understood the concept of duty.

Now let's get the rest of them, Sylvie's bishop had said yesterday.

'And how do you define "innocent" anyway?' he pressed on. 'Workers in factories that are making bombs? Or guns, or aircraft, or steel, or ball-bearings or tanks? The Gestapo? Hitler?' He was most definitely into hyperbole now. 'And let's not forget it was the Germans who started this war.'

'I rather think we started it at Versailles,' Ursula said quietly.

Teddy sighed, regretting his choleric response. Methinks he doth protest too much. 'Sometimes,' he said, 'I think if only I could go back in time and shoot Hitler, or, better still, kill him at birth.'

'But then, I suppose,' Ursula said, 'you could keep

going back, unpicking history all the way, until you arrived at Cain and Abel again.'

'Or the apple.'

'Shush,' someone said crossly as the first violinist made his way on to the platform. They joined in the applause, relieved to end the conversation. Ursula put her hand on his arm and whispered, 'I'm sorry. I haven't lost faith in the war. I just wondered how you felt. If you were, you know, all right.'

'Of course I am.' Teddy was grateful when, to much acclaim, Boult appeared. A great silence fell.

Ursula should congratulate him, not raise doubts. Operation Gomorrah was considered an enormous success by the crews. It was a turning point, it would push the war nearer to its conclusion, it would help those troops, the 'brown bodies', who at some future date were going to have to land again on European soil and battle their way to the end. 'A good prang,' his flight engineer, Geoff Smythson, had written in his log book. *A good show*, the solicitor said yesterday, slavering in anticipation of the poor pig.

The crews had been pleased, Teddy thought, glancing at his sister, now utterly absorbed in the music. Surely everyone was?

Later, much later, long after the war was over, he learned that it had been a 'firestorm'. He had not heard that word, not during the war. He learned that they had been sent deliberately to residential districts. That people were boiled in fountains and baked in cellars. They were burnt alive or suffocated, they were reduced to ash or melted fat. They were trapped like flies on flypaper as they tried to cross the molten tarmac of the streets where they lived. A good prang. ('An eye for an eye,' Mac said at the squadron reunion. Until everyone was blind, Teddy wondered?) Gomorrah. Armageddon. An Old Testament God of spite and vengeance. Once they started there was no going back. Hamburg wasn't a turning point, it was a staging post. In the end it led to Tokyo, it led to Hiroshima, and then later the whole argument about innocence became irrelevant when you could flick a switch on one continent and destroy thousands on another. At least Cain had to look at Abel's face.

The RAF had gone back for a second innings on the Tuesday night and found the city still ablaze – one vast inferno, like a glowing, incandescent carpet spread across the landscape, smothering everything beneath it.

It was like flying over an immense volcano containing the fiery heart of hell from which violent explosions would occasionally erupt. The City of Destruction. Its ferocity, its terrible awful beauty, almost returned poetry to Teddy. A medieval apocalypse, he thought.

'Navigator, come and look at this,' he said, persuading Sandy Worthington out from behind his curtain. 'You'll never see anything like it again.'

Keith didn't need to direct them in, they could see the conflagration from many miles away and as they flew over the boiling, bubbling cauldron of flames he said, 'Let's put another shovelful of coal on the fire, shall we, skipper?'

A filthy dense column of smoke rose as high as the aircraft, and they could feel the tremendous heat rising up from below. They could smell the smoke through their oxygen masks, and something else, even less welcome, and when they landed back at the squadron they discovered that *Q-Queenie*'s Perspex was covered in a thin film of soot.

The smoke and the soot of the fire had risen up to meet them thousands of feet in the air. And the something else, something that Teddy would never forget, something he could never talk about – the smell of burning flesh rising from the pyre.

He knew then in his secret heart that one day a reckoning would come due.

Sometimes a German fighter would infiltrate the bomber stream as it made its way back across the North Sea, a particularly mean trick. It might pick off an aircraft as it headed home or even as it came in to land, just as safety was at hand. A few weeks after the Battle of Hamburg, after dodging and weaving for months, *Q-Queenie* was finally caught on the way back from a raid on Berlin.

It had been a long hard struggle to get back from the Big City and they were all sleepy and cold. They had eaten their chocolate, drunk their coffee, taken their wakey-wakey pills, and it was a great relief when they finally saw the red light on top of the church spire in the village nearest to the airfield. Teddy presumed the light was there to prevent them crashing into the spire but they always regarded it as a beacon guiding them home. The flare path was lit up and they heard the cheery tones of a WAAF in the control tower clearing them to land, but no sooner had she spoken than the flare path was extinguished, the airfield plunged into darkness, and the call sign for intruders was broadcast.

Teddy switched off *Q-Queenie*'s lights and pulled back on the controls to take her up again. Somewhere, anywhere but there, because he could see tracer fire crossing in front of them and the gunners were yelling that there was a bandit, but neither of them seemed to know where he was and their guns were hosing all over the sky. There was no sky to corkscrew down into, not enough speed to do anything, and he thought perhaps the best thing he could do was just land any old how, pancake down on whatever was below them.

Before he could do anything, *Q-Queenie* was pummelled by cannon fire from the fighter. It must have hit her in the undercarriage because they landed on one wheel and she tipped over, one wing high, the other digging into the ground, and they left the runway and screamed through a field before hitting a tree that they all swore had never been there before but was real enough to flip them over, like a giant insect, and the world inside *Q-Queenie* was turned upside down.

There were a lot of groans coming from behind Teddy, but they were the groans of people who had been thrown around, bruised and battered, not mortally wounded. He could hear a lot of angry Norwegian. Only Keith was silent, and Sandy Worthington and their Geordie mid-upper kicked open the bottom – now top – escape hatch and helped to drag him through it.

As they exited the topsy-turvy aircraft, the flare-path lights came back on and Teddy was surprised to see that they were still within the boundary of the airfield and the blood wagon and fire engine were already racing out to them. Apart from the fact that they were upside down – or perhaps because of it – it was a miraculous landing. For this 'brave deed' he added to the fruit salad of ribbons on his uniform – a bar to go with his DFC.

Keith had lost a lot of blood, he'd been hit by the cannon fire before they crashed. He was deathly silent although his eyes were half open and his little finger was fluttering. No last words. *Well, good luck to you then.*

They laid him on the ground, and Teddy pulled him on to his lap and held him in his arms, awkwardly, a brutal *pietà*. Keith's luck had ceased to be widdershins and had become ordinary rotten stuff. And it had run out. Teddy knew he wasn't going to last more than a few seconds and saw the moment when the finger stopped fluttering and the half-open eyes lost the light, and he was sorry that he couldn't think of anything to say to Keith that might have made him feel better about leaving this life. But there wasn't anything really, was there?

When he got back to his quarters, Teddy stripped off his bloody uniform and emptied the pockets. His cigarettes, the silver hare and, finally, the tardily taken photograph of himself and Nancy and the dog on the promenade by the sea. A smear across the top, still wet. Keith's blood. It seemed precious, like a relic. 'Tea,' he told his granddaughter when she asked about it, not because she wouldn't have been interested but because it was a private thing.

He showed his feelings to the dog alone, pressing his

face into the fur of its neck to stifle his emotions. It suffered for a while and then struggled out of his arms.

'Sorry,' Teddy said, pulling himself together.

But that was several weeks away yet, in the future. *Now*, in the present, in the Royal Albert Hall, Beethoven was performing his secret ministry on Teddy.

Teddy resolved to simply *feel* the music and stopped searching for words to describe it, and by the time the fourth movement came around and Roy Henderson, the baritone, began to sing (*O Freude!*), the hairs on the back of his neck were standing up. In her seat beside him, Ursula was almost quivering with the power of emotion, like a coiled spring, a bird ready to rise from the ground at any moment. Towards the end of the final movement, when the magnificence of the Choral becomes almost unbearable, Teddy had the odd sensation that he might actually have to hold on to his sister to prevent her rising into the air and taking flight.

They left the Albert Hall and walked into the balmy evening. They were silent for a long time as the dusk gathered around them.

'Numinous,' Ursula said, breaking the silence eventually. 'There's a spark of the divine in the world – not God, we're done with God, but *something*. Is it love? Not silly romantic love, but something more profound . . .?'

'I think it's perhaps something we don't have a name for,' Teddy said. 'We want to name everything. Perhaps that's where we've gone wrong.'

'"And whatsoever Adam called every living creature,

that was the name thereof." Having dominion over everything has been a terrible curse.'

Afterwards – because it turned out that there was to be an afterwards for Teddy – he resolved that he would try always to be kind. It was the best he could do. It was all that he could do. And it might be love, after all.

1960

His Little Unremembered Acts of Kindness and of Love

It had begun with a headache, a terrible one, in the middle of the school day. This was before they moved to York and Nancy was still teaching at the secondary modern in Leeds. A wretched Monday in winter, a raw east wind and precious little daylight. 'A bit under the weather,' Nancy said when Teddy remarked over breakfast that she looked 'peaky'.

At lunchtime she went to the sickroom and the school nurse gave her a couple of aspirin, but they had no effect and she had to abandon teaching the first period of the afternoon and instead took up residence in the sickroom. 'Sounds like a migraine,' the school nurse said authoritatively. 'Just lie down in the dark and rest.' So she did, on the sickroom's uncomfortable little camp bed with its scratchy red blanket, the usual occupants of which were teenage girls with period pains. After half an hour or so she struggled to a sitting position and vomited all over the red blanket. 'Oh, God, I am *so* sorry,' she said to the nurse.

'Definitely a migraine,' the nurse said. She was the maternal sort and after cleaning up she patted Nancy's hand and said, 'You'll soon be as right as ninepence.'

She *did* feel a bit better after being sick and was well enough to drive home to Ayswick – rather cautiously – before the end of the school afternoon, although it felt as if a swarm of bees was busy inside her head.

When Nancy arrived home, Viola was already there with Ellen Crowther. Mrs Crowther was the local woman they had employed to pick up Viola from the village primary school and wait with her until one or other of them returned from work. Mrs Crowther's own 'brood' was grown and gone but she had a husband, who was a farmhand, and an ancient father-in-law ('the old man'), both of whom sounded more demanding than any child, even Viola. She was a witchy-looking woman, thinning black hair scraped into a knot and a twisted expression due to some childhood palsy. Despite these attributes she seemed rather characterless, worn away by service and obedience. 'Do you *like* Mrs Crowther?' Nancy once asked Viola and Viola gave her a puzzled look and said, 'Mrs who?'

Usually by the time Nancy got home Mrs Crowther was ready to leave, wrapped up in headscarf and brown belted gabardine mac, and out of the door like a greyhound from a trap before Nancy had time to say 'hello'. Her husband (and perhaps the old man too) seemed to be a stickler for punctuality, particularly when it came to tea being on the table. 'I'll get a row if I'm late,' were Mrs Crowther's usual words as she dashed off.

Arriving home earlier than usual, the bees still diligently at work in her head, Nancy must have entered the house more quietly than she realized as neither Viola nor Mrs Crowther noticed her. Even Bobby the dog failed to greet her. Viola was sitting at the big farmhouse table reading *Bunty*, holding a ham sandwich in one hand while twirling a lock of hair around a finger on the other – a surprisingly irritating habit that they had been unable to break her of. Mrs Crowther was writing what looked like a shopping list in a stubby joiner's pencil on the back of an envelope, a cup of tea to hand. Nancy felt oddly affected by this domestic tableau. The peaceful ordinariness of it, perhaps – the knitted cosy on the teapot, the way Mrs Crowther was stirring the sugar in her cup without taking her eyes off her shopping list. The frown of concentration on Viola's face as she assiduously ate her way through her sandwich while lost in this week's adventure of 'The Four Marys'.

For a moment, as she stood unseen in the doorway, Nancy experienced a sudden, odd sense of detachment. She was invisible, an observer, looking in on a life that she was somehow barred from. She began to feel dangerously untethered, as if she might simply float away at any moment and not be able to get back to where she belonged. She started to feel panic, but at that moment Viola looked up from her comic and spotted her. 'Mummy!' she exclaimed, her face lighting up. The spell was broken and Nancy crossed the threshold and entered the safety of the kitchen, the old Aga throwing out comfort and warmth to welcome her.

Mrs Crowther said, 'Goodness, you gave me a fright standing there. For a minute I thought you were a ghost. You're as white as any ghost would be,' she added (as if she was familiar with spirits). 'Are you feeling all right? Here – sit down. Let me pour you a cup of tea.'

'I had a migraine at school,' Nancy said, sinking into a chair at the table. The bees moved restlessly in her head, behind her eyes. Mrs Crowther poured the tea and before Nancy could protest she stirred three spoonfuls of sugar into the cup.

'Hot sweet tea,' Mrs Crowther said. 'Just what you need.' It was strange being ministered to by someone who was normally a blur of gabardine in the hallway. (Mrs Crowther proved to have unsuspected reservoirs of small talk.) 'Thank you,' Nancy said, enormously grateful for the tea, even with its heavy charge of sugar.

'You're home early,' Viola said. She was suspicious of any change in routine, disliking spontaneity. Was it because she was an only child? Or simply a child?

'Yes, darling, I am.' When the tea was drunk, and, on Mrs Crowther's recommendation, she had eaten a Rich Tea biscuit to settle her stomach ('Works a treat, doesn't it?'), she said to Mrs Crowther, 'I know it's an imposition, but would you mind hanging on until my husband gets home? I think I might go and lie down.'

She must have fallen fast asleep. When she woke it was dark, but the bedroom door was open and the light was on in the hall. The bees were silenced, gone to find a new queen. The clock by the bed said nine o'clock. She felt thick-headed but much better.

'Hello, you,' Teddy said when she came downstairs. 'Mrs Crowther told me you had a migraine, so I let you sleep.' (Nancy wondered if Mrs Crowther had been given 'a row' from her husband and the old man.) 'I gave her a bit extra for hanging on. I said this morning that you looked peaky – that must have been why. Shall I fry you a chop for your supper?'

She didn't have another migraine, just a few more headaches than normal, nothing as startling as that day in the sickroom. 'I expect your job is rather taxing,' the optician said when she visited him to discover why she was occasionally seeing a wave of light in her left eye, a little shimmering line of gold that was actually rather pretty. 'Optical migraine,' he said, peering into her eye, so close to her that she could smell the peppermint he had taken to mask (not very successfully) the oniony smell of his lunch. 'You don't necessarily experience pain with them, dear.' He was quite elderly, the avuncular sort, and had practised for years in their small local town. There was nothing, he said reassuringly, that he didn't know about eyes.

'And sometimes when I've been writing a lot on the blackboard,' Nancy said, 'my eyesight goes a bit blotchy, like Vaseline rubbed on glass, and I can't read or write properly.'

'Definitely an optical migraine,' he said.

'I had a proper migraine recently,' she said, 'and a few more headaches than usual.'

'There you go then,' he said.

'My mother used to have headaches,' she said, recalling

her mother dragging herself up the stairs to her darkened bedroom, her sad, uncomplaining smile when she said to them, 'One of my heads, I'm afraid.' That used to make them laugh (not when she was in pain, they were not cruel daughters). 'The Hydra,' they called her affection-ately. 'But a nice one,' Millie said. 'A lovely, darling Mummy Hydra.'

Later, Nancy wondered if she had sensed something, a kind of premonition, that had motivated her to choose that particular evening to suggest uprooting the three of them and moving into town, where life would be easier and more convenient. As she left the optician's, however, armed with a prescription for reading glasses ('Just the age you've reached, dear, nothing to worry about'), the thought uppermost in her mind was the pot of tea and the toasted teacake that she was going to treat herself to in the café around the corner before setting off on the rather arduous cycle home. It was a hot day and Teddy had the car. He was going to an agricultural show, a reluctant Viola in tow. She was awfully tired, Nancy thought, but the tea would buck her up.

It did, and as she was sorting out her change for a tip for the waitress she was struck with the thought that the only thing that was happening to her – to her and Teddy (and even Viola, although less urgently) – was that they were simply growing older. Otherwise their lives stayed the same. They were treading water, plodding along in a rut. Why shouldn't they do something different, shake themselves up a little?

'Plodding?' Teddy said, a fleeting spasm of distress taking

hold of his features. They were in bed – cocoa and library books, and so on – a good definition of 'plodding' in anyone's lexicon, Nancy supposed. She remembered Sylvie saying, 'Marriage blunts one so.'

'It's not an insult,' she said, but Teddy didn't look convinced.

One weekend, not long after they had made the move to York, Nancy was taking the Sunday roast from the oven when, with no warning at all, her left arm gave way and the pan and its contents clattered to the floor. Teddy must have heard the noise because he came rushing through to the kitchen and said, 'Are you all right?'

'Yes, yes, fine,' she said, surveying with dismay the carnage of lamb and potatoes, not to mention the hot fat that had splattered everywhere. 'Not burnt?' Teddy said anxiously. No, she reassured him, not burnt. 'I'm a clumsy dolt, I really am.'

'I'll fetch a cloth.'

'I suppose that I'm used to the Aga in the old house and I just – I don't know – misjudged something. Oh, the poor lamb,' she added sadly, as if the joint was an old friend. 'Do you think we can salvage it – scrape it up off the floor and pretend nothing happened?' The leg of lamb seemed to have crusted itself in every last bit of grit and dirt on what Nancy had previously thought was a clean kitchen floor. She silently berated herself for her sluttish housewifery. 'Could we wash it under the hot tap? We wouldn't have let it go to waste during the war. We still have carrots,' she added hopefully. 'And mint sauce.'

Teddy laughed and said, 'I think I'd better heat up a tin

of beans and scramble some eggs. I can't see Viola eating carrots for Sunday lunch.'

There had been other little things, numbness and tingle in that rogue left arm, more headaches and another awful migraine that started on a Friday evening and didn't clear until Monday morning. It prompted her into visiting their new GP, hoping for a prescription for strong painkillers. After some rather odd tests – walking in a straight line, moving her head in different directions, as if testing her for drunkenness – the GP said he wanted to refer her to the hospital. He was the youthful partner of an older doctor in the practice and was eager not to make mistakes. 'But no need for alarm,' he said. 'You're probably right about it being migraine.' No hurry either, apparently, and by the time the appointment card for the specialist came through the letter-box Nancy thought the hospital must have forgotten about her. She had told Teddy none of this. There seemed no point in worrying him. (He was a worrier, Nancy wasn't.) She supposed the results would be vague and she would end up like her mother, having 'heads'. She doubted she could suffer as patiently.

It was perfect spring weather on the day of Nancy's hospital appointment and when she left school at break time ('Back by lunchtime'), she decided to walk to the hospital. If she planned her route she could walk part of the way on the Bar Walls and enjoy the daffodils, recently come into flower and now in their 'golden pomp' – a phrase she recalled from an old column of Agrestis. Teddy had been 'enraptured' by the wild daffodils he had encountered unexpectedly on a woodland walk a couple of years ago.

Teddy had, so far, kept on his Nature Notes. It was a short piece once a month, he argued (to himself), and he could easily drive out to the countryside – they could all go, take a picnic, a pair of binoculars. 'It's not quite the same, I know, as being in the *middle* of it – "the middle of nowhere",' he added rather pointedly, 'but needs must. Until the *Recorder* can find someone to replace me.' They did find someone, a year later – a woman, in fact, although the new Agrestis never admitted to this change in his sex. But by then it was of no consequence to Teddy, very little was, and he left Agrestis behind without a backward glance.

The daffodils growing on the grass slopes beneath the Bar Walls were truly lovely. There were none in the garden in the new house for some reason (surely everyone had daffodils?) and Nancy determined that she must talk to Teddy about planting some. Lots of them (a host, in fact) in a great Wordsworthian drift. He would like that. To her surprise, he had taken to gardening, perusing seed catalogues and drawing up plans and sketches. Nancy gave him free rein, although he continued to consult her – 'How do you feel about gladioli?' 'What about a small pond?' 'Peas or beans or both?'

It was when she had come down from the walls at Monkgate Bar and was waiting to cross the road at the traffic lights that a black curtain suddenly descended and covered her left eye. More of a blind than a curtain – she had never thought before about where the word came from. Her own personal blackout. She sensed disaster.

'Struck blind' – it felt biblical, although Monkgate was hardly the road to Damascus.

She managed to find a bench nearby and sat quietly waiting to see what would happen next. A revelation of faith? It seemed unlikely. If she had gone completely blind she would have called out for help, but the loss of only one eye didn't seem cause enough to involve complete strangers. ('That's ridiculous,' Millie said when she told her. 'I would have been screeching my head off.' But Nancy was not Millie.) After ten minutes or so of sitting on the bench in a kind of quiet contemplation, the blackout blind lifted – as quickly and mysteriously as it had fallen – and the sight in her eye returned.

'Nerves scrambled or something,' she said to the consultant when she eventually arrived at the hospital. 'I suppose it was jolly good luck I wasn't driving, or cycling for that matter.' She found herself chatty with relief, the crisis past, the biblical disaster averted. 'Well,' the consultant said, 'let's get you checked out thoroughly anyway, shall we?' He was neither youthful nor maternal nor avuncular and had very little to say on the subject of migraines.

Oh, and then it all just went on so quickly, like some awful express train that wouldn't stop. They did more tests, and X-rays. They were vague with her, unsure about what they were seeing, they said. She was married, wasn't she? Why didn't she bring her husband along to the next appointment? 'Not if they don't give me a diagnosis,' she said to Bea on the phone. 'They're being cagey with me for no good reason.' She knew what happened with bad cases. They told spouses, siblings, even friends, anyone but the patient, so that they could 'go on living a normal life'. She'd known a WREN at Bletchley Park – Barbara Thoms – down-to-earth type, one of the cogs in the wheel. The many wheels. Nancy had been a bigger wheel, a decoder, one of the boys. Normally she wouldn't have had much to do with a lowly cog but they had both been county netball players, had tried, and failed, to get a team going at Bletchley. (Nancy had been a Half Blue at Cambridge.) Nancy had had her own table by the end of the war, was deputy head of the hut. She had known them all – Turing, Tony Kendrick, Peter Twinn. She had loved that world, occluded, secretive, self-sufficient, but she had always understood that it was temporary, that 'normal service would be resumed'. Would have to be resumed.

Poor Barbara developed a cancer, 'very rapid, incurable'. A woman's cancer, too embarrassing for her less down-to-earth mother to go into detail over. Mrs Thoms had told someone Barbara worked with and pretty soon all the girls in Barbara's section knew. Everyone except for Barbara. They were sworn to secrecy by Mrs Thoms because that was what her doctors had advised, 'so as not to cast a shadow over what's left of her life,' she explained to them. The poor girl kept on working until she couldn't go on any longer and then went home, to die, still in ignorance, still waiting in hope to be cured.

She had almost forgotten about Barbara when Mrs Thoms wrote and said she was dead and buried. 'A quiet funeral. She never knew what was wrong, that was a comfort.' Pah! Nancy thought. If she had some horrible disease that was going to kill her she didn't want to be kept in the dark, she wanted to *know*. In fact she would have it the other way round – *she* would know and her nearest and dearest wouldn't. Why should Teddy and Viola live beneath the 'shadow'?

'You need to see someone in Harley Street,' Bea said to her. 'I've still got a few connections in the medical world.' Bea had been married to a surgeon after the war but it hadn't lasted ('I don't think I'm cut out for marriage'). 'I'll find out who's best in the field, someone who won't mess you about. But you should tell Teddy, Nancy.'

'I shall, I promise.'

She had nearly died when she gave birth to Viola and had felt somehow that she was 'proofed' against disaster. Perhaps that was why it had taken her so long to chase this thing down. And all the time it was chasing her. And her mind, of all things. If only it could have been a breast, an arm, an eye. Even if it had meant an early death, at least she would have been able to keep her mind to the end. Sometimes, when she found herself mired in the twin duties of marriage and motherhood, she thought how her life had been compromised by love. Viola coming out of the womb on a wave of anger, Teddy always putting on a cheerful front, pretending that he wasn't brooding inside.

When they first moved into this house there had been a lovely lilac that graced the front garden, but Teddy had chopped it down when it was in full scented flower in the first April. 'But why?' she said, but then saw the look in his eyes and realized it was something from the war – the great fall from grace – and he was unlikely to explain it. Teddy's war was the one enigma that she would never

decode. But it was the 1960s, for heaven's sake, she sometimes thought, finding herself losing patience. She was
tired. She seemed to spend a good deal of her time
chivvying and encouraging people – Teddy, Viola, her
pupils. It was rather like being the captain of the netball
team that she had once been.

Teddy was not the only one who had sacrificed precious
years. She had gained a First in Parts I and II of the Tripos
at Newnham, she was a Wrangler, graduated with a double
first in Mathematics in '36, was awarded the Philippa
Fawcett Prize and then had been plucked, recruited to go
to the Government Code and Cypher School in the spring
of 1940. She had given up a brilliant career for the war
and then given it up again for Teddy and Viola.

'I'm going down to Lyme to give Gertie a hand with her
house move.'

'All right. That's good of you,' Teddy said.

'It's just packing the light stuff, crockery and ornaments
and so on. Only a couple of days. I thought it would be
nice to spend some time with her, just the two of us.'

The day after she returned home there was a card from
Gertie, a watercolour of violas on the front of it – 'Our
mother's favourite flower, of course, as you know.' No, she
had forgotten, and yet she had named her daughter Viola.
It had been for Shakespeare, not her mother. How could
a daughter forget such a thing? Or, at any rate, not
consciously remember. What would her own daughter
forget in time? Nancy felt a sudden sense of desolation.
She wished her mother was still here. This would be how
Viola would feel without a mother. It was unbearable.

Hot, painful tears welled up in her eyes. She brushed them away and told herself to pull her socks up.

She continued with Gertie's card – 'I just thought I should drop you a quick note,' she wrote. 'Teddy phoned looking for you while you were "here", I hope I fudged enough, made out I was a complete dimwit. Are you sure, darling, you shouldn't tell him what's happening? (Not interfering, just saying.) Much love, G. PS. Did you come to a decision about the sideboard?'

'You should tell him,' Millie said, 'you really should. I mean I covered for you *awfully* well, saying I'd just put you on the train and everything and what a wonderful time we had in the Lakes, but Teddy's going to find out, one way or another.'

It was her sisters not her husband that Nancy had turned to, little flurries of communication between different permutations of them. She could burden her sisters but she couldn't burden Teddy. He wasn't naïve, he probably suspected something, but she wasn't going to tell him until it was definitive. At heart she would always be a mathematician, her faith in absolutes. And if the worst came to the worst, then the less time he had to suffer knowing the better.

'You have to tell him, Nancy.'

'I will, Millie, of course I will.'

She may not have been in Dorset or the Lakes, but Nancy was most certainly in London with Bea. Not, it was true, taking in *a show, maybe an exhibition*, but sitting on the sofa in her sister's rather bohemian Chelsea bedsit, nursing a glass of whisky. Ursula, sitting next to Nancy, had brought a bottle with her. 'I thought we would need something stronger than tea,' she said.

'I always have gin,' Bea said. She had been divorced for some time now from her surgeon husband. She worked at the BBC and was happy being single, she said.

Millie arrived in a fluster and out of breath from rushing up the stairs. 'I got lost,' she said. 'Sorry.'

'Whisky or gin?' Bea offered. 'Or tea?'

'I'm tempted by all three, but gin, please. A stiff one.' She glanced over at Nancy but continued to address Bea. 'I need it, don't I? It's bad, isn't it?'

'Very bad,' Bea said, her voice pitchy.

'*Completely* bad?' Millie was using a funny clipped accent, either trying not to give way to emotion or imagining herself to be a character in a play or a film, one who was putting on a stiff upper lip – Celia Johnson in *Brief Encounter* came to mind. The call of duty, the moral imperative of doing the right thing. Nancy admired it and yet something in her now rebelled. Run away, she thought, forget duty. She imagined herself fleeing down Bea's steep, narrow staircase and out into the street, along the river, on and on until she had outpaced the dread thing on her heels.

A glint in Millie's eye and a little tremor in her hand as she took the glass of gin reassured Nancy that she wasn't play-acting.

'I *am* here,' she said to her. 'You can ask me.'

'I don't think I want to ask you,' Millie said. 'I don't think I want to know.' The glint turned into a tear that rolled down her cheek and Bea pushed her gently towards a chair and then sat on the carpet at her feet.

'Well, it is true,' Nancy said calmly. 'It's been confirmed and I'm afraid it is *completely* bad, as you put it. I'm sorry to say that it's the worst it could possibly be.'

Millie let out an awful sob and her hand flew to her mouth as if she could stop the sound escaping, but too late. Bea grabbed her other hand and they clung to each other. They looked as if they were facing shipwreck. 'Is there *nothing* to be done?' Ursula asked. 'Surely—'

'No,' Nancy said, cutting her short. They would all want to be hopeful, to see possibilities, and she had moved beyond possibilities. 'He said that if perhaps it had been detected at an earlier stage there might have been something. And he won't operate,' she said, holding up a hand to silence Bea, who was about to protest. 'They can't operate because of where it is, and now it's become tangled with blood vessels' – 'Oh God,' Millie said. She looked green, she was always the most squeamish of all of them – 'which makes it impossible. An operation would, at best, be the end of me.'

'And if death is the best, what is the worst?' Ursula puzzled. Millie gave a little gasp at the word 'death', as if uttering it was somehow blasphemous.

'I would probably be left almost completely incapacitated, mentally and physically—'

'Probably?' Bea said, still clinging to hope amongst the storm-tossed wreckage.

'Almost certainly,' Nancy said. 'Which would be the end of me too, in a different way. But even that would be no good as, because of its position, they wouldn't be able to cut it all out.' Millie looked as if she was going to retch.

'It would carry on growing. Really,' Nancy said, perhaps less kindly than she had intended, 'it would be better, better for *me*, if you accept this.'

She had divined in her heart that this was coming, ever since that first visit to Harley Street, when she was supposedly helping Gertie to move house. The consultant Bea had found, Dr Morton-Fraser, was a sensible sort of Scot. 'Comes highly recommended,' Bea had said. 'Reputation for being scrupulous. No stone unturned and so on.' There had been perhaps a little hope then, less so when she returned the following month (*Wordsworth's cottage and so on*) and he showed her the X-rays and she could see how much it had already grown in a short time. 'Perhaps if you had come to me a year ago,' he said, 'but even then who knows . . .' *Very rapid, incurable* – poor Barbara Thoms's diagnosis.

'I can't bear it,' Millie murmured as Bea went round topping up their glasses. Nancy felt a sudden flash of resentment. She was the one who had to bear it, not them.

She wanted to be left alone in peace, to disappear into her own quiet world and meditate upon death. Death. Yes, she could form that blunt, obscene word too. But instead she was the one who was going to have to be kind and strong and say that everything was going to be all right (which it clearly was not) and that she had 'come to terms with it'.

'It's going to be all right,' she said to Millie. 'I'm all right. I've come to terms with it and now you must.'

'And Teddy?' Ursula said, her voice breaking. 'He phoned me this morning, Nancy. He suspects you of having an affair, for heaven's sake. You must put him out of his misery.'

Nancy laughed bitterly and said, 'And put him in a worse misery?'

'Tell him as soon as possible, it's unfair keeping him in the dark this long.' (Ursula, Nancy thought rather irritably, always Teddy's greatest champion and protector.) 'Although I suppose not Viola—'

Oh, God. Viola, Nancy thought. She was quietly convulsed with despair.

'No, not Viola,' Bea said quickly. 'She's far too young to understand.'

'We'll be there for her,' Millie said wildly. 'We'll care for her—'

'But first you have to tell Teddy,' Ursula said insistently. 'You have to go home now and tell him.'

'Yes,' Nancy sighed. 'Yes, I will.'

They all accompanied her to King's Cross and saw her on the train. Bea kissed her tenderly, as if she had suddenly turned to thinnest glass and might shatter at any moment. 'Courage,' she said. Ursula seemed to have no fear of Nancy breaking and held her tight. 'You're going to have to help Teddy,' she said urgently. 'Help him to cope with it.' Oh, lord, Nancy thought wearily, would none of them just let her be weak and irredeemably selfish?

They stood on the platform waving as the train pulled out of the station, all of them in tears, Millie in floods. You would think I was going off to war, Nancy thought. The battle, however, was already fought and lost.

*   *   *

'Plodding?' she queried.

'I know what you've been up to,' he said. In all these years she had never really seen Teddy angry, not like this, certainly. Not with her.

She went into the kitchen, walked over to the sink, turned the tap on and filled a glass with water. She had rehearsed this moment on the train (an awful journey, stuck in a carriage full of beery smokers, leering at her), but when it came to it she didn't seem to have the words. She drank the water slowly to give herself more time.

'I *know*,' Teddy said, his voice tight with this new animosity.

She turned to face him and said, 'No, Teddy. You don't know. You don't know anything.'

At first, the tumour had appeared to Nancy to be a predator, an invader, worming its way through the fibres in her brain, consuming her, but now it was settled, now there were no more *possibilities*, it was no longer the enemy. It may not be a friend (far from it), but it was *part* of her. Hers and hers alone and they would be companions to the awful end.

She left work immediately. What, after all, would be the point of staying on, giving herself away to others? Viola, who was used to travelling to and from school with Nancy, was put out that suddenly she had to make her own way. Nancy taught her how to catch the bus ('But *why*?'), explaining that she wasn't very well and needed to take some time away from teaching to get better. It was harsh for Viola that she was being thrust into an independence that she should have grown into slowly, but it had to be about practicalities now, not sentiment. The iron had entered into Nancy's soul.

She bought clothes for Viola, two and three sizes ahead, made lists and notes – where her piano teacher lived, her friends' parents' addresses and phone numbers, her likes and dislikes. Teddy, of course, knew many of Viola's preferences but even he could not have imagined the full range.

She felt, ironically, remarkably well during the first few weeks that followed the confirmation of her death sentence. That was how she thought of it, although for everyone else's sake there were euphemisms. She tidied drawers and cupboards, threw away unnecessary clutter, pared down her own wardrobe. Would she last through next winter? Would she need these drawers stuffed with woollens and vests and thick stockings? She imagined her sisters would come and sort through her clothes when she was gone, the way they had all done for their mother after the funeral. It would be a help to them if she broke the backbone of it now. She didn't discuss these rather macabre tasks with anyone. It would upset them more than it upset her, for Nancy drew considerable satisfaction from thinking that she was leaving things in good order. She imagined Gertie looking around her bedroom after she was gone, saying, 'Good old Nancy, typical of her to leave everything ship-shape and Bristol fashion.' When it came to it, of course, Gertie said no such thing, too consumed by grief for such buoyant remarks.

Teddy was confounded by all this energy and hazarded that somehow the diagnosis had been a mistake ('records get mixed up all the time'). Or perhaps she was actually getting better. 'That would be a miracle, Teddy,' she said, as gently as she could. 'There is no cure.' Hope would be the worst thing for him. Her, too. She wanted to enjoy this respite for what it was, not for what it could never be.

'But you thought I was dead during the war,' he persisted. 'Did you give up hope?'

'Yes. Yes, I did. You know I did. And you said it yourself – I thought you were dead.'

'So then when I came back it was a miracle,' he said, as if he'd won the argument. But he had come back from a POW camp, not from the dead. There was no logic in him these days, but then what did it really matter? He would stop believing in miracles soon enough.

And then all the drawers were tidied, all the lists were made. When she stopped being busy she discovered that she craved simply being on her own in the house, filling the silence with the piano, occasionally Beethoven, mostly Chopin. Her playing was rusty, but day by day she saw small improvements and said to Teddy, 'At least some things *are* capable of remedy,' but he shied away from gallows humour.

One afternoon, when she was intent on the Polonaise in E flat – fiendishly difficult – Teddy came home early, something he was doing more and more, she had noticed. She could feel him trying to fill his heart and mind with her because that was where she would live on afterwards. (Not living, just a memory, an illusion.) And in her sisters' hearts, too. And a little of her in Viola, and that would fade and be forgotten. *Our mother's favourite flower, of course, as you know*. 'My favourite flower is the bluebell,' she said apropos of nothing to Viola one day, who said, 'Oh?' indifferently, more interested in watching *Blue Peter*. But then Teddy would die, her sisters would die, Viola would die and nothing of Nancy would remain. That was how it was. The tragedy of life was death. *Sic transit gloria mundi*. 'Penny for them?' Teddy said often, too often, when she was engaged in this philosophy (pointless, by its very nature). Better to be a dumb animal like Bobby and greet every new morning in ignorance. 'Oh, my thoughts are nonsense,' she said, making an effort to smile at Teddy. 'You would feel cheated out of your penny.'

It wasn't that she didn't want to share her thoughts with Teddy or spend time with him – and Viola, of course – but she was preparing to go into the darkness on her own, a place (not even a place, a nothing) where everything would cease to matter – cocoa, library books, Chopin. Love. That list, should she choose to make it, would be endless. She chose not to make it. She was done with lists. She put her morbid philosophy aside. She played Chopin instead.

'Is that the Revolutionary?' Teddy asked, interrupting her concentration so that she played a wrong note that sounded particularly harsh to her ears. 'My mother used to play it,' he said.

Sylvie had been a terrific pianist. Sometimes Nancy used to sneak next door to listen to her. When Sylvie was in a bad mood you didn't need to go to Fox Corner to hear her, Nancy's father said, you could hear her from the end of the lane. He said this fondly. ('There goes Mrs Todd!') Major Shawcross held Sylvie in great esteem ('a magnificent creature').

It hadn't struck Nancy at the time, but perhaps Sylvie, too, had wanted to be left alone, had resented the quiet little listener in the corner of her drawing room. She had seemed lost in the music, oblivious to Nancy's presence until she finished whatever piece she was playing. Nancy couldn't help but applaud. ('Bravo, Mrs Todd!')

'Oh, it's you, Nancy,' Sylvie would say, rather sharply.

'No, not the Revolutionary, it's the Heroic,' Nancy said, her hands resting impatiently on the keys. Time's wingèd chariot, she thought. She could hear the wings beating, heavy and creaking, like a great ponderous goose. She could feel her own strength ebbing away and was powerless to fight it. 'Your mother was accomplished,' she said. 'I'm a rank amateur, I'm afraid. And it's such a difficult piece.'

'Sounded pretty good to me,' Teddy said. He was lying, she knew. 'You reminded me of Vermeer, when I came into the room just now.'

'Vermeer? Why?'

'That painting in the National Gallery. *Lady at a Virginal* – something like that anyway.'

'*A Young Woman Seated at a Virginal,*' Nancy said.

'Yes. Your memory is always so precise.'

'Why Vermeer?' she prompted.

'It was the way you turned to look at me. The enigmatic expression on your face.'

'I always thought the girl in that picture had the look of a frog about her,' Nancy said, thinking, I look enigmatic because I'm dying.

'Isn't there one of a woman standing by a virginal too?' he puzzled. 'Or am I getting them mixed up?'

'No, there are two, the National has both.'

'Same woman?' Teddy said, looking ruminative. 'Same virginal?'

Oh, do go away, my love, Nancy thought. Stop spinning out conversations so that you'll have them to look back on, stop making *memories*. Leave me to Chopin. She sighed and closed the lid of the piano and said with false cheerfulness, 'Shall we have some tea?'

'I'll make it,' Teddy said eagerly. 'Would you like cake? Do we have cake?'

'Yes, I believe we do.'

'I want you to promise me something.'

'Anything,' Teddy said. A fatal promise to make, Nancy thought. They were sitting at the dining-room table. Teddy was going through the month's bills, while Nancy was sewing Cash's nametapes on to Viola's uniform. The long school holiday was nearly over, the new school year was about to begin. The rhythm of Nancy's life had always been the school year and it seemed strange that a new one was beginning that she wouldn't see the end of.

Viola B. Todd, the nametapes said in that familiar red cursive. 'B' for Beresford, Teddy's middle name, Sylvie's name before she became a Todd. Her father had been an artist – 'very famous in his day', according to Sylvie – although the family owned none of his work. Nancy had been delighted when, investigating the art gallery in York with Viola, she had found a portrait, some civic dignitary, long forgotten now, painted by Sylvie's father at the end of the last century. The tiny brass plaque beneath read 'Llewellyn A. Beresford 1845–1903'. And a ghostly monogram of the letters L, A and B was painted in the corner of the picture. 'Look,' Nancy said to Viola, 'this was painted by your great-grandfather' – but it was a relationship too distant to have any meaning for Viola.

Nancy began a new nametape, on the collar of a school blouse, and almost immediately pricked herself with the needle. She was a clumsy seamstress these days. And she could no longer follow a knitting pattern. She imagined the silent bees were secretly making a honeycomb in her brain.

'Are you all right?' Teddy asked, looking at the perfect little sphere of blood on her finger. She nodded and licked the drop away before it could stain the blouse.

'Promise me,' she continued, laying her sewing down, 'that when the time comes—' (Teddy flinched at the phrase) 'when the time comes you will help me.'

'Help you what?' He abandoned the gas bill he had been checking.

He knew perfectly well what. 'Help me to go, when it starts to get bad, if I can't help myself. And it will get bad, Teddy.'

'It might not.'

She could scream with frustration at the avoidance, the ducking and diving. She was dying of brain cancer, it was going to be brutal, savage (*completely* bad). Unless she was outrageously fortunate, she was not going to fade away in serene sleep. 'But if it *does* start to get bad,' she said patiently, 'then I want to go before I become a drooling imbecile.' (I want to die as *myself*, she thought.) 'You wouldn't let a dog suffer, so please don't let me.'

'You want me to put you down? Like a dog?' he said testily.

'That's not what I said. You know it isn't.'

'But you want me to kill you?'

'No. To help me kill myself.'

'And that's better in what way?'

Nancy pushed on. 'Only if it's difficult for me to do because I become incapacitated. Morphine or tablets, something like that, I'm not sure.' Or just stick a pillow over my face, for heaven's sake, and be done with it, she thought. But of course that would never do. 'It must clearly be by my own hand,' she said. 'Otherwise you'll be tried for murder.' (Now there was a barbarous word to lay before him.)

'But it's as good as,' he said. 'I don't really see the difference.'

His hands were clasped together and he stared at them as if assessing whether or not they could do the deed. After a considerable silence he said, 'I'm not sure I can.' Not looking at her, looking anywhere but at her, anguish on his face. You made the fatal promise, Nancy thought, you promised anything. You made another promise too, she thought. For better or worse. And now we've come to worse. The worst. And a mean thought – how many had he killed during the war?

'Never mind,' she said, reaching across the table and putting forgiving hands on top of his, clenched now in a kind of rigor. 'It might not get bad after all, we'll just have to see.' He nodded gratefully as if she'd given him benediction.

*   *   *

He was a terrible coward. He had rained down destruction on thousands, on women and children – no different from his wife, his child, his mother, his sister. He had killed people from twenty thousand feet up in the sky, but to kill one person, one person who was asking to die? He had watched as the life went out of Keith, he didn't know if he could do that again. Even for Nancy. He had known her since he was three years old (*childhood sweethearts*), all of his conscious remembering life, and he was to be her executioner?

He had imagined them settling into an unchallenging old age. He couldn't picture himself but he could see Nancy growing thick in the waist, acquiring comfortable chins and grey hair. A little like Mrs Shawcross. She would strain her eyes to knit and to do the *Telegraph* crossword. He would dig up potatoes, she would pull up weeds. She was not a gardener but she couldn't be idle. They would be good companions and they would fade quietly away together and now she was just going to leave early. He remembered Sylvie's displeasure at Hugh's sudden easy death. *He just slipped away without a word.* 'To cease upon the midnight with no pain,' Teddy thought. Didn't Nancy deserve that?

She would have to seek her own solace, she realized. She was lying on Viola's bed, Viola asleep in the crook of her arm. Nancy was uncomfortable, it was still a small child's bed, Viola would need a bigger one soon but it wouldn't be Nancy who bought it. She had been reading *Anne of Green Gables* to Viola. Anne, too, had had to acquire iron in her soul. Sometimes, if she wasn't too sleepy at bedtime, Viola read to Nancy instead. Viola was a good reader, a bookworm – a phrase she hated. 'How can a worm be a nice thing to be?' Viola said. I would be a worm, Nancy thought, if that was the only existence on offer, and then laughed at herself for having reached such a pass. 'Without worms we wouldn't be able to grow food and everyone would starve,' Nancy said reasonably.

She must make sure that Teddy knew she wanted to be cremated. To go up in flames, a pyre, and be returned to the atomic world of elements. It would be better for Viola not to spend the rest of her childhood imagining her mother buried in the dark, damp earth, worms feeding on her flesh. Nancy's heart was heavier every day. To be thinking of such things (to feel obliged to think of such things) while lying with one's arms around one's child, *Anne of Green Gables* open on the bedspread, Viola's glass of milk half drunk on the bedside table (*cocoa, library books, and so on*).

In the past few weeks they had also read together *The Secret Garden* and *Heidi*. No coincidence that they were all tales about orphans. After *Anne* (if there was time) Nancy planned to move on to *Little Women* – not orphans, it was true, but strong, resourceful young women. All the Shawcross sisters had loved Louisa May Alcott. 'And fairy tales, too,' she said to Winnie, who had 'popped up for a quick weekend visit'. Winnie, the eldest of them all, lived in Kent. She had 'married well' to a self-styled 'captain of industry', a title that amused her sisters. But she was a good sort, kind-hearted and competent.

'Think about all those heroines who have to be quick-witted just to survive,' Nancy said. 'Red Riding Hood,

Cinderella, Snow White. People have the wrong idea about fairy tales, they think they're about being rescued by handsome princes, whereas really they're like Girl Guide handbooks.'

'Beauty and the Beast,' Winnie offered, warming to the subject. They were having tea and Winnie was slicing up a cherry Genoa she had brought with her. No one expected Nancy to bake any more. Which was as well as she could barely lift a kettle. Teddy came home every evening and cooked and did housework. Nancy was never hungry any more. Always tired. She used to be up with the lark, but now Teddy brought her tea in bed every morning and she lay there for hours after Teddy and Viola had left the house to get on with their lives.

'You look so well though,' Winnie said.

'I have headaches,' Nancy said, feeling rather defensive. She was tired of people telling her how well she looked, as if she were cheating somehow. Of course, Winnie didn't mean it like that, she chided herself.

'The Goose Girl,' Winnie said. 'Did she have a name? I can only remember the horse's name.'

'Falada. A funny name for a horse. But I don't know about the goose girl herself. Nameless, I think.'

'Shall I be mother and pour?' Winnie said. Even the simplest of sentences could be like a dagger to Nancy's heart.

'Please.' Would this be the last time that she ever saw her eldest sister, she wondered? Soon (now even) it would become a cascade of last times. It was imperative that she go quickly, early, sidestepping the awfulness of all the farewells. She could throw herself beneath the wheels of an express train (but then think of the poor driver). Could she walk into the sea or cast herself into a river? But by instinct she might swim.

'The girl with the brothers who were turned into swans,' Winnie said. 'What was she called? She was very brave.'

'She was. Elise. "The Wild Swans".' What about poison? Too horrible, Nancy thought, too uncertain – she might gag on it rather than swallow it.

'Hansel and Gretel,' Winnie said. 'But just Gretel really. Hansel wasn't too bright, was he?'

'No, he got himself locked up. Sisters are always cleverer than their brothers in fairy stories.' Hanging was supposed to be quick, but deeply distressing for whoever found you, which might well be – probably would be – either Teddy or (unthinkable) Viola.

'Goldilocks,' Winnie said. 'Was she foolish rather than enterprising?'

'Foolish, I think,' Nancy said. 'She had to be rescued.' She was going to have to rescue herself. She must start a cache – sleeping tablets and painkillers, anything she could get her hands on. She must take them while she was still capable, still in control. It was difficult to assess what would constitute a fatal dose. It wasn't the kind of thing you could ask, although she had a different GP now, a Dr Webster, who was the older, wiser partner of the GP she had first seen ('a young buck', Dr Webster called him). Thankfully, Dr Webster was happy to talk about the reality of what was to come.

But what if she had left it too late? Was it already too late? 'Gerda in "The Snow Queen",' she said to Winnie. 'She was very resourceful.'

* * *

The Fourier series, theorems, lemmas, graphs, Parseval's theorem, natural numbers – words hummed in her brain. She had understood them all once, but now their meaning was lost to her. The bees were back, an endless infuriating buzzing that she tried to drown out with the piano. She had played nothing but the Heroic all day. It was incredibly challenging but she was determined to master it.

She was playing with great vigour. *Con brio*. It sounded almost perfect to her ears. How extraordinary, how wonderful that she had become so proficient at such a difficult piece. It was as if this, and this only, had been her life's work. She finished with an enormous flourish.

'Hello, you,' Teddy said, coming into the room. 'Fancy a cup of tea?' He was carrying a tray, Viola trotting at his heels. 'Shall I help you into an armchair?' He was fussing. He put the tray down and led her to a chair by the window. 'You like this one, don't you?' he said. 'You can see the birds on the bird table.' She wished he wouldn't stare at her like that, as if he was trying to see something behind her eyes. He settled her feet on a footstool, her tea on a table by the side of her. Tea in a beaker. Cups and saucers had suddenly become fiddly, confusing.

'Do you want a biscuit, Mummy?' Viola was hovering at her elbow. 'Chocolate bourbon or pink wafers?'

'Or there's some of Win's cake left,' Teddy said. 'It goes on without end. It would have done better than the loaves and fishes for feeding the five thousand.' Nancy ignored both offers. She was feeling rather annoyed that neither of them had congratulated her on her magnificent playing. (*Bravo, Mrs Todd!*) Yet her triumph with the Chopin was fading already. The bees were making her sleepy, all that buzzing. Honey was oozing through her brain.

Time folded in on itself. Where had Teddy gone? Wasn't he here a minute ago? It felt as if everyone had just left the room. Or perhaps it was Nancy herself who had left the room. But there was no room, there was only something she didn't have a name for. Nothing. And then there wasn't even that. And then the bees took flight and blessed her in farewell and Nancy stopped. Dead.

'A stiff whisky, that's my prescription. Pour one for me too.' Their GP, Dr Webster, who was 'looking forward to retirement, a bit of golf, some watercolour painting'. He was the old-fashioned sort. He had given his blessing to Nancy when she refused the operation and had been generous with the morphine and held back on homilies.

A crisp October morning. Spider webs were spangled across the plants in the garden. It was going to be a beautiful day.

Bobby, their Labrador, paced between the rooms, confused by the upset in his regime. Routine was the first thing to be discarded by a death.

Teddy poured the whisky and handed one to the doctor. He raised his glass and for an odd, rather awful moment Teddy thought he was going to say 'Cheers,' but instead he said, 'Let us toast Nancy,' and it was still odd and rather awful, but made sense somehow, and Teddy raised his glass and said, 'To Nancy.'

' "From this world to that which is to come",' Dr Webster said, surprising Teddy with *Pilgrim's Progress*. 'She was a good woman. Such a bright mind, and a kind nature.' Teddy downed the whisky in one, he wasn't ready for eulogies. 'You should call the police,' he said.

'Now why on earth would I do that?'

'Because I killed her,' Teddy said.

'You helped her on her way with a little extra dose of morphine. If that was a crime I would be serving several life sentences.'

'I killed her,' Teddy said stubbornly.

'Now listen to me. She was a few hours away from death.' The GP looked alarmed, Teddy noticed. It was him, after all, who had been so generous with his liquid-morphine prescriptions over the last few weeks for her awful headaches. 'Nancy was in distress,' the doctor continued. 'You did the right thing.' He had visited Nancy the previous evening and given his opinion that it 'wouldn't be long now', and added, 'Do you have enough morphine?'

Enough, Teddy thought?

He had been in the kitchen, making a shepherd's pie, when he heard the terrible cacophony coming from the living room. Before he could run through to investigate, a tearful Viola appeared in the kitchen and said, 'There's something wrong with Mummy.'

Nancy was bashing at the piano keys as if she was trying to destroy the instrument. Her hands were clawed almost into fists and when he had taken hold of them in an effort to quieten her she had looked at him with a strange, lop-sided smile on her face and tried to form words. It seemed important to her that he understood, but it was Viola standing beside him that translated her spastic mumble. 'The Heroic,' she said.

He led her gently into an armchair by the window and they ministered to her with tea and biscuits, but when he looked into her eyes he knew that the thing she had feared the most had happened to her. Nancy was no longer Nancy.

He had helped her to bed early but she had woken before midnight, moaning and calling out, whether from pain or distress he couldn't tell. Both, he supposed. The shell, the shade of the woman who had once been his wife was shouting out nonsense, not even words – just barks and growls like an animal.

He made warm milk, put in a tot of rum and emptied several of the morphine vials into it. Then he sat Nancy up and wrapped a bed jacket around her thin shoulders. 'Drink up,' he said, excessively cheerful. 'This will make you feel much better.'

He didn't spot Viola, woken by the inhuman noises her mother was making, standing sleepily in the doorway of the bedroom in bare feet and cotton pyjamas.

Instead of falling into the deep sleep that Teddy had hoped would be the precursor of death, Nancy grew suddenly much more agitated, throwing herself around in the bed, tearing at the bedspread, her nightdress, her hair, as if she was trying to rid herself of a burning demon. He added more morphine to the milk that remained in the beaker but her thrashing arms sent it flying across the room. She started screaming, an unholy noise, unstoppable, her wide-open mouth a black maw, as if she finally had become the demon that was in her brain. In desperation Teddy grabbed a pillow and pressed it against her face, at first tentatively and then more firmly, unable to bear the idea that at the end, the very end, she should be denied peace, denied the ceasing upon the midnight with no pain. He pressed down hard on the pillow. This is what it meant to kill someone. Hand-to-hand combat. Until death us do part.

She was still. He removed the pillow. The fight was out of her, or perhaps the morphine had worked, but she lay still. He felt her pulse. Stopped. His own heart was thundering. Her face was peaceful, the pain and animal distress had fallen away. She was Nancy again. She was herself.

Viola padded silently back to bed. 'The true nightmares occur when we are awake,' according to the narrator of *Every Third Thought*, her last novel. ('Her best yet,' *Good Housekeeping*.)

'And what would happen to that little girl upstairs if you were arrested and stood trial?' Dr Webster said. She had any number of aunts she could live with, Teddy thought. Any one of them would probably do a better job than he would. 'If something happens to you as well,' Nancy had said to him, 'then I think Viola should go and live with Gertie.' ('Not that anything *is* going to happen to you, of course!')

Out of all the aunts available Gertie seemed almost the oddest choice – Millie taking first place in the race for unsuitability. 'Why Gertie?' he asked.

'She's sensible and practical and patient,' Nancy said, ticking off Gertie's virtues on her fingers. 'But at the same time she's adventurous and not frightened by things. She'll be able to teach Viola how to be brave.' Viola wasn't brave, they both knew that, but neither of them ever said it.

What right did Teddy have to talk about bravery, he thought, pouring both himself and Dr Webster another whisky.

'I'll make out the death certificate,' the GP said. 'You should probably telephone an undertaker, or I'll do it for you if you'd prefer?'

'No,' Teddy said. 'I'll do it.'

After the doctor had left, Teddy went upstairs to Viola's room. She was still fast asleep. He couldn't bring himself to wake her in order to give her the worst news she would probably ever hear. He stroked her forehead, slightly damp, and kissed it lightly. 'I love you,' he said. They should have been his last words to Nancy, but he had been too taken up in the awful final struggle to say anything to her. Viola stirred and muttered something, but didn't wake.

2012

Love, Mercy, Pity, Peace

The Queen was sailing slowly down the Thames.

'The Queen,' Viola said. 'She's on the television.' She was keeping her interpretation of events simple – the flotilla on the river, the rain, the admirable perseverance of monarchy. 'You can't really see the television though, can you?' She talked very loudly and slowly to Teddy as if he was a particularly stupid child. She was sitting next to his bed in one of the care home's high-backed armchairs. It always disturbed her to sit in this chair. It was meant for the elderly and she dreaded being counted amongst that number now that she was old enough to qualify for Saga holidays and lunch clubs in church halls, old enough to wear beige anoraks and pull-on 'slacks'. (As if.) She was old enough to move into Fanning Court. God forbid.

Teddy could no longer sit in the chair. He could no longer leave the bed, no longer do anything. He was approaching the end of his twilight, entering into the final darkness. Viola imagined the synapses in her father's brain flaring and dimming like the slow death of a star. Soon Teddy would burn out completely and implode and become a black hole. Viola was hazy on the subject of astrophysics, but she liked the image.

He was labelled, a plastic hospital bracelet around his wrist. Sunny and Bertie had both worn them in the maternity ward. Other people kept things like that – first baby teeth, first shoes, primitive nursery paintings, school reports – regarding them as precious relics of childhood, but Viola had managed to discard everything as she went. (Yes, she regretted it. All right?)

'DNR,' it said on Ted's plastic bracelet, indicating he had lingered on, long past his sell-by date. Oh God, life was awful. A memory of last night came back to her, although the memory of last night hadn't ever gone away. She shuddered at it now. She had embarrassed herself dreadfully. 'Humiliated' would be a better word.

She had arrived in York from Harrogate in the evening, hoping to see some friends. Yes, she did have friends, against the odds. She was going to phone them and say casually, 'How about meeting up? A drink?', pretending it was an impromptu idea, when in fact she had been planning it for several days. She was trying to be more spontaneous – what she thought of as spontaneity in her earlier years she now recognized as mere torpor. ('Shall we go to the beach?' 'Yeah, OK.') She was also trying to revive a social life that she had once had but which she had woefully neglected since her success. ('So busy with stuff, sorry.')

She hadn't seen these particular friends for a long time – years (and years) – and they had parted on rather bad terms. They had all been in a 'Women's Wholefood Cooperative', which basically meant that they bought big ugly sacks of chaff and husks, masquerading as muesli, and then divided it up between them. They didn't have much in common, apart from the Steiner school and CND, which sounded like a lot, but wasn't for Viola.

Arriving in York, she realized that she had forgotten that it was both a Saturday and a bank-holiday weekend and found York bedecked in Jubilee adornment, a frenzy of bunting and red, white and blue. Weekends were also when the city was besieged by rampaging hordes of stags and hens coming down from the even-more-northern north.

She checked in to the Cedar Court Hotel, which used to be the headquarters of the North Eastern Railway. Everything became a hotel eventually. Dust and sand and hotels. She had hoped for a room with a view, one of the ones that faced on to the Bar Walls, but there were none available. If she was in a Forster novel she would meet the love of her life at this point (she would also be forty years younger) and be wrenched emotionally and at the end she would have her view. Not that she wanted to be wrenched emotionally (she had given up men), nor indeed meet the love of her life, but she would have liked a view. The girl who checked her in at reception had almost certainly never heard of Forster, although she might have heard of Viola Romaine, but Viola didn't feel up to testing that theory. Viola felt as if she spent her life wading through a sea of ignorance, shallow but without a shore in sight.

Yes, she was making elitist assumptions. No, she didn't have a right to. The receptionist (who had heard of neither Forster nor Viola Romaine, but had 'enjoyed' *Fifty Shades of Grey*, a fact that would have made Viola apoplectic) handed her a key card and said she would get someone to show her to her room. 'Anything else I can do for you, Mrs Romaine?'

After the divorce Viola had kept Wilf's name (and half the proceeds from the sale of the house, of course) on the grounds that it was more interesting than the prosaic 'Todd'. 'How do you spell Romaine? Like the lettuce?' someone asked her the other day. Her father's aunt, the writer of those endless ghastly Augustus books, had taken the name 'Fox' – much nicer than a lettuce, why hadn't she thought of that? Viola Fox. Perhaps she could use it as a pseudonym, write a different kind of book – a serious one that didn't sell but was critically lauded. ('A text that challenges our epistemological assumptions about the nature of fiction,' *TLS*.)

They had married a month after first meeting. 'An immense passion,' Viola explained to her disappointed yet strangely envious women's group. 'Passion' was a word that appealed to Viola – the word possibly more than the passion itself. It was doomed and Brontëesque and she felt she hadn't had enough of that in her life. She yearned for the Romantic. It was neither passion nor romance with Wilf Romaine, merely wishful thinking.

Wilf Romaine had seemed a firebrand, but it turned out that really he was just bombastic. He was polemical, a political activist, CND, Labour Party, etcetera, who made much of being the son of a coal miner. But, as Viola felt it necessary to point out to him not long into their marriage, being the son of a coal miner didn't actually make you a coal miner yourself. Instead he was a lecturer in Communications (a meaningless discipline) at a further education college, with type 2 diabetes and a drink problem. He had seemed fierce and noble but in the end he was as disappointing as everyone else.

'Did he hit you?' Gregory, her therapist, asked. Gregory was very keen on domestic violence as cause and effect.

'Yes,' Viola said, because that sounded infinitely more interesting than the cold, damp truth of mutual indifference. As you got older and time went on, you realized that the distinction between truth and fiction didn't really matter because eventually everything disappeared into the soupy, amnesiac mess of history. Personal or political, it made no difference.

Her children left home and she moved to Whitby, although technically Sunny didn't leave home, Viola did. That was when she became a writer. Even Viola had to acknowledge that she needed to shake herself out of her indolent state of mind, engage with the realities of life – which was the kind of thing The Voice of Reason would say, of course. Writing felt like something she knew, although she only knew it from the other side – reading – and it took her a while to realize that writing and reading were completely different activities – polar opposites, in fact. And just because she could do joined-up hand-writing, she discovered, didn't mean that she could write books. But she persevered, perhaps for the first time in her life.

She had had a good apprenticeship – early reader, only child, semi-orphan, and a nature that was essentially voyeuristic. As a child she had loitered in doorways, listening and observing. ('Writers are just vultures!', *People's Friend*, 2009.) *Sparrows at Dawn* was sent to an agent, who rejected it, and then another one and another one until finally one wrote back and said it was 'interesting', and although the agent made 'interesting' sound like an insult she did nonetheless sell it to a publisher who made a (modest) two-book deal, and less than a year later *Sparrows at Dawn* was a solid, tangible item in the phenomenal world rather than a jumble of ideas in Viola's head. ('What next?' Bertie said to Teddy. '*Badgers for Breakfast? Rabbits at Bedtime?*')

Her father did not seem as impressed by this achievement as she would have liked. She had sent him an early proof copy and then on publication day had come over to York, where he took her out for a meal and, surprisingly, ordered champagne 'to celebrate', but his critique of the novel was lacking in enthusiasm. She had wanted him to be overwhelmed and astonished by her talent instead of the 'Very good' he awarded it, managing to make it sound like the opposite. He also failed (apparently) to understand that the book – young girl, brilliant and precocious, troubled relationship with her single-parent father, etcetera – was about *them*. Surely he knew that? Why didn't he *say* something? Instead, on the way back to his house he sang, 'And that singular anomaly, the lady novelist, I don't think she'd be missed – I'm sure she'd not be missed!' as if the whole thing was amusing. Gilbert and Sullivan, he said. 'I've got a little list.' Haven't we all, she thought.

Sparrows at Dawn had limited success. 'Overly senti-mental', 'Rather baggy'. She had written herself into a hole, but she wrote herself out again with her second novel, *The Children of Adam*, 'a bittersweet tragi-comedy about life in a commune in the Sixties'. She had back-dated her experiences to a more fashionable decade and told it from the point of view of a four-year-old child. 'But isn't that my story, not yours?' Bertie said, rather aggrieved. It was hugely popular ('For some reason,' Bertie puzzled to Teddy) and was made into a very English and largely forgotten film with Michael Gambon and Greta Scacchi.

And that was that, the beginning of her brilliant career.

Her bedroom at the Cedar Court was large and rather dark and must have once been someone's office. She phoned the friends she had thought to meet up with and found that their phone number no longer worked, which was an indication of how long it was since she'd been in touch. To be honest (she was trying more of that too), she was relieved. All that catching up they would have been forced to do. And she had moved on so far from those days and they probably hadn't. If she thought about them, she imagined them still dressed in thick jumpers and long skirts with clogs on their feet, curtains of hair hanging down over their faces, still dishing out horse feed from sacks (although actually one was a barrister in North Square and the other one was dead).

She lay down on the hotel bed and stared at the ceiling. It was only six o'clock and the summer evening light would, depressingly, go on for ever. She could lie here and stare at the ceiling or watch television and order room service. Neither appealed, so she decided to brave a Saturday bank-holiday evening in York, not a light undertaking. At least it wasn't a race day, an event that also attracted large groups of inappropriately dressed young women, who could be distinguished from the regular hens by their fascinators, a ludicrous item of headgear if ever there was one. And they were all so fat! How did they manage in toilet cubicles and cinema seats? You could be squashed to death by one of them if you weren't careful.

It was early yet but when she left the hotel Viola discovered that the stags and hens were already out in force, already astonishingly drunk. She shuddered to think what kind of state they would be in later. Some of the stags were in fancy dress – a whole group (a bunch she should call them, she supposed) of men dressed in banana costumes were streaming down the steps into the Slug and Lettuce by the river. Most, though, were just in blokey uniform – clean jeans and T-shirts, reeking of aftershave, muscle already turning to flab. The girls were tribal, wearing T-shirts that picked out their affiliations in rhinestones – 'Claire's Hen Party', 'Hens in the City', 'The Only Way is Darlington' – the last a particularly deluded group, in Viola's opinion. Pink was the order of the day for the girls – pink cowboy hats, pink T-shirts, pink tutus, pink sashes. They were the kind of girls who thought cupcakes were sophisticated. Cupcakes were another bugbear of Viola's. They were just buns, for heaven's sake! Why all the fuss? To make money, of course.

She caught sight of the deely-boppers (pink, naturally)

on the heads of a flock of girls ('Hannah's Horny Hens')
who were flapping around at the traffic lights on Lendal
Bridge, uncertain where to take their patronage next. Viola
hadn't seen deely-boppers since the Eighties. Bertie had a
pair when she was a child, silver tinsel balls that bobbed
around on her little head like insect feelers. And – Viola
suddenly remembered – a pair of spangled silver wings
that went with them. A moth, not a butterfly, Bertie said.
A little jab to the heart. You had to be careful of the jabs
– if you had enough of them they could weaken the fabric
of the heart, open up fault lines, fissures and rifts, and
before you knew where you were the whole brittle
structure could shatter into a thousand tiny pieces. Viola's
heart was being held together by sticking plaster and glue.
Was that a good image? She wasn't sure.

Bertie, against Viola's advice, had insisted on sleeping in
her silver wings. The next morning, when she discovered
they were crushed beyond repair, she had sobbed
inconsolably. 'Well you should have listened to me,
shouldn't you?' Viola had said. 'I told you that would
happen.'

Sow and reap, Viola. Sow and reap.

Bringing up the rear of Hannah's Horny Hens there
was a couple of older, rather disconsolate-looking women
– a mother of the bride and an aunt or prospective
mother-in-law, perhaps. Their sagging bodies struggled
uncomfortably with the tight pink T-shirts, let alone the
rhinestone epithet inscribed across their wobbling
bosoms. ('Good corsetry,' Viola Romaine confides
conspiratorially, 'that's the secret to looking good for
the older woman.' *Sunday Express, Life and Style*, 2010.

That was not what she said! Completely misquoted.)

Would this be herself one day, Viola wondered? After all, Bertie might decide, in her own post-ironic fashion, to have a traditional hen night ('Bertie's Babes') and inflict humiliation on her retinue. She would have to meet someone to marry first, of course. It was beginning to look as if Viola would never know the redemption of being a grandmother. Sunny may as well have been a monk from the sound of it and Bertie didn't seem to date at all, or if she did she certainly didn't tell her mother about it.

Hannah's Horny Hens seemed to come to an unspoken decision and the bevy wheeled away down Rougier Street. As they passed in front of her Viola realized, to her embarrassment, that the wobbling deely-boppers she was staring at were actually stubby little penises. Without warning the penises lit up and began to flash and the hens cawed raucously at each other. Viola found herself blushing as she hurried on to the familiar comfort of Bettys. A sanctuary from dystopia, a reliably clean, well-lighted place.

She ate a chicken salad and drank two glasses of wine. She was no longer a vegetarian. It was difficult to stay slim on all those pulses. A man was playing the piano – very well, not just the usual lounge songs but some Chopin and Rachmaninov. Chopin reminded Viola of her mother and always made her horribly sad. Viola gave up piano lessons after Nancy's death. If she'd kept them up she might have had a musical career. A concert pianist – well, why not?

Viola went downstairs to the toilets. There was a

fragment of a mirror down there, the mirror that used to be behind the bar when this was 'Bettys Bar' during the war. The RAF crews used to scratch their names on the glass. Her father had told her about Bettys Bar, how he used to drink here during the war, but she hadn't really listened to his reminiscences. Now the mirror was a relic. Nearly all of these men who had left their names behind would be dead now. Many of them would have died during the war, Viola supposed. She peered at the near-illegible names. Had her father left his name behind here? She wished she had asked him about his war when he was still *compos mentis*. She might have been able to use his memories as the basis of a novel. One that everyone would respect. People always took war novels seriously.

When she sat back down at her table she found that a group of men dressed as condoms were staggering across St Helen's Square. They were in one of the best-preserved medieval cities in Europe and they were dressed as condoms. What was wrong with Benidorm? Or Magaluf? ('You want everyone to behave better, but you don't behave better yourself,' Bertie said.)

One of the condom men squashed himself like an insect against the large plate-glass of Bettys and leered at the diners. The pianist glanced up from his keyboard and then continued serenely with Debussy. A van drew up in the centre of St Helen's Square and disgorged several people dressed as zombies. The zombies proceeded to chase the men who were dressed as condoms. The condom men didn't seem very surprised, as if they were *expecting* to be chased by zombies. ('They pay for it,' Bertie said.) Was this fun? Viola despaired. It was possible, she thought, that she had won the race to reach the end of civilization. There was no prize. Obviously.

But not quite yet. The finishing line was in sight but Viola was still to stumble over it. She left Bettys and negotiated her way back across Lendal Bridge, where the atmosphere was decidedly rowdier now. Somehow or other she became accidentally entangled with Amy's Single Ladies, a brood who were utterly dishevelled by drink and being led by the eponymous Amy herself, tiara askew, a sash across a cheap bustier proclaiming her 'The Bride' and an L-plate attached to her not-insignificant rump. What had happened to girls? Was this what Emily Davison had thrown herself beneath a horse for? So girls could wear light-up penises on their heads and eat cupcakes? Really? Every time they encountered a male of the species they each held up a finger and screamed, 'Put a ring on it!' before hanging on to each other because they were collapsing with the humour of it. 'I'm going to wet myself!' one of them shrieked.

A herd of stags streamed around Viola. 'Cheer up, you old bag!' one of them yelled at her. 'You might get lucky if you stop looking so miserable.' Viola stomped on, a boiling fury inside. The cracks and fissures spreading, crazing the surface of her heart. She was an overstrung piano, all the wires about to rupture and spring apart in a dreadful cataclysm of metaphors.

How could people be so stupid and ignorant? ('Why are you angry all the time?' Sunny asked her long ago. 'Why not?' she snapped.) And why didn't her children love her? Why did no one love her? And why was she so lonely and bored and, let's face it, downright wretched and—

She went flying, tripping on a paving slab, landing heavily, bone on stone, on her hands and knees, like a leaden cat, everything in her head silenced by the shock for a moment. Her knees hurt so much she didn't want to move. Were her kneecaps broken? A stag made some ribald comment about the position she was in and a ripe Geordie accent, a woman, told him to fuck off. Viola sat back, kneeling on the pavement, knees screaming. A pink T-shirt appeared at eye-level. Rhinestones spelled out 'Slutz Go Nutz in York'. A woman – a girl really, younger than her smoker's voice, her face smiley and concerned – hunkered down next to Viola and said, 'Are you all right, pet?'

Not really, Viola thought, not at all. She burst into tears, right there on the stones of York, her expensive Wolford tights ripped, her knees raw and bloody. She couldn't stop. It was awful. Tears retched out of her insides as if she'd suddenly tapped into some ancient aquifer of grief. But it wasn't just the tears that horrified her, it was the words that came out of her mouth. The primeval howl, the alpha and omega of all human invocation. Not a howl but a whimper. 'I want my mother,' she whispered. 'I want my mother.'

'You can have mine, pet,' someone said and the hens all burst into laughter, but nonetheless, sensing a woman ruined, possibly by drink, possibly not, the hens closed ranks and clustered protectively around her. Someone helped her to her feet, someone else passed a tissue, a third passed a bottle of Evian that turned out to contain neat vodka. One of the older hens, a broiler with a wrinkled neck and a face that seemed to have collapsed and who was wearing a T-shirt declaring her to be 'Mother of the Bride', handed Viola a pack of Wet Wipes. They ascertained where she was heading and she was shepherded tenderly back to Cedar Court by her posse of Slutz. The doorman made a futile attempt to stop them breaching his defences, but they were already pouring over the threshold and spilling into the foyer. Viola fumbled for her key card and one of the hens lifted it up triumphantly and waved it at the nervous receptionist.

'She's a bit tired and emotional,' one of the hens explained. 'Poor old thing,' a young one, a spring chicken, said. Old thing! I'm only sixty, Viola wanted to protest, it's the new forty. But she didn't have any protest left in her.

She had an alarming vision of the hens continuing the party in her room, but eventually she managed to persuade them to leave her at the door to the lift. The Mother of the Bride pressed something into her hand, a tiny tissue-wrapped gift. 'Valium,' the Mother said, 'but just take a half. They're high-strength. I've built up a tolerance.' A still-teary Viola hiccuped her gratitude.

In the refuge of her room she forwent her usual nightly routine – make-up off, teeth cleaned, hair brushed – and instead crawled wearily between sheets that were snapping with starch and recklessly washed down a whole Valium with two little bottles of vodka from the minibar. She feared nightmares, but instead she fell into a surprisingly delicious sleep. Golden slumbers kissed her eyes, silver moths flitted around her head and she dreamed a powerful dream.

* * *

She woke early, showered, dressed, ordered a large pot of coffee and assessed the damage. She felt as if she had been, if not in a war, then certainly in a bloody skirmish. What else did she feel? She checked herself all over. Her wrists felt mildly sprained and her knees were horribly stiff and sore, as if someone had hammered them all night. Her head felt stuffed with wool – the Mother of the Bride's Valium, she supposed – but otherwise intact. Then she looked inside herself. Completely fucked, she concluded.

She checked out, relieved that there was no sign of the staff who had witnessed her humiliating fall from grace last night. How were the Slutz this morning, she wondered? Hopelessly hung-over, probably still asleep. (Although actually they were helping themselves enthusiastically to an eat-all-you-can full-English buffet breakfast in a superior Travelodge and getting ready to rampage through Primark. They were from Gateshead, they had stamina.)

Viola asked the doorman for a taxi to Poplar Hill. Spending the day with her father would be penance for last night. She would watch the Diamond Jubilee with him for extra contrition.

Her father was clearly exhausted, sleeping almost all the time now, like an aged dog. Why didn't he just go? Was he hanging on for a hundred? Two more years of this? It was mere existence – an amoeba had more life. 'The triumph of the human spirit,' the new nursing sister said, new enough to talk about 'positive outcomes' and 'enhancement programmes' – emollient management-speak, meaningless to most of the residents of Poplar Hill, who were either dying or demented or both. It was called a 'care home' but there was precious little of either to be had when you were run by a profit-based health-care provider employing minimum-wage staff. And, by the way, neither poplar nor hill were anywhere to be seen. This was a particular bugbear which Viola found herself bringing up at regular intervals, when really it was the least of her criticisms and just made her seem like another mad woman to the – mainly foreign – care workers. ('Polish and Tagalog spoken,' it said in the Poplar Hill brochure.)

'It's so stuffy in here,' she said to Teddy. He muttered something that might have been agreement. The heating was turned up impossibly high, intensifying the loathsome smells that made you gag the minute you walked into the building and helpfully incubating the millions of germs that must be circulating. There were the usual animal odours of urine and faeces as well as the reek of something rotted and spoiled that no amount of disinfectant could cover up. The scent of old age, Viola presumed. When she visited Poplar Hill she kept a handkerchief up her sleeve doused in Chanel that she sniffed occasionally, like a nosegay against the plague.

The doors to the rooms were kept open so that each room was a little vignette, the wreckage inside on display, like some awful zoo or a museum of horrors. Some people lay in bed and barely moved, while others moaned and shouted. Then there were those who were propped in chairs, their heads lolling on their chests like sleeping toddlers, and somewhere, unseen, a woman was meowing like a cat. As you walked along the corridors you had to slalom around the walking wounded (as Viola thought of them), the lost souls who simply shuffled up and down all day with no idea who they were or where they were going (nowhere, clearly). None of them knew the code for the security keypad on the locked door of the wing (1-2-3-4 – how hard could it be?), and if they had known they couldn't have remembered and if they could have remembered it would still have been meaningless because their brains were full of holes, like lace. Occasionally Viola had found them gathered, like zombies (slow ones, they weren't going to be chasing anyone, paid or not), at the door, staring mutely through the wired glass at a world that was forbidden to them now. They were prisoners, serving the lees of their life sentences. The walking dead.

To intensify the unpleasant atmosphere of the wing there was a blaring cacophony of competing televisions coming from every room, all with the volume turned up high – *Deal or No Deal* trying to shout down *Escape to the Country* and no one really caring what they watched because they couldn't make sense of any of it. There was always a buzzer going off somewhere, long and insistent, as a resident tried to get the attention of someone, anyone.

There was also a communal lounge where residents were parked in front of an even bigger, louder television set. For reasons Viola couldn't fathom, the lounge also contained a large cage that imprisoned a pair of lovebirds that no one ever paid any attention to. She had disliked Fanning Court, the sheltered-housing complex that she had cajoled her father into almost twenty years ago now, but compared to the nursing home – oh sorry, *care* home – it was a lost Eden. 'Why this is hell,' she said conversationally to her father, 'nor am I out of it, and nor are you.' She smiled brightly at a care assistant going past the open door. Who in their right mind could think that euthanasia was a bad thing? Shipman had spoiled it for everyone.

But however awful it was in Poplar Hill, it meant that Viola didn't have to be the one who coped, who changed nappies and spoon-fed pap and tried to think of ways to entertain in the long hours in between. She had never been much good at that stuff with her children so it seemed unlikely she would develop the skills now for someone at the other end of life. She just wasn't cut out to look after others.

Viola imagined herself as someone whose insides were made of a hard substance, as if soft organs and tissue had calcified at some point in the long-ago past. *The Petrification of Viola Romaine.* Good title for something. Her life, she supposed. But who would write it? And how could she stop them?

To be honest (with herself at any rate), she didn't really *like* people. (' "L'enfer, c'est les autres," Viola Romaine laughs lightly, yet this is clearly not true as she writes with great sympathy about the human condition.' *Red* magazine, 2011.) In her defence (Viola frequently thought of herself in the third person, as if presenting herself to a jury), in her defence, she was regularly moved to tears these days by tales of cruelty to animals, which, if nothing else, proved she wasn't a sociopath. (The jury was reserving judgement.) If you read the tabloids, which Viola did

– 'Important to know the enemy,' she would have said to the jury, but actually the red-tops were a much better read than the smugly self-satisfied broadsheets – it seemed as though there were people all over the place who were starving horses to death or putting puppies into tumble dryers or popping kittens into microwaves as though they were snacks.

These stories left Viola in a state of unresolved horror that wasn't quite matched by how she felt about, for example, cruelty to children. She had to keep this fact to herself, it was a taboo, like voting Tory. Not even Gregory, her therapist, knew. Especially not Gregory as he would have had a field day with it. *Her Secret Self: How to Hide Your True Nature* by Viola Romaine.

Her excuse (Did she need one? Yes, probably) was that she had been exiled from love after her mother died. 'After I lost my wife,' was the way her father would have put it, as if he had accidentally mislaid Nancy. *Exile from Love*, that was the title of one of Viola's early novels. 'A poignant tale of struggle and loss,' according to *Woman's Own*. That was where the best of her was to be found, in her books. ('Almost as good as Jodi Picoult,' *Mumsnet*.) Her readers (almost exclusively women) – and she had many, devoted, etcetera – all thought she was a nice – nay, wonderful – person. It was alarming. It made her feel guilty, as if she had made promises that she could never live up to.

She had been making this visit to Poplar Hill every week for three years now and would have been quite happy never to set foot in the place, but didn't want to be seen as neglectful. Viola derived no pleasure from being with her father. She had always been wary of him for one reason or another, but now that he was a wreck, more child than colossus, he felt like an utter stranger. The Ancient Mariner was lucky – his albatross was already dead before it was hung round his neck.

She had come from Harrogate by train today because she was on her way to somewhere else. She made a mental note. *On the Way to Somewhere Else* – good title. Harrogate was the kind of place that won Britain in Bloom competitions and where what poverty there was was swept neatly out of sight. Viola still harboured a regret that she had never made it beyond the borders of Yorkshire, never lived a London life, sophisticated and metropolitan (or so she imagined).

Her brief sojourn in a squat with deadbeat Dominic hardly counted. That had been in Islington, before it was fashionable, and she had hardly left the house. 'Postnatal depression,' she told people afterwards, a legitimate badge of suffering to parade, although really it was just straightforward depression. ('I think I was born depressed,' she tells *Psychologies* magazine. 'I think it's given me a greater understanding of people.')

If she lived in London these days she would be invited to parties, to lunches and 'do's. She sold too well ('international bestseller') to be embraced by the glitterati, but it would be nice not to feel that she was a populist barbarian knocking on the gates. ('I'm a northerner and proud of it,' *Daily Express* interview, March 2006. Was she? Not really.)

She would rather have been brought up in the plush Home Counties, at Fox Corner, semi-mythical now in her memory, everyone's memory. She was six when Sylvie died and the house was sold. Her mother's childhood home, Jackdaws, followed a few years later when Mrs Shawcross succumbed to genteel senility and lived out her days in Dorset with the tolerant Gertie. It was her father's fault, he had chosen to settle up here after the war. She had never asked why. Too late now. Too late for everything.

The Queen sailed on heroically, through wind and rain. 'Her Diamond Jubilee,' Viola said to Teddy. 'She's been on the throne for *sixty* years. That's a *long* time. Can you remember her Coronation?' Viola was barely a year old when the Queen was crowned and had never known another monarch. She would see Charles ascend to the throne, she supposed, possibly William if she lived long enough, but she wouldn't see one of his children taking over. Life was finite. Civilizations rose and fell and in the end everything was dust and sand. Nothing beside remained. Hotels, maybe.

Viola fell into (an admittedly self-indulgent) existential gloom and was only pulled out of it when her father started to choke. She panicked and tried to help him sit up. There was hardly any water in the jug on his table even though it was supposed to be kept topped up. The 'residents' (a ridiculous word, as if they had chosen to live here) were probably all suffering from dehydration. Not to mention starvation. 'Three nutritious meals a day' it said on the Poplar Hill website. There were menus pinned to a noticeboard every day – shepherd's pie, fish and sautéed potatoes, chicken casserole. They made it sound like real food, when in fact every meal that Viola had seen was a kind of beige slop and jelly for afters. Her father didn't seem to eat any more, a Breatharian by default. Viola had been briefly (very briefly, obviously) attracted to Breatharianism, as she was to all things cultish. Living on air had seemed like a good way to lose weight. It was an absurd idea and in her defence – she turned to the jury – she had been going through a particularly 'bad patch' in her life. That was before she discovered that all you had to do to lose weight was to eat less. ('Svelte,' according to the *Mail on Sunday*, 'and still the proud possessor of a good pair of pins, even though she's got a bus pass now.' She hadn't. She took taxis. And chauffeur-driven cars. And she would have preferred it if the 'good' had been 'great'.)

Viola poured the dregs of the water jug into a plastic cup and stirred in the thickener that turned any liquid into disgusting gloop but was supposed to prevent her father from choking. She held the cup to his lips so that he could take a sip of the gloop.

'Do you find old age in itself repellent,' Gregory asked, 'or just your father's?' 'Both,' she said. 'And your own?' Yes, all right, she was terrified of growing old. ('You *are* old,' Bertie said.) Was this going to be her fate too when she reached the endgame? Lunch clubs and chairs for the elderly and then finally being administered gloop by someone who spoke Tagalog? Not someone who truly *cared*. You reap what you sow, her father used to say. Bertie certainly wouldn't take her in. Perhaps she could go and live in Bali with Sunny. He was a Buddhist, his religion obliged him to be compassionate, didn't it? 'It's more a state of mind than a religion,' Bertie said.

Imagine if that was a law and everyone had to obey it.

Smiley, concerned faces everywhere asking if you were all right. Would it be utopian or just rather irritating?

It was ten years since she had seen Sunny. A decade! How had that happened? What kind of mother let a decade go by without seeing her child? She had tried a couple of times over the years. When she was on a book tour in Australia, for instance, but he said he was 'going to be in Thailand' while she was there. Perhaps she could stop off in Thailand on the way out, she suggested? He was 'hiking in the north', she wouldn't be able to get to him, he said. 'I wouldn't call that trying hard,' Bertie said. Righteous, like her grandfather, of course.

'You gave him up,' Bertie said. It was true, she had handed him over to the vile Villiers. 'But in my defence—' But the members of the jury were not listening.

The *Spirit of Chartwell* had moored near Tower Bridge. 'The Queen's stopped,' Viola informed her father. 'It's still raining cats and dogs. You, in particular, would admire her stoicism if you could see her.'

He mumbled something. It sounded as if his mouth was full of stones. He could no longer see well enough to watch television and even if he had been able to see he found it difficult to connect one moment to the next, as if everything fragmented in the moment of trying to hold on to it. Books were out of the question. Before the last bout of pneumonia, when he'd still been able to see large-print books, she discovered that he'd been reading the first chapter of *Barchester Towers* over and over again, looping round and coming to it fresh each time. Perhaps his brain was becoming economical with time, conserving what little was left as it approached its last days. But time was an artificial construct, wasn't it? Zeno's arrow staggering and stuttering its way to some fictional end point in the future. In reality that arrow had no target, they weren't on a journey and there was no final destination where everything would suddenly fall transcendentally into place, the mysteries revealed. They were all just lost souls, wandering the halls, gathering silently at the exit. No promised land, no paradise regained. 'It's all so *pointless*,' she said to her father, but he seemed to have nodded off. Viola sighed and replaced the untouched gloop on his overbed table.

'And now it's just boats, ships, passing in front of her. All kinds of different ones. Quite boring ones.' Viola's phone rang. 'Bertie' the screen said. Viola thought about not answering, answered.

'Are you watching the Thames Pageant with Grandpa Ted?' Bertie asked.

'Yes, I'm in his room.'

'It's rubbish, isn't it? And the poor Queen, she's almost as old as Grandpa Ted and she's having to suffer all this.'

'She'll catch her death in all that rain,' Viola said. She had spouted socialism and republicanism most of her adult life, but lately had revealed a strange affection for the royal family. And she had voted Tory in the last election, although it would have taken torture to drag that fact out into the open. 'In my defence, it was a tactical vote,' she explained to the jury. They were not convinced. UKIP were still beyond the pale, but never say never.

People didn't mellow in old age, they simply decomposed, as far as Viola could see.

'Anyway,' Bertie said, indicating she had already run out of things to say to her mother, 'can you put me on to Grandpa Ted?'

'He won't understand you.'

'Just put me on anyway.'

If Viola could start again – there are no second chances, life's not a rehearsal, blah, blah, blah – yes, but if she *could*, if she could retake the journey that wasn't really a journey, what would she do? She would learn how to love. *Learning to Love*, a painful but ultimately redemptive journey, displaying warmth and compassion as the author learns how to overcome loneliness and despair. The steps she takes to mend her relationship with her children are particularly rewarding. (Half the members of the jury had nodded off by now.) She had tried, she really had. She had *worked* on herself. Years of therapy and fresh starts, although nothing that really required an effort on her part. She wanted someone else to effect change in her. It seemed a shame you couldn't just get an injection that would suddenly make everything all right. ('Try heroin,' Bertie said.) She hadn't turned to the Church yet, but now that she had voted Tory (tactical!), Anglicanism would probably be next. But it didn't seem to matter how many new beginnings she had, Viola always somehow found herself in the same place, and no matter how hard she tried, the earliest template of herself always seemed to trump later versions. So why bother? Really?

'Pointless,' she said again as she tried to open the

window further, but it had a lock that prevented it moving more than a couple of inches, as if the powers-that-be were trying to prevent elves falling out rather than normal-sized, if slightly shrunken, old people. They were on the first floor and the view was of the huge industrial bins that contained God knows what kind of unpalatable refuse.

Her father must miss having fresh air, he had always been so into the outdoors. He loved nature. She felt a sudden spark of sympathy for him and stamped on it.

When she was a child, they drove out to the country nearly every weekend and walked for miles while he battered her with information about flowers and animals and trees. Oh God, how she had hated those nature walks. He wrote a column for years for some obscure rural magazine. Of course, if she had listened to him she might have learned some useful stuff, but she didn't listen on principle because there was nothing he could ever say about anything that would make up for his losing her mother. *I want my mother*. The desperate cry of a child in the night. ('Oh, for God's sake, get over it,' Bertie said. Unnecessarily harsh, in Viola's opinion.)

'You used the word "wary" earlier, in the context of your father,' Gregory said. He was yet another incarnation of The Voice of Reason, of course, a voice that had been pursuing her all her life.

'Wary?' he prompted her.

'Did I use that word?'

'Yes.'

She supposed he was trying to truffle out abuse or something equally traumatic and dramatic. But it was her father's provident character that had made her want to keep her distance from him. His stoicism (yes, that much-overused word), his cheerful frugality – the bees, the chickens, the home-grown vegetables. Chores had to be done ('I'll wash if you dry'). Leftovers had to be used up ('Well, let's see, there's a bit of ham and some cold potatoes in the fridge, why don't you pop outside and see if our feathered friends have given us any eggs?'). And his persistent patience with her as if she were a mulish dog. ('Come on, now, Viola, if you come and sit down and do your homework, we'll see if we can't find you a treat afterwards.')

'He sounds sensible, Viola.'

'You're supposed to be on my side.' (Sensible! What a horrid word.)

'Am I?' Gregory said mildly.

Was there no one who would ever sympathize with her tales of woe? Even people that she paid a fortune to precisely for that task? 'And he cut my hair off after my mother died.'

'Himself?'

'No, he took me to a hairdresser.' Nancy used to take her to Swallow and Barry in Stonegate and then they would go to Bettys and eat meringues filled with cream. She had ordered a meringue in Bettys last night. It was very good but it was not the meringue *perdu* of her childhood.

Swallow and Barry had a little counter downstairs where they sold jewelled tortoiseshell combs and clips and it smelt of some lovely grown-up perfume, and upstairs the hairdresser always said how nice her long hair was and then he trimmed the ends neatly so it would be 'even nicer'. It was a place of luxury and indulgence where people told her she was pretty and everyone loved Nancy, but after she died her father said he couldn't do her plaits every morning and she needed something more 'manageable', so he took her to a horrible little salon near where they lived. It was painted lilac, the sort of place that nowadays would be called 'A Cut Above' or 'Curlz' but then was called 'Jennifer's', and she clearly remembered that it was cold and the mauve paint was peeling.

She left with an awful short style that didn't suit her, made her look like a plain pudding, her lost hair abandoned on the cracked lino of Jennifer's. No meringues in Bettys, only lemon barley water and chocolate bourbons at home. She had wept and wept and—

'Couldn't you brush your own hair?'

'I'm sorry?'

'Couldn't you brush your own hair?'

'I was nine years old. So, no. Not properly.' Nancy had brushed her hair attentively, every morning and every evening before bed. It had been a lovely communion that they shared.

Bertie had long hair when she was small. By default really as Viola had never taken her to a hairdresser. Viola remembered rushing to get her children off to school in the mornings, always an appalling hour of chaos with Bertie being slow and Sunny being obnoxious. ('Why don't you get up a bit earlier?' her father suggested. Right, as if she got enough sleep as it was.) Bertie hated the ritual tug-of-war with the little Mason and Pearson, a brush that wasn't really up to the task. She fidgeted endlessly and yowled when the brush snagged so she usually went off to school with it sticking out all over the place. It was a Steiner school, all the children arrived looking vaguely unkempt so it didn't seem to matter that much.

Viola winced at a long-forgotten memory that resurfaced unexpectedly – yelling at Bertie, 'Well brush it yourself if you're not prepared to stand still!' before throwing the brush across the room. How old was Bertie then? Six? Seven?

Oh, Viola.

This memory, coming out of the blue, was another little jab to Viola's heart, already severely damaged by the previous evening's revels. ('Was I really such a terrible mother?' she asked Bertie. 'Why the past tense?' Bertie said. Sow and reap.) Another jab. The fissure in Viola's ossified heart widened into a crevasse. Jab, jab. Of course, it wasn't that people didn't love her (although it certainly *felt* as if they didn't), she hadn't been exiled from love, she had exiled herself. She wasn't stupid, she knew that. What was the next step then, The Voice of Reason asked? Was it perhaps to begin—

'Oh, shut the fuck up,' Viola said wearily.

When Bertie went to stay with Viola's father ('I *lived* with him, I didn't *stay* with him'), true to precedent, he took her to a hairdresser and she returned with an old-fashioned bob held back with a plastic hair slide. She loved it, she reported, but Viola suspected that she only said that to annoy her. 'She can look after it herself now,' her father said. He was obsessed with self-sufficiency, of course, with people being *responsible* for themselves.

He started to snore.

'I'm still interested in the word "wary"?' Gregory said.

Viola sighed. 'Maybe it was the wrong word.'

Everyone liked her father. He was good. He was kind. She had watched him kill her mother.

'Do you want to talk about that, Viola?'

The insubstantial pageant started to drizzle limply to an end and a pair of carers came into the room and said, 'Ready for bed, Ted?' like a children's rhyme. 'He's already in bed,' Viola pointed out and the carers laughed as if she'd said something funny. They were both Filipino ('Tagalog spoken here') and laughed no matter what you said. Were the Philippines really such a happy place or were the carers just happy not to be there? Or did they not understand a word she said? It was only six o'clock – even his bedtime was that of a little boy. One of them was carrying an adult nappy and they waited silently for her to leave the room. ('Preserving the dignity of our residents is of paramount importance.')

Once her father had been cleaned up and tucked in, Viola went back to say goodbye. 'I won't be here next week,' she said, although it seemed pointless to talk to him about anything that involved the future, pointless to talk to him about anything really. 'I'm not going home,' she added, 'I'm going to a literary festival in Singapore.'

He said something, it could have been 'Sunny'.

'Yes, it will be hot,' she said, even though she knew that wasn't what he meant. Sun, son, Sunny. It was just 'a hop and a skip' from Singapore to Bali, Bertie said. If she was already going that far, why wasn't Viola going to see her 'only son'? (And Bertie called *her* a passive aggressive!) It was four hours actually, but it wasn't the time or the distance unless you thought of those things as metaphorical. Which Viola did.

'Right, well, I'll be off now,' Viola said, glancing with relief at her watch. 'I've got a taxi booked to pick me up.' She kissed Teddy lightly on the forehead, the proximity of escape making her almost affectionate. He was cool and dry to the touch, already half-embalmed and mummified. His hand twitched, but that was the only acknowledgement he gave her.

Downstairs, at the main exit door, an old woman, one of the walking dead, was treading water, looking out at what would have made quite a nice garden for the 'residents' if it hadn't been given over to staff parking. Viola recognized her as someone called Agnes. She had still been in possession of her mind when her father first moved to Poplar Hill and used to sit in his room and chat to him. Now she had the dead stare of a fish and was fluent in gibberish.

'Hello, there,' Viola said pleasantly. Experience had taught her that it was difficult to converse with someone whose eyes slid past you as if you were the ghost, not them, but she pressed on. 'Would you mind moving?' she said. 'I'd like to leave and you are a bit in the way.' Agnes said something but it was like listening to Bertie talking in her sleep. 'You're not allowed out,' Viola said, trying to nudge her out of the way, but Agnes stood her ground, immoveable as a cow or a horse. Viola sighed and said, 'Be it on your own head then,' and keyed in the magic exit number on the security pad ('4-3-2-1'). Agnes slipped swiftly out, her speediness impressive, already halfway down the drive by the time Viola was climbing into her taxi. You had to admire her fugitive spirit.

The new nursing sister came jogging awkwardly out of the building and said to Viola, 'You haven't seen Agnes, have you?' Viola shrugged and said, 'Sorry.'

She caught the last train to London and missed the sub-headline in *The Press* the next day. The news item was buried amongst photos of the weekend's street parties and reports of the Jubilee celebrations and Viola did not read that 'An eighty-year-old resident of a care home who suffers from Alzheimer's disease has been reported missing. She was spotted by a motorist wandering on the hard shoulder of the A64 and police are trying to trace her whereabouts through CCTV. The woman, who has not been named, is a resident of Poplar Hill Care Home. A spokesperson for the care home said a full investigation is underway as to how the woman had been able to get out of a secure ward and declined to comment further.'

Viola was in Changi airport by then. Another fugitive.

She took a taxi from King's Cross to the Mandarin Oriental in Knightsbridge. She had suggested to Bertie that they meet up while she was in town. 'Dinner? At Dinner – the Heston Blumenthal place at the Mandarin?' (Talk about calling a spade a spade.) 'My treat!'

'Can't, sorry,' Bertie said. 'I'm busy.'

'Too busy for your own mother?' Viola said lightly. (Sow and reap.) The horror of Saturday night came surging back. Gregory said she had 'abandonment issues'. ('As in you abandoned us?' Bertie said.) She felt sick.

Give Viola three wishes and what would she ask for?

Her children back as babies. Her children back as babies. Her children back as babies.

Somewhere high over the Indian Ocean she remembered the powerful dream from last night. She was in a train station, not a modern one, it felt like the past, dark and sooty. Sunny was with her, five or six years old, wearing that funny little red duffel coat he'd had, a stripy scarf around his neck. (Yes, she had dressed him badly, she admitted it, all right?) The station was busy, people were rushing to catch the train, to get home. They were impeded by a turnstile and a ticket collector in a booth. There were steps that led down to the platform and the train, which were both out of sight. It was Viola and Sunny's job to help the people catch the train, herding them like sheep-dogs and shouting encouragement at them. And then the rush slowed to a trickle and finally stopped. They could hear the last of the train's doors slam down below and the guard blew his whistle and Sunny turned to her and, with a beaming grin on his face, said, 'We did it, Mum! Everyone got on the train.' Viola had absolutely no idea what the dream meant.

'Are you all right, Mrs Romaine?' the lovely Asian flight attendant was asking her. They were all lovely to you in First Class. Viola supposed that was what you paid for. Tears were streaming down her cheeks. 'Sad film,' she said, indicating her blank TV screen. 'Do you think I could have a cup of tea?'

She negotiated passport control and baggage retrieval and

walked towards the exit, pulling her suitcase behind her. The automatic doors to the Arrivals hall swished quietly open. There was a driver on the other side of the barrier holding up a sign with her name on it. He would take her to a very nice hotel, and then tomorrow or the next day – she seemed to have lost her schedule – she would do a 'Meet the Author' event and give a reading, 'a little preview' from her new book, *Every Third Thought*, out next month. She seemed to recall she was also down for a couple of panel events as well. 'The role of the writer in the contemporary world.' 'Popular versus literary – a false divide?' Something like that. It was always something like that. Literary festivals, bookshops, interviews, online chats, you were just filling up other people's empty spaces really. But they were filling up your empty spaces too.

She approached the driver. He would have no idea who she was unless she identified herself. She swerved away from him, carried on as if that was her intention all along, took the escalator back up to the check-in area, found the Singapore Airlines ticketing desk and bought a ticket to Denpasar.

She imagined the look on Sunny's face. ('Surprise, surprise!') They would get everyone on the train. Somehow or other.

30 March 1944

The Last Flight

The Fall

He had just whistled for the dog when he spotted a pair of hares in the grassy field that lay on the western side of the farmhouse. March hares, boxing like bare-knuckle fighters, the spring madness upon them. He caught sight of a third hare. Then a fourth. Once when he was a boy he had counted seven at one time, in the meadow at Fox Corner. The meadow had gone now, Pamela reported, ploughed up for winter wheat for hungry wartime mouths. The flax and larkspur, buttercups, corn poppies, red campion, the ox-eye daisies, all gone, never to come back.

The hares might be convinced by the new season but it didn't feel much like spring yet to Teddy. Pale clouds scudded across a washed-out sky. They were driven by a sharp east wind that was blowing all the way from the North Sea across the flat landscape, whipping soil off the dry tops of the bare furrows. It was the kind of weather that lowered the spirits, although Teddy's were lifted a little by the sight of the jousting hares and the high, fluty notes of a blackbird answering his own whistle from somewhere unseen.

The dog heard his whistle too – Lucky always heard him whistle – and was making a headlong dash in his direction, blithely unaware of the hares' sparring match taking place in the field. The dog roamed far and wide these days, quite at home in the countryside, although equally at home, apparently, in the Waafery. When the dog reached him it sat promptly, gazing up at his face, waiting for its next orders.

'Let's go,' Teddy said. 'We're on ops tonight. Me,' he added. 'Not you.' Once was enough.

When he looked again the hares had disappeared.

The orders had come down from Bomber Command HQ at High Wycombe this morning, but only a small handful of people on the station – Teddy one of them – was ever given early notice of the target.

As a wing commander he was discouraged from flying too frequently, 'or we'd be losing a wing commander a week', as the CO put it. All pre-war notions of hierarchy in the RAF had long since been upended. You could be a wing commander at twenty-three, dead at twenty-four.

He was on his third tour. There had been no obligation to sign up for it, he could have returned to instructing, he could have requested a desk job. It was 'madness', Sylvie wrote. He tended to agree with her. He had flown now on over seventy raids and had come to be regarded as untouchable by many on the squadron. This was how myths were made these days, Teddy thought, simply by staying alive longer than anyone else. Perhaps that was his role now, to be the ju-ju, to be the magic. To keep as many safe as possible. Perhaps he *was* immortal. He tested this theory by getting himself on the battle-order as often as possible, despite protests from higher up.

He was back with the first squadron he had served with, but now they were to be found not on the comfortable brick-built, pre-war RAF base that had housed them near the beginning of the war, but in a hastily erected township commandeered from corrugated iron and mud. It would only take a few years after they left (for leave they surely would – even the Hundred Years War had come to an end) for it to return to fields. To the brown, the green and the gold.

If he went on a sortie he flew in *F-Fox*. She was a good sound aircraft that had already beaten the odds by carrying one crew safely through their tour, but really he just liked the name and its associations with home. Ursula reported that Sylvie, who once upon a time loved the foxes at Fox Corner, had been laying poison down for them after they had committed a particularly successful raid on the hen-house. 'She might come back as a fox in the next life,' Ursula wrote, 'and then she'll be very sorry.' She 'liked the idea' of reincarnation, his sister said, but of course she couldn't actually believe in it. That was the trouble with faith, Teddy thought, by its very nature it was impossible. He didn't believe in anything any more. Trees, perhaps. Trees and rocks and water. The rising of the sun and the running of the deer.

He mourned for the foxes, he would have placed them above a coop of chickens in the order of things. Above many people, too.

He had sidestepped Christmas at Fox Corner, saying that he had to remain on the station, which was only half a lie, and he had not seen their potentially vulpine mother for many months – not, in fact, since the irritating lunch at Fox Corner after Hamburg. He realized that he had ceased to have any affection for Sylvie. 'One does,' Ursula said.

F-Fox's ground crew always issued dire warnings to anyone who had been allowed to borrow her – 'bring the Wing Co's kite back safely or else' – although really as far as the ground crew were concerned the aircraft belonged to them and they admonished Teddy himself in much the same terms.

Sometimes Teddy went up in one of the ropier old kites to test further his theory of immortality. His regular ground crew were unhappy if he flew with the new, the untested and the shaky. He occasionally piloted a sprog crew but usually he took the dickey seat and flew as a reassuring second pilot with them. It wasn't unlucky if he was in it – quite the opposite. 'We'll be safe now the Wing Co's with us,' he heard them say. He remembered Keith and his widdershins luck that had let him down in the end.

He made his way out to the dispersal pan to visit *F-Fox* and her ground crew.

It was the first flight for the crew Teddy was going up with. They had been delivered fresh out of the box from the OTU at Rufforth that morning. They had been assigned their own aircraft, but the ground crew had declared her unserviceable after her air test and Teddy had offered *F-Fox* to them, along with himself. They were as cheerful and excited as puppies at the prospect.

A bowser was already feeding fuel into *F-Fox*'s wing tanks. The ground crew knew roughly where they would be going by the amount being taken on board, but never talked about the target to the aircrew. They kept everything close to themselves. Perhaps they thought it was bad luck. Some of them would be keeping a long vigil through the night, usually huddled around an inadequate stove in their bleak little hut at dispersal, snoozing fitfully on a camp bed or even sitting on an upturned toolbox, waiting anxiously for *F-Fox*'s return. Waiting for Teddy.

A trolley of bombs trundled towards the aircraft, a miniature train, and the armourers started winching the bombs into the bomb-bay. Someone had chalked on one of the bombs, 'This is for Ernie, Adolf,' and Teddy wondered who Ernie was but didn't ask and no one said. One of the erks, a cheerful Liverpudlian, was at the top of a ladder, preoccupied with polishing the Perspex on the rear-turret with a pair of 'blackouts' – the large serviceable knickers that the WAAFs wore. He had discovered – perhaps it was best not to imagine how – that they were the best material for this vital job. A little speck of dirt on the Perspex could be mistaken by the gunner for a German fighter and before you knew it he'd be shooting his guns off all over the sky, betraying their position to the enemy. The erk caught sight of Teddy and said, 'Everything OK, skip?'

Teddy answered with a breezy affirmative. Calm

confidence, that was the best demeanour for a captain, pull everyone along behind you in your optimistic wake. And try and learn everyone's names. And be kind. Because why not?

He had made a vow, a private promise to the world in the long dark watches of the night, that if he did survive then in the great afterward he would always try to be kind, to live a good quiet life. Like Candide, he would cultivate his garden. Quietly. And that would be his redemption. Even if he could add only a feather to the balance it would be some kind of repayment for being spared. When it was all over and the reckoning fell due, it may be that he would be in need of that feather.

He knew that he was just stooging around, doing nothing useful. These fits of restlessness, mental and physical, seemed to be increasing all the time. Sometimes he found himself drifting off, lost not so much in thought as no thought at all, and without realizing it he found himself now at the pigeon loft. The homing pigeons were kept in a shed behind the crews' Nissan-hut sleeping quarters and were looked after by one of the cooks, who was a pigeon fancier and missed his own racing birds, back in Dewsbury.

Teddy made the dog stay outside the shed. It always barked at the birds and set them fluttering nervously, even though they were generally, by their nature, a steadfast, even heroic sort of creature. The theory was that the pigeons on board an aircraft could be used to relay messages and that in the event of ditching or parachuting out you could write your location down and put it in a little canister and the bird would carry this precious information home. It seemed to Teddy, however, that it was highly unlikely that if you were trying to evade in enemy territory anyone would find you because of some incoherent scribble. You would have to know where you were, for a start, and the bird would have to overcome tremendous odds just to make it back to British shores. (He wondered if the girl from the Air Ministry had any figures for *that*.) The Germans kept hawks along the French coast solely for the purpose of bringing the poor birds down.

And, of course, you would have to remember to get a bird out of the basket that was stowed in the fuselage and stuff it into a container that was not much bigger than a vacuum flask (a tricky feat in itself). Baling out of a crippled bomber involved – at best – a mad life-or-death scramble to clip on parachutes, throw off escape hatches, help the wounded out, while all the time the aircraft was on fire or in an uncontrollable dive. The poor pigeons would not be uppermost in anyone's mind in those last few desperate seconds. He wondered how many of them had been left behind, helplessly trapped in their baskets, abandoned to burn or drown or simply disintegrate in a little cloud of feathers when an aircraft exploded. Everyone knew not to put the pigeons on the Wing Co's kite.

Teddy was soothed by the soft cooing and the earthy ammoniac smell of the dim shed. He took one of the compliant birds from its hatch and stroked it gently. It suffered his attentions without protest. When he put it back it eyed him steadily and he wondered what it was thinking. Not much, he supposed. When he came back outside, into the harsh daylight, the dog sniffed him suspiciously for signs of infidelity.

It was lunchtime and he set off for the mess. He had little appetite these days but he forced the food down in a dutiful fashion. There was a particularly stodgy kind of steamed sponge pudding containing prunes that translated as 'plum duff' on the blackboard menu and which sat heavily in his stomach afterwards. He remembered with pleasure something called a *Far Breton* that he had eaten beneath a hot French sun. The French could transform even prunes into something delicious. He had made an emergency landing at Elvington, where the French crews were stationed, and discovered that their cooks were also French and they treated their rations with a good deal more élan than the RAF canteen staff. And what's more, they took their meals with a glass of red wine, Algerian, but wine nonetheless. They would not have tolerated a plum duff.

The crews had spent the rest of the afternoon resting – writing letters, playing darts, listening to the wireless in the mess, always tuned to the BBC Forces programme. Some slept. A lot of them had been on ops last night and had not fallen into their beds until well after first light.

Meanwhile the target was being revealed to the pilots and navigators in a preliminary briefing. There were specialist briefings for the wireless operators and bomb-aimers. Teddy more than half expected the op to be scrubbed – they were into the moon period and the skies were clear, but soon, with the shorter nights of spring, it would be impossible to fly the long raids deep into

Germany. He supposed that this was Harris's last hurrah in the Battle of Berlin. The long gruelling series of winter raids with their high toll was nearly over. Seventy-eight bombers lost to Leipzig last month, seventy-three to Berlin last week. Nearly a thousand crew lost since November. Every one a young man. 'Flowers of the Forest', the lament played at the funeral of a Canadian navigator that Teddy and Mac both knew on their first tour. Walter. Walt. His nickname was Disney. Teddy didn't think that he'd ever known his real name, although he must surely have had one. It seemed so long ago now, and yet it wasn't.

The CO had asked them to accompany Disney's body to Stonefall and act as pallbearers. A Scots piper had been found in Leeds and played at the graveside. Disney had been killed by flak on a raid over Bremen. The flight-engineer navigator had used astro-navigation to get them home, unable to consult Disney's maps and charts because they were so sodden with his blood that they were useless.

They were burning burnt-out towns, bombing bombed-out cities. It had been a good idea. Defeat them in the air and save the world from the horror of land warfare, from Ypres, the Somme, Passchendaele. But it wasn't working. When they were knocked down they got up again, the stuff of nightmares, an endless harvest of dragon's teeth sprouting on the plain of Ares. And so they continued throwing the birds against the wall. And still the wall stood.

An air vice-marshal had dropped in on the squadron. He had lots of medals and braid – 'scrambled egg' – on display. 'Like to show my face to the men,' he said. Teddy didn't remember ever seeing his face before.

His mind was on Nancy. He had received a letter that morning – many words, as usual, yet saying nothing, also as usual, but at the end a reference to their engagement and how she would 'understand if your feelings have changed'. ('You write to me so rarely, darling.') Was she really saying that *her* feelings had changed? His CO said, 'Ted? Ready?' disrupting his wool-gathering, and they made their way to the briefing hut, the vice-marshal striding authoritatively ahead. He was accompanied by his rather glamorous WAAF driver, who surprised Teddy by winking at him.

The crews were already assembled, ticked off on a roll at the door by the RAF police. Once everyone was in the doors would be locked and the windows shuttered. The air vice-marshal's driver was left to kick her heels outside. Security was tight before a raid. No one could leave the station or make phone calls. Keeping the target secret was vital, although it was often jokingly said that if you wanted to know the next target you only need go to Bettys Bar. The reality was that one way or another the Germans were tracking them from the moment they took off. They listened on their radio frequencies, jammed the Gee, tracked the H2S and caught them in the net of their own radar that stretched along the coast of Europe. Toe to toe, blow for blow.

When they entered the briefing hut there was a great clattering of chairs as the crews, some hundred and twenty of them, stood to attention. The room – a Nissan hut – was the usual smoky, sweaty fug. More scraping and bumping of chairs as everyone sat down again. The map on the wall was hidden by a blackout curtain and the CO always drew it back with a theatrical flourish as if it was part of a conjuring trick, before pronouncing the by now time-honoured words, 'Gentlemen, your target for tonight is . . .'

Nuremberg? There was a rumble of discontent from the more experienced crews, a few 'Jesus's and 'Christ's, an Australian 'Strewth', despite the presence of the scrambled egg. It was a long flight, deep into the enemy's heartland, nearly three times further than going to the Ruhr. The red ribbon stretched almost straight to the target with hardly any of the usual zigzagging.

The senior intelligence officer, a stern-faced WAAF who took her duties very seriously, stood up and told them all about the importance of the target. It was seven long months since it had been attacked and was largely intact, despite being home to a huge SS barracks as well as 'the famous' MAN armament works, and now that the Siemens factory in Berlin had been bombed they had stepped up production of searchlights, electric motors 'and so on' at their Nuremberg works.

The city was symbolic, where Hitler held his mass rallies, and was close to the enemy's heart, the intelligence officer continued. It would hit their morale hard. The aiming point was the railway yards but the creep-back would find the medieval city, 'the Altstadt', she said, making a poor stab at German pronunciation. They were carrying high loads of incendiaries and the old wooden buildings would burn well.

Dürer's birthplace was in the Altstadt. Teddy had grown up with two of Dürer's prints. They had hung in the morning room at Fox Corner – one of a hare and one of a pair of red squirrels. The intelligence officer didn't mention Dürer, she was more interested in the flak and searchlight positions that were marked on the map with green and red celluloid overlays. The crews, too, paid careful attention to them, their unease growing all the time as they looked at the long straight red ribbon.

But it was the moon that was really upsetting them, upsetting Teddy too. It was an unusually bright half-moon and it was going to be shining down on them like a bright coin through a long dark night. Their unhappiness was compounded when they were told they were to fly through the Cologne gap. It was 'unlikely' to be heavily defended this late in the year, they were told. Really, Teddy thought? The route passed close to the Ruhr and Frankfurt defences, to night fighter airfields and their beacons, Ida and Otto, around which the German fighters circled, waiting, like hawks after pigeons.

The Met officer took the stage and gave details of wind speeds, cloud conditions and the weather likely to be encountered. He said there was a 'possibility' of fairly good cloud cover on the way there and back that 'might' hide them from the fighters. The word 'possibility' made them shift nervously in their seats. The word 'might' made it worse. 'Fairly' wasn't too promising either. It would be clear over the target, he said, even though the first Pathfinders had already reported cumulus at eight thousand feet, information that wasn't passed on to the crews. They needed it to be the other way round – cloud on that long leg to hide them from the fighters and the moon illuminating their target.

The CO had confided in Teddy that he was 'certain' the op would be scrubbed. Teddy didn't know why it had been considered in the first place. Churchill liked the target. Harris liked the target. Teddy didn't. He didn't suppose Harris and Churchill cared much for his opinion.

The specialist leaders made a few pertinent remarks. The navigators were taken over the route and the turning points. The sparks were reminded of their frequencies for the night. The bombing leaders detailed the payload and ratio of high explosive to incendiaries and the timing and phasing of attacks, the colours of the target indicators that they were to drop their bombs on. Everyone was reminded of the colours of the day. They all knew of crews shot down by friendly fire for shooting off the wrong colours of the day.

Then Teddy was up. A constant course of two hundred and sixty-five miles over well-defended enemy territory in bright moonlight with little chance of cloud cover. For the sake of morale (the quietly confident leader) he tried to spin these bleak facts into something less dire – highlighting again the importance of the city as an industrial and transport centre, the blow to enemy morale, and so on. The long leg will suggest a number of other possible targets to the fighters so they will be distracted from the Cologne gap. The sheer simplicity of the long leg will fool them and the lack of doglegs will conserve fuel, and that means that you can carry heavier bomb loads. And, being more direct, it will mean less fatigue for you, you will get there quicker, and the quicker you get there the quicker you will get safely back here. And keep a tight bomber stream. Always.

He sat down again. They trusted him, he could see it on their haggard faces. There was no going back for them now so it was best that they went out in a good frame of mind. There was nothing worse than setting out oppressed by the feeling that you were for the chop. He remembered Duisburg, the last op of his first tour, how his crew had been jittery, convinced they were going for a burton. Two of them had, of course. George and Vic. Of *J-Jig*'s original crew there was only himself and Mac left. He had a letter from Mac, telling him that he had got married, honeymooned at Niagara, 'little one on the way'. The war was over for Mac.

Kenny had gone on to train new air-gunners at a gunnery school and had written a letter to Teddy in his almost illiterate hand. 'Me – an instructor! Who'd have thought it?' A few weeks later he was in an aircraft that crash-landed on return from a cross-country training exercise. Three crew members survived. Kenny wasn't one of them. One of his many sisters wrote to Teddy, 'Wee Kenny is an angel now,' in a hand almost as poor as Kenny's. If only that were true, Teddy thought, if only the ranks of Spenser's bright squadrons were being swelled by those of Bomber Command. But they weren't. The dead were dead. And they were legion.

Kenny should have kept his mangy black cat instead of giving it to Vic Bennett's baby. A letter had wound its way to him eventually, not from Lil but from Mrs Bennett, a reluctantly proud new grandmother. 'A girl, not much to look at but she'll do.' A Margaret, not an Edward, and Teddy was relieved that he didn't have a namesake. *Margaret, are you grieving over Goldengrove unleaving?*

* * *

The CO gave a few encouraging words, the vice-marshal made some hearty remarks as befitted someone sporting so much scrambled egg, a medic standing at the door handed out wakey-wakey pills as they went past. And that was that.

There was the traditional last supper, not much of a feast tonight – sausages and a rubbery egg. No bacon. Teddy thought of Sylvie's pig, of the smell of roasting pork.

They were sealed off now, a bad time when your thoughts could overshadow everything. Teddy had a few games of dominoes with a flight-lieutenant in the officers' mess. It was mindless enough to satisfy both of them but it was a relief when it was time to go to the crew room and get kitted up.

Thick woollen long johns and vest, knee-length socks, roll-neck pullover shirt, battledress, sheepskin flying boots, three layers of gloves – silk, chamois, woollen. Half their items of clothing weren't even uniform at all. It gave some of them a raffish, almost piratical air – rather offset by the way they waddled around as if in nappies. Then they added even more – the Mae West, the parachute harness – until walking itself became difficult.

Checked there was a whistle on their collars, dog tags round their necks. Then from the WAAF orderlies they collected their flasks of coffee, sandwiches, boiled sweets, chewing gum, Fry's chocolate. They were given their 'escape kits' – silk maps printed on scarves or hand-kerchiefs for the countries they were flying over, local money, compasses concealed in pens and buttons, phrase sheets. Teddy had kept a scrap of paper left over from a long raid to Chemnitz when it was feared that if they came down they might be picked up by Russians, who wouldn't know what to make of them and would shoot them while they were making up their minds. It said (apparently), 'I am an Englishman.'

They picked up their parachutes and a pretty WAAF gave Teddy a silk neck scarf and said shyly, 'Take that for me, will you, sir? Then I can say it's flown over Germany and bombed the enemy.' It smelt sweet. 'April violets,' she said. Like a knight taking a favour from some fair damsel in a tale of chivalry, he thought, and stuffed it in his pocket. He never saw it again, it must have fallen out at some point. The time for tales of chivalry was long over.

They emptied their pockets of everything that might identify them. It was an act that always seemed symbolic to Teddy – crossing the threshold between being individuals and becoming fliers, anonymous, inter-changeable. Englishmen. And Aussies and Kiwis and Canucks. Indians, West Indians, South Africans, Poles, French, Czechs, Rhodesians, Norwegians. The Yanks. In fact, the whole of Western civilization was ranged against Germany. You had to wonder how that could have happened to the country of Beethoven and Bach and how they would feel about it if they had an afterward. *Alle Menschen werden Brüder.* Ursula's question, 'Do you think it's possible? One day?' No. He didn't. Not really.

A WAAF stood at the door of the crew room and called for *F-Fox* and *L-London*'s crews and they all piled aboard the old charabanc she was driving. Sometimes transport seemed as haphazard as some of their clothing.

Lucky had been left in the arms of a particularly attractive WAAF, an R/T girl called Stella. He liked Stella, thought there might be something between them. Last week Teddy had escorted her to a dance in the mess at a neighbouring station. A peck on the cheek on their return and a 'Thank you, sir, that was jolly good fun.' Nothing more. There had been a sickening incident the day before at their own airfield, a WAAF who had been decapitated by a propeller blade. Teddy shied away from remembering it even now. It had left everyone sombre, particularly – naturally – the WAAFs. Stella was a good sort, liked dogs and horses. Sometimes the awfulness of war led to sex, at other times it didn't. It was hard to fathom a reason for the different outcomes. He regretted not going to bed with Stella and wondered if she felt the same. He had had a short-lived – very short-lived – affair with a friend of Stella's called Julia. It had involved a lot of sex. Very good sex. A secret memory.

They reached *F-Fox* at dispersal and dismounted from the bus. Even at this point Teddy was expecting the red light that would tell them that the raid had been scrubbed. But apparently this was not to be, so he carried on, going over the aircraft with the new pilot, the flight engineer and the ground crew. The engineer was called Roy, Teddy reminded himself. The mid-upper was a Canadian called Joe, the tail-end Charlie was – helpfully – called Charlie. He looked about twelve years old. The tail-gunner's Perspex was getting a final polish with the blackouts.

Teddy offered cigarettes all round. Only the bomb-aimer didn't smoke. 'Clifford,' he reminded Teddy when he could see him struggling. 'Clifford,' Teddy murmured. All of the ground crew smoked like chimneys. Teddy wished that he could take them up on a raid, a safe one from which they would all be guaranteed to return. It seemed a shame that they never experienced what 'their' aircraft went through, never saw the view through that well-polished Perspex. At the end of the war, the RAF did 'Cook's tours', flying the earthbound personnel over Germany so they could see the havoc that they had helped to wreak. Ursula managed to wangle her way on to one, Teddy had no idea how but he wasn't surprised. The war had proved his sister to be rather good at negotiating the great game of bureaucracy. It was terrible, she reported, to see a country in total ruin.

Teddy's sprogs all urinated on the wheel of *F-Fox* and then looked slightly abashed when they realized that Teddy wasn't going to partake of this masculine ritual. He was their sadhu, Teddy thought, a guru. He could have told them to climb up to the control-tower roof and throw themselves off in an orderly sequence and they would have done. He sighed and fumbled with his enormous amount of clothing and took an unnecessary piss against the wheel. The sprogs gave each other covert grins of relief.

Then the ground crew made their usual unshowy, optimistic farewells, shaking hands all round. 'Good luck, see you in the morning.'

Teddy stood next to the pilot for take-off. The pilot was called Fraser, from Edinburgh, a student at St Andrews. A different kind of Scot from Kenny Nielson. No second dickey flight for him, instead his wing commander riding shotgun. He remembered the crew of *W-William. This aircraft took off at 16.20 hours and failed to return. It has therefore been reported as missing.*

The Bristol Hercules engines whined as the propellers made their first few jerky revolutions before catching and turning to the familiar staccato. Good engines, Teddy told Fraser when they were doing their checks. Fraser, of necessity, was interested in the *mechanics of bombing.*

Port outer, port inner, followed by starboard inner, starboard outer. Once all the checks were done – the mag drops and oil pressures and so on – Fraser asked control for permission to taxi. He glanced at Teddy as if he needed his approval more than he needed the control tower's and Teddy gave him a thumbs-up. The chocks were removed and they edged forward to join the procession on the perimeter track, the engines throbbing and rumbling, a vibration that passed through muscle into bone and lodged in the heart and lungs. There was something magnificent about it to Teddy's mind.

They were fifth in line to take off and they swung on to the runway, engines to full boost, waiting, a greyhound in a trap, ready to go when the controller's Aldis light showed green. Teddy was still expecting the red light from the control tower, cancelling the op. It never came. Sometimes they were even recalled once they were in the air. Not this time.

The usual flare-path farewell party had gathered at the controller's caravan. Assorted WAAFs, cookhouse and ground crew. The CO was there, the air vice-marshal too, saluting every aircraft as it passed. Those who are about to die do not salute you back, Teddy thought. Instead he gave a thumbs-up to Stella, who was also there, holding Lucky in her arms, and as they rolled down the runway she lifted one of the dog's paws and waved it. Better than any scrambled egg's salute in Teddy's book. He laughed and Fraser glanced at him in alarm. Taking off was a serious business, especially when it was your first operational sortie and your wing commander was your second pilot. And that same Wing Co was showing signs of eccentric behaviour.

The green light showed and they began to lumber along the runway like an overweight bird, trying to reach the necessary 105mph that would 'unstick' twelve tons of metal and petrol and explosive from the earth. Teddy helped with the engine throttles and felt the usual relief as Fraser eased back on the yoke and *F-Fox* strained to drag herself off the ground. Unconsciously, Teddy touched the little silver hare in his breast pocket.

They roared towards the farmhouse and Teddy looked for the farmer's daughter but could see no sign of her. He felt a chill. She was always there. He could see the flat fields in the dusk, the bare brown earth, the darkening horizon. The farmhouse. The farmyard. They banked and began to circle, stacking and gathering themselves before heading for the coast, and as *F-Fox*'s wing dipped to port he caught sight of her. She was gazing up at them, waving blindly, waving at them all. They were safe. He waved back, although he knew she couldn't see him.

The squadrons in the north had to take off an hour earlier than those on the more southerly airfields and then had to fly due south to meet at the rendezvous point. It gave them some relatively safe time to get on with their routine tasks. Once they were in the air there were no idle moments, all that gloomy introspection that could take hold on the ground disappeared. The flight engineer was kept busy synchronizing the engines, calculating fuel stocks, changing petrol tanks. The IFF was switched on to identify them as friend rather than foe to the RAF's own fighters. The spark wound out the trailing wireless aerial and the navigator put his head down, working on accurate fixes, comparing the actual winds to those forecast. Once they were over the sea the bomb-aimer started chucking Window out. They were still flying with their navigation lights on and Teddy could see the red and green lights twinkling on the wingtips of other aircraft.

They ground their way over the North Sea, climbing all the time. The waves were highlighted by the moon and the wings of *F-Fox* glinted like polished silver. They may as well have had a searchlight shining on them. The gunners tested their Brownings in short bursts over the sea. The bombs were fused, the navigation lights switched off. At five thousand feet they put their oxygen masks on and Teddy heard the familiar rasping breathing over the intercom.

They were bowled across Belgium by a following wind. Visibility was so good that they could see many of the other aircraft in the bomber stream. It was as close to a daylight raid as Teddy had ever been. His life took place at night. The wide-awake moon could be seen reflected in lakes and rivers as they passed over them, escorting them, mile after spot-lit mile. *There's not a trace upon her face of diffidence or shyness.* Hugh had loved his Gilbert and Sullivan gramophone records. There had been an amateur performance of *The Mikado* put on in the local village hall and their father had astonished them all by taking the role of Ko-Ko, the Lord High Executioner. He had relished the complete change of character it had afforded him, leering and prancing and singing around the stage. 'Quite the Jekyll and Hyde,' Sylvie said. Mrs Shawcross had played Katisha. Again, another thespian revelation.

They reached the first turning point near Charleroi and not long after that the slaughter began.

There were fighters everywhere, like angry wasps whose nest had been disturbed. It was a shock to meet them so early, and so many of them. Not a nest that had been disturbed but a swarm that seemed to have been waiting for them.

'I can see an aircraft going down in flames off the port bow,' the mid-upper gunner reported.

'Log that, navigator,' Fraser said.

'OK, skipper.'

The rear-gunner's voice this time, 'One going down on the starboard beam.'

'Log that, navigator.'

Teddy, standing next to Fraser, could see stricken aircraft everywhere. The sky was scattered with the bright white stars of explosions.

'Are they scarecrows, sir?' the bomb-aimer asked. Fraser was 'skipper', Teddy noticed, and the crew had plumped for 'sir' for Teddy so as not to confuse them with each other. They had all heard the rumour that the Germans were using 'scarecrows' – anti-aircraft shells simulating exploding bombers – but it had always seemed unlikely to Teddy. He saw some of the bright white stars belching the dirty, oily red flames that were only too familiar to him. His sprog crew had never seen a bomber shot down until now. Baptism of fire, he thought.

Some floated down like large leaves, others plummeted straight to the earth. A fellow Halifax over on their port beam flew past with all four engines on fire, spilling streams of burning petrol, but too far away to see if there were any crew aboard. Suddenly its wings collapsed like a drop-leaf table and it fell from the sky like a dead bird.

'Not scarecrows, aircraft, I'm afraid,' he said and heard several gasps of horror on the intercom. Perhaps he should have let them continue with their delusions. Aircraft everywhere were going down on fire, or exploding, often with no sign that they even knew they had been attacked. The mid-upper continued to count them and the navigator to tick them in his log until Teddy intervened and said, 'That's enough,' because he could tell from their breathing that the crew were beginning to panic.

On their port beam an aircraft on fire from aft to stern flew by, straight and level but upside down. Teddy saw a Lancaster erupt in sheets of white flame and drop on to a Halifax below it. Both went cartwheeling down to earth together, gigantic pinwheels of fire. Teddy could see what must be a Pathfinder spooling down to earth, its red and green marker flares exploding prettily as it hit the ground. He had never been a witness to this much carnage. Aircraft went down in the distance usually, stars flaring and dying.

Crews simply disappeared, they weren't there next morning for their bacon and eggs, you didn't give too much thought to *how* they disappeared. The horror and terror of those last moments were hidden. Now they were inescapable.

The Pathfinder puzzled Teddy, it should be at the head of the Main Force. Either it was in the wrong place or they were. He asked the navigator to check the winds again. It seemed to Teddy that they had drifted north of that red ribbon. He sensed the confusion in the navigator's reply. He found himself wishing for Mac's experience.

Down below he could see the blazing wreckage of aircraft on the ground stretching back for fifty or sixty miles.

Then, as further proof of the scarecrow myth, over on the starboard beam they saw a Lancaster, illuminated by the cruel moon – it may as well have been coned by a searchlight – being stalked stealthily by a German fighter from underneath, invisible to her oblivious rear-gunner. The fighter had an upward-pointing cannon, the first Teddy had ever seen. Of course – that was why so many aircraft were going down so suddenly. The cannon looked as though they were pointing straight into the vulnerable bellies of the bombers, but if they could hit the wings, where the fuel tanks were, then the bombers didn't stand a chance.

He watched helplessly as the fighter opened fire before peeling quickly away from its victim. The Lancaster's wings exploded into great gouts of white fire and *F-Fox* lurched violently.

Before they had a chance to recover they were raked by

cannon fire, ripping and clattering along the flimsy aluminium fuselage, and without warning they pitched into a vertical dive. Teddy thought that Fraser must be trying to evade the fighter, but when he glanced at him he saw to his horror that he was slumped over the controls. There was no sign of any injury, he could have been asleep for all Teddy could tell. He shouted for help over the intercom – it was almost impossible to get at the controls with Fraser in this position and he had to try to hold his inert body back and at the same time haul back on the controls, while the G-force was like a ton of concrete on his head.

Both the spark and the engineer fought their way forward and started tussling with the motionless Fraser. The pilot's seat was quite high up in the aircraft and it was a snug fit to cram yourself into it with all your kit on. To extricate someone from that position seemed like a near-impossible task, especially as Teddy was perched on the edge of the seat and at one point he thought he might have to crouch on poor Fraser's lap. Somehow or other they wrestled the pilot out and Teddy took his seat. There was no blood anywhere, for which he was grateful.

They were screaming earthward at 300mph now, *F-Fox* almost standing on her head. Teddy yelled for the flight engineer and they both wrapped themselves around the yoke and hung on to it for dear life. Teddy worried that the wings would simply be pulled off, but finally, after what seemed like an eternity but must have been a handful of seconds, their combined strength was just enough to actuate the elevators and bring the nose back up again and they levelled out and started a ponderous climb back up.

There were a lot of expletives on the intercom and Teddy did a crew check and told them rather tersely, 'The pilot's been hit, I'm afraid. I'm taking over. Navigator, plot a new course for the target, please.' The gods alone knew where they were now, and possibly not even them.

The spark and the flight engineer had dragged Fraser to the crew rest position. 'Still breathing, skipper,' the spark reported. He was no longer 'sir', he noticed. He was the skipper. The captain.

Dismayed muttering from the bomb-aimer alerted Teddy to something he had never seen before. Vapour trails. They were never usually seen below twenty-five thousand feet and now they were everywhere, pouring from the tails of the bombers. The contrails were bright banners, marking them as targets even more clearly than the moon, if that was possible.

The bomber stream had long ago begun to disintegrate. The more experienced pilots had realized that rather than being the safest place to be, it had become the most dangerous. Teddy began to elbow his way out to the edge of it at the same time as he pushed higher. *Keep a tight bomber stream. Always.* His last command to his squadron. He hoped they weren't blindly following his instructions. Teddy was working the sky as much as he could. *F-Fox* couldn't quite make the height of the Lancasters but in the thin air and with good engines he got pretty close. Nonetheless they were spotted.

'One coming in, skipper.'

'OK, navigator.'

'Nine hundred feet. Eight hundred,' the navigator

counted off the distance of the approaching blip on his radar screen. 'Seven hundred, six hundred.'

'See anything yet, gunners?'

'No, skipper,' from both.

'Five hundred, four hundred.'

'Got him, skipper,' from the mid-upper gunner. 'Port upper quarter. Corkscrew port. Go, go, go.'

'Up the revs, engineer.'

'A hundred on, skip.'

'Hang on everybody,' Teddy said as he rammed the controls forward, rolling the aircraft and dropping the wing down to port. The G-force pinned him to his seat. They spun down, the altimeter unwinding until at the bottom of the dive he rolled the aircraft to starboard, pulled the ailerons back and they lumbered upwards again. He was trying to find cloud to hide in but the mid-upper was shouting, 'Starboard upper quarter, corkscrew starboard, go, go, go!'

Sometimes the amount of turbulence alone that was created was enough to put a fighter off, but not this one. As soon as they had climbed again, there was a shout from the rear-gunner, 'Bandit at rear port, dive to port!'

The gunners' Brownings were drumming away and the aircraft filled with the stink of cordite. The sky around *F-Fox* was crowded with bullet and cannon tracer. Teddy threw the heavy aircraft around in the sky, dropping into a starboard dive and then heeling into a port curve, clawing his way back up the sky, trying to shake the fighter off their shoulder. He felt exhausted from the sheer physical effort needed to control the aircraft. Needs must, he heard his mother say. The gunners were out of ammunition but then the mid-upper reported, 'Port bandit broken away, skipper,' and then, 'Starboard bandit moved on too, skipper.' On to another poor sod, Teddy thought and said, 'Well done, gunners.'

Their luck finally ran out. They never reached the target. Teddy wasn't sure they would ever have found it anyway. Many didn't, he learned later.

It happened very quickly. One minute they were in the dark void of the sky, no sign of the bomber stream any more, and the next they were coned and were being hit by flak – huge, hollow bangs as if the fuselage was being battered by a sledgehammer. They must have found the Ruhr's defences. Dazzled and blinded by the searchlights, all Teddy could do was fling the aircraft into another dive. He could feel poor *F-Fox* protesting, he had already tested her beyond her limits and he was expecting her to break up any second. He suspected that he, too, had been tested beyond his limits but suddenly they were out of the awful light and back into the welcome dark.

The port wing was on fire and they were rapidly losing height. Teddy knew instinctively that there was going to be no soft landing this time, no ditching, no WAAF guiding them into a friendly airfield. *F-Fox* was going to her death. He gave the order to abandon the aircraft.

The navigator kicked off the escape hatch and he and the spark strapped a parachute on to the injured pilot and pushed him out. The spark followed quickly, then the navigator. The mid-upper climbed down from his turret and followed. The rear-gunner reported that his turret was shot up and he couldn't get it to revolve.

The bomb-aimer crawled up from the nose, fighting gravity, and went to see if he could help the rear-gunner manually release the turret.

Flames had begun to lick the inside of the fuselage. They had come out of the dive but were still losing height. Teddy was expecting *F-Fox* to explode at any moment. There was no word from the bomb-aimer or the rear-gunner. Clifford and Charlie, their names suddenly came back to him.

He was fighting *F-Fox* now, trying to keep her flying straight and level. Clifford appeared by his side and said the fire had prevented him from getting to the rear-gunner and Teddy told him to jump. He disappeared through the hatch.

It was all a blur after that, there was a curtain of flames behind him, he could feel them beginning to scorch his seat. The intercom was no longer working but he carried on wrestling with *F-Fox* to give the rear-gunner a last-ditch chance to get out. The captain was always the last to leave.

And then, when he thought he was resigned to death – quite accepting of it – the instinct for life kicked in and the jaws of death were forced open. He found himself tearing off the twin umbilicals of oxygen and intercom and flinging himself out of his seat and was more or less sucked from *F-Fox's* belly through the escape hatch.

The silence of the night sky was stunning after the noise inside the aircraft. He was alone, floating in the dark, the great peaceful dark. The moon was shining benignly on him. Below a river ran like silver, Germany laid out like a map in the moonlight, growing closer and closer as he drifted towards it like a feathery dandelion head.

Above him the fiery form of *F-Fox* continued to glide on her downward path. Teddy wondered if the rear-gunner was still inside. He shouldn't have abandoned him. The aircraft found the ground before Teddy did and he watched as it exploded in a glittering starburst of light. He would live, he realized. There would be an afterward after all. He gave thanks to whichever god had stepped in to save him.

2012

All the Way to Bright

'. . . geofencing . . . we should want to do because . . . the new normal . . . client–agency relationship or on the other hand . . . as well as near-field communication . . .'

The man who was speaking had a degree in jargon and a doctorate in nonsense. His words were floating in the air, language devoid of meaning, sucking out the oxygen, making Bertie feel mildly hypoxic. The man speaking, the Nonsense Man, as she thought of him, was called Angus and came 'from Scottish stock' – hence the name – although his accent was pure English public school. 'Harrow, actually,' and Bertie knew these things because she had been on a date with him, a date procured by that well-known pander, Match.com. Which was why she was now slouched at the back of the room, trying to look as if she wasn't there.

She had taken an almost instant dislike to him over a dinner at Nopi which, when the bill arrived, he had been more than happy to go Dutch on, thereby failing one of her first requirements of a suitor, which was to behave like a gentleman. She wanted doors opening, meals paid for, flowers. Billets-doux (lovely words, made her think of doves – bill and coo). She wanted to be courted. Gallantry. What a lovely word. Fat chance of any of that. She snorted to herself and the man seated next to her in the 'industry seminar' gave her a nervous glance.

'Bertie?' the Nonsense Man had said over dinner. 'What kind of name is that?'

'A very good one.' And after a long, rather tedious silence, 'Roberta, after my grandmother.' Roberta was Bertie's middle name, she wasn't about to give Angus the Moon.

Just the wrong side of sensible, she had gone home with him (classic mistake) to his flat in Battersea, a flat which was all shiny glass surfaces as if it had been designed in the future, and then she had proceeded to have rather disagreeable, drunken sex with him which, naturally, had led to self-loathing and a stealthy dawn exit, a walk of shame along the Thames, to *ease her payne*. She had been surprised at how many other people were out and about *along the shoare of silver streaming Themmes*, although Spenser's nymphs, the Daughters of the Flood, were notable by their absence, unless they were a university team of grunting female rowers, hammering their way through the brown water as if they were being chased by a river monster. What kind of woman got up at six in the morning to row, Bertie wondered? A better woman than her, she supposed.

Spenser handed over to Wordsworth who met her at Westminster Bridge, where, early on a morning late in May, London really was all bright and glittering in the smokeless air, if only for a little while.

She was surprised, to put it mildly, when she looked over the bridge and saw a gilded, swan-necked barge being rowed towards her. As she watched the boat sweep smoothly beneath the bridge, Bertie wondered if perhaps she had time-travelled back to Tudor times.

'*Gloriana*,' a voice said. She hadn't noticed the man who had come to stand next to her. 'It's the Queen's barge,' he said, 'for the flotilla. Rehearsing, I expect.' Of course, she thought. The river pageant. London was *en fête* for the Diamond Jubilee. So many lovely words, Bertie thought – 'gilded', 'jubilee', 'flotilla', 'diamond', 'pageant', '*Gloriana*'. It was almost too much to bear.

'I thought I'd stepped back in time for a moment,' she said.

'Would you like to?' he asked, sounding like someone who was inviting her to enter a time machine that he had handily parked around the corner.

'Well . . .' she said.

'. . . Transactional supply-based relationships and com-moditization . . .'

Bertie worked in an advertising agency and for reasons now already forgotten to her was in Belgravia, where Angus was facilitating a 'Hackathon'. (Yes, really.)

Angus's father was a QC and his mother a hospital consultant, and the family – a brother and two sisters – had been brought up in Primrose Hill, where Angus had a 'pretty normal childhood'. Bertie had immediately mistrusted him. Nobody had a normal childhood.

He was in marketing, 'an innovator', which didn't seem like a proper job to Bertie. 'I'm in library services,' she said, because that was always a conversation killer.

'On the website,' he puzzled, 'it says you're in "community education".'

'Same thing,' she said. 'More or less.' She could never remember what her cover story was, she would have made a dreadful spy. 'Community library,' she amended and his eyes duly glazed over at this information and he turned his attention to the twice-cooked baby chicken on his plate. Surely once was enough for the poor thing?

'. . . bluejacking . . . roadblocking . . .'

Angus was currently wearing a black T-shirt with a picture of Nipper, the HMV dog, on it. Beneath Nipper – and she really wished she didn't know this – Angus's chest was waxed. Nipper himself was beneath the Lloyd's insurance building in Kingston-upon-Thames. Bertie hoped that she didn't end up buried beneath a building. Or worse, excavated and put on show, like all those poor Egyptian mummies or the people from Pompeii, immortalized in their helpless death throes. Grandpa Ted wanted a woodland burial. ('An oak, if possible.') 'He'll get what we give him,' Viola said. 'It's not as if he's going to know, is it?' (But what if he did?) The fight over his corpse had already begun and he wasn't even dead yet. Bertie loved her grandfather. Her grandfather loved Bertie. It was the simplest arrangement.

'. . . standout talkability . . .'

What on earth was she doing with her life? Could she just get up and leave?

'. . . hot linking . . .'

Viola was the last person she would ever tell about the men she dated. Bertie was thirty-seven – 'and counting', as

Viola always reminded her in that giddy girls'-school manner she had sometimes. 'Just jump right in! You don't want to miss out on motherhood.' Bertie's friends who were married with children – all her friends, in fact; Bertie had spent what seemed like nearly every weekend for the last five years at either weddings or christenings – all seemed in thrall to their children, each one a version of the Second Coming. None of these children seemed particularly attractive to Bertie and she worried that if she had a baby she wouldn't like it. Viola came to mind. She hadn't loved them, or it certainly hadn't felt like it, and she definitely didn't like them (although she seemed to like no one). 'Liking doesn't really come into it,' Grandpa Ted had told her when he was still capable of giving advice. 'You'll be besotted with your own.' Bertie wasn't sure that she wanted to be besotted by anyone, particularly someone small and helpless.

'Your grandmother was besotted with Viola,' her grandfather said. So, it just went to show, anything was possible.

A long time ago now, before he left on his hegira, Sunny had got a girl pregnant. Viola had been aghast and then when the girl had a termination she was equally aghast. 'No pleasing some people,' Sunny said.

Viola had started sending Bertie links to donor websites – sperm supermarkets where you could simply pick a gene packet off the shelf – Scandinavian, 71 kilos, 6' 1", blond hair, blue/green eyes, teacher – and pop it in 'Your Basket'. 'Danish is best, apparently,' Viola advised.

Of course, Viola was terrified that if she didn't have grandchildren her genes would die and nothing of her would be left. She would cease to exist. Pouf! Viola was sixty now, always waiting for people to say, 'Never!' Which they didn't. 'You may not think so now,' Viola said to her, 'but when you get to fifty and turn around and find it's too late for motherhood, you'll be *devastated*.' Why did her mother always have to be so unnecessarily melodramatic? Because no one would listen if she wasn't?

Of course, no one was more surprised than Bertie when two years later she had twins (and, yes, besotted), after marrying a perfectly straightforward man, a doctor (yes, that man on Westminster Bridge), and becoming, well . . . happy. But that wasn't now. Now was Angus pumping the air with evangelical fervour as if he were at a prayer meeting and exhorting them to consider 'sellsumers'. Bertie tried to divert herself by thinking of rhymes for Nonsense Man (Japan, frying-pan, catamaran, watering-can), but in the end she had to pull out scraps from the ragbag of loveliness that she was forced to carry around these days to protect herself from the evil materialist universe. (Was advertising the right profession for her?)

Where the bee sucks, there suck I

She could just go. She had a meeting at two and it would take her for ever to cross London. The creatives were presenting ideas to the client for a new toothpaste. Surely there was enough toothpaste in the world already? Did people really need so much choice that they could never get to the end of choosing? As if the world needed more of anything. Yes, it was official – she was in the wrong profession. If Bertie was a god (a favourite fantasy), she would be manufacturing things there was a shortage of – bees, tigers, dormice – not flip-flops and phone covers and toothpaste. No, don't go down that road, she thought, the creation fantasy was so vast and wide that she could be lost in it for ever.

'. . . monetize . . . materialism . . .'

the frost performs its secret ministry, unhelped by any wind

'. . . always-on consumers . . .'

whose woods these are I think I know

'. . . staggered event-related . . .'

loveliest of trees, the cherry now is hung with bloom along the bough

'. . . outcome-specific media burst . . .'

as kingfishers catch fire, dragonflies draw flame

'Brand-relevant content . . . re-energize consumers' perceptions of the . . .'

On Wenlock Edge the wood's in trouble

'. . . by doing that you can take it all the way to bright . . .'

There's a certain Slant of light

'. . . Chi-squared Automatic Interaction Detection . . .'

What?

Dear God. When did language and meaning divorce each other and decide to go their separate ways? Bertie's ragbag of loveliness was almost depleted for the day and it wasn't even lunchtime.

O how full of briers is this working-day world!

'Oh, I'm so sorry,' she said when the nervous man sitting next to her twitched. 'Did I say that out loud?'

'Yes.'

She stood up rather abruptly, and whispered 'Sorry' to the twitchy man. 'I have to go. I just remembered I left my real self on the Tube. She'll be wondering what's happened. She's lost without me.'

Angus caught sight of her and frowned as if he was trying to remember who she was. She gave him a little wave, waggling her fingers in a way which she hoped looked ironic, but it seemed to confuse him even more.

On the Tube – on the Piccadilly line, although that was probably not relevant – there was no sign of her real self, but there was a copy of the *Daily Mail* that someone had left behind. It was folded open to a page with a headline that blared, 'Could the universe collapse TODAY? Physicists claim that risk is "more likely than ever and may have already started".' (How on earth would you tell?) It was a curious usage of the upper case. Bertie would have put the emphasis on 'collapse'. It was how Viola spoke ('You'll be DEVASTATED').

Rummaging around at the bottom of her ragbag for some crumb, Bertie couldn't even find a bit of wild thyme blowing around in there.

'Are you watching the Thames Pageant with Grandpa Ted?'

'Yes, I'm in his room,' her mother said.

'It's rubbish, isn't it? And the poor Queen, she's almost as old as Grandpa Ted and she's having to suffer all this.'

'She'll catch her death in all that rain,' Viola said.

Was that what happened, Bertie wondered? Did you have to catch your death, like a runaway horse, and it took some people, like Grandpa Ted, a long time to get hold of it but others managed to grab the reins straight away?

Like the grandmother she had never known – nimble-footed Nancy, jumping on the back of death, a bold rider, so quickly that she must have taken everyone by surprise. Death itself, perhaps.

'Anyway,' Bertie said, 'can you put me on to Grandpa Ted?'

'He won't understand you.'

'Just put me on anyway. Hello, Grandpa Ted. It's Bertie here.'

On the day, of course, the gilded barge had been forsaken by the Queen for a more prosaic Thames cruiser, *Gloriana* having been deemed too small for all the hangers-on – the protection officers and ladies-in-waiting and lackeys – that were necessary when a queen took to the river. Bertie had intended to join the flocks of people on the banks of the Thames – to be part of something bigger than herself, something that she would remember in the future in the same way that you knew where you had been at midnight on the Millennium. (Drunk, in Soho House, something she regretted now. Obviously.) It had rained, however, relentlessly, for the whole day, and Bertie had watched the admirable perseverance of monarchy on the television, the medium through which she had also experienced Diana's funeral, the Twin Towers falling and the last Royal Wedding. One day, she thought, she would actually *be* somewhere when something happened and it wouldn't be rendered second-hand through a lens. Even if it was a dreadful spectacle – a bomb, a tsunami, a war – she would at least know the grandeur of horror.

Grandpa Ted's brother, Jimmy, dead before Bertie could meet him, had been one of the first to go into Belsen and then after the war he left for Madison Avenue and joined one of the original ad agencies as a copywriter. To have lived a life of such polarities made her envious. Nowadays you just did a degree in Media Studies.

And Grandpa Ted himself, of course, mind and body crumbling a little more every day, like a magnificent, neglected ruin, had once been a bomber pilot, flying into the jaws of death every night. '"The jaws of death" – is that a terrible cliché?' she asked him on their farewell tour, an elegiac revisiting of his old haunts, over ten years ago now. ('Why doesn't he just die?' Viola wailed. 'How long does it *take* to say goodbye?') It had given Bertie an insight into her grandfather's life, into history itself, which although gratifying had also left her existential nerves jangled and confused. 'Promise me you'll make the most of your life,' he had said to Bertie. Had she? Hardly.

She muted the inane BBC commentary and said, 'How are you, Grandpa Ted?' She imagined him lying in bed in that horrible nursing home, living this unwelcome remnant of his life. Bertie wished she could rescue him, swoop in and carry him off, but he was too ill and frail now. Her grandfather had lived at Fanning Court for nearly twenty years, then he fell and broke a leg which led to pneumonia which should have led to an easeful death ('The old people's friend,' Viola said wistfully), but he pulled through it. ('He's immortal,' Viola said.) He was a lesser person than before, near enough helpless, and he was discharged into the dubious arms of the nursing home, which was where, Bertie supposed, he would die. 'Every time I see him I think it might be the last time,' Viola said hopefully.

He deserved a better place to leave this life than Poplar Hill. 'And where is this mythical poplar and this mythical hill?' Viola was always ranting, as if the problems with the place were a matter of semantics.

Viola was furious at how much the nursing home cost. The sheltered flat was sold but all the money was being 'swallowed up' by the nursing-home fees.

'But you have plenty of money,' Bertie said.

'That's not the point. He should care enough about me to leave me something.' ('That's not the POINT. He should CARE enough about me to leave me SOMETHING.') 'A legacy. There'll be nothing left by the time he dies.'

'Well, nothing left of him, at any rate,' Bertie said. 'And you don't really mean to be so horrible,' she added.

'Yes, I do,' Viola said.

'Are you watching the flotilla on television, Grandpa Ted? The Jubilee?' (Oh God, her intonation sounded like her mother's.) 'Sunny sends his love,' she reported and her grandfather seemed to chuckle (or perhaps he was choking) because he had always understood Sunny better than any of them. Grandpa Ted may have been pulsing slowly towards the end of his life but he was still palpably himself, something her mother seemed incapable of understanding. Sunny hadn't actually sent his love but he would have done if he'd known she was talking to their grandfather. Sunny loved his grandfather. His grandfather loved Sunny. It was the most complicated arrangement.

'I'm going to Singapore tomorrow.' Her mother's rather shrill tones suddenly replaced her grandfather's silence and Bertie recoiled from the phone.

'Singapore?'

'A literary festival.'

Viola used to sound embarrassingly pleased with herself when she talked about the more glamorous end of publishing. 'A meeting in London with a film producer', 'lunch at The Ivy with my publishers', 'the main stage at Cheltenham'. Now she just sounded oddly defeated.

'I'll be in London tonight,' she said. 'I could take you to dinner. At Dinner.'

'Sorry, I'm busy.' It was the truth but Bertie would have said it anyway. Her mother sounded disappointed, which was interesting as for over thirty years it had been the other way round.

'Are you going to see Sunny?' she asked her.

'Sunny?'

'Your only son.'

'Singapore isn't Bali, it's a completely different country,' Viola said, although she sounded unsure. Geography never had been her strong point.

'It's a hop and a skip away though. You'll be well over halfway there when you get to Singapore. It's not as if you have anything else to do. And you should,' Bertie added, 'and quickly because you may not know this but the universe has already started collapsing. There are signs everywhere. I have to go.'

'No, you don't.'

'No, I don't but I am. Say goodbye to Grandpa Ted for me.'

The Queen had reached Tower Bridge. Bertie turned the television off, alert for signs of the universe collapsing.

* * *

There was an old Aga in the kitchen that pumped out heat. She thought of it as akin to a big friendly animal. Next to the Aga was a small armchair covered in a crocheted blanket and on the blanket a large tabby cat was sound asleep. The stone-flagged floor was warmed by hand-hooked rugs. A Welsh dresser held blue-and-white crockery and on the large scrubbed deal table was a little china jug of sweet peas and marigolds from the garden. Bertie was standing at the ancient Belfast sink patiently drying pots and laying them on the wooden draining-board.

She could see the garden from the kitchen window. The garden was a little corner of Eden, the scarlet flowers of runner beans, the neat mounds of strawberry plants and tangled rows of peas. An apple tree next to the—

A siren interrupted this delightful reverie. Bertie was on her way back from lunch at the Wolseley with a production company. On Piccadilly, she discovered, there was a sense of occasion in the air. Or threat, it was hard to tell the difference. Police and military everywhere and crowds corralled on the pavement. A motorcycle escort signalled importance. A huge car containing royalty swept past. 'The Bomber Memorial,' someone explained when she asked. Of course, the Queen was dedicating the new Bomber Memorial today, midway between the Jubilee and the start of the Olympics, a patriotic summer of red, white and blue for London.

Later, on television (because this was another second-hand spectacle) she watched the ceremony on the news, saw all the fragile old men struggling to hold back tears and couldn't hold back her own as each one reminded her of her grandfather and the mysterious past.

Bertie waited patiently with the crowds on the pavement. Bomber Command had waited seventy years, she supposed she could wait a few minutes. A formation of Tornado fighter jets roared overhead, thrillingly noisy, and were followed by a lone Lancaster that dropped the contents of its bomb-bay over London. Poppies bloomed in a stain of red on the blue-and-white summer sky.

Bertie was on her way home from work when Viola phoned. 'We've been summoned,' she said portentously.

'Summoned?'

'Asked to come. By the nursing home,' Viola said. She sounded excited. She loved drama as long as it didn't threaten her.

'Grandpa Ted?' Bertie said, suddenly alert. 'What's happened?'

'Well . . .' Viola said, as if about to embark on a thrilling narrative when in fact all that had happened was that Teddy had fallen asleep yesterday evening and couldn't be woken this morning. 'They said to get there as soon as possible but I won't be able to get a flight until the morning. It'll be late tomorrow night before I can get to York.'

'I'll set off and drive there now,' Bertie said.

It wasn't them who had been summoned, Bertie thought, it was her grandfather. The angels had finally called him in.

'They took their time about it,' Viola said.

2012
The Last Flight

Dharma

'There is a Hindu legend that tells us that there was once a time when all men were gods, but they abused their divinity. Brahma, the god of creation, concluded that people had lost the right to their divinity and decided to take it away from them. Wanting to hide it somewhere where they wouldn't be able to find it, he called a council of all the gods to advise him. Some suggested that they bury it deep in the earth, others that they sink it in the ocean, others still suggested it be placed on top of the highest mountain, but Brahma said that mankind was ingenious and would dig down far into the earth, trawl the deepest oceans and climb every mountain in an effort to find it again.

'The gods were on the point of giving up when Brahma said, "I know where we will hide man's divinity, we will hide it inside him. He will search the whole world but never look inside and find what is already within." '

Viola wasn't really listening. Sunny liked to finish his yoga sessions with what she thought of as a 'little sermon'. Words of wisdom from the enlightened, pulled from all over the place – Hinduism, Sufism, Buddhism, even Christianity. The Balinese themselves, she had learned, were Hindu. Viola had been under the misapprehension that they were Buddhists. 'We're all the Buddha,' Sunny said. 'It sounds preachy in print,' Viola wrote in an email to Bertie, 'but actually it's sort of uplifting. He would have made rather a good vicar.' Who was this new docile version of her mother, Bertie wondered?

Sunny taught at a place called the Bright Way in Ubud. To begin with Viola had avoided the sessions at the Bright Way. She was staying at an outrageously expensive 'wellness retreat' hotel a half-hour's drive away, where they had their own yoga teacher – and where the private, individual classes were held in something called the 'yoga bale', a pleasant airy pavilion constructed from polished teak, situated amongst trees in which birds trilled and cackled in an exotic fashion and insects droned or clacked like wind-up mechanical toys.

At the Bright Way, on the other hand, classes took place in a huge upstairs room that was hot and stuffy, even with all the windows flung open in an effort to catch a breeze. It was quite basic or the product of a 'simple ascetic', depending on your viewpoint – Viola's or that of the Bright Way's website.

Despite the size of the room, it was always crowded, mostly with women – athletic young Australians and middle-aged Americans. Most of the latter seemed to be doing what Bertie called 'their eat-pray-love shit'.

Sunny qualified as a yoga teacher years ago in India and he was currently teaching on Bali. He was, apparently, a 'respected teacher on the international circuit'. He frequently travelled to America and Australia to hold retreats that were always booked up. Everyone was in retreat, it seemed to Viola.

Sunny was all over the Internet if you knew where to look – if you knew who to look for – because although you would have thought that Sun (or even Sunny) might be a good name for someone who did what he was doing, he was known to all and sundry as 'Ed'. 'Sun Edward Todd,' he said reasonably to Viola, 'it's my name.' And that was only a small part of his transformation. The physique of a dancer, the shaven head, the oriental tattoos, the wash of an Australian accent were all a complete surprise to her. A changeling. And women loved him! They were like groupies, especially the eat-pray-love crowd. Viola hadn't seen Sunny for nearly ten years and in the interim he had turned into a complete human being. ('Perhaps the two things aren't unrelated,' Bertie said.)

'Thank you for this practice. Namaste,' Sunny said, bowing with his hands in prayer. There were a lot of murmured thank-yous and Namastes in return. (They took it so seriously!) Sunny leaped up from his lotus pose with alarming fluidity. Viola struggled to her feet, not from a lotus pose, merely a stiff and uncomfortable cross-legged position that reminded her of school assemblies.

Sunny lived in a village quite close to her outrageously expensive hotel yet seemed to have no intention of inviting Viola into his home so she decided, reluctantly, that the only way she was going to get to spend time with him was by coming along to his classes and putting up with the inane adoration of his other 'students' – to which he appeared sublimely indifferent – not to mention the hideous physical challenges of the class. She had done yoga before, of course – who hadn't? – but it had usually taken place in draughty church halls or community centres and had involved not much more than a bit of cautious stretching and then lying down and 'visualizing' yourself in a place where you felt 'safe and at peace'. This was always a challenge for Viola and while other people (women, always women) were lying on a tropical beach somewhere or in a deckchair in their garden, Viola's imagination was running around fretfully looking for something – anything – that it could recognize as peaceful and safe.

When Sunny finished his Hindu homily and they'd all *Namasted* each other to death, the American woman who had occupied the mat next to Viola ('Shirlee with two "e"s') turned to her and said, 'Ed's a wonderful teacher, isn't he?' The boy who couldn't be taught anything, Viola thought. 'I'm his mother,' she said. How long since Viola had said those words? Not since Sunny was in school, probably.

– Oh –

A sudden horrible memory of the Casualty department at St James's hospital in Leeds came back to her. Sunny had just started college and she had thought it must be drugs when the hospital phoned her, but apparently he had been found wandering in the street with blood dripping from his arm from a botched attempt at cutting his wrist. 'I'm his mother!' she had yelled at the doctor treating him when he told her that it was best that Sunny didn't see anyone 'just now'.

'Why?' she had asked him when she was finally allowed into his cubicle. Why did he do it? The usual inarticulate shrug. 'Don't know.' When pressed – 'Because my life's shit?'

Did he still have the scar? Was it hidden by the complicated dragon that curled up his arm?

Shirlee with two 'e's laughed and said, 'I don't think of him as having a mother.'

'Everyone has a mother.'

'Not God,' Shirlee said.

'Even God,' Viola said. Perhaps that's where it had all started to go wrong.

Of course, no one would know by observing them that they were mother and son. Sunny called her 'Viola' and she didn't really call him anything. He treated her exactly the same as he treated everyone else in the class, with a detached kind of concern. ('Do you have arthritis in your knees?' No, she didn't, thank you very much.)

'Surprise?' she said when she eventually tracked him down.

'It is,' he said. They had hugged warily, as if one of them might have a knife.

Only Bertie and Sunny knew where she was. She hadn't bothered to tell the staff at Poplar Hill that she was on a different continent from her ailing father. She was at the other end of a phone if they needed to contact her.

She had stepped out of her life. If she'd known how easy it was she would have done it long ago. She had sent an email to her agent and asked her to tell people that she was having an operation (she was, she was having her mind removed) and to make her apologies all round. She didn't want people to think she had absconded, disappeared, like Agatha Christie. The last thing she wanted was people looking for her. No, that wasn't true – the last thing she wanted was people finding her.

The incredibly expensive hotel where Viola was staying had been converted from an old estate and sat at the top of a gorge from where there were lovely views along the river a long way below. There were security guards and personal butlers and nothing was any trouble at all. She had a villa – the largest, the most expensive – all to herself. It was far too big, it could have accommodated several families, but she liked the solitude. When she got up in the morning she could make coffee in the high-end espresso machine in the 'living area' (surely everywhere was a living area?) and drink it while she watched the mist rising from the valley below and listened to the birds calling to each other across the forest. Then someone would bring her something delicious for breakfast and she would go to the spa and be massaged or walk down the ancient stone steps to the 'sacred river'. She wasn't sure why it was sacred. Sunny said all rivers are sacred. Everything was sacred, apparently.

'Even dog shit?'

'Yes, even dog shit.'

She was compiling a list of things that might not be sacred. Hiroshima, jihadist massacres, kittens in microwaves. Those are acts, Sunny said, not things. But weren't acts committed by people and weren't people sacred? Or was it just trees and rivers?

In the afternoons she slept (an alarming amount) and then woke up and had the hotel car drive her to Ubud, where she joined Sunny's class. He didn't even save her a place on the mat-crowded floor, so that if she arrived late there was no room for her and she had to sit in the little office and read the books they had in a small 'library' (i.e. a shelf). All the books had some kind of spiritual slant, needless to say. There was a handwritten sign attached to the shelf that said, 'Please, dear friend, leave these books in the condition that you found them,' which was ridiculous as no book could ever be left in the condition that you found it in because it was changed every time it was read by someone.

The class, if there was space for her, lasted for two hours (it was designed with punishment in mind) and afterwards the driver would take her back to the hotel and she would watch the family of monkeys that came out from the forest every evening to play on the old estate walls around her villa. She would eat dinner too, of course. The 'eat' part was easy. The praying and loving were harder.

Once or twice she had been to Sunny's early-morning meditation class, which was less crowded but even more difficult.

'Don't think, Viola,' Sunny said.

How could anyone not think?

'Don't not think either.'

'I think, therefore I am,' Viola said, clinging doggedly on to an outmoded Cartesian universe. If she stopped thinking, she might cease to exist.

'Just let go,' Sunny said.

Let go? Of what? She had nothing to hold on to to begin with.

And then! The flowing river, the calling birds, the mechanical insects, the chattering monkeys all finally did their job and her mind stopped working and it was the most unbelievable relief.

In the car, on the way to Sunny's class, her phone surprised her by ringing. It was the nursing home.

The end was nigh. She had been waiting for her father to die so her life could begin, but as we could all have told her it doesn't work like that. She knew that anyway. Really.

'The Buddha asked a Shramana, "How long is the human lifespan?" He replied, "A few days." The Buddha said, "You have not yet understood the Way." He asked another Shramana, "How long is the human lifespan?" The reply was, "The space of a meal." The Buddha said, "You have not yet understood the Way." He asked another Shramana, "How long is the human lifespan?" He replied, "The length of a single breath." The Buddha said, "Excellent. You have understood the Way."'

The words flowed over Viola. She had no idea what they meant. She had taken Sunny's class as usual. She saw no reason not to. It would be tomorrow morning before she would be able to get on a flight back to Britain. She waited until Sunny had *Namaste*d everyone, the eat-pray-love brigade behaving as if he was bestowing a blessing on them before they trooped reluctantly out into the heat and humidity of the early evening. Viola stayed.

'Viola?' Sunny said and smiled solicitously at her as if she were an invalid. 'The nursing home called,' she said. 'My father's dying.'

'Grandpa Ted?' Sunny's brow furrowed and he bit his lip and for a moment she saw the shade of a younger Sunny. 'Are you going back?'

'Yes. Although I expect Bertie will get there long before me. Are you going to come?'

'No,' Sunny said.

There were many things Viola could have said at this point. She had thought of all of them while gazing at the forest, the sacred river, the birds, 'I'm sorry' being foremost, but instead she told him about the dream.

'And then you turned to me and you were smiling and you said, "We did it, Mum! Everyone got on the train."'

'I don't think it was about the train.'

'No,' Viola agreed. 'It was how I felt when you spoke to me.'

'Which was?'

'Overwhelmed by love. For you.'

Oh, Viola. At last.

Bertie had brought a copy of *The Last Chronicle of Barset* with her and sat at Teddy's bedside reading to him. She knew it was one of his favourite books and she supposed it didn't matter much whether or not he could understand the words because it might be soothing for him to hear the familiar rhythms of Trollope's prose.

He made a little sound, not speech, but something, as

if he was confused. She put the book down on his bed-spread and held one of his fragile, clawed hands in hers. 'It's Bertie Moon here, Grandpa,' she said. The flesh on his hands was like melted tallow and the veins were great blue ropes. His other hand was held up at a right angle and he waved it around gently as if he was asking to be excused. Which he was, she supposed.

He was a baby once, she thought. New and perfect, cradled in his mother's arms. The mysterious Sylvie. Now he was a feathery husk, ready to blow away. His eyes were half open, milky, like an old dog, and his mouth had grown beaky with the extremity of age, opening and closing, a fish out of water. Bertie could feel a continual tremor running through him, an electrical current, the faint buzz of life. Or death, perhaps. Energy was gathering around him, the air was static with it.

Teddy was fighting *F-Fox*, trying to keep her flying straight and level. She wanted to give up. The bomb-aimer – Clifford – appeared by his side and said the fire had prevented him from getting to the rear-gunner. Teddy knew nothing about the boy except that he looked terrified out of his mind and Teddy thought he had been brave to go and help the rear-gunner – Charlie – who he also knew nothing about. The only thing Teddy could think at that moment was that those boys had to be saved. He told Clifford to jump, but he had lost his parachute and Teddy said, 'Take mine. Take it, go on, jump!' and Clifford hesitated but obeyed his captain and took the parachute and disappeared through the escape hatch.

He was St George and England was his Cleolinda but

the dragon was overpowering him, burning him up with its fiery breath. There was a curtain of flames behind him. He could feel them beginning to scorch his seat. The intercom was no longer working and he didn't know if the rear-gunner had got out or not so he carried on wrestling with *F-Fox*.

The room was lit by just one dim lamp. It was nearly midnight and the nursing home had been overcome by sleep, disturbed only by the occasional shriek of terror that sounded like a small animal being attacked.

Her grandfather was dying of old age, Bertie thought. Worn out. Not cancer or a heart attack or an accident or a catastrophe. Old age seemed like a hard way to go. There were long gaps between each rasping breath now. Sometimes he seemed to panic and say something and Bertie squeezed his hand and stroked his cheek and murmured to him about the bluebell wood she had never seen and the people she had never met who would be waiting for him. Hugh and Sylvie, Nancy and Ursula. Of the dogs, of the long sunny days. Was that where he was bound? To long sunlit days at Fox Corner? Or eternal darkness? Or just nothing, for even darkness had a quality to it whereas nothing was truly nothing. Were Spenser's bright squadrons of angels waiting to welcome him? Were all the mysteries about to be revealed? They were questions that no one had ever answered and no one ever would.

She fed him scraps from her ragbag because words were all that were left now. Perhaps he could use them to pay the ferryman. *Much have I travell'd in the realms of gold. The world is charged with the grandeur of God. Full fathom five thy father lies. Little lamb, who made thee? Though worlds of wanwood leafmeal lie. On that best portion of a good man's life, his little nameless unremembered acts of kindness and of love. Farther and farther, all the birds of Oxfordshire and Gloucestershire.*

The air rippled and shimmered. Time narrowed to a pinpoint. It was about to happen. *Because the Holy Ghost over the bent world broods with warm breast and with ah! bright wings.*

Moments left, Teddy thought. A handful of heartbeats. That was what life was. A heartbeat followed by a heartbeat. A breath followed by a breath. One moment followed by another moment and then there was a last moment. Life was as fragile as a bird's heartbeat, fleeting as the bluebells in the wood. It didn't matter, he realized, he didn't mind, he was going where millions had gone before and where millions would follow after. He shared his fate with the many.

And now. This moment. This moment was infinite. He was part of the infinite. The tree and the rock and the water. The rising of the sun and the running of the deer. *Now.*

The trumpets sound the end of the revels. The baseless fabric begins to disintegrate. The stuff that dreams are made of starts to rend and tear and the walls of a cloud-capped tower tremble. Little showers of dust begin to fall. Birds rise in the air and fly away.

Sunny is sitting on the veranda of the room he rents,

meditating in the dark before dawn. He is moving out soon. His Australian girlfriend, also a yoga teacher, is six months pregnant and has already gone back to Sydney. Sunny is going to join her there in a few weeks. He's going to accompany Viola to the airport later this morning and see her on the plane and before he says goodbye to her he will give her the gift of this knowledge to take home with her. His other gift to her will be the little silver hare that he has kept all these years. Against the odds. 'For luck. For protection.' His Australian girlfriend is the Buddha. She is carrying the Buddha inside her.

He takes in a sudden breath as if he has been asleep and has woken suddenly.

An alarming crack appears in the gorgeous palace. The first wall shivers and crumbles. The second wall buckles and falls, stones tumble to the ground.

Viola is drinking her coffee, waiting for the dawn, waiting for the mist to lift from the river and the birds to start calling. She's thinking about her mother. She's thinking about her children. She's thinking about her father. She is overcome by the pain of love. The birds commence their dawn chorus. Something is happening. Something is changing. For a moment she is gripped by panic. *Don't be afraid*, she thinks. And she isn't.

The third wall comes down with a great crash, sending up a cloud of dust and debris.

Bertie is holding her grandfather's hand, willing him to

feel her love because isn't that what everyone would want to be the last thing that they feel? She leans over and kisses his hollow cheek. Something tremendous is happening, something catastrophic. She is going to be a witness of it. Time starts to tilt. *Now*, she thinks.

The fourth wall of the solemn temple falls as quietly as feathers.

He could no longer fight *F-Fox*. The aircraft was mortally wounded, a bird shot out of the air. *Ah! bright wings*. He heard the words quite clearly as if someone in the cockpit had spoken them. He had made it to the coast. Beneath him the moon glinted off the North Sea like a thousand diamonds. He was reconciled to this moment, to this now. The noise in the aircraft had ceased, the heat from the flames had disappeared. There was just a beautiful, unearthly silence. He thought of the wood and the blue-bells, the owl and the fox, a Hornby train trundling around his bedroom floor, the smell of a cake baking in the oven. The skylark ascending on his thread of song.

F-Fox fell with Teddy still inside her, a blaze of light in the dark, a bright star, an exaltation, until her fires were finally quenched by the waves. It was over. Teddy sank to the silent sea-bed and joined all the tarnished treasure that lay there unseen, forty fathoms deep. He was lost for ever, only a small silver hare to keep him company in the dark.

And with a massive roar the fifth wall comes down and the house of fiction falls, taking Viola and Sunny and Bertie with it. They melt into the thin air and disappear. Pouf!

The books that Viola wrote vanish from bookshelves as if by magic. Dominic Villiers marries a girl who wears pearls and a twinset and drinks himself to death. Nancy marries a barrister in 1950 and has two sons. During a routine examination, her brain cancer is discovered and successfully removed. Her mind is less keen, her intelligence less bright, but she is still Nancy.

A man, a doctor, standing on Westminster Bridge turns away after the Jubilee barge, *Gloriana*, has passed beneath the bridge. For a moment he thinks someone is standing beside him but there is no one there, only a fluctuation in the air. He feels as if he has just lost something but can't imagine what it might be. An Australian yoga teacher on Bali worries that she will never find someone to love, never have a child. An old woman called Agnes dies in Poplar Hill nursing home, dreaming of escape. Sylvie overdoses on sleeping tablets on VE Day, unable to come to terms with a future that doesn't contain Teddy. Her best boy.

Across the world millions of lives are altered by the absence of the dead, but three members of Teddy's last crew – Clifford, the bomb-aimer, Fraser, the injured pilot, and Charlie, the tail-end Charlie, all bale out successfully from *F-Fox* and see out the rest of the war in a POW camp. On their return they all marry and have children, fractals of the future.

Fifty-five thousand, five hundred and seventy-three dead from Bomber Command. Seven million German dead, including the five hundred thousand killed by the Allied bombing campaign. The sixty million dead overall of the Second World War, including eleven million murdered in the Holocaust. The sixteen million of the First World War, over four million in Vietnam, forty million to the Mongol conquests, three and a half million to the Hundred Years War, the fall of Rome took seven million, the Napoleonic Wars took four million, twenty million to the Taiping Rebellion. And so on and so on and so on, all the way back to the Garden when Cain killed Abel.

All the birds who were never born, all the songs that were never sung and so can only exist in the imagination.

And this one is Teddy's.

1947

Daughters of Elysium

The hawthorn in the lane was just coming into blossom and Ursula said, 'Oh, look, the hawthorn's flowering. Teddy would have loved to see that.'

'Oh, don't,' Nancy said, the tears starting. 'I can't believe he's gone from this world for ever.' They walked, arm in arm, Lucky running backwards and forwards, excited to be in the lively warm air. 'I wish we had a grave to visit,' Nancy said.

'I'm glad we don't,' Ursula said. 'Now we can imagine him as free as the air.'

'I can only imagine him at the bottom of the North Sea, cold and lonely.'

'Of his bones are coral made,' Ursula said.

A tremulous 'Oh' from Nancy.

'Those are pearls that were his eyes.'

'Stop, do stop, please.'

'Sorry. Do you want to walk across the remains of the meadow?'

*   *   *

'Look!' Nancy exclaimed, letting go of Ursula's arm and pointing towards the sky. 'There. A lark – a skylark. Listen,' she added in a thrilled whisper, as though she might disturb the bird.

'Beautiful,' Ursula murmured.

In thrall to the skylark, they watched as it soared, flying further and further away until it was no more than a speck in the blue sky and then it was just the memory of the speck.

Nancy sighed. 'Sometimes I wonder,' she said, 'about reincarnation. I know it's absurd, but wouldn't it be wonderful if Teddy came back as something else – as that skylark, say. I mean we don't *know*, do we? That *could* have been Teddy saluting us, letting us know that he's all right. That he still *is* in some way. Do *you* believe in reincarnation?'

'No,' Ursula said. 'I believe we have just one life, and I believe that Teddy lived his perfectly.'

And when all else is gone, Art remains. Even Augustus.

The Adventures of Augustus

The Awful Consequences

"I SN'T THAT Augustus?" Miss Slee whispered in Mr Swift's ear. Quite a loud whisper, the kind that makes people in surrounding seats turn and look at you with interest.

Mr Swift's features were impassive although he couldn't quite suppress a slight shudder at the spectacle before him. Miss Slee leaned further forward in her seat to catch Mrs Swift's attention. "That *is* Augustus, isn't it?" she persisted, in an even louder whisper. "Your *son*," she added. It didn't really qualify any longer as a whisper. More of a shout. Mrs Swift's expression remained inscrutable. The rest of the audience were as transfixed as Augustus's parents by the scene unfolding before them on the stage of the village hall.

"England Through the Ages" had reached the Armada, and Elizabeth I was giving her rousing speech to the troops at Tilbury. Gloriana had commandeered Boadicea's chariot – a makeshift sort of affair – and was brandishing a trident that had been borrowed from Britannia. These two noble emblems of womanhood (played by Augustus's sister, Phyllis, and Lady Lamington from the Hall) had not volunteered their possessions and were standing at either side of the stage glowering at Gloriana.

The rest of the pageant players were gamely carrying on, despite the fact that half the scenery had collapsed and several dogs were wandering aimlessly around on the stage.

The vicar, sitting on the other side of Mrs Swift, said to her, "But I thought Mrs Brewster had taken on the role of Queen Elizabeth. Who *is* that on stage?"

Gloriana's red wig had slipped down to one side and, having no proper costume, she had wrapped herself in a Roman centurion's cloak. Again, an item not voluntarily relinquished by said centurion. Her surprisingly grubby knees were visible beneath the cloak and there was what looked to all intents and purposes to be a catapult in her pocket.

"You're doing jolly well, you lot," this dishevelled Gloriana yelled in a rather unqueenly way. "Killin'' all these spaniels and stuff." "*Spaniards*," Mrs Garrett could be heard hissing from the side of the stage. Gloriana brandished Britannia's trident high and shouted, "Now let's go and kill the rest of 'em!" A marauding horde of children poured on to the stage, roaring and shouting and in some cases squeaking. The dogs barked excitedly at the sight of them. Some – nay, many – of those children had previously been of good character but now seemed to have come under the hypnotic spell of Gloriana. As, apparently, had many members of the audience, who were viewing her with open-mouthed horror.

"Are the children supposed to be the Spaniards?" the vicar asked Mrs Swift. " 'Invading hordes'," he said, consulting the programme notes.

"I'm not sure I know who anyone is supposed to be any more," Mrs Swift said, distracted by the hideous sight of the red wig slipping further down her son's face.

"Are they the same children," the vicar puzzled, "who were also the Saxons and the Vikings and the Normans? It's hard to tell now that they're all covered in green paint. What do you suppose that represents? England's green and pleasant land?"

"I doubt it," Mrs Swift said and gave a little cry of alarm as Boadicea's chariot, not robust to begin with, suddenly collapsed and Gloriana toppled ingloriously to the stage, taking the remaining scenery with her. A small West Highland terrier ran on stage and with excellent timing snatched the red wig in its mouth and ran off with it, accompanied by some off-stage shrieking.

"That *is* Augustus," Miss Slee said.

"I have never seen that boy in my life before," Mr Swift said resolutely.

"Neither have I," Mrs Swift said.

In retrospect, Mr Swift said gloomily, you could see that it was bound to end in disaster.

"And it all started so well," Mrs Swift said.

"It always does," Mr Swift said.

The whole village had been in a state of great excitement. It had been discovered by Mr Robinson, who ran the local history society, that the village was much older than anyone had thought, the proof coming from the remains of a Roman villa that had been unearthed in a field on the outskirts of the village. "Evidence of early occupation by our Roman conquerors," Mr Robinson said.

"A viller," Augustus reported back to his little gang of pals. His cohorts – Norman, George and Roderick – had recently decided to give themselves a name. They had considered and rejected the Pirates, the Outlaws and the Robbers, and after much discussion (endless, some might have said) and one or two mild scuffles, they had finally settled on the Apaches as a name that conveyed their bold fearlessness. (Or bloodthirsty murderousness, Mr Swift said.)

"Roman conkers," Augustus explained further. There was a murmur of interest from the Apaches. Every autumn the playing fields of their school became the battleground for the annual Conker Wars, a particularly savage form of warfare that inevitably ended with several of the injured in Matron's office.

Mr Robinson had been invited to dinner by Mr and Mrs Swift, along with the vicar, who was the genial, slightly confused sort of vicar that was very common in the area, and Miss Slee, a forthright, rather mannish spinster whose weekend hobby was "rambling". ("Ramblin'?" Augustus said scornfully to his parents. "How is that a *hobby*? You're always sayin' to me, 'Stop ramblin' on, Augustus,' and *then*," he tugged on the imaginary lapels of an imaginary barrister's gown, "and then you say, 'Why don't you get a sensible hobby, Augustus?' ")

Also sipping the Swifts' sherry were Mr and Mrs Brewster, who were new to the village, and Colonel

Stewart, who was generally disagreeable to all and sundry and had a particular dislike of small boys. "A *soirée*," Mrs Brewster exclaimed, when invited. "How charming." Mrs Brewster cut a rather striking figure. She was tall, with a head of impressive red curls and a rather theatrical manner. She was very keen on amateur dramatics, apparently.

"Not just the Romans," Mr Brewster said, eyeing the near-empty sherry decanter anxiously. "Angles, Saxons, Vikings, Normans, it's been one invading horde after another." The Brewsters were "new money" according to Miss Carlton, a shrew-faced elderly spinster who eyed Mr Brewster eyeing the decanter. She was a "teetotaller", which seemed to make her rather irritable. She had induced Augustus and the rest of his little tribe to sign a pledge that they would never partake of alcohol in exchange for a halfpenny-worth of lemon sherbets. "Fair trade," the Apaches were agreed. "Bringing up the rear" at the *soirée* was the Swifts' next-door neighbour, Mrs Garrett.

"Previously," Mr Robinson said, holding forth again, "we had only been able to date ourselves back to Domesday."

"Doom's Day," Augustus murmured to himself appreciatively. "Day of Doom." He was much taken by words that seemed to hold within them the promise of almost infinite mayhem. His eavesdropping was rudely interrupted by Cook knocking him on the head with a soup spoon – her preferred weapon – and shooing him away. "That boy *lurks*," he had heard her complaining to their housemaid, Mavis. "He's a regular little spy."

Augustus felt rather gratified by this compliment. Naturally, he *was* going to be a spy when he grew up. As well as a pilot, a train driver, an explorer and "a collector of things".

"What kind of things?" Mrs Swift had asked at the breakfast table that morning, and immediately regretted the question as Augustus launched into an enthusiastic list that included mouse skeletons, gold farthings, molluscs, twine, diamonds and glass eyeballs.

"I've never heard of gold farthings," Mr Swift said.

"That's why I'll collect 'em. They'll be worth a king's ransom."

"What if they don't exist?" Mr Swift said.

"Then they'll be worth even more."

"Did you drop him on his head when he was a baby?" Mr Swift asked Augustus's mother. Mrs Swift muttered something that sounded like "I wish I had," and added, much louder, "Do stop *fiddling* with the marmalade pot, Augustus."

"Go away," Cook said to him. She was still in high dudgeon over the Charlotte *Russe* she had planned for "dessert", which was what they ate when they had guests. When they didn't have guests it was simply "pudding". Augustus said it wasn't his *fault* that he had eaten all the sponge finger biscuits. He had been going to take just one and then somehow when he looked again they had all gone! How did that happen? (How did it happen so often?) To Cook's chagrin, the Charlotte *Russe* had been demoted into a more banal mousse. "What will they think?" she grumbled.

"They'll think they're jolly lucky," Augustus said, under the understandable misapprehension that "mousse" was "moose", which sounded like a more exciting item of food than the usual fare served up at the Swifts' dining table. Indeed, "moose" was the kind of prey that the Apaches might hunt with their bows and arrows before spit-roasting it over a camp-fire. (Augustus's own bow and arrow were currently confiscated due to an unfortunate incident.)

"There are no moose in this country," Mr Swift pointed out.

"How do you know," Augustus said, "if you've never seen one?"

"You have the makings of a fine empiricist," his father had told him, after a particularly challenging discussion about cricket balls and greenhouse glass. ("But if you didn't *see* who threw the ball then how could you *know* it was me?" "Because it's always you," Mr Swift said wearily.)

Mrs Garrett clapped her hands suddenly and said, "A pageant!" (Augustus had returned to loitering, a soup spoon was no deterrent to an Apache.) "We should have a pageant to celebrate the village's history."

The assembled company were in voluble agreement. "It will depict the whole history of Britain as experienced from the point of view of a typically English village," Mrs Garrett enthused.

"I myself," Mrs Brewster said, "have played several queens in theatrical productions."

Mrs Swift murmured something inaudible.

"But none of those awful boys must be in it," Colonel Stewart said.

"Oh, goodness no, I quite agree," Miss Carlton said. "Oh, I'm sorry," she said hastily to Mr Swift, "one of them is yours, isn't he?"

"Well . . ." Mr Swift demurred, "we found him on the front doorstep actually." Augustus frowned at this paternal betrayal. There were sympathetic murmurs all round and Mrs Swift said agreeably, "Of course we didn't. It was the back doorstep." There was much laughter at this remark. Augustus's frown deepened. *Had* he been found on a doorstep? Front or back seemed irrelevant. He was an abandoned orphan. He was rather pleased with that idea. Perhaps his real parents were incredibly rich and had been hunting for him ever since accidentally leaving him on Mr and Mrs Swift's doorstep.

"Oh, I'm sure we can find something for all the children to do," Mrs Garrett said. Mrs Garrett was a somewhat troubling figure in Augustus's world. Until recently she had been merely the rather stout and friendly widow who lived next door. She was fond of children (an unusual trait in a grown-up) and had a very good greenhouse full of peaches and grapes that the Apaches were always attempting to raid, to the fury of her gardener. She was also generous with sweets and cakes, again an unusual habit in a grown-up. But, unfortunately, she was also the leader of the local "chapter" of Afor Arod. The words were Saxon, according to Mrs Garrett, for "fierce" and "bold", which none of the members were. If you could imagine a Scout pack consisting of only the outcasts and rejects of boyhood society then that would be Afor Arod: the goody-goodies, the fat, the toadies, the swots – and girls.

They were a peace-loving alternative to the "rather militaristic" Scouts, according to Mrs Garrett, who was a stalwart of the Peace Pledge Union. "Cooperation and harmony," she said. Augustus's mother thought this would be "good" for Augustus as these were traits that he was "singularly lacking". Not true! he protested. "Look at the Apaches."

"Quite," Mrs Swift said and dragged him along to a meeting.

This was so unfair, he thought bitterly as he watched a group of children dancing in a circle. Dancing! No one had mentioned dancing.

"Oh, a new friend for us!" Mrs Garrett declared as if she had never seen him before when in fact she encountered Augustus on an almost daily basis.

And then Augustus met his nemesis. He spied a little girl in the corner of the room, a little girl with the curliest curls and the sweetest dimples. "Madge – hello." She was doing some kind of sewing. "Cross-stitch – a badge, would you like me to make you one, Augustus?" Augustus nodded dumbly, looking even more idiotic than usual.

And now he lived in horror that the rest of the Apaches would catch him in the midst of any of the Afor Arod's ghastly pastimes – the aforesaid dancing and sewing, the chanting and poetry writing. Nature walks – which, it turned out, did not mean the raiding of birds' nests or the indiscriminate shooting at things with catapults, no *mayhem*, in fact.

The whole thing was odious, but he was helplessly in thrall to Madge. ("Oh, thank you for helping me wind my wool, Augustus.")

"A pageant," he reported back to the Apaches. "Invading hordes," he added. He moved a pear drop from one cheek to the other, a movement that generally signalled deep thought. "Got an idea," he said casually. "If we—

'Oh, do stop,' Teddy said to Ursula.

'He's nothing like you, you know,' his sister said, laughing.

'I know that,' Teddy said. 'But please stop reading now.'

Author's Note

When I first decided that I wanted to write a novel set during the Second World War I rather grandiosely believed that I could somehow cover the whole conflict in less than half the length of *War and Peace*. When I realized this was too daunting a challenge – for both reader and writer – I chose the two aspects of the war that interested me most and which I thought provided the richest material – the London Blitz and the strategic bombing campaign against Germany. *Life After Life* is about Ursula Todd and what she goes through during the Blitz, while *A God in Ruins* (I like to think of it as a 'companion' piece rather than a sequel) is about Ursula's brother Teddy and his life as a Halifax pilot in Bomber Command. Neither novel is exclusively about the war, indeed in both novels we spend a long time either arriving at the outbreak of hostilities or an equally long time dealing with the after-math. Nonetheless it is Ursula's and Teddy's individual and shared experiences of the war that permeate their lives.

Ursula lived many versions of her life in the previous novel, which gave me a certain freedom when it came to

Teddy's own life, many of the details of which are different in this book. I like to think of *A God in Ruins* as one of Ursula's lives, an unwritten one. This sounds like novelist trickery, as indeed it perhaps is, but there's nothing wrong with a bit of trickery.

Teddy captains a Halifax and so it goes almost without saying that he is stationed in Yorkshire where most of the Halifax airfields were situated. (The Lancaster gets all the glamour and glory. I would refer you to Teddy's grumbles on this subject rather than mine.) Teddy's Halifax is part of Bomber Command No. 4 Group, one of two groups based in Yorkshire (the other was No. 6 Group – the RCAF). I have not tied Teddy down to a named airfield or squadron, in order to allow myself a little authorial latitude. I imagined him, however, as part of 76 Squadron and I used the squadron's operational records (in the National Archives) when it was based either at Linton-on-Ouse or at Holme-on-Spalding-Moor as a guide for his war.

For the reader's interest, I have appended a short bibliography of some of the sources that I used for this novel. I read many vivid first-hand accounts of individual aircrew's experience to which I am indebted; histories and accounts that draw on personal experiences, as well as the more official histories. The stories of the men who served in Bomber Command are all extraordinary, documenting as they do not only the prized virtue of stoicism but a heroism and determination (and modesty) that seem almost alien to us nowadays, although of course we have not been tested the way they were. The average age of these men (boys, really), all volunteers, was twenty-two.

They experienced some of the worst combat conditions imaginable and fewer than half of them survived. (Of aircrew flying at the beginning of the war, only 10 per cent would see the end of it.) One cannot fail to be moved by the sacrifice of their lives and I suppose that was what first impelled me to write this novel.

There is nothing that happens during the chapters set during the war in *A God in Ruins* that isn't in some way based on a real-life incident that I came across in the course of my research (even the most horrific, even the most outlandish), although nearly always modified in some way. It is sometimes difficult to remember that you are writing fiction, not history, as it is only too easy to get caught up in the finer (and not so finer) technicalities, but the needs of the novel should always trump one's own peculiar obsessions. The Bristol Hercules engine became mine but that, too, I handed on to Teddy.

I readily admit to borrowing from everyone, but particularly from a harrowing account of ditching in Geoffrey Jones's *Raider* when, in January 1944, the (unnamed) crew of Halifax II JD165 (*S Sugar*) from 102 (Ceylon) Squadron based at Pocklington spent three days adrift in the North Sea on their return from a raid on Berlin. I also learned a lot about what it was like to be caught in a thunderstorm from Keith Lowe's *Inferno*. I fudged a few things, the date of the introduction of those darned Bristol engines for a start, and for the most part ignored the continual developments in technical and navigational aids so that the reader wasn't continually tripping over heavy-handed references to, for example H2S, Fishpond or Monica, all the time. Some things I haven't explained

– for the same reason, but also because I haven't necessarily understood them myself (best to be honest here, I think).

The bottom line is that it's fiction. Personally I think that all novels are not only fiction but they are about fiction too. (Not, I don't think, as post-modernly self-referential as it sounds.) I get tired of hearing that a new novel is 'experimental' or it 'reinvents the form', as if Laurence Sterne or Gertrude Stein or indeed James Joyce never wrote a word. Every time a writer throws themselves at the first line of a novel they are embarking on an experiment. An adventure. I believe in the rich textural (and textual) interplay of plot, character, narrative, theme and image and all the other ingredients that get thrown in the pot, but I don't believe that necessarily makes me a traditionalist (as if we're not all in a tradition, the tradition of novel writing).

Everyone always asks you what a novel is 'about'. In the 'Author's Note' that accompanied *Life After Life* I griped that it's about itself and I didn't spend two years writing it in order to précis it in a couple of sentences. But, of course, it *is* about something. If you asked me that question about *A God in Ruins* I would say that it's about fiction (and how we must imagine what we cannot know) and the Fall (of Man. From grace). There are, you will probably notice, a lot of references in the book to Utopia, to Eden, to an Arcadian past, to *Paradise Lost* and *Pilgrim's Progress*. Even the book that Teddy's daughter, Viola, throws at his head at one point is Enid Blyton's *The Land of Far-Beyond*, which is itself based on *Pilgrim's Progress*. So much of this is only semi-deliberate, as if there is a part of the writing brain that knows what it's doing and another part that is woefully ignorant. I see only now how much rising and falling there is in the text. Everyone and everything ascending in flight or falling to earth. (And the birds! Flock upon flock!)

Imagery is for me of paramount importance in a text, not complex imagery that jumps up and down and demands to have its hand shaken but a more subtle web that weaves its way throughout, often enigmatically, and knits everything together. The 'red thread' of blood that binds the Todds echoes the red ribbon of the long leg to Nuremburg that echoes the thin red cords of Teddy's sheltered housing – a pattern that I hadn't even noticed until the final read-through of the novel and yet makes perfect sense to me now. (Just don't ask me why there are so many geese. I have absolutely no idea.)

And, of course, there is a great conceit hidden at the heart of the book to do with fiction and the imagination, which is revealed only at the end but which is in a way the whole *raison d'être* of the novel. I think that you can only be so mulishly fictive if you genuinely care about what you are writing, otherwise you are occupying a two-dimensional space where the text ceases to be an interface between the self and the wider world. If this is a refutation of modernism or post-modernism or whatever has superseded post-modernism, then so be it. Any category designed to constrain should be thrown out. ('Constraint' and 'restraint' are words that appear continually throughout this novel – and their opposite, 'freedom' – something else I only realized when I had finished. I thought about taking them out and decided against it. They're there for a reason.)

War is Man's greatest fall from grace, of course, especially perhaps when we feel a moral imperative to fight it and find ourselves twisted into ethical knots. We can never doubt (ever) the courage of those men in the Halifaxes and Stirlings and Lancasters but the bombing war was undoubtedly a brutish affair, a crude method employing a blunt weapon, continually hampered by the weather and lack of technology (despite massive advances that war always precipitates). The large gap between what was claimed for the results of the bombing campaign and what was actually achieved was never fully understood at the time, and certainly not, I suspect, by those men flying the bombers.

The rationale behind the deliberate move away from attempted precision bombing of legitimate targets (near impossible at night with little technology) towards attacking the civilian population was that killing the workers in the factories and destroying their environment was itself a form of economic warfare. It was a campaign that began with the best of intentions – to avoid the attrition of the First World War trenches – and yet it became itself a war of attrition, escalating all the time, an ever-open maw that could never have enough – man-power, technology, raw materials – all of which might possibly have been more fruitfully directed elsewhere, particularly perhaps in those last months – almost apocalyptic for Europe – when Harris's obsession with pulverizing a dying Germany into annihilation seems more like a biblical punishment than a military strategy (although I am not one of Harris's detractors). Hindsight is indeed a wonderful thing but unfortunately it is unavailable to view in the midst of battle.

We have been plagued by questions about the morality of the strategic bombing offensive ever since the end of the war (aided perhaps by Churchill's diplomatic back-pedalling from responsibility for the policy) and whether our war on savagery did not, in the end, become itself savage as we attacked the very people – the old, the young, women – that civilization is supposed to defend. But the bottom line is that war *is* savage. For everyone. Innocent or guilty.

This is a novel, not a polemic (and I am no historian) and I have accordingly left the doubts and ambiguities for the characters and the text to voice.

And, as a final note, I'm sure that most readers will recognize that Augustus owes a debt to William Brown of *Just William* fame. Augustus is a poorly drawn shade of William, who remains for me one of the greatest fictional characters ever created. Richmal Crompton, I salute you.

Acknowledgements

Lt Col M. Keech BEM R Signals
Squadron Leader Stephen Beddoes RAF
Suzanne Keyte, Archivist, Royal Albert Hall
Anne Thomson, Archivist, Newnham College, Cambridge
Ian Reed, Director of the Yorkshire Air Museum, who
answered my (probably annoying) questions so fully.

The Yorkshire Air Museum (www.yorkshireairmuseum.
org), based at Elvington on one of the many wartime airfields, is a wonderful place for anyone interested in the
Halifax, or indeed the war in general. The museum has
done a brilliant job of bringing the poor old 'Halibag' back
to life and I must thank Phil Kemp for the delightfully
informative tour he gave me of the interior of *Friday 13th*
– sadly not the original aircraft, which was sold for scrap
like all the Halifaxes that survived the war.

And thanks also, of course, to my agent, Peter Straus, and
my editor, Marianne Velmans, and everyone at Transworld,
particularly Larry Finlay, Alison Barrow and Martin Myers.

Thank you also to Reagan Arthur at Little, Brown, Kim Witherspoon at Inkwell Management, Kristin Cochrane at Doubleday Canada and Camilla Ferrier at the Marsh Agency.

It goes without saying that all mistakes, intentional or not, are mine.

Sources

Chorley, W. R., *Bomber Command Losses of the Second World War, Vol. IV, 1943* (Midland Counties, 1996)

Chorley, W. R., *Bomber Command Losses of the Second World War, Vol. V, 1943* (Midland Counties, 1997)

Chorley, W. R., *Bomber Command Losses of the Second World War, Vol. IX, Roll of Honour* (Midland Publishing, 2007)

Middlebrook, Martin and Everitt, Chris, *The Bomber Command War Diaries: An Operational Reference Book 1939–1945* (Penguin, 1990)

Webster, Sir Charles and Frankland, Noble, *The Strategic Air Offensive, Vols I and II* (The Naval and Military Press, 2006)

Hastings, Max, *Bomber Command* (Pan Books, 2010)

Overy, Richard, *The Bombing War* (Allen Lane, 2013)

Ashcroft, Michael, *Heroes of the Skies* (Headline, 2012)

Bishop, Patrick, *Bomber Boys* (Harper Perennial, 2007)

Delve, Ken, *Bomber Command* (Pen and Sword Aviation, 2005)

Jones, Geoffrey, *Raider, the Halifax and its Fliers* (William Kimber, 1978)

Lomas, Harry, *One Wing High, Halifax Bomber, the Navigator's Story* (Airlife, 1995)

Nichol, John and Rennell, Tony, *Tail-End Charlies: The Last Battles of the Bomber War 1944–45* (Penguin Books, 2005)

Riva, R. V., *Tail Gunner* (Sutton, 2003)

Rolfe, Mel, *Hell on Earth* (Grub Street, 1999)

Taylor, James and Davidson, Martin, *Bomber Crew* (Hodder and Stoughton, 2004)

Wilson, Kevin, *Bomber Boys* (Cassell Military Paperbacks, 2005)

Wilson, Kevin, *Men of Air: The Doomed Youth of Bomber Command, 1944* (Weidenfeld and Nicolson, 2007)

Lowe, Keith, *Inferno: The Destruction of Hamburg, 1943* (Viking, 2007)

Messenger, Charles, *Cologne: The First 1000 Bomber Raid* (Ian Allan, 1982)

Middlebrook, Martin, *The Battle of Hamburg* (Penguin, 1984)

Middlebrook, Martin, *The Nuremberg Raid* (Pen and Sword Aviation, 2009)

Nichol, John, *The Red Line* (Harper Collins, 2013)

Ledig, Gert, *Payback* (Granta, 2003)

Sebald, W. G., *On the Natural History of Destruction* (Notting Hill Editions, 2012)

Beck, Pip, *Keeping Watch* (Crecy Publishing, 2004)

Lee, Janet, *War Girls: The First Aid Nursing Yeomanry in the First World War* (Manchester University Press, 2012)

Pickering, Sylvia, *Bomber Command WAAF* (Woodfield, 2004)

Blanchett, Chris, *From Hull, Hell and Halifax: An Illustrated History of No. 6 Group, 1937–48* (Midland, 2006)

Chorley, W. R., *In Brave Company: 158 Squadron Operations* (W. R. Chorley, 1990)

Chorley, W. R., *To See the Dawn Breaking: 76 Squadron Operations* (W. R. Chorley, 1981)

Jones, Geoffrey, *Night Flight: Halifax Squadrons at War* (William Kimber, 1981)

Lake, John, *Halifax Squadrons of World War Two* (Osprey, 1999)

Otter, Patrick, *Yorkshire Airfields in the Second World War* (Countryside Books, 2007)

Pilot's and Flight Engineer's Notes, Halifax III and IV (Air Ministry, 1944)

Rapier, Brian, *White Rose Base* (Aero Litho, 1972)

Robinson, Ian, *Home is the Halifax* (Grub Street, 2010)

Wadsworth, Michael, *Heroes of Bomber Command, Yorkshire* (Countryside Books, 2007)

Wingham, Tom, *Halifax Down!* (Grub Street, 2009)

Baden-Powell, Robert, *Scouting for Boys* (OUP, 2005)

Beer, Stewart, *An Exaltation of Skylarks* (SMH Books, 1995)

Cornell, Simon, *Hare* (Reaktion Books, 2007)

Danziger, Danny, *The Goldfish Club* (Sphere, 2012)

Hart-Davis, Duff, *Fauna Britannica* (Weidenfeld and Nicolson, 2002)

Mabey, Richard, *Flora Britannica* (Chatto and Windus, 1997)

McKay, Sinclair, *The Secret Life of Bletchley Park* (Aurum Press, 2011)

Wallen, Martin, *Fox* (Reaktion, 2006)
Williamson, Henry, *The Story of a Norfolk Farm* (Clive Holloway Books, 1941)

From the National Archives

The Operations Record Books for 76 Squadron – AIR/27/650 (May '42 and December '42), AIR/27/651 (February '43 and December '43), AIR/27/652 (March '44)

DVDs

Forgotten Bombers of the Royal Air Force (Simply Home Entertainment, 2003)
Halifax at War (Simply Home Entertainment, 2010)
The History of Bomber Command (Delta Leisure Group, 2009)
Nightbombers (Oracle, 2003)
Now It Can Be Told (IWM, 2009)
The Royal Air Force at War, the unseen films vols 1–3 (IWM, 2004)
Target for Tonight (IWM, 2007)

Reading Groups

For a list of topics for reading groups, please go to
www.kateatkinson.co.uk ('Resources')

By Kate Atkinson

Behind the Scenes at the Museum

A surprising, tragicomic and subversive family saga set in York, Kate Atkinson's prizewinning first novel, like all her novels, has a mystery at its heart.

'Little short of a masterpiece'
Daily Mail

Human Croquet

A multilayered, moving novel about the forest of Arden, a girl who drops in and out of time, and the heartrending mystery of a lost mother.

'Brilliant and engrossing'
Penelope Fitzgerald

Emotionally Weird

Set in Dundee, this clever, comic novel depicts student life in all its wild chaos, and a girl's poignant quest for her father.

'Achingly funny . . . executed with wit and mischief'
Meera Syal

Not the End of the World

Kate Atkinson's first collection of short
stories – playful and profound.

'Moving and funny, and crammed with incidental wisdom'
Sunday Times

Life After Life

What if you had the chance to live your life again
and again, until you finally got it right?

'Grips the reader's imagination on the first page and never
lets go. If you wish to be moved and astonished, read it'
Hilary Mantel

A God in Ruins

The life of Teddy Todd – would be poet, heroic World War II
bomber pilot, husband, father, and grandfather – as he
navigates the perils and progress of the twentieth century.

'Kate Atkinson's finest work, and confirmation that her
genre-defying writing continues to surprise and dazzle'
Observer

Featuring Jackson Brodie:

Case Histories

The first novel to feature Jackson Brodie, the former police detective, who finds himself investigating three separate cold murder cases in Cambridge, while still haunted by a tragedy in his own past.

'The best mystery of the decade'
Stephen King

One Good Turn

Jackson Brodie, in Edinburgh during the Festival, is drawn into a vortex of crimes and mysteries, each containing a kernel of the next, like a set of nesting Russian dolls.

'The most fun I've had with a novel this year'
Ian Rankin

When Will There Be Good News?

A six-year-old girl witnesses an appalling crime. Thirty years later, Jackson Brodie is on a fatal journey that will hurtle him into its aftermath.

'Genius . . . insightful, often funny, life-affirming'
Sunday Telegraph

Started Early, Took My Dog

Jackson Brodie returns to Yorkshire, in search of someone else's roots, while shopping mall security chief Tracy Waterhouse makes an impulse purchase that will turn her life upside down.

'The best British crime novel of the year'
Heat

BEHIND THE SCENES AT THE MUSEUM

Kate Atkinson

'An astounding book . . . without doubt
one of the finest novels I have read for years'
The Times

Ruby Lennox was conceived grudgingly by Bunty and born while her
father, George, was in the Dog and Hare in Doncaster telling a woman
in an emerald dress and a D-cup that he wasn't married. Bunty had
never wanted to marry George, but here she was, stuck in a flat above
the pet shop in an ancient street beneath York Minster, with sensible
and sardonic Patricia aged five, greedy cross-patch Gillian who
refused to be ignored, and Ruby . . .

Ruby tells the story of The Family, from the day at the end of the
nineteenth century when a travelling French photographer catches frail,
beautiful Alice and her children, like flowers in amber, to the
startling, witty and memorable events of Ruby's own life.

'Little short of a masterpiece . . . fizzing with wit and energy, Kate
Atkinson's hilarious novel made me laugh and cry'
Daily Mail

'Enchanting. It hops with sprightly omniscience from past to future
and back again . . . takes in tragedy, history, mystery and comedy
through the sarky, perky, pessimistic voice of Ruby Lennox'
Sunday Times

HUMAN CROQUET
Kate Atkinson

'Vivid and intriguing . . . a tour de force'
Independent

Once it had been the great forest of Lythe. And here, in the
beginning, lived the Fairfaxes, grandly, at Fairfax Manor.

But over the centuries the forest had been destroyed, replaced
by Streets of Trees. The Fairfaxes have dwindled too; now they
live in 'Arden' at the end of Hawthorne Close and are hardly a
family at all.

But Isobel Fairfax, who drops into pockets of time and out again,
knows about the past. She is sixteen and waiting for the return
of her mother – the thin, dangerous Eliza with her scent of
nicotine, Arpège and sex, whose disappearance is part of the
mystery that still remains at the heart of the forest.

'Vivid, richly imaginative, hilarious and frightening by turns'
Cressida Connolly, Observer

'Wonderfully eloquent and forceful . . . brilliant and engrossing'
Penelope Fitzgerald, Evening Standard

LIFE AFTER LIFE
Kate Atkinson

'If you wish to be moved and astonished, read it'
Hilary Mantel

*What if you had the chance to live your life again and again, until
you finally got it right?*

During a snowstorm in England in 1910, a baby is born
and dies before she can take her first breath.

During a snowstorm in England in 1910, the same baby
is born and lives to tell the tale.

What if there were second chances? And third chances?
In fact an infinite number of chances to live your life? Would
you eventually be able to save the world from its own inevitable
destiny? And would you even want to?

'Truly brilliant'
The Times

'Her most ambitious and most gripping work'
Guardian

'A dizzying and dazzling tour de force'
Daily Mail

'Deliriously inventive . . . magnificently tender and humane'
Observer